The Asset Within
Hera McLeod

Seeking Different Press

Author's Note

Hi, I'm so glad you found this book. Thanks for picking it up.

If you're new to my books or this series, I'm especially thankful and excited for you to meet *these* characters. This is the first book in the Global Security series. While I'm an unapologetic lover of romance novels, my characters are messy, authentic, and my books will always have thought provoking themes that dance along side the romance. I center marginalized characters in my books, and believe there are pieces of all of us that live on the margins and deserve to take center stage.

This is a work of fiction and any resemblance of real people or situations is coincidence; however, I draw on personal experiences for authenticity. I'm a Black woman and I spent years as a case officer in the Central Intelligence Agency. This is an untold story of Black patriotism, redemptive love, and an unapologetically Black spy novel.

And finally, I'd be so honored if you could leave a review after you've read the book.

Love,
Hera

Content Warnings

The content warnings for *The Asset Within* are sexual content, profanity, death of a parent, violence, police brutality, and brief descriptions of sexual assault.

Chapter 1
Calculated Risks

Following Farhad through the dark alley that *allegedly* leads to his apartment could be the very last thing I'll ever do. I'm sitting at a dive bar in the middle of Brasilia, Brazil where I expected to meet an Iranian Diplomat and his son for the type of debrief that I've conducted hundreds of times. But instead of meeting at the bar as planned, his son is insisting I follow him to his apartment.

When I took an oath to be a case officer for the Central Intelligence Agency several years ago, I knew it wouldn't always be safe. But following an Iranian college student into the sketchy alley leading back to his apartment – well, this is a decision I never anticipated having to make. I've jumped out of moving cars, quickly aborted asset meetings after spotting surveillance, and recruited several high value intelligence targets. I'm a survivalist at my core but taking this risk could get me the best nugget of intelligence in my entire agency career.

Frozen with fear and anxiety, with the weight of a possible nuclear war on my shoulders, my feet feel like they're taking root in the ground below me. I rock on the dirty bar stool, irrationally thinking that maybe the rocking will unstick my feet and help propel me forward into the darkness. Farhad, with toasted brown skin and dark soulful eyes, stares back at me. There's a deep furrow in his thick brows and a tormented look on his face. I watch him closely, needing his body language to lend the trust his words can't. Sweat beading on his forehead, he ever so slightly sways back and forth. Watching his eyes dart back and forth, from me to the streets around us, is making me dizzy.

I take a deep breath and mentally open a list of pros and cons in my head. I was the only Black female case officer in my graduating class at The Farm. The Farm is what agency employees affectionately call the lengthy training required to legally be allowed to spot, assess, develop, recruit, and debrief foreign assets. I am the *only* Black person — and the *only* woman — stationed in Brazil. Every move I make is second guessed, questioned, and criticized by my White colleagues.

Farhad sighs deeply, snapping me back to this moment.

He's staring at me – fuck.

I take another deep breath, studying Farhad with my eyes inch by inch so that he can be clearly identified in the report I'll have to write and in hopes that something on his face will give me a clue to nudge me toward the right decision. His thick beard and mustache are so well groomed, with flecks of red shooting out like fireworks embedded in darkness, that his face looks like a beautiful mosaic of color. The sadness in his eyes, though, is gripping and draws me into them.

All I have is his word, and I don't know this dude from Adam. This could be a total setup. Farhad could drag me into that alley, beat me up, and kill me. On the other hand, if he is telling me the truth, he's probably just as scared as I am.

His eyes...

My heart feels like it's twisting out of my chest as I'm watching him shift and fidget as though he needs to use the bathroom.

"Where's your father? Why isn't he *here* like we planned?" I say, continuing to search Farhad's face.

"My father...is scared to see you here."

Farhad's deep, soulful eyes begin to water, making me feel like he's reaching into my heart and grabbing a hold of it with his bare hands. He's not a small man, standing at least a couple inches above six feet and with shoulders that look like he isn't a stranger to the gym. Despite his size, though, he has a youthful innocence about him that seems at odds with his large stature.

Farhad's voice is strained when he speaks, like he's been screaming too much or perhaps hasn't been sleeping. His thick eyebrows, with only a tiny space in between them avoiding the distinction of a unibrow, point upward toward faint tracks of worry lines on his forehead. Despite the worry lines, he looks like he's just barely entered adulthood – like a scared child who's trapped in the body of a young adult.

With his tears still tugging on my emotions, I feel the invisible roots that held my feet in place on the floor release, and I pull myself from the stool to stand closer to eye level with him.

"They will kill all of us if they see me here with you. They will do anything to keep my father from talking...and giving you what he has."

Farhad places his hand on the table in front of me. It shakes so violently that the motion makes it seem like a mini earthquake is happening in the exact spot where we are standing.

I've got to get this dude out of here before someone else notices us.

I place my hand on top of his, which slows the movement but doesn't appear to do much to ease the terror behind his eyes and continue scanning our surroundings.

Bar Versão Brasileira is a sports dive bar with outdoor seating. When I chose this location, I expected to meet Farhad and his father Basir Assadi. Basir is a high-ranking Iranian Government official who passed word through his son that he wanted asylum for him and his family in return for "important intelligence." And while I'm always skeptical when someone says they have intelligence worthy of asylum, when an Iranian official recommends a meeting – you go.

"Andy can't handle this one. This is men's work," my coworker Todd said the evening prior, as he was trying to poach my case.

My coworkers all knew that this meeting could be a career maker, and they weren't above trying to shove me aside to take the glory.

What's even more infuriating is that had this been any of the men in the office, my boss Brody would have sent counter-surveillance. But because it was me, he didn't bother making the men leave their families to work alongside me.

This bar looks like a dozen others in the city, and I picked it because it's far enough away from embassy row to conduct a respectful surveillance detection route. It's also close enough to the US Embassy where, if I drive fast, I can get back to the embassy within about ten minutes - should something go terribly sideways.

Thinking of my escape plan and trailing my free hand over the agency issued Glock strapped to my belt loop, I relax a little.

I'm prepared - and dammit– I'm good at my job.

A personal pep talk seems appropriate right now, given that I could be staring down death in a few moments.

Since this bar isn't the type of place *any* respectable foreign dignitary would frequent, smelling of cheap beer with a nauseating hint of sweaty man funk, I think the likelihood of other Iranian officials spotting us here is slim. I'm unapologetically bougie enough to feel completely out of place, and on the verge of vomiting. But I'm always willing to rally for the sake of national security.

I'm not ready to walk away from Farhad and his family, even though this is the scariest decision I've ever had to make. And I know I can't walk back into the Embassy and admit that I punked out and couldn't go through with this meeting – even though following Farhad to his apartment is also wildly against protocol.

I place my hand back on the Glock, which is hiding under a large sweatshirt. In addition to my attire effectively hiding my gun, I also hope it helps me avoid getting hit on by the drunks around me, who likely wonder if I'm a call girl. While irritating, I never bother to correct these assumptions when out in public with potential targets. At The Farm, our instructors always told us that it was better to be assumed a prostitute than a spy.

This gun would make me feel so much safer if I'd ever actually fired one outside of training. If all hell breaks loose, what if I can't hit the target? I've done well when shooting a gun full of paintballs at moving cardboard targets, but the thought of hitting human flesh with a real bullet makes me queasy.

"Baby girl, a Glock isn't that powerful of a weapon. If you ever need to use it, just make sure it's a kill shot." This was what my father always told me before I deployed as an officer.

Dalton Lynam, my dad, is a retired CIA officer. He was a chemical engineer in Directorate of Science and Technology (DS&T) who never let me forget that he made several of the bricks that were used to build the Russian Embassy in Washington, DC. While my dad fits the stereotype of an engineering nerd, more disheveled and brilliant than organized and pocket protecting, he'd always be packing a weapon on his business trips and made sure I could shoot before I deployed.

I shake my head, attempting to focus on the task at hand instead of my father's weapon advice. Before this change of plans, I planned to order a variety of greasy Brazilian street food from the menu, hoping that — if nothing else — Farhad, his dad and I could bond over the acquired taste of chicken hearts on a stick. I'll never get used to the consistency of a chicken heart. It feels like a blob of bloody Jell-O jiggling down your throat, but I've learned to fake it like a native and smile as it slithers down.

Basir doesn't speak Portuguese or English, so we planned on Farhad coming along to help translate. Farhad's English isn't perfect, but he loves practicing more than I love speaking about nuclear proliferation in Portuguese. Farhad considers himself a music head. We met a few weeks prior when he approached me outside of a diplomatic event. When he mentioned he was Basir's son, whom I already knew was a well-known Iranian Diplomat with access to Iranian nuclear plans, I kept him talking. In a self-deprecating way, he joked about how he learned English from the American rap videos he was able to view outside of Iran or illegally download on his computer.

I push the glasses up on my face and adjust my baseball cap, which covers enough of my light brown curls to be an effective light disguise. Since it isn't common for a Black woman to have hazel blue eyes, I wear tinted glasses every time I want to hide my identity in public.

"Onde fica sua casa?" I figure asking Farhad where his house is in Portuguese might not draw as much attention as if I continue speaking English.

Farhad points to an apartment building within line of sight of the dive bar. It's safe...or so he says.

"Trust me, please," Farhad begs, barely audible.

He speaks so clearly that I wonder if he practiced exactly what he needed to say to get me to trust and follow him. As scared as I am, I know that it's probably more dangerous for Farhad to be out in public with me. Should I ever be in trouble, my government would do whatever they could to extract me from danger. But Farhad and his family? They are surely on their own if my intelligence is correct.

"Sim, vamos." I quickly stand, right hand on my weapon to avoid dropping it on the sticky bar floor.

I throw a wad of cash on the table to cover the cost of my drink. I'm taking a leap of faith, but there is something about Farhad that makes me want to trust him.

God, please don't let 28 years be all that I have.

I follow him down the dark path toward his apartment, trying to remember every prayer my catholic school education taught me.

As we walk, I feel like my head is on a swivel – turning in every direction. I want to take in every detail of the alley, looking for ways to escape or clues of danger. There are streetlights that line the alley, but most of them are burnt out, and there's only one that offers any light at all. It flickers as though it, too, is about to die out. The smell of stale urine hits me in the face as we get closer to the stairwell of his apartment building. I'm thankful for the poorly maintained bushes that line the walkway, as this hides us from the people that still sit at that bar.

I turn my face, covering my nose with the sleeve of my sweatshirt, to avoid vomiting as Farhad fishes for his keys in his coat pocket. The stairwell smells so bad that I'm sure people must be using it as a urinal. After we get inside, I follow Farhad up two flights of stairs in the garden-style apartment building. The lighting on the inside isn't much better than the outside, with only a few dim ceiling lights illuminating the dark hallways. We're both sweating, mine a mixture of nerves, the intense heat, and the lack of ventilation or central A/C in this building.

"I'm sorry. This place is not nice." Farhad looks back at me before quickly looking down and hesitating a moment before turning the keys in the door.

"It's ok. I'm just glad you and your family are safe. Let's try and keep it that way." I place my hand on Farhad's shoulder, which to my surprise seems to make his tense body relax a bit.

A timid smile appears on Farhad's face causing the corner of his lips to turn up just slightly. As he pushes the door slightly ajar, a petite woman, looking to be in her mid-fifties appears. Her skin is light brown and her eyes strikingly like Farhad's. A hijab covers her hair, which immediately draws me to her grief-stricken eyes and the worry lines that surround them. She flashes a nervous smile causing me to relax a bit.

Farhad wasn't kidding when he told me the place wasn't nice. The small size and the conditions of the apartment aren't what I expected for the Assadi family. Basir is high up in the Iranian government, but this place looks like a dirty bachelor pad. Clothes are strewn all over, and the suitcases that line the single hallway leading to the bedroom indicate there is either nowhere to store them *or* this family doesn't feel safe enough to settle in. I don't blame them for the unsettled feeling because just looking around this apartment causes the hairs to stand up on the back of my neck. They aren't safe – *we* aren't safe.

Moments after walking through the door, Basir emerges from the bedroom. He's smaller than I imagined, standing about two inches shorter than me around 5'5". Like his wife, his eyes have dark circles under them and are bloodshot as though he hasn't slept in a long time. Basir's hair is peppered with gray, and his shoulders slump as though he's spent way too many years hunched over a computer. I'm shocked at his choice of clothing - just an undershirt and a pair of shorts that only look a tad more modest than boxers. It's hot as hell in there, but his attire is still shocking considering that he knew there was a possibility that I'd come over.

"My father...he left Iran with little more than the clothing on his back, and he's been afraid to leave the apartment," Farhad explains quickly, seemingly reacting to the expression of shock on my face.

Andy, fix your face girl.

I've never been amazing at hiding my emotions. My facial expression is likely betraying my attempts to appear unphased by the hurricane of clothing that I just stepped over when I entered this tiny apartment. I don't want the Assadi family to feel worse than they already do so I force a smile on my face and clasp my hands together to stop myself from shaking.

"It's ok. I understand – you all have been through a lot. Please don't feel like you need to explain this to me." I start toward the couch that Farhad is clearing of clutter.

As soon as my butt hits the couch cushion, Basir is ready to jump right into business. He pulls out a series of maps with red marks on what look like hundreds of locations, hands shaking as he unfolds them. To my surprise, these aren't maps of Iran like I'd expected but instead of The United States of America and several of our NATO allies. Next to the maps there's a syringe, filled with a liquid substance of some sort.

"What *is* this," I ask, looking between Farhad – the maps – and the syringe.

"Before my dad left, he took a copy of the maps and...the vial."

What the hell is this?

Basir pushes the syringe toward me, as though he wants me to give myself a shot with a dirty syringe.

No way, there must be something lost in translation here – because that's crazy.

There is no way I'm injecting myself with that thing when I don't know what it is. The introduction of this syringe suddenly has me worried that this family might be trying to kill me.

"You...must...take," Basir struggles to say, grabbing the syringe and handing it to me.

My eyes scan the 500 square foot apartment, and I spot a teenage girl typing on a computer. I don't reach for the syringe, despite Basir's insistence that I take it. I'm still trying to process this situation, while Basir turns to Farhad and the two of them begin speaking in Farsi. But as they speak, I'm still distracted by the girl.

"Farhad, what is she doing?" I rise from the couch and slowly start walking toward the girl to get a look at what she's doing on her computer.

"Fariba – what are you doing?" Farhad asks the girl, who I assume is his sister given that she has the same eyes as her brother and their mother.

Fariba, who'd been giggling quietly to herself and rapidly typing, quickly looks up, her eyes wide, and puts the computer next to her on the ground. She has a confused and scared look on her face, her thick eyebrows creasing in the center.

"It's just Orkut – my friends...I...I was just..." Tears begin to form in Fariba's eyes as Basir shouts at his daughter in Farsi.

"Fariba, I need you to shut down the computer immediately. We need to get out of here." I look between Farhad and Fariba, needing them both to help relay the message to their parents.

"What? Why? None of my friends would ever tell anyone where we are." The tears now streaming quickly down Fariba's face, and her body starting to tremble.

"They don't have to. Simply being on that site gives your location away, and if someone was looking for your family – they found you." I place a hand on her shoulder while gesturing to Farhad to get the suitcases that line the hallway.

Basir hadn't been to work in two weeks, and the Iranian Ministry of Foreign Affairs would certainly be trying to track the family's every move to ascertain his current location. If he hadn't shown up for a day, they might have assumed he was ill. But after this long, they know he's trying to defect, and they'd rather have him and his entire family dead if that's what it takes to protect their intelligence.

Turning toward his son, Basir whispers frantically to him in Farsi.

"My father says...he says...he's sorry," Farhad says, eyes widening as his father continues speaking.

I look between the two of them, acutely aware that the translation doesn't seem quite right. Farhad is arguing with this father as his father lunges for the syringe that's still on the coffee table next to where we were just sitting.

"Baba, No," Farhad screams, holding onto his father's shoulders.

Farhad takes the syringe from his father and hands it to me, "This is what everyone is looking for and my father wants you to have it – to keep it safe."

I grab it and put it on the table next to me, looking skeptically between the two of them.

"No – put it somewhere safe. No, no...can't keep out," Farhad says, his English deteriorating.

"Okay, okay, grab some things to take with you, but only what's important because we don't have a lot of time."

I pat the vial, giving Farhad what I hope is a re-assuring smile.

"The vial is my dad's only chance to get us out of here. You must keep safe," Farhad says, his dark eyes pleading with me.

"I will, it's right here. We will take it with us," I say, glancing back at the vial and making a mental note to grab it from the counter before leaving the apartment.

As the Assadi family springs into action, like this isn't their first rodeo, I look around the apartment for alternate exits and ways to barricade the door.

"My mother is worried. She wants to know where we will go." Farhad moves from comforting his father to taking his mother by the hand.

"I'm going to make sure you are safe. I'll take you to the embassy. While inside the embassy compound, you're on US soil, and you're safe while we plan our next move."

I know I shouldn't promise political asylum, but I also can't just leave them here in this apartment like sitting ducks either. I really hope that Basir is getting some real clothes on. Running around the streets of Brasilia with a half-naked Iranian defector is going to draw more attention than we need. Still waiting for everyone to pack, I walk over to the window and slightly part the curtains. At the site of a fire escape, I audibly sigh with relief. Fire escapes are rare in Brasilia, but because this tiny apartment sits on top of a restaurant – thankfully it's required.

I walk back to the middle of the room and rest my hand on my Glock, which remains safely hidden under my sweatshirt. As soon as I start to feel as though we could make it out of there alive, I hear footsteps in the hallway. My eyes meet Farhad's as I quickly raise my finger to my lips and push him toward the bedroom with the rest of his family. I try to quiet my breathing as my right-hand hovers over my gun. Slowly walking toward the door, looking for anything I can shove in front of it, the floor creaks loudly. There's a shadow of two feet in the crack at the bottom of the door.

As I grab my gun, to pull it out of the holster, a burly, light brown man kicks open the door. I can hear my heartbeat thumping in my ears as everything moves in slow motion.

Do what it takes to survive.

The voices of all my instructors ring in my ears.

My father's voice follows - *Make sure it's a kill shot, baby girl.*

The man has a long whip in one hand and a large knife in the other. He scans the room, like he's looking past me, while also coming straight for me with that whip.

What the hell!? A whip?!

I struggle to grab the gun because I'm busy dodging the damned whip that's dancing dangerously by my head. I shift right, but the whip hits my face – my chest – my back.

My entire body feels like it was enveloped in fire, and I struggle to catch my breath through the intense pain shooting through every inch of my body. As I go for the gun again, trying to shove him off me, he stabs me in the side.

Oh, good GOD, I'm in so much pain – but Andy, you cannot stop.

I grab a glass vase from the kitchen table, which is the heaviest and closest thing I can find and launch it at his head. He shakes his shiny, bald head violently and starts back toward me, like he barely feels the impact of the vase.

As I attempt to run far enough away to collect myself, the bald guy makes a quick move toward the kitchen counter and dives to grab the vial Farhad gave me. I hear screams from the Assadi family as several of them attempt to throw things at the assailant.

The bald guy is running at me again with his knife in one hand and the vial in the other. I reach to grab the vial from him, but fall backward while trying to dodge his knife. Before I can regain my footing, he stabs my leg with the vial and a menacing smile flashes across his face. As the bald man pulls the now empty syringe out of my leg, he grabs me by the wrist and tries to pull me out of the apartment. The shock masks the pain and I try to fight the man off me by kicking and reaching for any weapon I can get my hands on. Farhad runs out of the bedroom with a bat and clocks the man across the face. He falls over with blood spilling out of his head. With a knife still lodged in my side, I pull out my gun.

BANG – BANG - BANG

Kill shots to the chest - the stomach - and finally his head.

Pulling the knife out of me, I double over in pain and brace myself on the kitchen counter. After taking a moment to catch my breath, I run to my purse, pull out a tampon, and shove it into the gaping hole the knife left behind.

The paintball bruises during training didn't prepare me for this.

Still bleeding and in the type of pain that steals your breath, I slide from the counter to the floor and grab a t-shirt from a nearby pile of clothing to press against the wound. I need to get us out of here.

Farhad rushes over and lifts me off the ground. His eyes widen and the color drains from his face as he looks at me intensely. Basir runs to the other side of me, stepping over the dead body next to us. He lifts up the empty vial and his face drains of most of its color as he looks between me and the vial.

"I'm sorry – I told my dad it was too dangerous to even bring that thing out. He says he's sorry and to forgive him for this," Farhad's eyes look into mine apologetically.

Time seems to stand still for a moment as the two men, father and son, hover over me. There isn't time for me to diagnose what this all means because that crazy man with a whip probably has friends on their way – and I don't want to meet his friends.

But what was in that vial? We can figure that out later – we have to get out of here.

"I'm ok – I'm ok. Let's get out of here," I say, trying to ignore the crazy shit that just happened.

I am not okay.

I don't have the time or energy to think about what that bald man put into my leg.

Oh God, what if I die before I can get us to safety?

Cameron...

It shocks me that Cameron has entered my thoughts at a time like this because I haven't spoken to him in years. I've worked *hard* to push the image of him, and how I felt about him, far into the recesses of my memory. But as I slump against Farhad, bleeding out from several locations, my mind wanders to the last time Cameron and I saw each other.

Forcing myself back into the moment, I shove the memory of Cameron safely back to the furthest corner of my mind.

He is not your person anymore. He won't help you.

Allowing Farhad to help me walk, I point toward the fire escape, and we all crawl out the tiny window and down the stairs. Blood soils my clothes, but at this point I can't tell which part of my body it's coming from.

As soon as we all clear off the fire escape, we run toward my car. It's pitch-black outside, which makes finding my car in the now-crowded parking lot even harder than it should be.

Who am I kidding - I can't even find my car in a crowded mall parking lot when I'm not bleeding to death.

This realization causes more panic to circulate through my body. I'm also getting dizzy from all the blood loss, or maybe because this is terrifying.

When I finally spot the car, surprised I found it at all, I make a mad dash. I'm not sure how I'm still standing so the fact that I'm running is even more shocking. Farhad runs over to support my body as I struggle to pull my keys from my pants pocket. My shirt is blood soaked and even pulling the keys from my pocket feels like someone is sticking their finger in the gaping wound at my side.

"Get in!" I slide in the driver seat after opening the door.

This manual shift jalopy of a car is a piece of crap, which is a good thing since now it's covered in my blood. I borrowed the embassy's rental car because it doesn't have identifiable diplomatic plates. I'm certain that over a dozen people have gotten into an accident in this car as several parts only remain in place because of duct tape magic. The car screeches out of the parking lot and toward the embassy.

"Andy, you're bleeding. This is bad, you need to go to hospital," Farhad says, grabbing some paper towels from the floor of the car trying to stop the bleeding.

I'm not going to the hospital. That would decrease my chances of getting everyone to safety and if the dude I just killed has friends on the way – the hospital is one of the first places they'll look for us. I glance in my rear-view mirror and notice a vehicle behind us that makes several turns with us. I don't need to do a traditional surveillance detection route to know we're being followed.

Of course, the big, whip wielding crazy man brought his friends.

Slamming my foot on the gas, I weave in and out of cars to lose the guy tailing us. Once we arrive at the embassy gates, my breathing is shallow, and I feel like I'm trying to suck air through a pinhole. I'm dizzy even while sitting still and worry I'll pass out before we get inside the gates. I press the call button to the guard station and Mark, one of the young Marines, answers.

"Andy, is that you? You're the only one who ever drives that beat up old car," Mark's voice is scratchy, like he'd been sleeping when I pushed the call button.

"Mark, I need you to let us in. I have people with me, and I'm hurt. Please hurry." I wheeze as I struggle to get the words out, starting to see dark spots in my vision.

My hands shake as I grab the steering wheel tighter. Tears threaten to burst from my eyes, but I maintain composure. I don't want to scare the Assadis more by having a complete emotional and physical breakdown in this car. When the gates finally open, I drive the car just inside and pull the emergency brake before everything goes black.

Chapter 2
The Sandbox

"Cameron"

"**D**ude, get out there and hang with us," my friend and teammate Theo calls to me as I finish trying to shave my face.

I'm so tired of breathing in this grimy air and feeling sand particles on my skin every time I shave. All the guys keep telling me to just let my facial hair grow, but they don't understand what it's like to have a beard that grows patchy and makes you look like a damned chia pet when it's long.

Fuck this place. And fuck this crappy mission.

Shindand Air Base is in the middle of the Herat Province of Afghanistan, seventy-five miles from the Iranian border. And for the last six months, my unit of Global Security Officers – Team 9 (GST 9) has been stuck here waiting for an Iranian defector to arrive with some Intelligence goods. The CIA sends Case Officers to collect Intelligence, but they send us to clean things up when things go wrong, or the mission is too dangerous for everyone else. I know I could've tapped out of this mission, as several others on my team have, but this is potentially the biggest operation I've ever worked on. It's my chance to prove that I'm ready to lead my own team.

After finishing in the tiny communal latrine that's small enough to touch the door from the toilet, I walk outside. The remote area of the base we're in is nothing more than a few small trailers surrounded by miles and miles of sand and barbed wire fencing. The Rock music playing from portable Bluetooth speakers in the communal area between the trailers isn't lightening my mood. At this point, the only thing that will cheer me up is if this dude shows the hell up so we can leave this awful place. I flop down on a dirty, camping chair just as an empty soda can hits me in the head.

"Dude, seriously?" I glare at Theo who's now doubled over laughing.

"Man – chill out and have some fun with us," Theo says, shoving me in the shoulder and nearly knocking me off my chair.

My dog Boss has been out here waiting with me and the nine other members of my team. He saunters over and rubs his body against my leg before flopping at my feet.

Yes, I actually mean 'saunter' because homeboy has swagger.

Boss is a red fox Labrador Retriever who I rescued after he was fired from the FBI K-9 unit. He washed out of the FBI due to his inconsistent work ethic and was described as a "moody disposition." Boss is like a human trapped in the body of a dog. He has expressive, dark chocolate eyes and is really picky about his food, refusing normal pet food and insisting the bougier dog life with steak and rice. I met Boss after a joint mission my team had with the FBI. I became obsessed with helping Boss redeem himself and agreed to give him a job with our team. People say that I saved him, but I think he saved me.

"Woo woo," Boss howls in sync with the 90s R&B coming from the small stereo at Theo's feet.

My team has been waiting for the asset to show up with the Intel that will inform our next move. Our mission is to take down the terrorist network that has its hands on the most powerful nuclear technology around – Solaris. And apparently this asset is bringing us a vial of the nuclear agent and information about several nuclear sites under the terrorist network's control. But since we've been here for weeks without a sign of this guy, I'm getting impatient and these guy's acting like they're on college spring break isn't helping.

I'm not here for *fun*. I'm here to serve my country and destroy terrorist cells – like the cell that killed my dad. He was at the Pentagon on September 11th, just going about his business another day at work when a plane flew into him, burning his body beyond recognition. I was supposed to be there that day. He wanted me to follow in his footsteps and was going to introduce me to some high-ranking officials in military Intelligence. That day changed my life, perhaps giving me a singular focus. And while I love the guys on my team, especially my dude Theo who'd been beside me for years, I'm not here to chill.

Leading my own team of GS-9 would make me the first Black officer to rise to that level and *this* is the opportunity to prove to my boss Scott Rove (whom everyone affectionately calls "Rove") that I'm ready.

Ignoring my irritation, Theo continues talking about what foods he wants to eat as soon as we get home. We've been on this base for so long that everything has started to taste like sand and chalk.

"A burger – a giant juicy burger with bacon and cheddar cheese...no, no, gouda cheese," Theo muses, licking his lips as he speaks.

"Roo, roo," Boss says, nodding his head like he also wants a juicy burger.

"Dude, all you think about is food," I say, throwing the empty can back at Theo before patting Boss on the head.

"Yeah...food and women. But right now, I just want that burger," Theo laughs, pretending to lick his fingers as though he's enjoying ketchup dripping from his fake burger.

We're so close to going home. This guy should've been here by now, but the Intel we received a few hours ago told us that he'd smuggled himself on a plane out of Iran about a week ago. That wasn't the agreed upon plan, and the fact that he's missed the rally window tells me our base isn't where he's coming. But until we have a location, we must wait – just in case he shows up as planned. I know that I'm a horrible person to be around right now, and the last thing I want to do is sour the entire team. We've all been in this hell hole for too long. But this guy wasted our time, and now instead of going home – we need to chase him somewhere else to finish the op.

Just as I start considering what I'll eat when we finally get home, the emergency satellite phone vibrates in my pocket. This phone only ever rings for one reason – when an officer is in trouble. Given that this phone hasn't gone off in at least six months, my heart begins to race with the adrenaline of what's to come.

"It's game time fellas," I yell to my teammates before answering the phone.

The mood in the group immediately shifts from grown men clowning to serious and all about business, as the men pack up and head toward the operations trailer for instructions from Rove. Boss follows the rest of the team and I trail behind, pulling out a pad to take notes from the caller.

"Hello? This is Global Security Unit 9 – what's your emergency?" I ask, patiently waiting for the caller to respond.

"GS-9, this is Officer Mark Samson from the Marine detachment in Brazil. Calling to report there's an officer down requiring extraction," the voice on the other hand responds.

"Confirm your coordinates officer and we will send a team," I respond, taking notes on the small pad I pull out of the zippered pocket of my camo pants.

"U.S. Embassy sir...and the officer has several assets with her that will also require extraction," Officer Sampson replies.

"Roger, have station send Rove the report," I say before closing the phone and heading toward the trailer outfitted as our command center to discuss with Rove.

Before I reach the trailer door, Rove comes bounding out with such force that a plume of dust bellows toward me. The serious look on Rove's face, his eyebrows nearly connecting and his cheeks flushed, stops me in my tracks. Whatever he's about to tell me isn't as routine as the call from the Marine made it seem.

"Guys – you have two hours to pack your shit and meet on the airfield. We found our guy," Rove shouts at the men who are filing out behind him.

"Hey, we also need to send a team to Brazil...there's apparently an officer requiring extraction," I respond, wondering how these two incidents happened at nearly the exact same time.

"Come inside Cam, we need to talk," Rove says, grabbing my shoulders and leading me into the trailer.

Inside the trailer, I see a map of Brazil on the screen and tell Rove about the call in to the satellite phone.

"Cam, we're headed to Brazil. The officer down is *Andy* – she found our guy," Rove says.

Andy? My Andy? No, it can't be...

My eyes widen as I realize that my past has just collided with my present and I'm headed to Brazil on the biggest mission of my career – and to see a woman I thought I'd never see again.

Andy found him. How? What?

Forcing myself to move, and get out of my head, I turn to follow the rest of the crew while panic threatens to take over my entire body. Like a giant barrier gate in a parking garage, Rove's muscled arm slams in front of me and blocks me from continuing.

"Not yet Cam – we need to talk before you get on that plane."

Here we go...

I turn around and wait for what feels like it's going to be more lecture than instructions from Rove.

"How bad?" I ask, bracing myself for the news as my blood pumps hard enough for me to hear my heartbeat pulse in my ears.

"She's alive, but they say she's hurt, and her injuries are bad...extraction is going to be difficult," Rove winces, studying my face.

I've got to get myself together or he isn't going to let me take the lead here.

"Okay, let's go," I say, tactfully removing all emotion to my face and turning into the soldier my father trained me to be.

"I don't know the extent of your history with her Cam, but whatever it is – you cannot let that cloud your judgement on this case. The moment I think you can't handle it, I'll remove you," Rove warns, letting the reality of what that means to me sink into the silence between us.

Before we took this case, Rove told me this was my chance to show him I could lead the team. If I blow this chance, I won't get another one with GS-9 and I'll either need to do something else or be content staying at this level for the rest of my career. Neither of the alternatives would be acceptable because I feel like I was born to do this work.

I've sacrificed so much – this can't have all been for nothing.

"I'm good, Rove. Let me do this," I respond, clenching my teeth so hard that the pulsing in my head is getting more intense.

"Around the same time that you got the call from the marine unit, we got reporting confirming that Andy arrived with Basir Assadi and his family on the embassy compound," Rove says, with a hint of annoyance that I can completely understand given how long we've been waiting here for this guy.

"Did station know she was meeting Basir?" I rubbed my hands through my hair, that was cut closer than usual and only starting to curl beyond the length considered a buzz cut.

Rubbing my hands through my hair was a nervous habit of mine that often left my hair looking like a disheveled curly afro. With the heat, and the guys starting to make jokes about how crazy my hair looked, I've been intentionally keeping it short.

"Chief of Station Brody knew exactly what he was sending Andy into, but something tells me she didn't know the full story. If she did, I'm guessing she wouldn't have walked into that without backup," Rove says.

Andy is a badass and I'm not so sure she'd have turned down an opportunity to debrief Basir. But Basir is a man whom over a dozen of the worst international terrorists want to get their hands on. And if this guy got out of the country with his entire family, he likely has something he expects will buy them all asylum.

He must have brought out a nuclear vial.

"You know if I'd known Basir would go there, I'd have told them to stand down until our arrival," Rove says, looking directly into my eyes.

I know Rove would never have sent anyone to debrief Basir without backup because he's a good boss and a good man. Rove has had my back out here and I'm grateful to him for a whole lot. When my dad died, he gave me an avenue to channel all my anger and his leadership has gotten me to the point where I am today. While I know I've earned my right to be a GS-9, I've often wondered if my admission into this unit was abbreviated because Rove and my dad served in the military together. Rove mentioned on one occasion that he owes his life to my dad and sometimes acts more like an uncle than a boss. Perhaps this operation feels so important to me because I want to prove to Rove and my dad that I deserve to be here, and I've earned the right to lead.

Unlike Rove, Chief of Station Brazil – a guy named Brody - is a notorious asshole who's known for trampling over his staff if it means he can get another career notch on his belt. I know of him because we had to handle another situation that occurred on his watch when he was COS Portugal. In that case, Body was covering up the sexual exploits of Reef Fontaine for an entire year. He'd have let Reef continue had the sick bastard not raped and beaten a young case officer who'd only arrived in station a week before the assault. Even after that situation, Brody wanted us to bury the incident so that his right-hand man could stay out of trouble. Luckily, Rove supported me when I reported what I'd seen and when I testified against Reef in the criminal trial that followed.

The entire intern class of 2001 called Reef "no briefs Reef" because he couldn't seem to ever keep his pants on and was constantly terrorizing the female interns. We all knew Reef was dirty and, in my book, anyone who was friends with Reef was *also* dirty. So, it doesn't surprise me to learn that Brody would send Andy into the fire. Brody likely saw Basir as his golden ticket to an Intelligence award. And Andy was the "perfect" agent to send in his eyes – Brown enough to blend with the locals and female enough that the local flavor of misogyny would be less likely to suspect her involvement. He's just the type to make her do all the hard work and then swoop in for the credit once the heavy lifting is done.

"Of course, Brody is all up in this…asshole," I say under my breath, not expecting anyone else to hear me.

"Look, I don't want to clean up after Brody again either – but this is our operation and we will finish what we started *and* get Andy home safely," Rove says.

"Alright, what are we waiting for them – let's roll," I say, ready to get to Brazil and handle this.

I jogged to my trailer and shoved the few loose things into the bag next to the door that stayed packed and ready to go. On my way to the airplane hangar where we all needed to meet, I thought about the last time I'd seen Andy. We'd had a big fight just a few weeks before graduating from college, which was something we'd started to do often toward the end. After my dad died, I lost it and felt like my entire future was in a spiral. Andy didn't want me to join GST because it's dangerous but joining felt like something I needed to do. Instead of just dealing with the loss of my dad, I pushed away the love of my life.

During one of my darkest moments, I'd thrown a plate on the floor. It shattered into pieces all over my apartment and shards of glass cut into my legs and feet. I remember staring at the plate, standing frozen in shock, as though I was watching someone else's life – while blood spilled out of me. Andy's screams startled me, and I'll never forget the look of horror and fear in her eyes, and she grabbed hold of me and tried to stop the bleeding. I'd been so out of it that I hadn't been able to stop her before she'd sliced open her foot trying to help me.

"Andy no – your foot...you need to get away from me," I begged, feeling radioactive.

"Cam, baby you're scaring me. You need to see a doctor," Andy cried, tears rushing down her cheeks and face.

She had good reason to be afraid for me, and perhaps also *of* me – or both. And I'd hated myself for that. The love and passion in her eyes when she'd looked at me was replaced by concern, pity, and fear. Once things calmed down that night, with me taking her to the school clinic to get stitches in her foot and subsequently getting stitches in my leg at the same time, we sat down to talk. That's when I made a mistake that I'm not sure she will ever allow me to fix. I blew up the relationship so that I couldn't pull her into the darkness with me.

"You know that chic you saw me with the other day?" I asked her.

Andy didn't respond, but I'll never forget the pain in her eyes and the tears she fought as she looked at me.

"We fucked and it was *amazing*," I lied, trying to remove any remorse that could give away the bold-faced lie I hoped she'd believe.

After hesitating for a moment, searching my face for a shred of emotion beneath the stony expression I'd plastered on my face, she picked up her purse and took off toward the door.

"Fuck you, Cameron. I've been here for you through your total emotional spiral and even put up with your obsession over your job – often at the expense of our relationship – and now this? I don't know if you did that shit or you're just fucking with me, but I'm not gonna sit here and keep waiting around for you to fix your shit" she'd said over her shoulder before slamming the door behind her.

Though I was still too wounded to properly make amends for what I'd done, the night before my first deployment with GS-9, I tried to apologize. Worried I'd die on a mission, and she'd never know how I felt about her, I went to her apartment. Loren met me at the door, arms folded and ready to read me the riot act for showing my face after the pain I'd caused her best friend.

"I'm sorry. Please, tell Andy I need to talk to her. Just this one last time and then if she never wants to see me again...I'll respect that," I'd begged.

Loren reluctantly moved out of the way, threatening to chop off my man parts if I upset her again, and I entered the apartment. I found Andy curled up on her couch next to Gina, face red and puffy from crying, with a cup of tea in her shaking hands. Loren and Gina refused to leave me alone with her in the room, so I kneeled in front of Andy and tried to ignore the audience.

"Andy, I'm sorry. I understand if you never want to see me again, but I need you to have this," I'd said, passing her a card with a number on it.

"Cam, what is this?" She'd asked.

"I'm deploying tonight," I'd whispered in her ear, "and I need you to know that if you ever need me – I'll come for you."

I hoped she'd never need me but also prayed that someday we'd see each other again.

Andy stared at me for several seconds, with glassy eyes full of pain that was quickly disguised by anger. It was the moment I realized she'd never look at me the way she had before.

"Andy please..." I'd begged, before Loren and Gina appeared at my sides to pull me off the floor and push me toward the door.

In the seven years since I uttered the lie, a day hasn't gone by where I haven't regretted it and wondered where we'd both be if I'd been honest. I never cheated on Andy. That girl I lied about was Theo's sister, who'd been in town visiting her brother. It took me years to realize that I needed to go to therapy to heal from the trauma of losing my father, and while I've tried several times over the years to come back and tell her the truth – it was too late.

It was Rove who'd insisted I see the agency therapist, which means he saved my life just as he claims my dad saved his. Rove made seeing a therapist a condition for me to continue service as it became clearer that I wasn't handling my father's death well. And being able to serve alongside Rove, with this elite team, has given me purpose and allowed me to finally feel as though I am avenging September 11th. I was supposed to be with my dad the day the plane flew into the Pentagon, and a thousand different scenarios for how that could've played out flipped through my head regularly.

"Cam, you comin' or are you gonna just stand there and watch all of us board the plane?" Theo asks, slamming his fist into my shoulder and jolting me out of my thoughts.

I didn't realize I was just standing there staring at the plane.

"Yeah, oh…sorry. Yes, I'm coming," I say, shaking my head before pulling my hand through my hair.

Once we get on the plane, Theo plops down into the seat next to me. I'm grateful for this dude and how easily he can make me smile. Even pushing thirty years old, the man still walks around like a teenage boy who suddenly grew several feet and has no idea how his large body will react in space.

"Oops, my bad," Theo says, as both of our seats shake at the force of his weight.

I chuckle before saying, "Thanks for staying ridiculous, bro."

Theo shrugs before flashing his classic, wonder boy smile and tossing his dirty blond hair behind a bandana. Theo has always been an enigma – he was one of the two percent of White students in our class at Howard, though he never lets any of us forget that he's a quarter Black even though he "passes" for White. My dude always looks like he's just stepped off a surfboard, but he's the most brilliant man I've ever met. Few people know this, likely because he's humble and doesn't flaunt his intelligence, but his IQ is high enough to qualify him for Mensa.

"Hey man, I'm sorry about your girl," Theo says, with sincerity in his tone.

I sigh audibly before responding, "she's not my girl anymore. You were there during all that…so you remember what happened."

"There's still time man," he responds, moving his sunglasses up and down on his eyes suggestively like a fool.

I roll my eyes at him, "let's just get her out of there safely and deal with our asset."

This isn't how I've pictured seeing her again and while I do want a chance to make amends with her – to apologize and prove that I've grown up and worked on myself – I can't allow that to be anywhere near the forefront of my thoughts right now. I also cannot allow myself to get distracted from the mission. Rove was clear that he'd remove me if I showed even an ounce of trouble handling my emotions.

"Get some rest guys – we have a lot of work ahead of us once we touch down in Brazil," Rove says.

He's right, but sleeping is going to be hard with all the thoughts racing through my head right now. Boss sits down beside me, likely sensing my anxiety spiking. I reach out to pat him and pull him to my side.

She will be okay – she will be okay – she will be okay.

I keep telling myself this before I drift off to sleep.

Chapter 3
Extraction

If I were dead, would my body still hurt this much?

I have no idea where I am, and I feel like a ton of bricks are laying on my eyelids. I need to get up and make sure we're safe.

What if we aren't safe?

What if we didn't make it inside the gates?

Oh God, what did that man inject me with?

I feel like I'm going to throw up because the room won't stop spinning. And every single part of my body hurts. The leg that was injected feels like it's on fire. Reaching my hand down, I feel my leg checking around for anything else that might give me more information about what's happening to me. My hands search my body to take inventory of the wounds.

The lights above my head are blinding, and my side feels like it's still being stabbed. This sensation only further contributes to my panic. Desperately reaching around, trying to free myself from the wires connecting me to this bed, a wave of nausea grips my stomach like a vice on my intestines.

Fighting off vomit, I take a deep breath and break free from the thin tubes connecting me to an IV bag. Just as I try to escape the bed, a large set of muscular arms wrap around my shoulders from behind.

No! Let go of me – noooo!

I'm not even sure if the words come out, or if I just think them as I struggle to break free from this bed. With every move I make, the arms tighten around me, and now I can't breathe.

"Let me go. Please, I can't...I can't breathe."

This time I hear my voice, raspy and strained. The room keeps spinning, and it's hard to make sense of the other voices that fill it. I'm shaking and can't seem to stop.

I'm so cold. What's happening to me?

The arms are still wrapped around me, and the room goes from spinning to turning dark. As the arms tighten their grip, the nausea comes back so strong that I can no longer stop the vomit from coming. I grab at my throat, still struggling to breathe and to break free. And before I can stop myself, I throw up, continuing to dry heave, while also still trying to get out of here.

"Andy *STOP* moving! You're safe. It's ok. It's me – Cam."

At the sound of Cameron's voice, I stop fighting and feel my body collapse into his arms. I close my eyes and the heat of the tears streaming down my cold face sting. My terror turns into embarrassment as I continue to shake. I bury my head into his chest and allow him to envelop my body in his arms as he lifts me back up into the bed. Just as he places me back into the bed, I shove him off me.

Why is he here? He's legit the last person I want to see me like this.

My brain feels like it's at war with my heart. I cannot seem to help the violent reaction my body is having to his proximity. My mind tries to make sense of why he's here and then I realize – the marines called his team. He's here because they've called in the clean-up crew and just my luck – my ex-boyfriend is on the clean-up crew. I'm thankful his team is here, because I know this is bad, but seeing him is a reminder of how angry I am at him. Even after all these years, I still feel like punching him in the teeth. But a weak shove, given the state I'm in right now, is all I can muster before grabbing my side in pain.

"Why are you here?" I say weakly, before leaning back into the bed.

He's here because that's his damned job.

"My team was called. You want to tell me how you ended up this way?" He asks, placing his arm gently on my shoulder before I swat it away.

His face flashes with a look that shows I've wounded him, but he quickly fixes his face into the stony expression I'd grown to hate toward the end of our relationship. I roll my eyes and look away from him, avoiding the memories that look brings.

I continue to lower myself back into the bed, feeling a bit less concerned about imminent danger.

"You want to tell *me* why this was important enough for them to send *your* team?"

"Andy, I can't explain more outside of the secure area, but we're going to have to get more information about what you were doing at Basir's house and what he told you," Cameron says, pulling a small notebook out of his pocket and jotting down a note.

I carefully turn away from him in the bed, hugging myself to try and calm the tremors I can't control. As he continues speaking, I think about everything I remember from Basir's house, trying to piece together what went wrong that led me to this and trying to figure out how Cameron even knows about Basir.

Oh my Gosh – my leg! What did the bald man inject into my leg?

My hand returns to my leg, still boiling lava hot while the rest of me is bone chilling cold. I need to get up from this bed. I need to get out of this room and talk to Basir. I can't let anyone get to him before me because I need to know what is inside of me. Knowing the agency, whatever he put there likely means more to them than my own life. Panic sets in as I put two and two together – they wouldn't have sent Cam's team for just a human extraction. Whatever is now in my leg makes *me* the Intelligence because Farhad said the vial was his family's key to asylum.

Cameron's team wouldn't have come for just anything. Even though it's obvious this is a bad scene, especially given the fact that there's a dead man in Basir's apartment, there are plenty of global security teams within this area of responsibility that should have deployed first. The fact that they were the ones that responded to the call, instead of regular security, tells me this isn't just an average extraction case.

But they wouldn't know I was injected with the vial, would they?

With Cam this close, my body reacts as though it's in mourning all over again. He was my best friend and the love of my life. If this were then, I'd pull him close to me and tell him about the injection. Now, I can't trust anyone with this information– including him. Cam's team is likely already debriefing Basir, and I pray Basir won't tell them about the injection until I have a chance to learn what was in it.

"It's ok. You're at the embassy – you made it, Andy. We're trying our best to bring the hospital services here because we can't take you off the compound safely yet," one of the nurses says, disrupting my thoughts.

I force a smile toward the middle-aged woman with warm green eyes, dressed in scrubs, who puts several blankets on top of me. I'm so thankful for the warm blankets wrapped around me, but it feels like no amount of heat can warm the chill that's deep inside my bones.

As soon as I lay back, more nurses gather around. One of them places an oxygen mask on my face while the others try to salvage the tubes that I pulled out of my arms. Cameron retreats to the far corner of the room, those kaleidoscope brown eyes wide and the color draining from his tan skin. One of his hands reaches up to pull off his winter beanie and the other rubs his head, which is covered in noticeably shorter curls than I've ever seen him with. He always kept his hair a little long, and I used to love the way his curls seemed to bounce along with his personality when he'd get excited about something. This new hair doesn't bounce at all, and I wonder if the bouncing curls left at the same time our relationship did.

As the nurses poke and prod me, I desperately inhale oxygen from the mask. I glance over at Cameron, tears welling up in my eyes. I hate crying in public, especially in front of Cameron, and force my eyes closed to stop from completely losing control of my emotions. The nurses step out of the room shortly after ensuring everything is hooked back up and I'm calm enough to take stable breaths. When they close the door behind them, Cameron timidly walks over to my bed. I shift my body closer to the other side of the bed to get as far from him as possible.

"How bad is it?" I ask, knowing my situation is worse than even he knows.

Did someone see me with Farhad?

Have local authorities found the man who attacked us?

What happened to the man who attacked us?

What was in that vial?

My mind races, and my thoughts are disconnected from my current surroundings. Every time I close my eyes, I see that man with the whip, that knife, and that dirty vial of who knows what being stabbed into my leg. I know I'm safe, especially being on the Embassy compound, but that doesn't stop the panic I feel. And I can't get out of my head. I have too many questions that none of the people around me can answer – which is why I need to be okay enough to get the hell out of this bed.

Cameron isn't making this situation better. He feels like home and like falling off a cliff at the same time. When we broke up, it took me months to feel even close to feeling like my whole self again. He used to be the only person who I ever wanted as my forever.

And there hasn't been anyone since...

But that last time I saw him, he was different. And right now, I have no idea which version of Cameron is here. And if *my* Cameron is even inside of him at all anymore.

"Why are you here? And why are you hovering over me instead of working" I ask him, closing my eyes to avoid the bright lights and having to see his eyes on me.

He doesn't respond and instead just shifts uncomfortably in his chair.

Stop looking at me – oh God...please stop. I can't handle the way you're looking at me.

He continues to watch me silently with intense eyes, and it physically hurts being this close to him without being able to allow myself to be held by him. If only his hurtful last words – those horrible last months - could've severed our connection completely. Maybe then I could see him for likely just what this was – a coworker and his team…here to clean up this mess I've walked into.

"I promised you that I'd come if you needed me. And so…I'm here," he says, his eyes filled with worry and his voice a gentle tone that makes me wonder if he's worried that I'll break.

He isn't going to tell me the real reason…

"I'm scared," I admit, the words slipping from my mouth moments before I realize I shouldn't have uttered them.

Cameron, who's giant six-foot five frame is overpowering the tiny chair beside the bed, places one of his hands on mine. With this simple touch, it feels like lightning bolts awaken feelings in me and I flinch, but this time I don't immediately pull away as he squeezes my hand.

"I hate you," I say, moving away from him and trying to force tears from betraying me.

Cameron doesn't respond, but only shifts his large frame in the chair which his body makes appear as though the chair was designed for a toddler. If he doesn't stop moving in it, I'm certain he'll end up falling out of it and crash onto the floor.

Eh, perhaps that would be karmic retribution.

I rub the tears from my eyes with my free hand and jump to change the conversation, "Where are the Assadis?"

I need to know that they're safe, or all of this happened for nothing. I'll deal with Cameron and whatever the hell happened between us when he touched me – at some point later.

Later, or perhaps never.

I closed this chapter years ago after he quite literally closed a door in my face, and I cannot open those old wounds. I need him to get away from me right now, because his touch is doing things to me.

"Don't worry, we aren't going to leave them behind." Cameron responds, staring at me with intensity and mesmerizing me momentarily with the swirl of light brown flecks dancing around in his eyes.

A hesitant smile flashes on his face, exposing just one of his dimples. "I'm glad you're alive. I…"

"Don't. Please. I can't do this right now. Don't pretend this is anything more than work."

I need to get out of here and away from him.

I start tugging at the wires again. I feel like I am on death's doorstep, and I don't want to go down an emotional rabbit hole with Cameron while I still have no idea what will happen to my assets. There's no way I am going to be left out of the plans related to their safety. I also can't stand to have his eyes on me right now. Action feels like medicine, and I need as much distraction as possible to keep my thoughts and feelings about Cam in check.

"Andy you're going to bleed to death if you don't chill the fuck out!" Cameron's warm eyes turn cold as the smile melts off his face and turns to a chilling glare.

There it is.

Cameron doesn't understand. He doesn't know what it was like to have to prove himself as the *only* woman in an office full of men. None of my coworkers have the balls to do what I did the other night, and I'll be damned if I'm going to let them swoop in and debrief my asset. I also don't trust them to protect the Assadi family, and I need to ensure they get out of Brasilia too. What Cam also doesn't know, a detail I'm not ready to tell any of them yet, is that whatever was in that vial is now inside me – and I can't risk station finding out about that.

"You don't get it. If I don't go up there, those guys are going to shit all over my case. You have no idea what it's like being the only woman in a sea of testosterone," I sneer, trying to push him out of my way.

"You think I don't know what it's like being *the only*? How many other Black GS officers have you *ever* seen? None – because it's just me," he responds, his eyebrows flaring upward.

"I don't want to get into the oppression Olympics with you Cam. I just need to go do my job," I reply, rolling my eyes.

Cameron and I had many conversations in the past about what it's like often being the only Black person in the room at the agency. While I often felt like he was one of the only people who could understand how I felt, it's frustrating how he still seems to miss how his gender allows him to move through spaces in ways I cannot.

"Cam, you don't get to weigh in on my life decisions. You gave up that right the night you decided to blow up our relationship."

Cameron drops my hand and puts both of his hands up as though he's being stopped by a police officer.

"Just get away from me and leave me alone," I say, shoving him a little harder this time to push past him to get out of the bed.

Adrenaline still pumps through my veins as I piece together the events of the night. With each movement, I feel like my organs are going to spill out of the stab wound in my side. Turning my head away from Cameron to shield the pain on my face, I grab the machine I was hooked up to and wheel it with me out of the room. My leg is still on fire and while I know I should tell the doctors everything, I'm scared of what will happen to me if I do.

"Andy, wait! Can you at least let me help you if you are going to insist on getting up and walking out of here?" Cameron jumps out of his chair and starts down the hall with me.

As I approach the secure office door, a 600 square foot vault that requires badge access, I pull my badge out of my hospital gown pocket. Luckily, I'd grabbed it off the bedside table before walking out. Swiping my yellow badge over the reader, I press my entire body against the heavy vault door to open it.

Inside, my boss Chief of Station (COS) Triden Brody sits at his desk surrounded by several of my coworkers. Everyone looks disheveled and tired as though Brody dragged them all out of a peaceful slumber. As usual, I'm the only woman and the only Black person (besides Cameron, who's now standing beside me) in the room. Though it's normal here to be the only one, I still scan the room and count every time I enter a space.

Five men...

and me.

Six White men...

Zero women today...

but me...

Tonight, I'm the only woman, so I know this will be a bro-fest that the dudes won't be happy about me breaking up.

"What the hell are you doing out of bed?" Brody asks as soon as he notices me standing at the door.

"Doing my job," I raise my voice, before immediately regretting taking that type of salty tone with my boss.

If you'd been doing yours, you'd have made sure I was here before meeting about my case.

"What are you all doing here?" I ask, continuing to scan the room as though it's going to give me clues to what I've missed.

I know I shouldn't be catching an attitude with Brody, but I'm so angry that I can't hold my tongue. I pull back my tone because I'm also deeply aware of the ever-present danger of being labeled "the angry Black woman." I take a deep breath, trying to calm down and avoid coughing up blood again. I'm not going to let one of my thirsty, male coworkers take credit for all my work by jumping in for the debrief and writing the Intelligence report.

Oh God...and the serum...what's in the serum?!?

"We aren't planning to debrief Basir until you all are safely back on American soil. Right now, we're focused on an extraction plan," Brody says dismissively, returning his focus to his computer.

I grab the IV fluid stand, and slowly drag it over to the couch by Brody's office door. Scanning the room, the men are huddled around Brody's computer.

Except Cameron...who hasn't taken his eyes off me since we entered the room.

Brody's office sits to the right of the vaulted door. It's large, complete with several bookshelves, two safes large enough for an average sized person to hide in, and a large desk in the back of the room. The window behind Brody's desk is covered with a blackout curtain, which always makes the room unusually dark. The small desk lamp doesn't provide enough light to avoid the cave-like feel of this room.

Brody's office is usually clean, but today it looks like a makeshift war room – maps strewn across the desk, hard copies of embassy rosters on the floor, an extra monitor showing GPS footage of the GRS team at Farhad's apartment, and a whiteboard with man scribble all over it.

"What's the team looking for in the apartment?" My question causes the room to fall silent, and everyone's eyes land on me.

Brody, whose blond hair is tousled indicating he didn't bother to comb out the bedhead, looks between me and the whiteboard with a list of Iranian officials. I swallow and look at the dozens of names on the board, most I don't recognize.

"Basir isn't just an Iranian Government official...he's a scientist," Cameron interjects, hovering by the office door as though he's afraid to make sudden moves.

"Well, Iranian official or not...they know he has something they want, and Basir knew that taking it would be his key to get out of Iran," Brody says.

I stumble back from the desk and sit on the couch. I feel a lump in my throat as though the words are clogged there. I don't know exactly *what* this technology is, but I have a strong suspicion it's now inside me – coursing through my veins.

"Do you think that whatever Basir brought with him is still in the apartment?" I ask the room, not directing my question toward any single person.

They aren't going to find what they're looking for in that apartment.

"We sure as hell hope they do because if they don't – it could mean one of the bad guys got it," Brody responds.

Conversation continues around me and luckily none of them assume I have anything to offer which allows me to listen without revealing what I know.

"Andy, did Basir say anything to you about a vial?" Brody asks, glancing over to me with a seriousness that pins me in place.

"A vial?" I ask, not wanting to give anything away.

"Basir left Iran with a vial filled with a serum that he claims is the key to some kind of revolutionary weapon production," Brody says, now looking back at the papers in front of him.

I feel like my heart just stopped as I quickly try to process what's just been said, "wait, what?"

On no...I know where the serum is, but these guys can't know.

"He contacted our team months ago when he was trying to find a way out. We didn't know he'd found a way until you found him Andy," Cam responds, back to studying my face.

"Did Basir say where the serum is? Did he say anything else about it?" I ask, trying to keep my voice from shaking and these guys finding out that *I* know where the serum is.

Here I thought Basir was just another defector, here to tell us all about his government job over the course of a series of debriefs, but the whole time he planned to turn over the vial in exchange for asylum.

"We haven't been able to locate the serum and Basir isn't being as forthcoming as we'd hoped," Brody replies.

Thank God.

The men continue jabbering among themselves, but I can no longer pay attention to them. The realization of my dire circumstances grips me. I just killed a man, who injected me with some sort of nuclear serum, after he busted down the door of my Iranian asset during a debrief. And now my freedom is in jeopardy because it's only a matter of time before my body is considered U.S. Government property. Basir wants asylum for him and his family and to get that kind of deal, he'll eventually have to tell them what happened with the vial.

"Oh snap...the dead guy is an Iranian henchman?" Theo exclaims, eyes wide and bringing his fist to his mouth.

Theo, a friend of Cameron's from college who joined the service with him, always tended to say the worst thing possible and then regret it shortly after. I guess he hadn't grown out of that. I used to like Theo because he always made me laugh and was a great counterbalance to Cameron's more serious personality. Almost as soon as the words leave his lips, Theo peers over at me and mouths an apology. I raise a hand and wave it off so that he will think I'm okay, but the room starts feeling way too crowded and like the walls are closing in on me.

Until the last few moments, I thought I'd be given temporary leave in the US to heal and debrief Basir, before returning to finish my tour in Brazil. But killing an Iranian diplomat/henchman, and now a vessel for whatever was in that vial, it's clear that I'm not coming back to Brazil or any other OCONUS location any time soon.

Will I even be safe at home?

Cameron places a gentle hand on my shoulder. "If it hadn't been him, it would've been you. I am glad it *wasn't you*."

Do they think I'm upset about shooting my attacker?

He's right. I killed that man in self-defense. But I have bigger problems than that Iranian henchman. I'm more worried about what is inside me and what my own government will do to get the information they need from me.

And why that henchman injected me with the serum he was apparently supposed to be taking back to Iran with him...

"Did anyone see me — identify me?" My heart races and sweat begins to bead on my chest beneath the hospital scrubs.

"We aren't sure but given the number of people present at your meeting place who could have seen you with the son..." Brody's voice trails off as his eyes dart from Cameron to the rest of the security team.

Closing my eyes, I try to remember every detail in that restaurant – the wooden bar stools, the smell of Brazilian Brahma Beer mixed with the aroma of the grease and meat cooking on the grill. With my eyes still closed, I scour my memory.

Was someone watching me?

Did anyone else look out of place?

I count every person, every car, and every window where someone could've watched from the shadows.

To anyone who saw me there, especially without the vial recovered – they'd know that I could be the one who had it. I don't even want it, but why did Basir want me to have it?

"*One, two, three*"...still counting how many people would have seen me there. My voice is now audible to those around me, and I feel the level of danger increase with each possible witness in my memory.

The meticulous steps I took that night, required for operational security, continue looping through my head like a movie set to rewind. I didn't spot surveillance, but I can't be sure Basir and his family didn't bring surveillance or that our communication wasn't intercepted, and we walked right into an ambush.

And my lazy co-workers should've been there to watch my back.

I shoot my boss a side-eye, intentionally trying to express my irritation all over my face.

Brody stares back at me, as though he's trying to read my expression. Typically, I plaster a smile on my face to avoid the men in my office telling me to smile more. I'm an intense person, and my blackness doesn't give me the luxury of being myself at work. To navigate this environment, without constantly being misunderstood, I usually try hard to make myself less intimidating. This is likely the first time my coworkers have seen me without my work filter, because at this moment I don't have the energy to put on my usual act.

Everyone is looking at me as though they're worry that any comment could make me snap – they aren't wrong to think that. I look at Cam, whose eyes show his concern by the deep crease between his eyebrows, and then at the floor. I sink deeper into the couch and clutch the pillows to try and anchor myself in place. I don't want to go back to the nurse's station. I *deserve* a seat at this table.

Todd, my officemate — who's always sure to let people know he is a Harvard graduate — interjects, "Shouldn't I do an initial debrief with the Assadi's to obtain more information about the vial and negotiate resettlement? I mean, I *am* the best at conducting debriefs out of everyone in this office."

Todd tosses his straight, shoulder length brown hair to the side and shoots a menacing smirk toward me. I loathe Todd. He's notorious for mansplaining, and he always acts as though his Harvard degree is proof that he's the smartest in the room. While he's rarely the largest man in the room, standing only a couple inches taller than me at 5'8", he always walks into a room with his chest first. His arms are always slightly outstretched as though he wants people to think his lateral muscles are too large for them to hang normally at his sides. I hate just about everything about this guy and it's growing increasingly difficult to fake as though he doesn't irritate the living hell out of me.

"I didn't see any of you stand up and volunteer to provide counter surveillance on the night I got my ass beat by that man who was trying to kill me — so thanks, but I got this."

For additional dramatic impact, of which I have zero shame, I lift my hospital gown enough for them to see the bloodstained bandages covering my stab wound.

"Uh...well," Todd starts to speak but is sharply cut off.

"No, Todd. Shut the hell up, man." Cameron, who towers over Todd in height, stands up while delivering this warning.

Though Todd cowers back after Cameron's show of bravado, I still ponder whether I can get away with punching him in the jaw. Per usual, Todd tries capitalizing on the moment and feels entitled to take over my case just because he is him. Todd is a lazy opportunist, and I'm hell-bent on blocking him from getting yet another ill-deserved win.

"Brody, they trust me. There's no way they're gonna talk to Todd," I grab my side as I lift myself off the couch and walk back toward Brody's large, wooden desk.

"Andy, if you don't relax and sit down, I'm going to send you back to the med unit and have them chain you to the bed." Holding up his hand and pointing toward the couch, Brody sternly peers at me over the rims of his reading glasses.

Fuck you, Todd.

I bite my lip to avoid cursing out loud and retreat toward the door a few steps.

"We aren't going to debrief them here anyway. We don't have enough time," Brody's eyes dart to the clock hanging on the wall before turning them toward Rove.

"Extraction will be complicated because the Brazilian authorities are not looking at this as self defense – but instead just as a murder. The apartment was registered to Farhad so he is likely already a suspect, but if anyone saw Andy with him, she will be a suspect too," Rove explains, directing his words at Cameron instead of me.

"Do we know whether they have issued any kind of warrant?" Cameron asks, also acting as though I'm not in the room or capable of discussing my own extraction.

"Guys, stop treating me like I'm not standing right the F here. I'm a person – stop talking about me like I'm an object on your chess board," I say, raising my voice.

My face is getting hot. The way these guys are acting is making me feel as though I've been transported back to childhood – powerless.

Feeling dizzy, and not wanting anyone in the room to know this, I slowly start making my way toward the door. Now that Brody destroyed Todd's attempt to hijack my case, at least for now, maybe it's safe to go back to the med unit. Certainly, it's safer than staying and giving them the satisfaction of seeing my body completely fail me. I need them believing that I'm fully capable of handling my own debrief.

With each step, the room spins faster and faster. I close my eyes momentarily to regain composure, and then make a quick move toward the door. Getting on the other side of the door before blacking out is critical for my professional integrity in this situation. If I can just sit on the steps outside the office, I think I'll be okay.

I can feel Cameron's eyes on the back of my head, and he's close enough that his breath gently brushes the back of my neck.

He smells good.

Fuck, I don't WANT to smell him.

"I will be right back," Cameron says to everyone else as he follows me out the door.

As soon as the vault door closes behind us, I grab the wall to stabilize myself. I involuntarily cry out, the pain overwhelming. It feels like I'm back in that apartment and the man with the whip is stabbing me in the side all over again. I'm disoriented and suddenly not even sure where I am. I know I'm not in the apartment, but this feels so real and when I close my eyes, I can see the man coming at me again.

Am I losing my mind too?

"I think I need help — I can't see...oh...*help!*"

My words are labored, frantic, and I have no control over my body as the room begins to spot.

I can't lose consciousness. I can't...

I slump down toward the ground and reach out for Cameron as warm tears run down my cheeks. Before hitting the ground, Cameron sweeps me up into his arms and bounds down the stairs toward the med unit. Blood soaks my shirt, as I slip in and out of consciousness.

"It's going to be okay, Andy. You're okay... I promise."

I appreciate that Cameron is trying to reassure me, but I have no control over my own body. Terrified over this complete lack of control, I start to worry that I won't live long enough to make it home. For all I know, that serum could be a ticking time bomb.

Once we arrive at the med unit, the nurse meets us at the doorway. She opens the doors and pulls machines and IV bags toward us as Cameron lays me on the gurney. I watch the panicked bodies rush around me, blurry and whizzing past, trying to push me to respond to the poking and prodding. I can't speak because breathing is taking every ounce of energy I have left. Trying hard to remain conscious, my eyes flutter. I'm trapped in a body that isn't responding to my desperate attempts to move. Then suddenly, despite my best efforts, I'm gone again.

Chapter 4
Lifeline

"Cameron"

I need to grow my hair back because running my hands through the buzz cut isn't at all easing my anxiety about this situation. I can't remember the last time I've gotten a good night's sleep. My head feels like someone is stabbing me in the sinuses with a blunt kitchen knife and I can hear my pulse thumping loudly in my ears. My migraines can get bad and if I don't find a way to sleep, I'll be useless to everyone.

As I rub at my temples, trying to calm the stabbing pain, I glance toward Andy who's laying in the hospital bed next to me. She's hooked up to the tubes again and as I scan her face and neck, I take note of the bruises and gashes.

She's still the most beautiful woman I've ever seen.

I don't deserve her forgiveness. While I've hoped to have the opportunity to show her how much I love her, I didn't want it to be like this. Though irrational, given how thoroughly I betrayed her trust, I still held out hope that one day she'd contact me.

...or respond to one of my many attempts to contact her over the years.

I wish things hadn't gotten so messed up between us, and that I could've been mature enough to just handle my shit without pushing her away from me. Seeing her again reminds me of how much I miss her.

Like a pathetic, lovesick puppy, I've been following her social media and trying to keep tabs on her through mutual friends. For years, I've convinced myself that what happened was for the best and that perhaps I've remembered our relationship through unrealistic rose-colored glasses. The alternative – admitting that I ruined the best relationship with the best woman I'll ever have in my life – is just too painful. But looking at her now, after all these years, it's clear that I've never stopped loving this woman. There is no way I'm going to stand by while men like Brody and Todd try to exploit her, making selfish decisions that negatively impact her safety.

I feel helpless. She collapsed in my arms like a rag doll. She was there one moment, giving those guys what they deserved and just a moment later she was gone. And all I can do is sit here and watch her chest rise and fall as if my gaze will keep her alive.

"What's wrong with her?" I ask the nurses, who scurry around the room checking her vitals.

"She's going into hypovolemic shock from rapid blood loss. We need to get a hold of the doctor on call," one of the nurses responds, scrolling through her cell phone contacts presumably looking for the doctor.

As they wait for the doctor, I desperately search the room, thinking of ways to help. Everyone on my team had to go through a paramilitary emergency medical course so that each of us could stabilize patients on the battlefield until they could be transported to a proper hospital. So, I know enough to know that Andy doesn't have time for us to keep waiting. I grab her tiny, cold hand in mine while nurses continue to scramble for a solution.

"She's lost a lot of blood. We can't find a good vein easily," the nurse who's been furiously poking Andy's arm says.

These nurses don't seem to know what they're doing, or perhaps the chaos of the whole situation is causing them to lose their focus.

I can relate to that.

"We don't have enough here. We need the doctor to bring more from the hospital," another said from across the room.

"Take mine. We're both O positive," I say, feeling hopeful because this is something I can do that doesn't involve me sitting in a panic with everyone else in the room.

Stay calm son...don't let your emotions keep you from making the right moves.

In these moments when I can feel myself starting to panic, my dad's voice always pops into my head. He was the most stoic man I've ever met. I remember Rove laughing with my dad about a time when a bomb went off in their camp while they were serving together during Desert Storm. They were having burgers. Everyone else dropped everything and ran for cover, and as everyone huddled inside the safe zone, they all noticed that my dad continued eating his burger.

"Well, I wasn't going to leave a perfectly good piece of meat in the sand," my dad said, offering a moment of humor in the middle of what Rove described as living hell.

The man was unflappable and my entire life I've wavered between wishing I could be that way and cursing the fact that he never seemed to see the value in my capacity to feel deep emotions. To him, I was "too soft" but there are times when I believe that ability to understand people and empathize allows me to make the best decisions in this line of business. Of course, it's taken years in therapy for me to accept that I will never be like my father and that maybe that's not actually a bad thing.

The nurses argue back and forth about protocol, and I notice that they're no longer even looking in my direction. I can't just sit here and let her die, so I do what needs to be done. Their bickering creates the perfect distraction, while I grab Andy's arm and quickly drive the needle in. She lets out a quiet whimper, which makes me wince.

"I'm sorry," I whisper in her ear.

But thank God she's conscious enough to feel something.

Then, I shove another needle into my arm and blood begins to flow between us. I'm not sure how long we sit there, my blood pumping rapidly into her arm, before the nurses realize what I've done. I feel lightheaded but notice that Andy has started to move. One of the nurses runs across the room, so quickly it's as though she leaps into the air and flies to disconnect my arm from the tube transferring life back into Andy. Turning to Andy and shining a small light into her eyes, the nurse scolds me.

"What's happening...where am I," Andy asks, eyes still closed and wincing as the nurses continue to poke and prod.

"The wound on your abdomen opened up, and you lost enough blood to send you into shock," the doctor, who's just arrived, explains.

"She needs to go to the hospital," one of the nurses interjects.

"We can't take her to the hospital here. It's too dangerous," I interrupt, cutting off any consideration of exposing her location to local authorities, Iranian officials, or possibly even terrorists searching the area.

The doctor nods in understanding, "very well, then you're going to need to load up and get her out of here immediately or she's not going to survive this."

This probably isn't this doctor's first rodeo here.

I roll down the sleeves of my shirt, covering up a few drops of blood I hadn't bothered to clean and grab the satellite phone out of my pocket to dial Rove's number. The team doesn't have time to keep searching that apartment. Anything worth finding is likely already gone anyway. We need to get Andy out of here and debrief Basir somewhere safer for everyone.

"We have to leave now—Andy lost a lot of blood, and the doctor said he can't keep her stable for long here," I bark into the phone.

"The guys have already packed up – by the time we got there it had already been swept. Nothing but clothes and personal items the family left behind," Rove says, frustration in his voice.

"Did you find cameras or anything that would've revealed that Andy was in that apartment and connected to this?" I ask, hoping nobody saw her.

There's silence on the phone for a few moments before Rove continues.

"Our guys weren't there in time to wipe the footage from the apartment cameras and by the time we did arrive, the guard in the security booth had a bullet in his head."

Shit...

Andy's eyes shift toward me, and I can tell she's studying my face. Even though we've been apart for years, I'm afraid she still knows me well enough to tell that I'm worried. Turning my back, trying not to worry her more than she likely already is, I end the call with Rove with a simple acknowledgement that we'll head toward the airfield as soon as the doctor clears Andy for transport.

"Did they find anything? Did they see the vial?" Andy asks, with a clarity that's surprising given the state she was in a little over an hour ago.

"No, the place had already been swept when they arrived. Did you get anything from Basir before you left?" I ask, wondering if there's something she hasn't told me.

Andy is silent and I *know* there is something she isn't saying.

"Andy, Brody asked you if saw the vial and you didn't respond. What aren't you telling us?" I ask, trying to read her body language to figure out what's going on with her.

Her entire body stiffens in the bed and she turns away from me, curling into herself with her arms folded against her body. She closes her eyes, and I can hear her taking rapid breaths as the machines begin to beep wildly.

"Andy, what's wrong? What's happening right now?" I ask, reaching for her.

"Boy, you need to stop whatever you are doing. No more questions right now. She isn't stable and whatever Intelligence you are looking for – that can wait son," the doctor says, placing his body in front of me like a wall between Andy and me.

"Boy? Fout tone," I mutter under my breath, knowing that the doctor likely won't understand the creole expletive my mother always said when she didn't think we were listening.

"What was that?" The doctor asks, raising an eyebrow.

I clear my throat before responding, "um, nothing. We, we need to get her out of here. Do you think she can be cleared to leave in the next ten minutes?"

"I'll do my best, but perhaps it would be best if you cleared out," the doctor says, glaring at me.

I take a deep breath, and back away from the doctor. I can feel my anxiety rising and that's not helping this situation. My priority is to get Andy out of here so instead of continuing to argue with the doctor, I raise my hands in surrender and back out of the room.

You cannot get removed from this case – keep your cool man. But what is Andy hiding?

I shove the door a little harder than I expect on the way out, causing it to fly open and slam into the wall on the other side. I take a deep breath of the fresh night air and wonder what time it is. The parking lot is empty, and the embassy is still silent enough to hear my own heartbeat in my ears.

How did I end up in this situation?!?

The first time in years I get the chance to see Andy and it just so happens to be in the middle of the biggest case of my entire career. It's like the universe is testing me, throwing my past in my face, and forcing me to make amends while also proving I'm ready to lead my own team. Taking a few deep breaths, avoiding what feels like a bout of panic bubbling just beneath the surface, I pull out my phone and press forward.

"Marine one," the voice of one of the marines answered in a sleepy voice.

"Bring the van around the back. I think we're ready to load up and head out," I respond, rubbing a hand through my hair and pacing on the sidewalk.

"Sure thing, boss. The driver told me he was ready whenever you called. I'll send him around," the marine says, yawning audibly into my ear.

"Hey man, I hope you're able to get some rest soon. Thank you for helping us out today," I say, hoping that my sincere appreciation comes through.

Several of the marines here have pulled an extra-long shift these past couple of days. The entire embassy compound has been in a state of high alert that started the moment Andy drove through the embassy gates with Basir and his family. In addition to pulling extra shifts to secure the compound, several of them have also worked through their time off to join my team searching the apartment.

Just as I see the van round the corner toward where I'm standing, the embassy doors burst open, and nurses wheel the stretcher where Andy is laying toward where I'm standing. As she passes me, she grabs a hold on my shirt, startling me.

"Cam – I need you to do something for me," she says weakly, still holding a fist full of my polo in her hand.

"Okay, what do you need?" I ask, looking around us to make sure nobody is within earshot in case she makes me agree to something insane.

"You can't let Brody or Todd...or anyone else debrief Basir before I do, okay?" She pleads, her deep blue grey eyes fixed intensely on mine.

I'm confused and wonder what is isn't saying. I know she doesn't want the guys to take credit for her work, but her insistence while she's in this state seems a little too extreme.

"Promise me, Cam," she says, glancing toward the nurses who've been busy securing the stretcher in preparation to board the van.

"Okay, I'll try," I reply, unsure what sort of power I will have in this situation.

"Cam please, I need you to do this *one* thing," she insists, now pulling on my collar tight enough to start restricting blood flow.

"Okay, okay...I will," I reply.

Andy shoots the nurses around us an arresting look with her now piercing blue green eyes. She's the only person I've ever seen whose eyes can change color with her mood. They all keep their distance as we wait to depart. After looking into my eyes for a moment longer, she shoves me away from her with enough force it shocks me.

"Damn woman, over here asking me for help whilst also shoving me like we're in a bar fight," I say under my breath, glancing over at her just in time to catch her looking at me with a look that seems halfway between disgust and anger.

The look in her eyes makes me feel like someone's just punched me in the gut and knocked the wind out of me. I turn away from her, embarrassed at how this one look is making me feel, and find myself wondering and longing for her to look at me the way she used to look at me...before I ruined everything.

Chapter 5
Sirens and Cicadas

"Andy"

When the cicadas come out in Brasilia, they're so loud that it sounds like a siren. The first time I heard them, I ran out of my apartment wondering if I needed to find a bomb shelter and take cover until the threat passed. When I looked around and saw the locals milling about calmly at the fresh market across the street from my building, I was so confused.

Why aren't they running?

How come nobody else is freaking out?

When I asked a man walking past me about the alarm, he laughed and explained that the cicadas get loud during mating season.

While I wait to leave this place, the cicada's siren-like music is all I can hear. Given the current situation, the noise is appropriate — perhaps they're warning us to get out of this country with all due necessary urgency and speed.

Just as the sound starts to lull me deeper into my thoughts, Cameron walks back over to me and pushes me for details I've been avoiding speaking out loud.

"Andy — I just spent months in the middle of a Fucking desert...waiting for Basir to cross the border with that vial. If you have more information, you need to tell me," he says, voice raised and face flushing.

I flinch at the tone of his voice, surprising even myself with my reaction.

Is he angry at me?

"Wait, back up...are you getting angry with me?" I ask, raising my tone to match his to ensure he knows who's in charge here.

Immediately regretting asking him for anything, I wrap my arms around myself protectively and fix my face in an expression meant to intimidate.

"I'm sorry Andy, I'm not mad – I don't want to hurt you. I just...I just want to understand..." Cameron's voice trails off as he retreats a few steps from me and raises his hands in a surrendering motion.

You've already hurt me.

"I don't *need* to do anything just because you ask," I respond, defensively.

"Look, there are some really terrible people...and organizations... looking for that vial, and I'm not even just talking about the Iranian government," he says, rubbing his hand through his hair.

"What do you mean?" I ask nervously, hoping that he's not about to share something that's going to make my situation even worse.

"That vial everyone is after – it's an essential nuclear agent the Iranians developed under the guise economy sustaining nuclear energy. But when the larger global community found out about it, just about every terrorist organization on the planet started coming for it," he replies, his voice low and eyes darting around as if worrying someone else might hear him.

"What do you mean, 'coming for it'?" I ask, head spinning and trying to make sense of all this.

"There were a few bad actors inside the Iranian government who took control of production and were ready to sell it to the highest bidder, regardless of intention," he replies, pinning me in place with his eyes as they reflect the bright lights from the embassy exterior.

"Did they sell it?" I ask, trying to piece this all together.

"My team was in Afghanistan for an operation called 'Solaris'. The facility in Iran where Basir worked, and where the serum was being stored, was raided and all the vials were stolen. A terrorist group, Solaris, were allegedly responsible for the break-in," he explains.

"If Solaris stole all the vials, how did Basir have one?" I ask, starting to hear my heartbeat pulsing loudly in my ears.

"All vials were reported stolen but Basir got out with one. We've been communicating with Basir for months and were waiting for him to cross the border and head to our base with the vial," he replies, a look of irritation spreading across his face.

"Okay, so then why didn't he follow through with the plan and come to *you all* instead of *me?*" I ask, wishing like hell he'd chosen to follow through with his original plan.

"Well, that's the part I don't have an answer for. I have no idea why he broke the plan and came here," he says, placing a hand to his head and looking past me as though he was trying to make sense of this himself.

"So, Basir brought the vial out in exchange for asylum for his entire family. Did your team promise that?" I ask, wondering what will happen to the Assadi family now that Basir doesn't actually have a vial to hand over.

Would he tell them the vial is inside me for exchange for asylum?

Cameron moves to close the distance between us, lowering his voice, "I don't even know how much I'm allowed to share with you — but I can say that we knew Basir would come out with that vial. We were waiting for him. We just don't know why he came *here*. And we don't know what happened to the vial because he hasn't given it to any of us."

I wish he'd come to you first.

"We told him to take a vial, destroy the rest of the lab, and meet us at the rally point with his family," he says, shaking his head.

When Farhad approached me and told me that his father wanted to share some intelligence, I had no idea that I'd end up being the intelligence.

Why did Basir choose to come to me?

"Wait, I ran a trace on Farhad after he first approached me. None of the information I found mentioned your team had anything to do with this," I say, also remembering that Brody insisted I meet up with Basir.

"You wouldn't have had access to it, but Brody would have. Operation Solaris is compartmented and only a handful of people knew Basir was coming out," Cameron says, his eyebrows furrowing.

"And of course, he didn't bother to mention it to me because he didn't want to wait for your team," I say, taking a deep breath to try and calm myself down.

Anger over my current situation starts to boil at the surface, making me feel like it will burst through my skin. I wonder what this all means for me, since the nuclear agent that everyone is looking for is *inside* me.

Can I trust Cameron?

Can I trust my own government?

Do I have a choice?

I don't want to be property of the U.S. Government, but I also have no idea what this thing is going to do to me – or if I can even deal with this alone. When Basir handed the vial to me in the apartment he told me not to keep it out. Did he know that man would inject me with it? Did he know that was even a possibility? None of this makes sense and it's clear there are major parts of this story that neither me nor Cameron have.

"If you knew where the vial was, would you tell me?" Cam asks, tilting his head to study me again.

"Stop interrogating me Cam," I snap, avoiding his questions again and feeling panicked that he keeps insisting.

Does he already know?

"Andy, are you serious right now? Do you realize how dangerous this is?" Cameron asks, looking at me with a mix of confusion and irritation.

"Are *you* serious right now Cam? I just got the shit beat out of me and nearly died and all you can think about right now is your job and pumping me for information. Fuck yourself," I say, reaching out and shoving him in the shoulder as hard as I can to push him away from my bed.

The machine at my bedside starts beeping loudly and I feel lightheaded from shoving him. At the sign of distress, the nurses run to my side. One of them body-checks Cameron further out of the way with so much force that he trips over the sidewalk curb and stumbles backward. The doors of the Marine van, hollowed out in the back to make room for the stretcher, fly open. I'm getting pushed and prodded again, and my entire body still hurts.

I know I should tell someone what's inside me, because what if it kills me before I can...

Cameron is back at my side and tries to grab ahold of my hand. Every bump in the pavement as they load me into the van feels like someone's sticking their dirty fingers in my open wounds. I'm too weak to fight him off this time so I just allow him to take hold of my hand.

All these men are literally salivating over that vial, like the first one to find it will strike gold. Typically, at least somewhat in control of my own operations, I feel more vulnerable than ever. I can't help the Assadi's right now like I promised because I can't even help myself.

My body is still shaking — the Brazilian night chill in the air is biting, and the warm blankets the nurses cover me in aren't enough to keep my teeth from chattering. This makes me feel out of control and chilled to my bones, worried I'll never feel safe or warm again.

I look over at Cameron, who's still silent. His eyes are bloodshot, and tears threaten the corners. I've never known Cameron to be a crier. When his father died, he didn't cry for months and then when he did it was like an explosion. I remember telling him at the time that this wasn't healthy and worrying he'd put himself in an early grave with his insistence on emotional suppression.

As my eyelids begin to feel heavy, Cameron places a gentle hand on my shoulder and finally responds.

"It's going to be OK. I'm not going to let anyone hurt you. And I promise that I'll do what I can to hold off the Basir debrief for as long as possible."

He turns away, but I can see him wipe his eyes.

"Okay – we're ready to roll," a Marine says, slamming the van doors and knocking on them to indicate the driver is free to go.

As the van slowly rolls through the opening gates, I watch Cameron. The nurses instruct me to keep taking slow, deep breaths into the oxygen mask. Cameron grabs one of my hands and strokes my hair with the other. I close my eyes, savoring this feeling of being cared for without my intruding and complicated thoughts destroying this moment. I desperately need just one moment to step outside the reality that I am completely alone.

"Rest, we'll talk when we get you home," Cameron says.

I nod, take a deep breath, and drift to sleep.

Cameron, is that you?

I'm calling to him because he's right in front of me, but he doesn't respond. I'm back in college. No, I'm not me. I'm watching me – with Cameron.

We're in his bedroom at the frat house and it's noisy because there's a party happening downstairs. We're about to have sex, for the first time. Cameron doesn't know this is, also, my first time ever. I haven't told him because I'm embarrassed.

He locks the door, turning around and flashing that one dimpled, crooked smile. I'm sitting on the bed, heart racing and nervous.

Not me now, college me. While dream me is here watching. Even though I know the girl on the bed is me, it still feels weird to be here with them – like voyeurism – but I cannot take my eyes off them.

Andy no! He's going to break your heart! I try to call to college me. But she can't hear me, just like he can't.

"Can I take off your clothes? I want to see you," he says.

College me is shy. Her face flushes as she looks at the ground.

You first – she says.

Cameron lifts his shirt over his head, revealing a chiseled six pack. His eyes are locked on college me, as he removes his pants and sits next to her. College me starts to take off her shirt, but he reaches to stop her. Then he gently starts trailing kisses from her neck down to her breasts as he gently unbuttons her shirt.

Wait, something is wrong. The room is spinning, the walls are melting, and the entire place is changing into somewhere else – Basir's apartment.

Oh no, we need to get out of here.

Andy! Cameron! No!

A large man enters the room – Cameron jumps in front of college me before the man shoves him to the side like he's swatting a fly.

I'm trapped in this room but cannot help Cameron or college me. He's going to kill them, and I am going to have to watch it.

Then I see a vial, and the man is now coming for me. Someone is holding me on a table and I can't move. Cameron and college me have disappeared – no, they melted through the floor.

What is happening to me? Is this real? Is this a nightmare?

Get off me – no, please don't put that in me!

I feel the needle stab me in the leg and my entire body explodes.

I'm screaming and there's a noise so loud that I can barely hear myself. Arms wrap around me, and I scream louder.

"No, no, get away from me," I scream.

Now someone is coming at me with a vial. I need to get out of here but I'm being held down. I kick and scream and claw at the man holding me on this table.

I'm going to die here.

I see the needle clearly before it's driven into my arm. And then the darkness and silence envelop me like an unwelcome restraint.

Chapter 6
Safehouse

"Cameron"

Running my hand through my hair, I pace back and forth in the area in front of my seat aboard the Air Medical flight they've contracted. Typically, these types of planes carry multiple patients, but for this special case – Uncle Sam splurged and didn't make us share. A raging headache is still threatening behind one of my eyes, the pressure of the flight making things worse. The plane reeks of diesel fuel that makes me feel like I'm going to throw up. I've never been able to deal with strong smells.

Boss, because his nose is one of his most valuable assets, stayed behind in Brazil to help the rest of the team search the apartment and its surroundings for the vial or any other evidence we needed to destroy. And in moments like these, I am acutely aware of how much I rely on Boss to help reduce my anxiety. That dog always seems to know just when to make me laugh or insist on belly rubs to take me out of my thoughts.

Andy is lucky they've given her meds to knock her out because she'd probably be complaining about the smell too if she were awake. The doctor's say the cocktail they gave her could have her toggling between barely conscious and completely knocked out for days. I promised Andy that I'd keep everyone away from Basir, but I am not sure I can do that given that I even want to run and debrief the guy. Waiting days for her to come back to a state of consciousness seems like a dangerous amount of time.

What if Basir can give us information on where the vial is? Time isn't exactly on our side here.

I consider what to do next and it feels like there are no great options that don't include doing something that could make Andy angrier than she already is at me. I also cannot betray her trust and expect things to improve between us. I also don't know if she realizes how important it is that we find that vial. Rove and the team have been scouring that apartment and the surrounding areas for the past day as well as listening to the Intelligence chatter and we've gotten nowhere. The next logical option is to question Basir. I flop down on the seat and place my head in my hands, taking deep breaths to try and calm down.

I've always wished I could have a chill personality like my younger brother Gabe. Nothing ever seems to faze him. When I was seven years old and he was five, the two of us had gotten separated from our parents at the state fair. Though I've always felt responsible for him and was able to hold it together that day until we found our parents, my heart felt like it was going to explode from my chest that day. It was the first time I had a panic attack. Gabe, in stark contrast, told me he remembers that day feeling like an exciting adventure. Perhaps he never had to worry because I did enough worrying for both of us.

A blood curdling scream, that sounds like a mixture between a dying wild animal and a human, jolts me from my thoughts. My head pops up and I look over at Andy, whom I quickly realize is the source of the noise.

"Andy...Cameron...NO," she screams, flailing around on the bed, and swiping her arms in the air.

As the monitors start alarming, I run over to try and hold onto her so that she doesn't disconnect the IVs and monitors.

"Andy stop, you're okay. Wake up, you're safe," I try holding her tight as she scratches and claws at my arms.

"No, don't try to wake her," a nurse says, bringing out a shot of what I can only assume is intended to calm her down and put her back into a peaceful sleep.

"What is that? I thought she was supposed to have meds that would help her relax?" I ask, confused because what's happening now certainly doesn't look like anything close to a peaceful sleep.

The nurse doesn't respond to me, and instead continues toward Andy with the vial of medicine.

Andy's eyes are open and looking right at me, but it doesn't look like she realizes it's me holding onto her. As soon as she turns away from me, confusion and fear in her eyes, she spots the needle in the nurse's hand and starts fighting harder and screaming even louder.

"Get off me! Please don't...don't put that in me, please..." She howls and thrashes as though her life depends on it.

"Wait, do you have to do that? Didn't you all just give her a bunch of meds before we took off? She doesn't want it," I protest, worried about them putting something in her that she is clearly not consenting to.

"Sir, you need to move, or we are going to strap you to that wall over there. Unless you *want* this woman to die on this table you need to get out of my way," the large nurse who body checked me earlier says, giving me a stern and authoritative look.

"But she doesn't want it," I continue.

"Well sir, are you authorized to make medical decisions on her behalf?" The large nurse asks, sticking out her chest and placing her hands on her hips.

"No, but..." I say, before realizing that Andy and I don't have any relationship and she probably wouldn't want me making any decisions for her.

What if I were her husband? No...I screwed any chance at that happening...

"She isn't fully awake and isn't in a healthy enough state to consent to anything right now," another nurse says, seeming to appear from the back of the plane for backup.

It's clear that I can't handle whatever is going on with Andy now, so I reluctantly move far enough back for the nurse to continue. The nurse jabs the needle into Andy's arm so hard that I cringe, and Andy goes completely limp, her head flopping back on the stretcher.

My God, did they kill her?

I reach a hand to that space between her jaw and neck, checking for a pulse. She feels so cold, but there's a pulse.

"Why is she so cold?" I ask, looking at the large nurse who reminds me of Mrs. Worch, my strict, fourth grade teacher whose short, fiery red hair came with a matching personality.

"Her temperature is running a bit colder than expected, but I assure you that she is resting now. You should sit down and rest too," the Worch doppelganger responds, raising an eyebrow at me and glancing toward my seat.

I flash the same sheepish smile I'd give Mrs. Worch as a kid and walk back over to my seat.

Andy is alright. It's going to be okay...

I recline my chair back, thankful for the leg room to stretch out my legs, and drift into some version of sleep. It feels like my eyes are closed for only moments, though my watch tells me it's been a few hours, when I hear the pilot's voice boom over the loudspeakers.

"We're approaching descent, everyone please take a seat and attendants make sure the cabin is secure," he says, before nurses and flight attendants begin buzzing around the cabin to find their seats.

My satellite phone buzzes in my pocket and Rove's name flashes on the screen. Opening the text thread, I look for my next instructions.

(Rove) *We're taking her to Blue Castle*

(Me) *What? Isn't that a little extreme?*

(Rove) Just get your ass there. Get there and sleep. We debrief in the morning.

(Me) Roger

"Blue Castle" is the codename for the safe house at Camp David. It's remote and Camp David is a fortress — nobody's getting in there unless approved. It also houses an extensive bomb shelter and command center. This is *not* usual protocol. I assumed we'd head to one of the safe houses in Virginia. I've debriefed hundreds of people at safehouses all over the world but have yet to see Blue Castle.

The jolt of the plane as the landing gear touches ground snaps me from my thoughts. Andy is still passed out on the stretcher, her hair flowing across the pillow like a waterfall of wild curls.

I hope she can forgive me.

Rove will never let me stay on this case if I can't get it together. I need to be able to keep my feelings for Andy separate from my obligations as an officer for my country.

But I still pray she'll forgive me.

The doors of the plane open, and a dozen armed, black Chevy SUVs with blacked out windows — a tell-tale sign of secret service presence – pull up next to us.

Where the hell is my team?

Why do we need this type of backup for patient transport?

Who are all these people?

The nurses put Andy in the back of a black van, outfitted as an ambulance. Just as I move to follow her, Theo hops out of one of the Chevy's, jogs over to me, and blocks me.

"Nope, nice try buddy – you're coming with me. Take this," he says, handing me a Glock.

"Wait Theo...I thought you and the rest of the crew stayed behind to keep looking for that vial?" I asked, wondering if Rove sent Theo back because he didn't trust me to escort Andy alone.

"Nah Bro, we cleaned that apartment out and there was no trace of the vial or any paperwork that might help get us any closer to gaining the upper hand on Solaris. We were on a plane out of Brazil about an hour before yawl even left," Theo responded, his goofy top knot full of wavy hair bobbing around on top of his head.

"So, what's the plan now?" I ask, watching Andy as she's loaded into the black van.

"We debrief Basir. Ain't shit else we can do without talking to that guy," Theo replies.

Shit...

I follow Theo, begrudgingly, and hop into the passenger seat.

Clearing my throat, I say, "don't you think we ought to wait for Andy to lead the Basir debrief?"

"Dude, I know Andy is...well, Andy...but remember what this mission means for us," Theo warns.

"Is it that obvious?" I ask, letting my guard down for the moment.

Given that Theo is my teammate and has been my best friend since college, he knows the history and was around to witness the numerous times I've tried to contact her over the years.

"Anyone with eyes can tell that you aren't over that woman, Cam," Theo responds, patting me on the shoulder.

I sigh, combing a hand through my hair, before responding, "She still doesn't want anything to do with me. But seriously, she went through hell for this case...she should lead the debrief."

"Dude, you think Brody is gonna wait for her to wake up from whatever medical induced coma they put her in? We don't have time for all that nonsense and that dude Brody is sketchy as fuck," Theo says, glancing over at me and raising an eyebrow.

Damn man, the secret service is thick right now. What's the deal?" I ask, looking around at the entourage of secret service escorting us to Blue Castle.

"Hey man, I just follow orders — I have no idea why they brought the extra guns," Theo says, shrugging.

Theo, like my brother Gabe, has a naturally chill vibe. Perhaps that's why we are such good friends. He always seems to know exactly what to say to put things into perspective and help infuse some chill into my mood. Chaos could be unfolding around the man and if Rove tells him to run left into the eye of the problem – Theo will run left without a second thought.

Theo's always been this way too. In college, everyone would be stressed about exams and Theo would roll in after partying all night without a care in the world. And he'd *still* ace the exam. It's one of the reasons he's the perfect teammate because he'll run into the fire after any of us, and never be too stressed to get the job done.

People who don't know him as well as I do, might assume he's a meat head because he prefers playing "would you rather" and drinking beer while laughing at immature jokes than debating politics. In college, we called him an "uh oh Oreo" because he was the pale kid in a Black fraternity and all his closest friends were also Black. Theo was raised by two moms, one Black and one White. His biological mom is White, and they'd used a Biracial Black donor, so Theo always responded with, "though the cookies look vanilla – there's some chocolate in this body fellas".

Theo tears out of the parking lot along with several other SUVs. We race down the streets and through the empty beltway from Andrews Air Force Base to Camp David. The caravan isn't driving like they have precious cargo, but instead like we're running for their lives.

"Theo, what can you tell me," I ask, craving as much information as I can get prior to a meeting with Basir.

"Our team arrived an hour before your plane, and the secret service was already swarming the place," Theo responds.

Theo confirms that in addition to not finding anything in Basir's apartment, four cameras could've caught Andy at the scene – all of which were wiped or taken before they could get to them.

"There are a lot of cooks who've entered the kitchen on this one, man. This was clearly in CIA jurisdiction but now it seems the White House and the DOD want to get their hands in it," Theo says, swirling his hand to point at all the secret service vehicles trailing Andy's van.

"And Rove hasn't shut that shit down yet? You know how he hates it when the ants start crawling all over our cases," I respond, glancing down at my watch.

It's just past 5am when we arrive at the gates of Camp David, which means a trip that should've taken an hour and a half at normal speeds took us under an hour. We pull up to a cabin in the woods and Theo hands me the key.

"There's a control center attached to where Andy is staying. Stay in the control center man, don't make this messy. And if you choose chaos and make this messy, please lie and tell Rove that you stayed on the couch in the control center," Theo says, smirking.

I sigh, laughing to myself at how ridiculous that sounds.

Choose chaos? As if Andy would let me choose chaos.

"And take a shower dude, you smell like a horse's ass," Theo says, punching me in the shoulder and plugging his nose dramatically.

"Fuck off man, I smell like roses," I joke, laughing and shoving him back.

"Whatever man, ain't no chaos that's gonna happen tonight with you smelling like that," Theo says, trotting back to the truck before jumping in and peeling out of the parking area.

I count seven cameras hiding amongst the surrounding trees as I approach a cabin with two front doors - one labeled "A" and the other "B". Inspecting the ring of keys Theo handed me, I notice that the "A" key also has the inscription "ops center".

"Well, I guess this is the one I'm supposed to go to," I say to myself, wondering if there are people on the cameras who are wondering why I'm talking to myself like a nervous fool.

When the door opens, the entire cabin seems to shake a little bit as though it's made of flimsy tin. It reminds me of the bunkers we had in Afghanistan. They were so thin that I could hear the wind whistling all night sometimes, constantly worried that the next harsh wind would blow the entire thing away with me inside. Gently closing the door behind me, trying not to make the thing move again, I set down my duffle bag at the door and inspect the space. It's a small room, no more than about 400 sq feet with a couch, a computer, a small table next to a rolling white board, and a large window that overlooks the safehouse that shares the cabin. Having been in these types of spaces, I suspect Andy won't be able to see what's behind the window on her side.

Theo was right, I do need a shower and hope that I find one in what I assume is a bathroom behind the door in front of me. I spent the entire flight sweating through my clothes. Perhaps the shower could also wash the insanity of the past few days off me. Glancing through the window between the rooms, I watch as nurses transfer Andy from a stretcher to the bed. Her arms flop around, and she looks like a lifeless doll while they scurry around her, adjusting wires hooked to monitors and poking her with needles and other medical instruments.

Good God, more blood? Why do they keep taking more blood vials from her?

The door swings open, causing me to temporarily lose my balance with the tiny earthquake-like moment beneath my feet, snapping me to attention. Rove bounds through the door, closing it way too hard.

"You close that door any harder you might knock this tin can of a cabin completely down," I say, looking over at Rove, who also looks sweaty and intense now.

Rove looks like he hasn't slept in a few days either. His peppered grey and black hair is tousled into greasy spikes all over his head, and he's hunched over and panting to try and catch his breath.

"You okay man?" I ask, moving to him and placing a hand on his shoulder.

"Yeah, yes. I just...oof, I think we all need to get some rest," he responds, walking the few steps to the table in the middle of the room before flopping down into one of the folding chairs next to it.

Rove places a cloth lock bag on the table before fishing a small key out of his pocket to unlock the back. He pulls several manila folders out before jumping back out of his seat, causing the room to tremor again. I'm stunned at how he looks like he's in some sort of robotic trance and I don't know whether to stop him so that he doesn't keel over or let him keep going to see where this goes.

"Rove, what are you doing?" I ask, my eyes darting around the room as he continues posting photos one at a time before stepping back to look and the placement of each.

He doesn't respond, acting as though he can't even hear me.

"Didn't you say we'd debrief tomorrow?" I ask, wondering what gave Rove a renewed sense of urgency.

"No time for that," Rove responds, pinning another picture before standing back to look at it and then moving on to the next.

"Who are these people?" I ask, walking closer to examine the faces now staring back at me from the photos.

Oh snap, we both smell like we need a shower.

I grimace and turn my head away from Rove so he doesn't see my face turn what I suspect is a shade of green from the pungent odor wafting between us.

"These are suspected members of the Solaris group — and finding any of them could lead us to where they're keeping those vials," he responds point -blank.

"What's happening here? Can you catch me up to where you are, man?" I ask, wondering if my fatigue from lack of sleep is making it harder for me to connect the dots here.

I rub at my eyes and look back at the wall as Rove continues buzzing around the room as though he hasn't heard my questions. It feels like there's some secret that I haven't been let in on and as the wheels churn in my head, it's clear I don't have enough information to make sense of all this.

"*Why* are we here Rove? Why was Andy taken to this safe house," I ask, raising my voice a little louder to try and get his attention, but not loud enough to make him think I'm being insubordinate or disrespectful.

Rove stops, as though I've just interrupted some sort of trance he's been in and puts the pictures down on the metal table in the middle of the room before flopping down on one of the chairs at the table. I finch with discomfort as the cabin shakes at even this seemingly small movement. Being deployed to war zones for the last several years, when a shelter tremors even a little, I can't calm the voice in the back of my head that worries there's been an attack. But I've learned that I can't let my team see the anxiety that's always boiling just under the surface of my skin.

Don't be weak son...my dad always said when my nerves started to show.

I swallow hard and take a deep breath before taking a seat in the chair Rove pulls out next to him.

"Cam, *Andy* has the vial that Basir brought out of Iran and that's why we needed to bring her here," Rove says, as my head whips around to look at him.

What? SHE has it? Why did she lie to me?

"Um, what?" I ask, blood boiling and still trying to process the fact that she kept this from me.

I asked her about it several times, told her my team was searching that apartment inch by inch – putting themselves in danger – only to learn she had it the entire time.

"I had an initial debrief with Basir hours ago before your plane touched down," Rove admits.

Of course, they did. And this is exactly why Andy didn't want anyone talking to him before she did.

Unable to stop myself, I sigh audibly. Sitting back in my chair, I begin to rub my forehead in a desperate attempt to ward off the migraine that's been gnawing at my temples for at least a couple hours.

"Basir had the vial in his apartment. He said he tried to give Andy the vial to keep it safe, but when they were attacked..." Rove's voice trails off and he looks physically pained about what he'll say next.

"When they were attacked, what? Where is the vial?" I ask, impatiently and still furious that Andy lied to me about having it.

Rove looks at me with blood shot eyes and I can see deep worry lines on his forehead as he continues, "Cam, the guy who attacked them in Basil's apartment injected Andy with the serum."

Injected? Did he just say...

"Wait, what? He did *what?*" I ask, feeling my face twist with confusion as I'm sure I've misheard him.

"I know, it sounds totally nuts. But he insists that the serum is inside Andy and is refusing to say more until he can speak with her," Rove responds, looking grimly at me before glancing toward the window connected to Andy's room.

I don't immediately respond because it feels like actual bombs are going off in my brain right now and I cannot find my next question because hundreds are tangled inside.

"I, um...what did you say?" I ask again, hoping this time he will tell me something that makes sense.

"So as you can understand...we can't just let Andy go home like none of this happened because our Intelligence...well, it's allegedly inside her," he says, grimacing.

Fuck...this is why she didn't want us talking to Basir.

"When was the last time you slept, Cam?" Rove asks, shifting the conversation.

"Um, ah...I don't know. It's been a...ah, some days," I respond, now feeling a little like I might throw up.

Concern flashes over Rove's eyes and I realize I haven't been hiding my panic from him as well as I'd hoped.

"Okay, here's what's going to happen right now. You're going to take your big, smelly ass into the shower here and then you're going to come back out and sleep. We have a lot of work to do, and I can't have you half zombie," he says, before jumping up and grabbing me by the shoulder to physically push me toward the bathroom.

Inside her? It's inside her?!?

Rove keeps pushing me toward the shower as I try to protest so I can get more information.

"No, I can't sleep until I at least know what our plan is at this point. I'm fine, I'll shower in a minute, and I promise I'll try and sleep after," I say, holding up my hands to stop him from shoving me again.

"Nothing is happening tonight, Cam. We took her here because she cannot be separated from the Intel at this point," Rove says, worry present in his thick, dark eyebrows that furrow so deeply that they almost touch the sides of his nose.

Fuck – she's probably panicking too.

I pause, trying again to collect myself while I process this news. I thought Andy just wanted to control her case and not have it sniped out from under her, but I realize I've been misreading this – Andy's probably more concerned about becoming a US Government lab rat. And there's no telling what will happen to her now that the government knows she's been injected with the vial.

And she doesn't trust me.

"Cam, I know you two have history, but you need to be able to separate whatever happened between the two of you...and keep history...history. I need your focus on this and you can't let your personal feelings stop you from doing the right thing here," he warned.

The right thing? What the hell does he mean by that?

"Yeah, um, of course," I say, hoping I can honestly carry through on what I've just agreed to do.

I love my job *and* my country, but I'd be lying if I said I didn't *also* still love Andy. There's no way I can just leave her in this alone, so I'll have to find a way to do both – protect her *and* successfully complete this mission. She can't die like this – I can't lose someone else the same way I lost my dad. Rove looks at me with a glimmer of disbelief in his eyes, raising an eyebrow before inspecting my face.

"Well, she doesn't even like me right now...so I think we're safe there," I say, telling no lies given that she refused my calls for three years before I gave up and stopped trying to contact her.

"Look, I don't give a rat's ass whether she *likes* you right now or not. Keep whatever school yard drama you all have in the past because right now you need to be all about business. When she wakes up, you need to go with her and get more information out of Basir," Rove says, giving me a serious look and patting me on the back before turning toward the door.

What's in Andy's best interest...might not be in the best interest of the US Government.

"Yeah, okay, I can do that," I say, certain Andy won't need me to force her to debrief Basir as she will want answers herself.

I watch Rove walk out the door, standing straight and doing what I've been taught a good soldier will do – shut off a part of my heart.

Chapter 7
Blue Castle

"Andy"

I wake up startled, completely discombobulated, and lying in an unfamiliar bed — in a place I've never seen before. Inspecting my body with my eyes and hands, I notice the IVs that were attached to my arms before we left Brazil are now gone. The room is plain, white, and scantily furnished. I'm alone, and this realization makes my heart race. Trying to make sense of how I got here, how long I've been here, and where the hell I am is making my head spin and ache violently.

How long have I been knocked out?

I reach under my shirt and pull out a few cords that are attached to a monitor next to the bed, and it instantly starts beeping loudly and flashing, which only makes my headache throb harder. I remember getting on the plane and expected the first place I'd see would either be my own bed or the inside of a hospital — but this is neither of those places.

As I stand up, I feel lightheaded, and the room starts to spin. A few seconds after I lay back down, closing my eyes to quiet the pounding in my head, the door loudly bursts open. Several nurses stampede through the door and the noise causes me to grab my throbbing head and cover my ears.

"Where am I? What is this place?" I ask, now squeezing my temples trying to get this pain to stop.

One of the nurses appears at my bedside and places her hand on my shoulder, "You made it home, Andy. We brought you to a safe house."

Home? This place is not my home.

"Can I call my parents? They'll be worried."

"Here's some medicine for the pain," a nurse says, handing me a few pills and pointing to a glass of water to my right.

"Can I leave? Can I get up?" I ask, starting to panic that this feels more like a prison than a hospital.

The nurse doesn't respond but instead reaches to try and hook me up to the monitors next to the bed.

"Wait, don't...please. I won't get up. Just please don't hook me back up to the monitors," I beg, grabbing the nurse's arm and looking into her eyes for any sign of humanity.

"I won't hook you back up, but you need to stay in the bed," she replies, lacking real bedside manner and sounding more like a prison guard.

"Can I use a phone to call my parents?" I ask, not even sure what phone I'd use if they let me since they took my purse and cellphone back in Brazil.

The nurse looked at me and shook her head in the negative, "No calls. Sorry."

She packs up her supplies and heads out of the room. Just as I close my eyes, the door opens again. This time, it's Jacob Mowry – my Jake. I haven't seen him in years, since we were at the Farm together.

"Jake? Hi..." I smile, relieved to see a familiar face.

"You scared the hell out of me Andy – I'm so glad you are okay," Jake says, sitting on the chair next to my bed.

Jake is a sweet man from the deep South – "a tiny town in Mississippi" that he actively avoids naming. His accent and presence always make me feel like I'm in a southern kitchen, filling me with warmth. I can practically smell the rum cake that he used to make at The Farm. We were in the same advisory group, but he never graduated. Several months in, he realized that being a core collector wasn't for him. He told me that he couldn't think quickly enough or come up with a believable enough lie when he had to. This didn't surprise me – there was always something about Jake that was too sweet to recruit assets to do something that we all knew could get them killed.

"I decided to work the desk, and I specialize in debriefs," Jack says, flashing a smile full of shiny, white teeth before making his eyebrows dance up and down.

I reach out to hug him and his cheeks turn the color of roses as he hugs me back.

"It's so good to see you Jake," I say, as he squeezes me to him.

I wince and stiffen from the pain shooting through my body from the pressure of the embrace.

"Oh gosh, Oh...I'm so sorry Andy. Are you okay?" He asks, horrified and retreating.

"Oh Jake, no – it's fine. I'm okay," I lie, my stab wound still throbbing from the contact.

I'm so not okay – but him treating me like a porcelain doll is going to make me feel worse.

I smile back at him and reach for the glass of water and plastic cup of pills sitting on a small table next to the bed, careful to steady my shaking hands. I pop the pills into my mouth and take a sip of the water. The cold water is a shock to my insides, and I grab my chest because it feels like it's freezing on its way down. The glass drops to the floor and shatters into pieces. I let out an involuntary scream, jumping back and recoiling in the bed.

"Oh Gosh, I'm sorry," I say, wrapping my arms around myself self-consciously.

As Jake goes to pick up the glass, I throw the blanket off me to help him. My hands are still shaking and I'm wobbling on my feet.

"Andy no," Jake says, blocking me from getting up with one of his arms.

I flop back down on the bed as he quickly runs across the room and grabs a broom, swiftly gathering the glass pieces and putting them into a garbage pail by the door.

"Andy, it's ok. You've been through a lot," he says, giving me a sympathetic look.

The way he looks at me makes me feel worse. His eyes are watering and the pity in his gaze has me wanting to melt into the bed and disappear. I can't even drink water without glass breaking all over the floor - or try to get up without alerting an army of nurses who then insist I get back in the bed.

I'm trapped here.

"Where are we? Can I go home?" My voice shakes as I cut right to the chase.

I'd give anything to be tucked next to the fire in my DC condominium with a glass of Cabernet Sauvignon or a steaming cup of coffee. It's warm outside, as DC heads into what is always a sweltering and humid summer, and yet I'm freezing. That chill I felt before we got on that plane is still here and it's like the cold has seeped into my bones and is pumping through my veins, threatening to turn me into an ice cube. And I'm trying to ignore the fact that my leg is throbbing at the site where the bald man injected me with the vial. And I can't even ask the nurses about it because I don't want anyone to know.

Jake clears his throat nervously, "uhh, we're at Blue Castle...in a safehouse on the compound."

Blue Castle – THE Blue Castle?

"What? Why would they..." my voice trails off as I place my hand to my mouth.

They know.

"Where's Cameron?" I ask, assuming he's failed to do the one thing I've asked him to do – stop anyone else from debriefing Basir.

God – how could I have been so dumb? Of course, these dudes would go talk to my asset without me.

"I'll try to make it as comfortable as possible, but we can't let you leave yet," Jake says, looking at me with concern in his eyes from under the brim of his baseball cap.

He conveniently ignores my inquiry about Cameron's whereabouts.

From the casual clothes he's wearing, jeans and a plain white tennis shirt, I assume it's a weekend. I take a deep breath and sit back in bed. There's a large blacked out window across from my bed, which probably means I'm being watched from the other side.

"I hope you guys are enjoying the show and my sexy outfit," I glare at the window, lifting the blanket just enough to show off the tattered and blood-stained scrubs I'm still wearing.

Jake snickers, also turning toward the glass, before getting up and closing the curtain.

"Thank you," I say, pulling the blanket back over myself.

Jake's face twists into a pained expression before asking, "Can you tell me about the night you were attacked? I know it's not going to be easy, but I think it might help us get you out of here sooner."

Telling Jake what actually happened that night isn't going to get me out of here soon, and I suspect that Jake is smart enough to know that. He pulls a notebook out of his back pocket and grabs a pen from the bedside table. I'm thankful Jake closed the curtain, even though whomever was on the other side of that window is surely still listening to us.

I'm not ready to talk about what happened because I haven't even processed it myself yet.

Well, at least they sent Jake – a friendly captor.

"I don't know who the guy was. I went to the Assadis' apartment because Basir wouldn't meet me in public. We were in the apartment for under fifteen minutes before that guy burst in with a crazy whip and a knife."

I can't say what happened next, and instead put my hand on my temple and try to calm the pounding in my head. It hurts so bad that I wonder if I hit it on something during the fight.

Or perhaps that vial was filled with poison, and this is a permanent side effect?

"Whoever the guy was, he used me as his voodoo doll, and I can't seem to stop thinking about why in hell he had a whip and a knife instead of a damn gun."

Jake sits silent for a few moments before speculating. "Andy, I don't think he wanted to kill you."

Silence passes between us for a few moments before I ask, "Jake, how much do you know?"

I look down, trying to avoid eye contact with Jake because there is no amount of clothing that can cover the shame I feel about this entire situation. I wonder if everyone is judging me for following Farhad that night or for not being a good enough shot to shoot before getting hit.

Jake lowers his voice before asking, "Andy, why didn't you tell the CIA that the man who attacked you also injected you with that vial? You know that now everyone is going to wonder why you withheld that information, right?"

Oh fantastic...so now I have turned into a suspect and a science experiment.

"I don't think I can do this right now Jake. COS Brody already knows what happened. What *more* do you all want from me?"

It's clear from my clothes and how awful I smell that this safe house is the first place we came to after our arrival in the United States. I want to take a shower and would've preferred a warm cup of coffee over the bitter cold water the nurses brought. I reach up to wipe the hair out of my face and am immediately grossed out over the hair grease that's now all over my hand.

"I want to go home," I repeat, grabbing Jake's arm to appeal to his humanity. Jake stares back at me, before quickly writing in his notebook.

"Andy, I can't...I um..." Jake struggles to explain why I'm being held in this place like a prisoner.

"Jake, what? Just say it," I beg, frustrated that he's being all cagey right now.

Jake is silent for a moment as he stares at his sneakers, as though he's inspecting them for dirt that he'll need to clean off later.

Why is he acting so weird?

"Andy, you know I love you and I want to believe that you aren't involved in this...terrorist shit...but I am just here doing my job," he says, his pale face turning a rose color and beads of sweat forming at his temples.

Wait, they think I'M the terrorist here?

Jake was never good at hiding his emotions, which is probably both one of the reasons I find him endearing *and* one of the primary reasons he failed clandestine training.

"Andy this is so crazy," he says, whispering like thinks this is something I don't already know.

When I look up at Jake, his light blue eyes are holding me in their gaze with sadness that makes me feel like he's squeezing my heart.

I can't answer him because I haven't said it out loud yet – not once. I've been afraid that if I do, the reality will set in and I won't be able to pretend this is just another, everyday operation.

"Jake, is Cameron still here?" I ask, suspecting that Cameron has more information than Jake.

Jake winces at the mention of Cameron. He knows what happened between Cameron and I in the months that followed our breakup, and was a witness to how horribly awkward it was when Cameron and I would still occasionally cross paths in the halls of Langley. On one occasion, when he saw Cameron round the corner by the coffee spot, he grabbed my waist and pulled me into a kiss. I'll never forget the look on Cameron's face as he saw us, or the laughter Jake and I shared afterward.

"Oh gosh, Jake – I know you're my work husband, but I feel like I just kissed my brother," I remember saying, before both of us broke out in laughter.

I know Jake is just an innocent messenger here, and I feel bad that I can't give him what he was sent to get. I can't give him the details he's looking for, nor am I sure I even have them. I don't know why that man injected me with that serum and everyone else seems to know more about this terrorist group than I do right now.

Oh Gosh...do they think I'm a part of Solaris?

"Jake, get Cameron, please. I want to speak to him," I say, pushing the words out between gritted teeth.

Jake looks at the ground, nods, and then gets up from the table before awkwardly leaving the room.

I pull the blanket further onto my body and allow the tears to flow freely down my face, while trying to stifle my sobs beneath the blanket. The walls feel like they're closing in on me, as I realize that I might be stuck here for a while.

I don't have any power over what happens to me next. They could force me into hiding, get rid of me, my career could be ruined, or I might never see my family again.

...or worse...

While all of these weren't entirely rational, the worst-case scenarios began flooding my thoughts. My family is likely already worried and demanding answers, since a day doesn't go by that I don't call my mother.

When Jake leaves the safe house, he locks the door behind him from the outside. I'm alone and being monitored as though I'm a fish swimming around a tiny little bowl. It seems like I'm here alone for hours before the door opens again. This time Cameron walks in, holding a duffle bag and a tray of food. I turn toward the wall to hide my tear-stained face. Cameron sets the tray of food on the table, places the duffle bag on the dresser, and walks over to stand beside the bed where I'm sitting.

Cameron looks at me with angry and bloodshot eyes before asking, "Andy, why didn't you tell the man who attacked you also injected you with that serum? Do you know how much danger you put my team in by not being honest?"

"What? Are you serious right now?" I ask, incredulous at the expectation that I should have trusted him with anything.

This entitled asshole...

"Andy, you clearly don't understand how much trouble you're in right now...how deeply you stepped into this. Why wouldn't you tell me?" Cameron asks, rubbing his hand through his hair before balling his fists as his sides.

"Wait, so you think that you were somehow entitled to my confidence? Because of what? Because we used to fuck?" I say, turning back to him and raising my voice with tears threatening to pour down my face.

Cameron visibly retreats and sadness flashes across his face so quickly that I almost miss it. He flops down in the seat next to me and sighs deeply before responding, 'I'm sorry. I know I don't deserve your confidence, but Andy, what exactly is your plan here?"

I don't have a plan.

Shaking my head, I let the silence between us sit in the air.

"Are you okay?" Cameron's voice is shaking and his face red as though he's just been running.

"Did you even try and stop them from debriefing Basir before I could do it?" I ask, ignoring his question.

"Andy, I was on the same plane as you and by the time we got here Basir had already told US authorities that you'd been injected with the serum. There was nothing I could do," he replies, holding up his arms as though to surrender.

Cameron is now out of the chair and pacing the room.

"I just wish you'd told me," he says, making me dizzy with the pacing.

"Why? What exactly do you think you could have done? Stopped that man from injecting me *after* it already happened? Are you going to tell me you're a time traveler now?" I ask, irritated and tired of all this.

"I'm sorry. I wish I could have stopped Basir from coming to you instead of following through with the original plan. But Andy, you are going to need to trust someone – you can't do this alone," he says, coming closer to my bed and hovering over me.

I hate the distance between us – I hate all of this. As I process what he's just told me, I wonder if my anger is – at least in part - residual anger from the past. I want to trust him, but he blew our entire relationship up and now he's here acting like he cares about me.

My brain is wise enough to remember how much of an asshole he was when we broke up, but it feels like my heart hasn't gotten them memo. As much as I'd love to shove him into a wall right now, I also really want him to wrap his arms around me like a warm blanket. He used to be my person – warm, loving, funny, sexy, brilliant...and then he wasn't. It was almost as though the day his father died, he went on some weird quest to turn into his father. He'd always accused his father of being cold, hard, and emotionless. And that's what he became to me – the cold hearted man who chose his career over me.

"Andy what the hell is going on with you?" Cameron asks, frustration in his voice.

After a few more moments of silence, I whisper my reply, "Cam I feel like I'm going crazy here. I don't know what was in that vial or why he shoved it into my leg."

It takes me several minutes to collect myself before continuing, "Cam, that guy...after he injected me with that serum he tried to take me with him. He didn't even try to kill the Assadi family – it was like he was singularly focused on *me*.

"Did Basir tell you why he broke the plan and came to you?" Cameron asks, intensity in his eyes.

"No, but that's one of the things I plan to ask him if you all ever let me debrief him," I respond, making sure there's an edge of irritation in my voice because I'm still pissed that Cameron was being such a jerk moments ago.

I look between him and the window to the observation area, curtain still drawn closed. I still feel like I'm sitting here naked.

"I'm scared," I admit, swallowing a painful lump in my throat.

It's the most honest thing I've admitted out loud since this happened.

Cameron looks back at me with a seriousness and void of emotion that confuses me. It's like I'm standing next to a robot version of him, completely opposite to the man I last saw on the tarmac in Brazil. I watch him as he goes between the Cameron robot and shows flashes of emotion and realize that I don't know this version of him at all.

"I know. I'm sorry. I'm scared too, but I am going to do the best I can to try and help you get untangled from this mess," he says, looking up at me and handing me a duffle bag.

"I brought you some food and clothes... I thought you might want to change." Cameron puts the bag beside the bed and points to the tray of food he placed on the bedside table.

I don't want the food, but I do want clean clothes. And I want to take a shower. I've always been the type to choose to be clean before eating. The way I smell right now, there's no way I could eat without the smell of my own funk making me nauseous.

As Cameron leans away from me, gesturing as though he wants to get up and leave, I grab him by the shirt stopping him. He looks at me raising an eyebrow as I hold his gaze — waiting for his humanity to return. I slowly place my hand on his chest, directly over his quickly beating heart, and he flinches away from me after a moment.

"What's going to happen to me?" I ask him.

Cameron's chest draws in a deep, low breath, "Andy, the vial you have inside you is a nuclear agent that over a dozen terrorist organizations would kill to get their hands on. Several foreign leaders would pay more than either of us will make in our entire careers to get their hands on that kind of power."

A nuclear agent?

My eyes widen, and I feel like I'm going to throw up.

"There isn't just a bounty on your head Andy – if any of these people get their hands on you..." his voice trailed off, as though he was afraid to complete the thought.

"Then...somehow...I become the key to a nuclear weapon?" I ask, not sure I really want the answer to this.

Lifting my hand to my mouth, I audibly gasp and try to process this new reality.

"Well since none of us know exactly how this thing works, and Basir refuses to give any more details to anyone except you — we need to get you well enough to do a real debrief so we can get more information and figure out what to do next," Cameron continues.

I swallow hard and sink deep into my thoughts.

"At this point, they're trying to assess whether they can let you walk out of here as Andora Lynam or if you need to be someone...*else*," Cameron's voice trails off as he looks from me to the bag of clothes that he'd handed me.

Or even if I get to walk out of here at all...

"Someone else?" I ask, still not fully processing.

"You have to know that you can't just walk out of this as though nothing happened right?" He asks.

"Yeah, I know..." I respond, putting my head in my hands.

I bite my lip, and stare at the wall, trying to distract myself by focusing on an antique clock above the door. It's yellow in the space that was once likely white, and it's missing the red dial that shows seconds. Staring at the clock, I wonder if the time is even right or if it's only there to make whoever is prisoner here feel oriented. It says two thirty, but since there aren't any windows leading outside – I can't tell if that means early afternoon or early in the morning. I've never described myself as claustrophobic, but right now I'm acutely aware of this trapped feeling that's making me feel as though the walls are closing in on me.

"You can go now," I say, trying to chill my own voice to match what he sounded like moments ago.

The U.S. Government effectively owns me right now, which was one of my biggest fears when this all started. And I know any eventual release will hinge on my cooperation.

Or at least all these men believing I'm cooperating.

"Did you hear me? You can go," I repeat.

Cameron stares at me, blinking slowly like I've just told him he has a third eye.

"You just said the Iranian Government and a dozen terrorists want to get their hands on me, so why are you still standing here," I ask, somewhat sarcastically because I know this is exactly the type of crap his team gets called in to deal with.

"Andy, I *do* care about you," he responds, his voice softening.

I don't respond because I have nothing to say that won't come out as a scream with almost a decade of pent-up anger behind it.

Cameron starts to pace back and forth, rubbing his temples. "Okay, whatever Andy."

"Cameron, I'm tired and I want to take a shower. I can't do this with you right now," I say, desperately wanting him to leave so I can have some peace and be alone with my thoughts.

Actively fighting to stop my voice and body from shaking, I slowly reach toward the set of towels next to the bed. Being enveloped in warm water and feeling clean for the first time in weeks seems like a fantasy. And I figure this might get Cameron to leave the room. There is no way he's going to stand there as I strip off all my clothes.

"Suit yourself," I say, slowly pulling my shirt over my head as he jerks and starts toward the door.

"I'm leaving, but I am staying in the room on the other side of this wall," he admits.

"Okay whatever Cam. Do what you gotta do," I say, now walking toward the bathroom with my towel.

He sighs audibly before saying, "If you need anything..."

"I won't - thank you," I say, still angry at him as I walk into the bathroom and close the door behind me.

Inside the bathroom, I lean against the door breathing deeply. Carefully taking off my clothes, uneasy at how unfamiliar this place is and acutely aware of how unsafe I feel. Peeling the scrubs off myself slowly, I try breathing through the pain. Blood and sweat made them stick to my body, and removing them reminds me of how much pain I'm still in. It feels like ripping a band aid off a bloody wound once it's fused itself to the broken flesh.

It's been days...a week maybe... since I was in Farhad's apartment, fighting for my life, but I can't shake the feeling of panic that lingers.

How long has it actually been – Fuck, I don't even know the actual time.

I don't really know, but from the look of my hair...and how filthy I feel... I assume it's been more than a few days.

I wince as the clothes skim my bandages on their way to the floor. The dressing on the bandages needs changing, but I don't want to call the nurses back for more poking and prodding. I turn the shower to the hottest setting, hell-bent on trying to wash away the horror and feeling warm at least for a moment.

Every time I close my eyes, I can see that man lunging at me — his dark, bloodshot eyes piercing through my skin and the deep wounds he left behind.

I actively shake my head, forcing the dark thoughts from my brain so that I can relax. I need this shower to feel like even a fraction of myself again.

Stepping in the shower, the hot water rushes through my long, sandy brown curls like a steaming waterfall. I lift my face toward the shower head, letting the warm water pour over my face and shoulders. I feel warm for the first time in what seems like months. I open the new bar of soap and lather it all over my skin, scrubbing hard to wipe away the dirt and trauma.

Just as I am starting to relax, a loud noise causes the entire cabin to shake. An involuntary scream comes from my mouth just before my hand flies up to stop the sounds from giving away my location. Crying and shaking, my body slides down the wall and onto the tile on the cold shower floor. I curl into a ball, trying to make myself as small as possible, as the water pours over my naked body. The cabin floor creaks as footsteps draw closer to the bathroom door.

No, no, no – please don't come in here.

I'm naked, soaking wet, overcome with fear, and weaponless with nowhere to hide. There's a loud knocking on the door, and I flinch - hand still covering my mouth, water from the shower pours over me and and salty tears stream down my cheeks.

"Andy, it's me — Cameron. Andy?"

I hear him but still can't speak or make my body move. All I can do is sit here, covered in physical reminders from the attack, unable to even call out for help. A few minutes pass, and I remain still on the floor.

"I'm coming in. Is that OK," Cameron asks, before slowly turning the doorknob and cracking open the door to the bathroom.

"Oh...okay," I sob, voice cracking and unable to catch a full breath.

I think I must be having a panic attack because I know I'm safe, but I cannot seem to get myself under control.

This isn't real – you're okay – this isn't real.

The door slowly opens and moments later the water stops running.

"I'm going to help you up now, OK?" Cameron leans into the shower and wraps a towel around my body.

I nod my head slowly, pulling the surrounding towel to cover more of myself. Cameron gently wraps one of his arms around my back, and the other under my knees.

I gasp and wince from pain as he tightens his arms around me to lift me off the floor.

"I'm going to go slowly. Hang onto me, and I'll lift you," Cameron whispers softly in my ear.

"Okay, I'm...I'm sorry," I say, burying my head into his shoulder and reaching my arms around his shoulders.

"No, no. Stop – don't apologize. It's okay," he says.

It's not okay – this is so very far from okay.

He slowly lifts me out of the shower and carries me to the bed. He covers me in warm blankets that feel like they've just come from the dryer. Then he sits next to me, wraps his arms back around me, and pulls me close to him.

"You're okay, I won't let anything happen to you," he says.

We stay like that for a while, and I notice that he waits and allows me to calm down. Laying on his chest, I feel my eyelids getting heavy.

"Do you need me to help you get dressed?" He asks.

"No, I...Oh God...no. Please...I can...I can dress myself," I say, feeling the embarrassment of what just happened.

Reaching past him to grab the duffle bag full of clothes, hands still shaking, I pull out a pair of sweatpants, a t-shirt and under garments. Since I didn't have a chance to gather anything from Brazil before leaving, these are standard issue, military-like clothes. The sweats are that vomit color brown we were issued during training and the t-shirt, plain white. I start toward the bathroom when Cameron stops me.

"That dressing on the wounds looks pretty bad. You either need to let me change them or we should really call the nurses to do it," he says, a look of concern on his face.

Remembering how horrible it felt when the nurses were swarming around, poking, and prodding me in Brazil – I opt for Cameron to help.

Well, it's not like he hasn't already seen me naked.

"Just let me put on clothes first and then you can help, okay," I say, feeling pretty defeated at the reality that I cannot do this alone.

Trying to maintain what's left of my pride, I start back toward the bathroom with the clothes bundled in my arms. When safely behind the closed door, I let the blanket fall to the floor. My leg is swollen and still warm to the touch. I can't tell whether the nausea is from whatever nuclear chemistry experiment is coursing through my veins, or the fact that I haven't eaten anything substantial in days. Stumbling against the door, adding vertigo to the list of things wrong with me right now, I dress swiftly to maintain the small crumb of dignity that comes with dressing myself.

As I walk from the bathroom back to the bed, Cameron is sitting with the first aid kit sprawled across the comforter. He pulls out fresh gauze and Neosporin, and gestures for me to get back in the bed. After slowly pulling up my shirt to access the stab wound in my side, he peels back the soiled bandage as I wince in pain.

"Got anything strong to drink – like perhaps Bourbon," I joke, craving anything that might numb this pain.

"I'll see what I can do. But in the meantime, try taking deep breaths," he responds.

I close my eyes and breathe deeply as he puts on Neosporin and applies fresh gauze to the wound on my side.

He draws his hand back and hesitates for a moment. The air between us feels thick with tension from words left unspoken over the years. I close my eyes, trying to avoid his gaze and disliking the heat I'm feeling in my cheeks from it.

"Andy, let me see your leg," he says, glancing down at the vomit brown sweats that now sickeningly make me feel like I might gag.

I hesitate because to show him I will need to take down my pants. I raise my eyebrow at him to which he responds with a stern look of annoyance.

"My leg is fine," I lie, protesting and trying to hold onto whatever control I have left over my own body.

My leg is swollen and has felt like it's going to explode into a heaping ball of flames since being injected with the serum. What's even stranger is that my leg can feel like this while the rest of my body feels like it's been freezing inside of a meat cooler. Showing Cameron my leg isn't something I want to do because ignoring this pain has been a large part of my ability to keep my shit together right now.

"Andy, I know this must be horrible. But please, let me see it. As part of GS training, we had emergency medical and while I'm not as talented as the nurses and doctors, I can at least help you so that we don't have to call them and you can get some sleep," he says, pleading with me through his eyes that are beaming those flecks of brown at me.

I sigh and look away from him as I pull down my pants enough to expose the top of my thigh at the injection point. I've avoided looking at it but as Cameron's eyes pin me to this table with their intensity, I glance toward my leg. It's worse than I imagined – purple and black bruising around the site and red streaking.

"Andy, this looks infected," he says, placing his hand gently on my thigh.

"It doesn't hurt that bad," I say, lying again.

"Andy, your leg is on fire – we need to figure out what is happening," he says, ignoring my attempts to downplay.

"It's fine, Cam. I just want to sleep – please don't make a big deal about this," I plead.

I quickly push his hand from my leg and pull up my pants. I'm so cold and even fully clothed with the blanket wrapped around me, I can't stop shaking. And I'm so tired. I don't think I can argue with Cameron right now. I just want to be warm and sleep.

He pulls out a thermometer from the first aid kit and insists I put it under my tongue.

95.2 – what the hell?

"We need to call the doctor, something isn't right," he says.

Without a fight, I flop back onto the pillow and pull the covers up to my neck. I can hear Cameron on the phone with the doctor. It sounds like I'll be able to sleep tonight, but tomorrow we will conduct another debrief with Basir to figure out what to do about the vial of crap in my leg. Once Cameron is off the phone, my eyes move from him to the dark window between my room and the control room.

"I'm going to bring you some warm blankets and the doctor instructed me to give you warm fluid and for you to stay put until he can get here. Don't worry. Everyone is gone for the night. I made sure before I came back," he says.

He walks across the room, adjusting the curtains that remain closed. Then he darts out the door and I assume across to the control room, before returning with blankets and hot tea. The cabin shakes when he closes the door firmly behind him. Even though I know what's causing the shaking now, I can't help but flinch at how unsettling the noise and rocking movement feels.

"I'm going to sleep on the couch in the control room. If you need something, or start feeling worse, just knock on the window and I'll come back," he says, heading toward the door.

"No, don't go," I say, before I can think through that response.

Shit...no, he should go.

Reaching up to grab the doorknob, he pauses. His hand hovers and it looks like he can't decide whether to leave or stay. Which is just long enough for me to panic when I realize that once he leaves, the door will lock from the outside and I will be back in this cell alone.

"You want me to stay?" He asks, understandably confused given how cranky I've been with him.

I want everyone around me to think I'm in control because that feels like the only way out of here or perhaps that's just how I've survived in this profession all these years. But nothing about what's happening to me feels like anything within my control. And as much as my body needs sleep right now, if he leaves that won't be possible. I can't even take a shower without having a panic attack. Swallowing my pride and praying this isn't as awkward and pathetic as it feels, I protest.

"Can you...stay? Please don't leave me here alone," I say, mortified as soon as the words exit my mouth.

What I wish I could say is that I need him — the way he was before — like none of this happened. I want to go back in time and just be Andy and Cam again, as we were — before our world changed in an instant. But I know he isn't that Cameron – and never will be again. And we can't go back to the before – because it happened and neither of us can make it as though it didn't.

Cameron hesitates, putting his hand on the doorknob before pulling it off several times.

"Andy, I...uh, promised Rove that I would keep some distance," Cameron admits.

"Oh, okay," I say, dejected and feeling like he's just stabbed me with the reminder that his career has always been more important than I will ever be to him.

Cameron sighs loudly enough for me to hear, before walking toward my bed and pulling up a chair.

"Andy, Rove is more than just my boss. That man has been like a father to me since before I joined the GS team. He and my dad served together in the military and him leading this team is one of the main reasons I joined," he admits.

I stay silent, raising an eyebrow to get him to continue. This is more than Cam was willing to disclose about himself at the end of our relationship and I'm afraid if I speak, he'll clam up and shut down like he did with me before we broke up.

"When my dad died, Rove...well...he pulled me out of a really dark place," he admits, his voice trailing off at the end.

"Why would that have anything to do with Rove mandating that you have distance from me?" I ask, unable to help myself.

He sighs again, and runs a hand through his already tousled curls, "Because he knows how much I still care about you and is worried that will cloud my operational judgement."

The silence between us returns as we just look at each other, his admission sitting in the room like a third person who's waiting impatiently to be acknowledged.

"Oh," I say, not sure what else to say.

"He's not wrong, Andy. Me being with you right now is a risk," he says, cutting through that silence like a wild horse that's just broken free.

"Okay, well go then. I certainly wouldn't want you risking your career for me," I respond, all the pain of our past hitting me in the chest like a bullet.

I can't do this right now with him.

"Andy, that's not...that didn't come out right. I *want* to be here. I just..." his voice trails off and he runs a nervous hand through his hair.

"It doesn't have to be all that serious, Cam. I'm not asking for..." my voice stops abruptly as I erase the image of Cameron naked in my bed from my head.

Cameron doesn't respond, but instead turns back toward me from the door and looks at me with an intensity that causes me to quickly look away.

"Rove doesn't need to know you stayed. And frankly, I don't need any of these men getting any nasty ideas or filling in the blanks with their own ridiculous, career harming narrative. I just...don't want to be in here alone," I continue, watching my hands to avoid looking back at him.

"I need the guys on my team to trust that I can remain objective because I don't want Rove to have to pull me from the case," he responds.

"Okay, I get that. Maybe...is Jake still here? Maybe it would be better if he stayed?" I ask, not wanting to make this weirder between us but sensing I have when he visibly finches at my suggestion.

"No, I'll stay," he immediately responds.

"Thank you," I say, taking a deep breath and shifting uncomfortably in this rock-hard bed.

Cameron sits back in the folding chair next to the bed and it looks like he's trying to get comfortable for the night. I laugh loudly as his large frame navigates different positions as though anything he does in that tiny chair will be suitable for him to sleep an entire night.

"Come here fool. This bed is likely only marginally softer than the floor, but I'm not going to make you stay in that chair all night when I'm the one who asked you to say," I say, moving closer to the wall and making space in the bed next to me.

"Oh, thank god," he says, flashing a dimpled smile before taking off his boots and laying beside me.

His hair is damp, and he smells like fresh, agency issued soap – like he stepped out of the shower just before I did.

"Is this, okay? I don't want to make you uncomfortable," he says, shifting his body a tiny bit closer but clearly trying to avoid making me uncomfortable by laying too close.

"Yes, it's fine. Do you have enough space?" I ask.

"I think I can manage, but I want you to be comfortable," he replies.

I nod and he reaches over to turn off the bedside light. He's still cautiously on top of the covers, as though he's afraid for our skin to touch while we lay next to each other.

"Thank you," I say, closing my eyes and trying to let go of the anxiety that still gnaws at my insides.

"Go to sleep – I'm here – you're going to be okay," he whispers in my ear.

Drifting to sleep to the sound of our hearts beating in sync, my body and heart remember what my mind has so desperately tried to forget.

Chapter 8
College Romance

Rowing down the Potomac River at 5am with several other people, all sculling in unison, is a magical experience. Once you get into a synchronized rhythm, the only sound you hear is the loud clunk of the oars and the splash of the water as the boat glides through the water. In 1998, as a college freshman, I walked onto the division one rowing team at George Washington University. I'd never rowed a day in my life, but I have powerful legs and the drive to push through an extremely ridiculous amount of pain. And through the pain and the morning meditation, these women have become part of my family.

"Andy – you brunchin' with us this morning?" my teammate Cara asks, throwing me a discolored rag so I can help wipe down the boat.

"No, I have a coffee date," I admit, blushing.

It's our final year together and we've spent almost every morning jogging from Thompson's boathouse, across from the Watergate Hotel, back to Foggy Bottom to eat breakfast together on campus. "Brunchin'" is when we get the latest gossip about who is dating whom – chat about our hopes and fears for post college employment or complain about how sore we are from the morning workout. But this morning, I have a date with Cameron. Cameron goes to Howard University, and we've been interns together at the Central Intelligence Agency (CIA) for a little over a year.

"Ohhhh, Howard guy?" Rachel asks, looking up from scrubbing.

Cara pipes in, "Yes! The dude who followed Andy for a month before mustering the courage to ask her out."

"Ahhh, the guy that she *hid* from us for almost an entire year," Dora teases, smacking me across the butt with her towel.

"His name is Cameron – and yes, him." I can't say his name without smiling.

I'm counting down the minutes until I can see Cameron. Though we've been dating for nearly a year, I only told my friends a few weeks ago. At the CIA, you form relationships with people you aren't allowed to acknowledge – even if you pass them on the street. And for the longest time, Cameron and I worried what publicly dating would mean for us. And so, we've spent the better part of a year hanging out in corners of the huge agency compound or in locations off campus where we wouldn't have to explain how we knew each other.

I enjoyed the time when Cameron and I weren't "out" with our relationship because it felt like something that was just ours. But once things started getting more serious, we both decided that we needed to come clean with our friends.

When I first confessed about our relationship to my closest friends, they wanted the whole story. Of course, I couldn't tell them that we'd met as interns at the CIA. Especially since we didn't even share a cover story – mine was that I was interning at The State Department and his was that he was interning at The Pentagon with the Department of Defense. So, Cameron and I decided to come up with our own "cover story" for how we met – telling everyone we met each other at a Kappa Alpha Psi party at Howard. And since I'm shamelessly willing to admit that there is something incredibly sexy about a Black man cane stepping – and Cameron is step captain of the Howard Kappa chapter- my friends totally bought it.

I told them how I fell in love with the boy from Louisiana – "Howard guy" – sprinkling truths throughout the story we'd both agreed to tell our friends. But the real story will remain just ours forever.

I saw Cameron in the halls of the agency for months before he finally spoke to me. Every morning, we'd pass each other in the cafeteria on my way to get coffee. I'd smile, before quickly looking down at my feet and heading back to my office.

"Hey, looks like we both like coffee," he said one morning, flashing one giant dimple and a crooked smile.

Well, that was awkward.

"Ha, yeah, I mean...coffee is good?" I smiled back before looking away, my face flushing.

"I'm Cameron – but my friends call me Cam," he said, holding out his hand to shake mine.

As our hands touched, I squeezed his hand firmly and he squeezed mine back. I felt the goosebumps forming on my arms like an electric current was passing between us. It was so shocking that I looked up – just in time for our eyes to meet. His eyes were striking - a soulful light brown with so many variations of the color that they reminded me of the kaleidoscopes I'd looked through as a child.

"Well then, since we both think coffee is delicious – does this mean we're close enough friends for me to call you Cam or is that going to have to wait until the second time we speak," I teased, giggling before immediately fearing that I sounded like a schoolgirl with a crush.

"Well, since I've been following you around for months trying to get the courage to speak to you – I think we might already be friends," he grinned, his voice giving away a hint of a southern drawl and made me feel like I was going to melt into the floor.

"Well then Cam – it's nice to officially meet you," I said, very willing to call his fine man a "friend".

After the day Cameron had the courage to say hello, we made a point to meet up for coffee every morning that we were both on the compound. Seeing Cam was always a beautiful start to my day. In addition to being fine as hell, he was smart and kind. And nobody had ever looked at me the way he did – like I was the only person in the room and the center of his world. When we were together, whatever I was stressed about – the statistics exam, my shitty boss, the chronic intercostal muscle pain from rowing, my parents' expectations, getting a job after college – never seemed that bad.

"You got this babe," he'd say, flashing his notoriously sexy crooked grin.

Our conversations were deep, and I felt like he was the only person who truly saw me. We'd commiserate about being the only two Black interns at the CIA, and how we both felt the need to prove ourselves while at the same time suffering from imposter syndrome. We traded stories about how close we were to our parents and how we were both deeply patriotic and drawn to serve our country.

Both 90s kids, there was no escaping the messaging we received in school about how America had vanquished communism and was the "land of the free". Though I'd always been somewhat skeptical about whether freedom was a unifying experience, given that not all Americans experienced America in the same way, my father always taught me that you cannot change anything from the outside. So, my patriotism was rooted in my deep desire to chase a version of America I dreamed of - a place where everyone was free to become whomever they wanted and afforded safety and belonging.

"I want you to meet my friends," Cameron said one day, as he sipped his coffee.

"How's that going to work," I asked, reminding him that we weren't supposed to acknowledge each other outside of the agency compound.

"We're throwing a Halloween party at the frat house this weekend – come," he said, smiling and grabbing my hand.

I could never resist that smile.

"I don't know…" I started to protest, really disliking the idea of introducing my friends to him at a crowded - and likely - smelly party.

"Andy come on - I care about you, and I hate that we can't just go out in public like a normal couple. There's no actual agency rule that prohibits us from being in a real relationship."

He wasn't wrong, but I was anxious about having to create a cover with my friends and pretend I wasn't already madly in love with this man - something I hadn't even admitted to Cameron yet.

"Okay, I'll come," I sighed, taking the paper from him that had the address to the party.

When my friends found out we were going to a Kappa party at Howard, you'd have thought I'd invited them to The White House. They were so excited about *this* party that they didn't ask a lot of details about my cover story – like the obvious detail of how I'd ended up at the Kappa party where I'd "allegedly" first met Cameron without them.

Since it was a Halloween party, we all wore costumes – I went as a Black Marilyn Monroe while Gina dressed as a "sexy nurse" and Loren a "sexy police officer". As soon as I walked into the party, the smell of stale cheap beer knocked me in the face, Cameron ran over to me. He was dressed as Steve Urkel from Family Matters, which made me laugh given how much of a nerd he was in real life. We stepped deeper into the crowded party, in the middle of the Shaw neighborhood in DC, and I wanted to run out. Crowds make me anxious, and Cameron knew this. But as soon as I tried to turn for the door, Cameron's strong hand wrapped around one of my wrists.

"Don't leave - you just got here," Cameron whispered in my ear, so close I could feel his breath on my neck.

He knew me well enough to know that this wasn't my scene. After introducing me and my two friends to a few of his friends, he took me by the hand and led me to the gardens in the back of the house.

I stepped out into the cold October air, folding my arms and shivering, and noticed the magical scene Cameron created for us. The garden surrounded a small patio that was lit up by white lights strung throughout the bushes. There were rose petals all over the ground and a bottle of Prosecco sat on ice next to two wine glasses. Cameron sat me down at a small, outdoor loveseat before covering me in a blanket and lighting an outdoor heater. He pulled his chair next to mine and shimmied himself beneath the large blanket with me.

As our friends partied, we spent the next two hours talking and cuddling under the moonlight in our Halloween costumes.

"Promise me that we'll always be this way," I said, hoping that things wouldn't change for us after college ended.

Cameron looked like he was panicking, and I immediately regretted saying something that sounded so permanent. Even with the cool fall air, he was warm and shifted nervously in the seat. I looked up at him, acutely aware that tears were forming in my eyes. After what felt like ages of awkward silence, Cameron finally spoke.

"Andy, you're the love of my life."

POP – someone snapped their rag loudly against the boat to snap me back to the present.

"Andy, Andy! Girl are you still with us?" Cara asks, waving her rag in my face to bring me back to the present.

Ick, do they ever wash these dirty boat rags?

Doing my best to ignore the teasing of my teammates, I quickly throw my water bottle and gloves into my backpack. Jumping on my bike, I wave goodbye to my coach and race up Virginia Avenue from the boathouse to my dorm. I only have 30 minutes to wash the Potomac River off me and try to look presentable before meeting Cameron at 8:30am for coffee. He has a meeting at The State Department at 9:30am for another job prospect and since GW is close to Main State, we're taking this increasingly rare opportunity to see each other. Both trying to secure post-graduation jobs, lately it seems like the only time we've seen each other has been passing each other in the halls of our internships.

Hair still damp from the shower, I gather up my wild curls into a messy top knot and grab the only clean business casual attire I can find - classic black pants, button down shirt, and my signature black leather jacket. I have a couple classes before I need to head over to the agency for a few hours. Unlike Cameron, I've already committed to the CIA and am in a program that allows me to work toward fulfilling my training requirement while finishing my last year of college.

Luckily the coffee spot he picked is right around the corner from my dorm. "Capitol Brew" has the best orange cranberry scones, and the coffee is good enough to please even an unapologetic coffee snob like me. Cameron is already sitting by the window next to two coffees and scones when I arrive.

"Hey you," I greet him, drawing his attention from the Washington Post he's reading.

At the sight of me, he gets up from his seat and wraps me in a warm bear hug, leaning in to kiss me on the cheek. He smells like the Louisiana peach soap I know he loves, and his embrace feels like a warm fire on a cold evening. I want him to hold onto me all day but know I only have him for an hour before we both head in opposite directions.

"Remind me why we can't just skip the day and lay in bed together all day," I ask, groaning from the exhaustion I feel from waking up at 4am.

Cameron draws back from the hug, and smiles, "because neither of us are independently wealthy, and we both need to find jobs post-graduation."

I huff, annoyed at his pragmatism.

"So, how's the job decision going," I ask, taking a sip of the delicious Dirty Chai Latte he had waiting for me.

"I wish there was a hybrid between military service and the Agency," Cameron sighs audibly, placing his head into his hands.

I want him to join me at the CIA because I want us to stay together. But I know his father, a five-star general in the Army, is pressuring him to "earn stripes" in the military. I know this level of pressure well. My father is an agency legend, and it feels like a forgone conclusion that I will serve there too. I don't want to pile the pressure on him, but I want him to choose our relationship.

And I want him to choose me.

So instead of telling him, I continue to ignore the giant elephant in a pink tutu that's been dancing between our conversations about the future for months. And the reality that within a year we could be headed in two opposite directions feels like an emotional gutting every time I think about it.

Just as I take a bite into my scone, and think about how to change the topic, the entire coffee shop erupts into chaos. People begin getting out of their seats, frantically trying to call on their cell phones, and crowding around the television screen in the corner of the cafe that's streaming a CNN live news report. Cameron and I get up to see what the commotion is, just as a second plane crashes into the World Trade Center. Cameron fishes his phone from his pocket. Both of us stand there, feet frozen in place, staring completely stunned as we watch history unfold on the television.

"I...I can't call out," Cameron stutters, his eyebrows curving into a worried bend.

"What? What do you mean?" I ask, looking at my phone to see if I have any signal.

Another cafe customer yells to the crowd that nobody's phones are working. Cameron continues trying to call out, trying to determine if his meeting is still taking place, when a group of police officers storm inside the cafe.

As some people around us loudly panic, others stand as if frozen by terror.

"We need everyone to shelter in place. There's been a report of a car bomb at the State Department," one officer said, with an eerie calm that confused me.

Is this guy human? Did he not just see the World Trade Center just explode into a million pieces?

I turn back toward the television. I can feel Cameron directly behind me with his arms wrapped protectively around my shoulders. I reach up to grab one of his hands and squeeze it tight – to comfort him and maybe also to remind myself that I'm awake and this is happening in real life.

We stand there transfixed on the screen for what feels like seconds, but when I glance back to the clock almost a half hour has passed. Looking around at all the faces, staring at the screen in horror, this cafe starts to look like a scene out of a zombie apocalypse movie. None of us seem to know what to do.

"Oh God! The Pentagon!" Someone in the cafe screams, as images of the Pentagon in flames flash across CNN on split screen.

I feel Cameron's entire body stiffen behind me. And when I look up at him, I can see the terror in his eyes and know exactly what he's thinking — his father is in the Pentagon.

Chapter 9
Intel

A loud thud, followed by rocking that feels like another minor earthquake, jolts me awake and for a moment I feel like I'm back inside my trailer in Afghanistan. But then Andy jolts up next to me, breathing heavy and loud enough for me to remember I'm not alone. I slowly sit up, rubbing my eyes and trying to process where I am when Andy starts shoving me in the side.

"Oh! No, no, no, no, no – get up Cam. GET UP," Andy whisper screams, continuing to shove me in the arm and trying to push me out of the bed.

"Ouch, what...wait...what time is it?" I ask, massaging the area of my arm that Andy shoved with a force I don't remember her capable of.

When I don't move fast enough for her liking, Andy keeps pushing me which causes me to fall out of the bed. Crawling around the floor to gather the t-shirt I'd thrown to the ground and stumbling around for my shoes, I try to move with an urgency that will calm Andy down. She's completely panicked, which is confusing given that the blinds are still firmly shut. Despite the insane circumstances that I'm aware are still looming over us, I slept well.

Can't tell her that, though.

"You need to get yourself put together. I don't want anyone knowing you stayed over here," she says, cheeks flushing like we did something more than sleep next to each other.

"Andy it's okay, it's probably just someone on my team coming to tell us about the plan for the Basir debrief. They know I'm staying next door in the command center so we can just tell them I was up early, and we were planning the debrief," I say, trying to bring down the urgency which would make us look more guilty than necessary.

"Cam – I cannot have these dudes thinking we had sex last night. You'll be a stud and I will be a *whore* – my credibility destroyed," she whispers, throwing a sock at me, and shoving my other boot into my arms while pushing me toward the door.

"Okay, I get it. I'll go cover with whomever that is and come back once I have more information about what's next," I say, putting on my shoes because walking back next door with my boots and socks in my arms would be more than I could easily explain.

"Andy, before I go...are you alright? Do I need to follow up with the doctor this morning?" I ask, wondering how she could go from being on the verge of unexplained hypothermia last night to punching me so hard in the arm that I think a bruise might be forming.

"Yes, I'm okay. I feel better this morning and I just want to get to this debrief and get some answers. So please, go next door and get the boss man to tell you when I can get out of this cage and do my job," she says, in a tone that reminds me of the Andy I met years ago.

She's the most intense, intelligent, and fiercely sexy woman I've ever met, and I cannot understand how I let her walk out of my life all those years ago. Was her request to have me stay last night an opening?

No dude, pretty sure she still hates you.

My strong, internal voice of reason occasionally takes on Theo's surfer dude voice because that is exactly what he'd say if he thought I was feeling myself too hard after one invite to stay with her. Now is my chance, though, to prove to her that I can be the man she fell in love with once.

But you have to keep an emotionally safe distance, right?

As the door hits me on the way out, I decide that this will be the day I'll build the courage to explain myself – and maybe she will forgive me. Sure, now is an awful time – given that we also need to deal with the very real threat looming over us...and inside of Andy's body...but I can't continue being close to her without telling her everything. And I can't go another several years without her in my life. I made a terrible mistake all those years ago, and months after when I tried to correct my mistake – she was already gone and refusing my calls.

Instead of Rove, whom I expected to see in the control room, I run smack into Jake. Jake, juggling donuts and coffee in his arms, almost falls to the ground as I come face to face with him at the door to the control center.

"Uh, oh hi. I didn't realize you'd still be here," Jake says, sheepishly and turning an irritating shade of pink.

"Where else would I be?" I ask, looking down at Jake who stands a few inches shorter than me.

This guy brings the complete dick out in me. Though I'm embarrassed of even my own reaction because it's Jake – I shouldn't be jealous of this guy and his friendship with Andy.

I puff out my chest enough to send Jake the message that's meant to intimidate. Because as much as the two of them don't give me romance vibes, I will never get the image of Jake sticking his tongue down Andy's throat in the halls of Langley out of my head.

Jake looks down, plastering a nervous grin on his face before he pushes past me on his way to Andy's room. I pivot quickly and follow. Andy is sitting on the bed, thankfully fully dressed, when Jake and I arrive in her room. Her curls are in a messy top knot and her face lights up at the sight of Jake, which makes me feel a pang of jealousy deep in my gut. I want her to glow when she sees me, like she used to do.

"I brought amenities," Jake sings, placing a box of donuts and a thermos full of coffee on the table.

"Coffee, my love language," Andy says, reaching immediately for the thermos and opening it to inhale the scent.

She moans as she closes her eyes, and I have to fight myself not to scowl at Jake. Andy's eyes shoot over to me with a warning before she mouths the words, "knock it off."

"Never come to a debrief without amenities…a lesson I could never forget from the farm," Jake says, giggling like a lovesick teenager as he sits next to Andy.

The two of them proceed to laugh and reminisce about their time at the farm and I start feeling as though I'm completely invisible while standing with the two of them.

"I'll never forget how angry that instructor Brandon was when you showed up with no food to that meeting. He came into Station ready to eat off your head," Andy says, now doubling over with laughter.

Jake shutters and says, "That man was terrifying, but he made his point – if you do nothing else…bring food or the asset won't want to talk to you."

As soon as the laughter dies down, Jake's eyes dart from Andy to me before prying, "So Cameron took the night shift?"

"Shut the hell up Jake – and get your mind out of the gutter. He spent the night on the couch in the control room," Andy responds defensively.

Nope, I spent the night right next to her Jake…

I interject, "get to the point Jake. You didn't just bring coffee and donuts to be nice. When do we leave for the debrief?"

Andy shifts her body uncomfortably on the bed at the mention of the debrief.

"You aren't going to love what I'm here to explain," Jake responds, avoiding eye contact with me, and instead focusing on Andy.

"Okay, just say it Jake," Andy says, taking another sip of coffee before placing the cup on the table.

My eyes shoot to Andy's hand, which is slightly shaking as she sets down the cup.

"Basir isn't here and...well...uh...they...um...," Jake stutters, his knee starting to bounce nervously.

Andy reaches over and places her hand on his shoulder, urging him to continue.

"It's okay Jake. I know you're just the messenger," she says, flashing him an understanding smile.

Even when she should be worried about herself, Andy always focuses more on those around her. And it's clear that her concern shifts to Jake, while I am still firmly focused on how whatever news Jake is here to deliver will impact Andy and this case.

"We have to transport you and it's going to feel like pretty heavy security," Jake says, now glancing in my direction.

"Okay, what do I need to do?" Andy asks, sighing deeply.

Jake instructs her to get dressed (as she is still wearing a t-shirt and those horrible brown sweats) and that he'll return when the van arrives for transport. Andy looks as though someone has punched her in the gut before folding her arms across her chest. I turn toward the door, prepared to be an active part of the preparations and security but stop abruptly at the door when I hear Andy's voice.

"Jake, can I go home...like, when this debrief is over...can I go if I want to go?" Andy asks, appearing to fight off tears.

Jake doesn't respond and instead shrugs before shaking his head in the negative. What I know of Jake, he isn't a shot caller and now I'm feeling a bit bad for the dude. They picked him to try and soften the blow that they're transporting her like a prisoner to her own asset debriefing. Frustrated, but not wanting to make Andy more anxious than she likely already is, I stalk out of the room, forcefully opening the door making this flimsy trailer shake.

Once I'm inside the control room, I turn to see Jake closely on my heels.

"What's your deal with me man?" Jake asks, puffing out his skinny, birdlike chest as though trying to compete with my earlier stance.

Oh, this dude...

I still cannot look at Jake without remembering Andy in his arms in the agency halls and his lips on hers.

Get that out of your head man...

"Where's Rove?" I ask, dismissing Jake by refusing to acknowledge his question.

Rove bounds through the door seconds later, as though he's just been running.

"Okay, we have the caravan ready to go. Jake, you can ride with Andy and Cam, you come with me and Theo in one of the trailing vehicles," Rove says, gesturing for both of us to follow him to the door.

"No, I'll ride with Andy – if you want me to debrief with her, we'll need time to prepare," I insist, reaching out to block Jake from leaving while glaring at him.

"Sure, okay…I can ride in the other car…chill out man," Jake says, retreating and putting up his arms in surrender.

As I move to leave, Rove stops me.

"I'm gonna allow you to ride with her because I need you to get the information from Basir. But this is the last time I should have to say this – *get* yourself together man," Rove warns, through gritted teeth.

"I'm fine – we aren't together and haven't been for years. I'm pretty sure she can't even stand me right now. So, no worries there," I respond, irritated that Rove doesn't trust me to do my job.

But this is my case too – and I have to see it through.

I swallow hard and collect myself before walking through the door. Once outside, I see several men holding Andy's arms and leading her to one of the SUVs in the caravan. While the agency is trying to spin the narrative that this is for Andy's safety, it looks as though she's a prisoner and the tears in her eyes indicate that she probably feels like one too. The man to Andy's right opens the door and they both help her into the car before standing guard outside. I make a point to shove one of the guards out of the way before I slide into the car across from Andy and close the door behind me.

Once inside, I hand Andy a bottle of water and a small backpack with a notepad and some writing utensils. The two of us exchange a knowing look, as I acknowledge how incredibly strange it was for those men to practically carry her to the car. We sit in silence for several minutes, with only the sounds of the road beneath us and traffic whizzing around.

"Are you okay," I ask, trying to imagine how she must feel right now and how it will be to walk into a debrief right after that scene.

Andy doesn't respond but instead just nods and looks out the window as the car pulls off the highway onto a local road.

More silence passes between us, while I contemplate what I can say to make her feel safe with me. I want to reach for her, but her body language looks as though she is building a force field around herself as she curls into herself. I recognize this because I've seen it before. When she doesn't want anyone to know how she feels, she shuts down.

Like when something would remind her of a childhood trauma that she didn't want people knowing still scared her. After watching her father profiled by a police officer and attacked in the streets, even years later she'd stiffen and go silent at the sound of a police siren. Though she shared this with me once, she didn't like talking about it and would shut down when I pressed for more details. But I knew her well enough back then and I loved her so much that I learned her tells – like the way her hands would shake, and her body would instinctively curl away from whatever bothered her.

My eyes shoot to her hand, ever so slightly shaking and then to her lip that she's been biting. When she notices my eyes following her, she brings a hand to her mouth, trying to cover from me what she knows she can't.

"Cam, I hate this. I'm scared and I don't want to be scared. I need to focus, and I cannot focus right now. Please stop asking me if I'm okay and just assume I'm not okay," she admits, clutching the water bottle I handed her.

"You know I won't let anything bad happen to you right," I say, reaching over to place my hand on hers to stop it from trembling.

"Do I?" She asks, looking up at me and rolling her eyes.

I deserved that, but it still stings.

"Andy, I'm sorry. I'm not…" my voice trails off and I pause to gather the courage that honesty would require.

"Cam. Stop, please. Don't. I can't…" her voice trails off and she turns her gaze back out the window.

"I'm not the man I was back then. Well, I mean…in all the ways that tore us apart. I'm sorry…when you told me to go see someone, I should've listened to you," I say, rubbing my forehead.

She stays silent and slowly turns back to look at me.

"I know now is not the best time for me to rehash all this – but Andy, I need you to trust me," I say, now taking her hands in mine.

Her hands are freezing, and she quickly pulls them from mine. I wonder if this is why she's been shaking. I start looking around the car for something I can cover her with – a jacket or blanket or *something*.

"Cam, I'm a *Case Officer*. It took me *years* to get to this point – to push through a load of misogynistic *horse shit* and finally earn just a small shred of respect from these guys. And today, I essentially just found out that I'm a prisoner without any choice in what happens to me – while at the same time about to conduct what is likely going to be the biggest debrief of my entire career – and you want to talk about what happened to us when we were basically *kids*? No Cam, this isn't the best time."

Andy turns away from me and pushes a few stray curls behind her ear before looking back out the window. Still shaking, she pulls the pen and paper out of the backpack and starts writing. I don't respond because I know she has every right to be angry at me. Without a word, I take off my coat and wrap it around her. While she accepts the jacket, she doesn't turn her attention back toward me.

"I need to prepare for this debrief. I know that Rove insisted you be here as my *minder* – or whatever – but I'm running this show and you'll follow my lead," Andy says, leaving no room for discussion.

"When the debrief is over, no matter what happens in there...I'm going to make sure you get to go home," I say, not entirely sure how I'll make that happen but really hoping it will make her feel better.

We spend the rest of the car ride in silence, with Andy writing in the notebook and me deep in thought. Once we arrive at a remote location that I've never seen before, I exit the car and ask Andy to remain inside until I come back.

"Where exactly do you think I can go," she says, shooting me an annoyed look before pointing to two, large security guards who stand so close to the door that I have to shove them out of the way to exit. There are six other SUVs surrounding us and Rove approaches me moments after I exit the vehicle.

"Are you ready?" Rove asks, surveilling their surroundings.

"What the hell is happening here, Rove? Why all these cars and why are they treating Andy like she's a prisoner?" I ask in response.

Rove leans in close to me as he speaks, "Something smells with this operation. I tried to shut out Brody and his team of minions but they're all over this like subway rats on a New York pizza. And Cam, I don't think they give one hell of beans about what happens to Andy."

I scan the parking area, acknowledging that we have an audience. Todd, the jerk who tried to take the case from Andy in Brazil, is standing next to Brody. I want to knock the smug smile off Todd's face, but I know that would make this situation a lot worse.

Ain't no way they'd let a Black man like me get away with that...

So instead, I shoot him a menacing glare and scrunch up my nose like I've just smelled a rotten animal's carcass.

"So, what's the plan?" I ask, trying to keep my lips still to ensure that the guys surrounding us can't read my lips.

"You go to the debrief with Andy. The two of you will walk down that path into the woods alone toward the cabin where they're housing Basir and his family. I'll block Brody and company. When you're finished, you'll take her out the trap door of the cabin and walk – well, maybe jog if you can - due north about 10 miles to a helipad. Theo will pick you all up and take you into the city where we have a spot where you both can hunker down until we sort this out."

Rove's face shows a level of concern that I haven't seen before, revealing fine lines between his thick eyebrows. His eyes dart around, and I try to casually lean in to get clarity and ask if he is completely nuts.

Andy is barely able to walk right now...he thinks we can jog?

"Geez Rove, ten miles? We can't do that before dark...and making that kind of mileage in this terrain is going to take us hours – especially in the state she's in," I whisper, praying he is about to tell me he's joking.

"You got other options man? Trust me when I tell you – you two need to disappear after this debrief," Rove says, his eyes intense and unrelenting.

What does he know that he isn't telling me?

"And Cam, you can't let Andy know what's happening until you're free from anyone tailing you – we don't have time for you two to argue. Things could get chaotic there because I think our comrades over there have big plans for her that don't include her safe return. I'll tell you both everything that I know once you're out of here and we have more time."

But will she trust me enough to follow me when I need her to follow?

"How are we going to get past...the minions?" I ask, my eyes scanning our surroundings.

"I'll handle them. Listen carefully Cam, use the code we planned for this operation on the door. Tell Farhad you're with me and he'll know what to do," Rove responds, leaning close enough that I can feel and smell his minty breath on my ear.

Brody lets out a loud whistle, calling the group to attention. But when I turn to open the car door to get Andy, I see her being dragged by the arm toward the group by a burly security guard. I narrow my eyes and shift to move toward her, but Rove shoots me a warning glance and holds up his arm to stop me.

"Play along," Rove mutters through gritted teeth and under his breath.

Andy has the small backpack I gave her across one of her shoulders. Rove shoves another backpack in my arms that I hope has enough water for both of us and a first aid kit for the trek. Knowing Rove, the bag also has a compass for backup and a GPS with coordinates of the rally point. Almost instinctively, my hand slides down my leg to the spot where I've holstered my knife. I always double check to make sure I've brought a backup weapon. My agency issued Glock is resting securely under my bomber jacket.

"Alright fellas – here's how this is gonna go down," Brody starts, placing his hands on his hips authoritatively and twirling around to address his minions.

I catch Andy's scowl and suspect it's a mix between her dislike for Brody and the fact that he didn't even acknowledge that not everyone standing here is a "fella".

Touché Andy, Brody is a prick.

Andy is the only woman amongst us, and Brody is making it clear with his language that to him she is insignificant to this operation. Andy clears her throat loudly and shakes her arm free from the man who's been holding it.

"Last I checked, Basir wanted to speak to me and *not* any of y'all – so, I think I got this," she says, glaring at Brody and rolling her eyes at Todd who is rocking back and forth like he is ready to pounce on her opportunity.

"Okay darling, we get it...calm down," Brody instructs in a patronizing tone.

"I'll stand guard outside of the cabin with my buddy Rick," Todd says, smirking.

"You'll stand *inside* the cabin to guard," Brody corrects.

"Nope – Basir made it clear that Andy was the only one he'd speak to. If we come in there with a parade – he's not going to cooperate. Andy and Cameron are the only two to enter the cabin," Rove says, pushing back on Brody.

"Fine...outside the cabin," Brody grunts, through gritted teeth.

Rove and Brody are technically peers, but this started as a GST 9 operation until our asset didn't follow the plan and ended up in Brody's jurisdiction. It's clear the two of them don't agree on how this should be handled, and I'm starting to see why Rove is so insistent on separating Andy from Brody and his team as soon as possible. Before this pissing contest gets out of hand, I swiftly walk over to Andy and ask her if she's ready to go. She nods affirmatively and I'm relieved when the two goons at her side take a step back so that I don't have to shove them out of our way.

"I think *she's* got this. We'll see you on the other side," I say, gesturing for Andy to come with me toward the dirt path leading to the cabin.

Chapter 10
Debrief

"Andy"

"Cameron, what the hell was that over there?" I ask in a low voice, following him down the dirt path.

Shaking his head and glancing over his shoulder at Todd and Rick, who are about five paces behind us, Cameron whispers, "not here – we'll talk later. Just keep walking, okay?"

As we approach the house, I take a deep breath trying to prepare myself for what Basir will tell us. I'm regretting not keeping Cameron's coat. Even with several layers of clothes and my own jacket, I still feel like I'm freezing from the inside out. My hands are shaking and if I can't figure out how to get them to stop, my asset is going to think I can't handle this.

Just as Cameron reaches out to knock on the door, I grab his hand to stop him.

"Cam – before we go in there, we have to get something straight. This is *my* debrief. I'm the Case Officer in this Operation and while I get that your team expected to take possession of the vial – this is *my* jurisdiction now and you *will take* the lead. Is that understood?" I ask, intentionally standing only a few inches from Cameron's face as I look into his eyes.

"Yeah, okay, yes. I understand. I'm here to make sure shit doesn't go down and if it does – I engage and get us to safety. But you lead the debrief," Cam acknowledges.

Cameron knocks on the door in a rhythmic tap that sounds like morse code, and it cracks open just wide enough for two, dark brown eyes to peer out. When Farhad sees me, his face brightens, and he opens the door wide enough for us to enter. But he keeps a cautious eye on Cameron as we walk to a small couch in the living room area of the cabin.

"Who is *he*," Farhad asks, sizing Cameron up with his eyes.

"This is Cameron – don't worry, you can trust him," I say, recognizing that while I don't know if I can trust him – he's certainly more trustworthy than the two morons standing just outside the cabin doors.

Cameron interjects, "I work with Rove."

Farhad doesn't respond, but his shoulders drop as though the association with Rove has earned Cameron some credibility. Cameron reaches for his bag, pulling out a tray of cookies and places them on a round table in front of the couch.

What hasn't Cameron told me about this operation?

"You must be Farhad. I was one of the men waiting for your father along the Iranian border in Afghanistan. I'm glad you all made it here safely," Cameron says, extending a hand to Farhad who offers his hand in return.

"Rove is a good man. So, if you are with Rove – you must be alright," Farhad says, as though to reassure himself.

Farhad gestures to the couch, asking us to sit while he gets his father. Voices can be heard in another room, which I assume are those of the rest of the family. This cabin seems like it's in the middle of nowhere and the surroundings are so quiet that the noises of the birds outside sound like musical accompaniment. The cabin looks like one from the movies with exposed logs on the ceiling and a giant deer head in the foyer. My eyes float around the surroundings, taking note of all the exits and what furniture could be used to barricade the doors should we need to stop an intruder.

One couch...

Two...no three...bar stools

A deer head?

My heart rate is quickening with the bird's loud chirps, remembering how the last debrief ended. Placing my hand over my chest, and taking a deep breath, I settle into the soft cushions of the couch.

"Are you alright," Cameron whispers in my ear as he sits next to me.

"Yeah, I'm fine," I say, dishonestly.

Basir emerges from one of the bedrooms and I quickly collect myself so that my nerves don't make him nervous. He's dressed in tan slacks with a black button-down shirt and dress shoes, a stark contrast from the clothing he'd worn when we first met in Brazil. He looks a lot better, like some of the stress weighing him down has melted off in the days since the family landed on US soil.

"It's nice to see you all," I say, getting up from the couch to acknowledge him but careful not to touch him as to respect their cultural norm.

Cameron, in contrast, reaches out offering a two-handed handshake. Having studied what is proper, I hold my breath while I wait to see whether either man will reach for the wrist of the other – a sign that the wrist-reacher wants something from the other. Luckily,

Cameron's hands remain in the proper place as do Basir's. Basir releases the handshake, nods his head at Cameron, and takes a seat in one of the large, plush chairs across from us. Farhad, who will translate for his father, sits in a chair to his father's right.

"My father, he...he wanted me to first tell you that he is sorry," Farhad says to me, as both he and his father look at me.

I swallow hard, not responding immediately because I'm unsure what he is apologizing for – his daughter drawing danger to the house or the fact that I was stabbed with the serum that was supposed to get his family asylum.

"Thank you...for that," I reply, shifting in my seat and rubbing the leg that was injected with the serum.

All three men immediately look at my leg, which prompts me to jump right into my first question.

"Basir, why did you come to Brazil instead of going to Afghanistan to meet Rove's team?" I ask, immediately cutting right to the chase.

Basir looks me in the eyes while speaking in Farsi while Farhad translates, "my father knew that the serum was our only chance at getting all of us asylum in the U.S.. And when he found out Andy was a target, a viable host, he knew that she was the only person he could trust to hand it to – who wouldn't have motive to hand it over to Solaris."

Cameron and I looked at each other, both silent and waiting for Farhad to continue translating.

"My father came to give you the vial and to warn you. He didn't know the Esfahani's had already come for you. That man who broke into the apartment wasn't coming for us, he was coming for *you*," Farhad says, pointing his finger at me passionately.

"What do you know about the man who attacked us?" I ask, looking between Basir and Farad.

"Esfahani, very bad," Basir says, before gesturing toward his son to elaborate.

"The Esfahani brothers are notorious hit men. They are like the rats of the middle east – some of them actual brothers and some not. Like a gang of hit men for hire. Once they have a target, they just keep coming," Farhad says, wincing as he looks at me with something that looks like sadness and fear in his deep brown eyes.

"Why not just come bring the vial to my team?" Cameron interjects, as I shoot him a warning look.

Both Farhad and Basir look at Cameron and don't respond to his question. They then turn back toward me to continue.

"My father was working for a nuclear lab in Iran. At first he thought they were developing nuclear energy, just like they were telling the rest of the world," Farhad translates, "but when he found out they were testing this serum for the rapid development...and using people...to make a nuclear weapon...he knew he had to get out of there."

"What do you mean using people?" I ask, starting to worry that the answers were going to make this all worse.

I look over at Cameron who's watching me closely and sitting at the edge of his seat as though he's anxiously waiting for me to let him speak again.

"The serum is useless unless it's mixed with human blood and there are only a few people on the planet with the exact biochemistry to make it work. Your blood is a match," Farhad says, looking between his father and me as he translates.

"How did they know I was a match?" I ask, wondering how in the hell the Iranian government knows anything about my blood.

Basir places his hands on his knees, wiping sweat from his palms before continuing.

Farhad says, "That's the thing, my dad found out that you were a target and after he did some digging, he realized that someone inside your government was providing the data."

"But how would they know I was a match?" I ask, still trying to untangle this in my head.

"They have our blood Andy. We are all required to take an agency physical before deploying. They have all the data they needed with that," Cameron says, placing his head in his palms in frustration.

My own government did this?

Farhad continues, "When my dad found out the Americans had a mole, he knew that the only way to get the vial out - and ensure he was handing it to someone who wasn't either affiliated with the Iranians or Solaris – was to hand it to someone who had incentive to destroy the network."

"Someone whose life depended the destruction of this technology – *me*," I say, gently placing my back on the sofa in an attempt to stop the room from spinning.

"Andy, please believe us. My dad wanted to warn you and to give you the vial for safe keeping – so that we could get to America. He didn't want this to happen," Farhad says, his dark brown eyes shining as the sun reflected against them through the windows.

I'm silent and trying to process this information. I've never conducted a debrief that felt as personal as this – literally life and death. I glance toward Cameron, nodding my head to show that I was okay with him asking his questions while I continued to process.

"So, Basir, can you explain what you know about what happened to the facility before you left?" Cameron asks, looking at Basir while glancing at me out of the corner of his eye.

"Two days before I got out, Solaris raided the facility and took everything. Everything except for the vial of the serum I'd brought home and the maps I took out with locations across the globe where other facilities were located," Farhad replies, after his father explains in Farsi.

"Are there others? Other matches that we know about, besides Andy?" Cameron asks, quickly looking back at me with pain in his eyes.

Basir shakes his head in the negative before responding, "No, no more. Just Andy."

Cameron's face is turning a shade that looks almost green, and I wonder if he's going to vomit. Silently looking between Cameron and Farhad, I cannot bring myself to reply to the news. I feel like my brain and voice are in some sort of war – panic fighting with my desire to remain professional. Cameron's leg starts to shake, the motion jolting me from my thoughts.

"You, okay?" Cameron mouths to me, again.

I nod and place my hand on his leg briefly to draw his attention to the shaking. I'm desperate to hide my own nerves and know he doesn't want his showing either. Directing my attention back to Farhad, I continue, "So, what now? How do we destroy this network? Do you even know if there is an antidote or what this stuff will do to me?"

And that's the question I've been too afraid to ask.

"No, no, no...not kill you," Basir says, looking at me before turning to Farhad and imploring him to continue.

Farhad jumps in to clarify, "They made it so the serum won't kill the host because they essentially need the host to continue to produce, so that there can be a continuous supply of the materials needed to build a viable weapon."

"If they haven't found a host...until now...how do they know it works?" Cameron asks, cautiously.

"They don't...yet. They'd need Andy to confirm, but from the vials of blood they were able to obtain from someone in your government – the Iranians think they found the key," Farhad responds, looking back at his father whose speaking rapidly and making translation tricky.

"Do you have names of anyone in our government who has turned?" Cam asks, his eyes nervously glancing to the door that we know is guarded by Brody's goons.

"No, we don't know who but Andy needs to be careful because whomever it is – they're probably working with Solaris. Solaris has all the technology now and we should assume Andy is their target," Farhad replies.

"And Solaris could've hired the Esfahani brothers," I say, making a mental note to get more information on those guys when I get back to a computer.

Both Basir and Farhad nod their affirmation.

"So then why did you tell us you'd meet us at the base if your plan all along was to just get to Andy?" Cameron asks, irritation in his voice.

"And while I work on getting rid of these places, what will happen to me with this stuff inside me? Is there a way to get it out?" I ask, my anxiety rising and making me feel as though I might drown in it.

Farhad takes a deep breath, "Well, we don't know exactly what it will do long term, but our hope is that you and your team will get your hands on the antidote before destroying the rest of the labs. We know there is an antidote...or that there was an antidote."

"But even with an antidote...would that make me a non-viable host if I took it?" I ask, hoping there's a way for me to remove myself as a target.

"No, you'll always be a host unless we can find and destroy all the vials and the technology allowing them to produce new ones," Farhad replies.

"Why didn't you just bring the antidote with you?" Cameron interjects, his voice holding a level of irritation that causes me to elbow him in the side.

"Sorry," he quickly whispers, glancing in my direction before retreating into the couch cushion.

"We couldn't...in the Solaris raid...it was taken along with everything else. And my dad didn't have access to it to take it out with the vial he was able to grab," Farhad says.

What? Someone took it?! Seriously??!?

I hear Cameron take a deep breath, and he looks like he's about to bite his tongue off as he glances at me.

I lean over and place my head in my hands. I feel like I'm going to throw up all over the shaggy white rug at my feet.

"Solaris took it, but we don't think it's been destroyed – just moved. My dad overheard someone saying that everything was being transported to the epicenter...the headquarters," Farhad responds.

"And where is that?" I ask, frustration boiling inside and threatening my composure.

"Well, we don't know yet. My father was never given the location. We have some location of other facilities, but to destroy the network someone will need to get on the inside," Farhad says, looking at me.

Cameron shifts in his seat and turns toward Basir before saying, "wait, are you suggesting that Andy go into the center of this? No way."

"There are still a few others who left...who might know more than my father...so maybe we can try them first," Farhad replies, looking at me apologetically.

"What do you know about this serum? How much time do I have to find this antidote? You said this wouldn't kill me, but do you actually know for sure if it's never been injected into a human before?" I ask, placing my hand on the injection site that still burns.

"It will mess with your body temperature, making you feel cold. This will get worse with blood draws and the short-term danger is body temperature dropping to dangerous levels. The good news is that if you were to enter one of these labs as a double, they have incentive to keep you alive and should know about the body temperature risk," Farhad explains.

That sounds as lovely as munching on a pack of metal nails for lunch.

I feel like I'm trapped in this hell loop of horrors with my body. While trying to take down this terrorist network, saving myself and my country, I also somehow must stay lucid. There's absolutely no telling what will happen to me and if the last day is any indication – I can be feeling completely fine one moment and like a frozen tundra that could crack into a million pieces the next.

This white, shaggy rug is so impractical that I want to intentionally spill the grape juice on the table just to make the agency change it.

To avoid looking at this ugly carpet, and momentarily disassociate from my present reality, I focus my eyes on the dark wooden floors, which are full of tiny nails as though someone tried to fix a dozen creaks instead of just changing out the old wood. At least now it makes sense why it feels like I've been sitting in a bath of ice water several times a day since that serum entered my body. Just as I start to shiver, one of the bedroom doors squeak open and Basir's wife enters the room with a large blanket. She carries it over, wrapping it around my shoulders. After a moment deep in my feelings, I look up to meet eyes with Basir. The sadness has returned, and I remember what drew me to this family in the first place. This man felt as though he was out of options, and he placed the safety of his family – and the fate of the free world it seems – in my hands when he came to me.

"I understand why you came to me, and I appreciate that you tried to warn me," I say quietly, looking between Farhad and Basir.

While I wish they'd given me a heads up sooner about the terrorist organizations that were after my blood, I cannot blame this family for doing what they could to save themselves. Basir weighed the risks and he decided coming to me was his best option, even if that choice was the one that led the threat right to me.

As I continue explaining my hope to carry out this mission, Cameron starts walking toward the front door and I notice his hand move to the gun he's been hiding under his jacket. The doorknob starts to jiggle, and I flinch at the unwelcome sound of danger. Cameron backs away from the door and places his finger to his lips to indicate that everyone should remain quiet.

"Farhad, I have to get Andy out of here immediately. You're safe, but when those men come through that door – you need to tell them you don't know where we went. Did Rove tell you the plan?" Cameron asks, grabbing my arm and leading me away from the door and toward the back of the cabin.

Farhad nods, pushing his father toward the back room. I look at Cameron with confusion, as he gathers our belongings and nudges me toward the back door. After closing the door behind his father, Farhad peers out one of the back shades to look behind the cabin.

"No, not this way. They're back there too. Go this way," Farhad says, reaching down to the floor and moving apart the floorboards I'd been staring at moments earlier.

What the hell? Who is this guy? And what in hell is going on?

Cameron shakes Farhad's hand and as we both move toward the exit through the floor and Farhad hands me what looks like a dozen rolled up pieces of paper and a flash drive.

"Here are maps and information that will help you find the sites that we know about. And Andy, there is a disease...corruption...it's inside your government. Be safe," Farhad whispers in my ear.

"Thank you – you be safe too," I respond, shoving what he's given me into my small backpack and pulling the drawstrings closed.

The floor closes behind us and Cameron grabs a small flashlight from his bag. Narrow stairs lead us down a dark room that opens to an even darker hallway.

"What is this place," I ask, swatting what feels like thick cobwebs from around my hair.

"It looks like an old tunnel, and I have no idea how Farhad knew about it, but I sure hope Todd and Dick...or whatever that guy's name was... don't know it's here," Cameron responds.

"Are you going to tell me what the hell is going on? Todd is a jerk, but this seems like a bit much" I say, wondering why it appears we are trying to escape guys who are supposed to be on our side.

As we walk down the hall, looking for obvious exits, there's a commotion above us. Cameron stops, pulling me to him as we crouch on the floor quietly. The walls around us are shaking and I close my eyes for a moment. Cameron wraps his arms around me and holds me tight as I burrow my head into his chest.

"Where are they?" A voice that sounds like Todd yells.

"They aren't here anymore...I...I don't know..." Farhad responds.

It sounds like chairs and tables are being shoved or maybe thrown around the house, and several men scream at each other. After a few minutes of utter chaos, another voice I don't recognize tells the Assadi family to stay put and notify them if we return. While Todd never allows anyone to forget about the fact that he went to Harvard, he's always lacked in the commonsense department. Given that they surrounded the house during what I can only assume was the entirety of our meeting, a logical person would assume we couldn't have gone far and certainly didn't leave through the doors. But clearly, Brody sent the fool.

Thank God.

Before continuing, we wait huddled in the corner and surrounded by loudly creaking wooden floors and the faint sounds of each other's breathing. Cameron's heart beats rapidly against the side of my head. My ears strain to hear the conversations whirling above us, hoping to obtain a morsel of information that might help me piece this all together.

"I told you she'd bolt," one of them says.

"What are we going to tell Brody?" Asks the other.

Sounds of the forest brush crunching drowns out their voices as they move out further away. There's a tap on the floorboard, in the same code that Cameron used to knock on the door. Cameron shifts his weight to stand, pulling me up with him.

"Let's go – we have a long walk. And I want to get as far away from here as we can tonight before we have to stop for the night," Cameron says, so casually that I want to scream and slap him at the same time.

"Wait a second buddy – you are gonna have to clue me in here," I say, folding my arms and digging my heels into the damp ground beneath me.

"Andy, I don't even know the whole story. Rove told me in the parking lot that we needed to get out of the debrief and meet Theo at a rally point. He seemed to think we couldn't trust our own guys. We have to walk 10 miles, through some pretty wicked terrain, in the next 24 hours so I suggest we get moving," He responds.

"Cam, did you miss the memo that I'm still recovering from a stab wound and I have a nuclear serum - that could cause my body to suddenly go into hypothermic shock – inside of me right now?" I ask, looking at him like he's lost his ever-loving mind.

And I'm not sure I trust you right now...or Rove...

Turning to face me, Cameron puts his hands on my shoulders and says, "Andy, I know I haven't given you many reasons to trust me but think about how you were being treated at Blue Castle and what just happened here. *Something* is wrong and those guys are going to hurt you if we go back there. Rove told me to take you to the rally point and right now – his plan seems better than the alternative."

My feet feel as though they are sinking into the floor, but I know he's right. I don't know who I can trust right now, but I know Brody isn't to be trusted. And at this moment, I don't feel safe anywhere. I cannot believe Cameron is asking me to follow him down this spider and rodent infested, dark tunnel.

"Andy, *please*. Come with me. Neither of us will make it out of here safely if we try to run back toward the danger," he pleads.

Just as I start debating my options in my own head, I hear loud voices above us followed by the sound of dogs barking. We clearly need to get out of here and I know I'm not safe with Brody and his men. Cameron and I exchange a knowing look.

Dogs...run.

Chapter 11
Escape

My eyes shoot upward, in unison with Andy's, at the sound of the dogs barking above us. I grab her hand, which is cold and clammy, and started running toward what appears to be our only way out – a dark, damp, smelly, tunnel. We're running for our lives, praying that the tunnel will lead us far enough away from the danger above.

And I'm praying the smell in here doesn't trigger a migraine...

While I hold onto Andy with one hand, I lift my flashlight with the other while also trying to shield my face. The tunnel smells like a family of giant sewer rats recently died in the walls that surrounded us. The smell is so rancid and offensive that it invades my nostrils, threatening to render both of us unconscious. As we reach a fork in the tunnel, I look back at Andy. The color is draining from her face, and she seems unsteady on her feet.

"Cam, wait," she says, slipping her hand out of mine, bending over, and placing her hands on her knees.

Andy's shaking, which coupled with the icy feel of her hands, worries me. These are early signs of hypothermia.

Basir said this wouldn't kill her, but then what the hell is this?!

Rove probably had no idea what this would do to Andy so we might not even have the supplies we'll need to get us through the night and to safety.

"Are you okay? Tell me what's happening?" I ask, my mind starting to race with possible solutions should her condition worsen.

"I'm *really* cold, and...and dizzy. I don't know how long I can run," she admits, panting and placing one of her hands on her forehead while the other reaches for me.

I try to steady her and prop her arm up on one of my shoulders. The smell hits me in the face again and I involuntarily start coughing.

"Cam, how are *you*? I know how you get with smells...are you going to be alright?" She asks.

"Yeah, I'll be good. We just need to find our way out of here before these dogs get us," I respond, pulling the collar of my shirt up to try and muffle some of the stench.

We can still hear the dogs barking in the distance and Andy looks up at me with pain and panic in her now blue green eyes, which glow in the darkness of the tunnel. I grab her hands in mine and try to rub them to warm her, knowing this won't be enough but giving myself time to think about our next move.

"Do you think you can make it a little further so we can get out of the tunnel? My satellite phone doesn't work down here, and if we make it to the surface we can call my team for help," I say, wrapping my entire body around hers to try and warm her.

"Okay, I'll try. I just can't run so fast," she responds, clinging to me with her teeth chattering.

I nod and pull out a map Rove mentioned was in the zipper pocket of the backpack. The GPS is toast along with the satellite phone until get out of this cave and have service, so I look at the map for clues on which direction to head.

"It looks like if we go to the right, there should be an exit just up ahead," I say, taking her hand back in mine and leading us forward.

We continue walking in silence, with only the sounds of our footsteps and the echoes of the dripping water around us. I haven't even heard the dogs in some time and after about an hour we finally make it to an opening. It's a rusted-out grate with dim light peeling out around it.

"Wait here until I make sure it's safe for us to come out," I say, holding Andy by the waist and helping her down to a seated position against the tunnel wall.

Andy slumps against the wall and crosses her arms tightly as though she's trying to stop herself from shaking. I take off my jacket and wrap it around her shoulders.

"Hang tight okay, I'll be right back. Please...stay with me. I'm going to get us out of this," I say, touching her face gently to get her attention.

She nods before closing her eyes and responding, "Okay...I'll be fine...just hurry."

She clearly isn't fine.

Her words sound like a whisper, and I don't think there's any way we'll make it to Rove's over ambitious rally point. We need another extraction plan, and we need one quickly. I run over to the grate and start pulling on it. It's stuck in place and barely budging. I pull harder, kick it, hang my entire weight on it – but it doesn't move. I can feel my heart racing, and I swallow the lump of panic in my throat. Andy is slumped over, and her lips are starting to lose color.

No, no, no, Cameron think!

This moment takes me back to that feeling I had as a little boy when I'd get lost in the woods by our house. No matter how many times I was told not to wonder off, I'd get too curious and then end up lost and panicked about it. I start to pace, racking my brain for a solution while I rub my hands through my hair. Typically, during GS missions I'm the one with a clear head, but this time it's not just me trying to get out of a bind – Andy is here too.

I can't fuck this up. I owe it to her to get her out of this.

Just when I think things cannot be more dire, I hear voices in the tunnel behind us. I stop moving to confirm whether they're the voices of our enemy. The barking dogs, followed by lights confirm what I've feared – they've caught up to us. I start cursing and punching the wall as I try to figure out a way to open this damned grate.

Andy's eyes pop open at the sound of the barking dogs closing in on us, and she lifts herself off the ground.

"Oh no, how long was I out...I should've been helping," she says, looking around and rubbing at her eyes.

"No, you needed to rest. But now that we have...visitors...we don't have the time I thought we did and this grate won't budge," I respond, pushing on the grate again and trying to disguise the growing panic in my voice.

Andy looks into my eyes, placing her hand on my shoulder, and then gently touches my face – a simple gesture that causes my head to spin with memories of what we'd been like together years prior. She always felt like home with just a simple touch and when I would get anxiety, she was always the person who could calm me down and make me feel grounded.

After leaving my side, Andy inspects the area around the grate. She pulls the flashlight out of her bag and runs her hand along the surface next to the grate.

"Cam, it's just dirt. We can dig around it to loosen it. Do you have a knife?" She asks, holding out her hand as though she expects me to just give it to her.

"Ummm, yeah...yes, I have knives," I respond, embarrassed that I've been unable to think of this seemingly obvious solution.

I'm thankful that despite the circumstances, she's clear headed enough to point out what should've been so obvious to me. I pull out my knife and Andy picks up what looks like a slab of metal that's laying on the ground. We both furiously dig, as the barking and yelling of those pursuing us draw closer.

The area around the grate is heavily packed with dirt and the first layer is hard to dig through. But I keep at it, stabbing with my knife as though I'm digging us out of a grave. I look across at Andy, whose hands are bloody as she scratches and claws at the dirt.

"Andy stop - you're hurting yourself. Please, just let me do it," I yell, while continuing to furiously dig at the wall.

Just as the dogs rounded the corner, I grab Andy by the arm and kick the grate loose. The grate flies outward and the tunnel walls around us started to crumble. A giant cloud of dust fills the air and invades our lungs. We both dive through the gaping hole just as the tunnel collapses, presumably burying alive the people and dogs that are still inside.

As we clear the tunnel, I throw myself on top of Andy to shield her from the rubble that's flying in all directions. There's an avalanche of rocks and dirt flying everywhere. I feel like my lungs are ablaze with all the dust and start to cough violently to clear it from my body. The only thing I can compare this to is when we were forced to run through a cabin lit up with pepper spray during training. I feel like every orifice on my head is trying desperately to expel the toxins. Andy's body shakes underneath me, as she coughs and attempts to catch her breath.

"Are you okay?" I ask, inspecting her with his eyes and hands to make sure she hadn't been hit.

At some point I expect her to start punching me if I don't stop asking her that.

"Yes, I think so...you?" She responds.

"Yeah, I'm good. But hot damn that was close," I laugh, trying to make her smile while still coughing and trying to catch my breath.

She giggles between coughs and pushes on my chest.

"Cam – can you...ease up? You're crushing me," she says, smiling awkwardly up at me.

"Oh gosh, I'm sorry," I respond, springing off her and starting to brush dust off myself.

As soon as I'm able to confirm that we've gotten out of the tunnel without further injuries, I feel around inside the backpack for the satellite phone and call Rove.

"Rove, man...you gotta send backup, and get us out of here. Andy's not doing well, and I don't even think we've gone more than about 3 miles on foot through this terrain," I say into the phone in a tone loud enough to highlight the urgency, without calling attention to our location.

"Okay, what's happening?" Rove asks.

I briefly explain what we've learned from Basir about the side effects of the serum and how they're likely to impact her body temperature before walking a few feet from Andy to elaborate upon my concerns.

"She's cold and shaking. For the last hour or so she's been stumbling a lot and she told me she feels dizzy and disoriented," I say, trying to keep my voice calm so that Andy doesn't get more upset than she likely already is.

"You need to hunker down – you're right, it's too dangerous for her to be walking around right now," Rove responds, his voice cracking due to spotty reception.

"Also – those fuckers almost caught up to us. That tunnel just collapsed as we got out, and while it looks like nobody's getting out of there the same way we did – I can't confirm whether anyone survived that mess. It was like someone set off a bomb in there," I explain, my voice shaking.

"Alright, I'll put some of our guys on this and see if they can figure out who was in that tunnel and whether or not any of them got out alive," Rove says.

Rove gives me coordinates of a nearby shed where we can hide, while he figures out how to get a team through these woods and to us without being detected. Rove also informs me that he packed a sleeping bag, camping blankets and a first aid kit that has some instant heat packs inside.

"But Cameron...that might be enough if she's getting hypothermic," Rove warns, hesitation in his voice.

I know exactly why Rove hesitates. In field training we were taught that skin to skin contact is one of the most effective ways to warm up body temperature. While Andy seems to no longer be in active disagreement with me, I'm not confident I'll be able to convince her to strip naked and lay skin to skin inside a sleeping bag with me.

"I know, I'll handle it...just get here," I respond to avoid the growing awkwardness at the reality that I'm talking to my boss while thinking about holding Andy's naked body.

God...does this make me a total perv? Get it together dude!

I shake my head, trying to make myself stop thinking about her being naked next to me because the last thing she needs is my hard dick pressing into her side right now. I reach into the bag to get a small pad to jot down the coordinates Rove reads to me. When I hang up the phone, I swivel around to look for Andy. She's standing, slumped against a nearby tree with her eyes fixed on me.

"Are they going to come for us?" She asks, her breathing shallow and voice raspy.

"Yes, but we're going to have to wait out the night. We need to find a way to warm you up," I respond, walking over to her and wrapping my arm around her to help her walk.

We leave the clearing and walk a few clicks down a steep hill toward a small shed that's hidden amongst a bunch of overgrown weeds. Rove didn't downplay the accommodations – the shed is tiny, has a rusted steel roof, and a broken-down barn style door that's hard to slide open. Inside, it's empty and has a hard, dirty wooden floor. Just about the only nice thing I can say about this place is that it will keep the wind off us. Certainly not the way either of us want to spend our night, but we don't have a better alternative. So, this little, barely standing hut will have to do.

Just as I drop my bag and move to pull out the sleeping bag, Andy collapses to the floor.

"Oh...God...oh no, I'm sorry...I..I...don't know," she stutters, struggling with her words and placing a hand to her forehead.

"Don't apologize – it's okay. I'm going to get firewood so that I can make a fire in that spot over there that looks like maybe it was once a working fireplace. I need you to get into the sleeping bag and hang on until I get back," I say.

I open the sleeping bag, helping Andy inside, and put all the camping blankets we have on top. I then grab the first aid kit, tearing open several heat packs and slip them inside with her. I run out of the shed, quickly gathering as much firewood as I can before rushing back into the shed. When I return to see her continuing to shake and lose even more color from her face, I know I need to set aside my pride and embarrassment and just get naked. As I start taking off my clothes, Andy's eyes get wide.

"*What* are you doing?" She asks, confused.

"We need to get your clothes off too," I reply, trying to remove all emotion from my voice so that she doesn't think I'm trying to assault her in this dingy, poor excuse for a cabin.

"What? Cam, no," she pleads, looking down at the ground as though she can't bear to look me in the eyes.

"You need to let me help you – you know if we don't get you warm...I just don't want to lose you," I admit, embarrassed as soon as the words leave my lips.

She studies my face for a moment, eyebrows bunching together with worry and fear. Once I remove my clothes down to my boxer briefs, I slowly walk toward her. She's still wrapped in the sleeping bag, so I crawl in with her and pull her close to me.

"Please Andy, please let me save you," I whisper softly in her ear.

Chapter 12
Survive

"Andy"

Cameron's body feels like a drink of water after days in a dry, hot desert. I don't have control over my own body as I cling to him like my life depends on the warmth he's generating.

God, he feels so good it hurts.

Pulling him closer doesn't feel like enough. So, when he starts pulling my shirt over my head, I let him – because I know I need this.

And I hate that that so much.

"Cam – I'm *really* cold," I say, cold tears escaping from my eyes like icicles falling from a frozen tree branch.

But actually...like the coldest I've been in my entire life.

"Basir warned us about this, but I didn't expect this to happen so quickly. But Rove is sending a team to get us. If there is something that can help, we'll find it okay," he responds, helping me to remove my pants so that there is no more bulky fabric between us.

I wrap one of my legs around him like a pretzel, which causes him to flinch.

"Oh, I'm sorry," I apologize, immediately moving my leg in mortification.

"Andy no...it's fine. It's just...I miss this," he admits.

When we were dating, it was how we'd sleep together – wrapped in each other's arms like a tangled, chocolate pretzel. Even without the serum I'm always cold and Cameron has always been like a furnace. We used to joke about how opposite we were in that way, but I always appreciated that he'd suffer through how hot he felt just to be close to me.

"Cam? Can we trust Rove and the rest of your team?" I ask, the truth that someone in my own government exposed me to this still eating away at me.

Hell, I am not even sure I can trust Cameron.

"I trust Rove with my life. I know this is a really fucked up situation, but I don't think you have to worry about anyone in the GS-9 crew being the mole here," Cameron says, with a level of confidence I don't share.

"How can I go back? How can I possibly go back to work knowing what these people did to me?" I ask, a shiver running through my body.

Cameron doesn't immediately respond, but after moments of silence he says, "Andy, I don't think you can. Just before we went into the debrief, Rove told me that I needed to get you out of there. I think we both just found out why."

"Did you know before the debrief that American officials were responsible for this?" I ask, feeling my body brace for the possibility that he was withholding information from me.

"No, I didn't even know you'd been injected with the serum until after we'd gotten to Blue Castle. I had no idea why they'd taken you there," he admits, in a tone that sounds sincere.

"Okay, so what do we do now?" I ask, feeling hopeless about my options.

"We wait here and survive until my team can get us help, and then we regroup back in the city and come up with a plan," he responds.

There are moments when I feel focused, like this is just another operation, and then moments where the reality of my situation seeps into my pores and I feel like there's no way out. Feeling this vulnerable, physically naked and emotionally bare, feels like new rock bottom. But surprisingly, there's comfort in Cameron's arms, even though my heart is still very broken.

Struggling to keep my eyes open, my head falls against his bare chest. I'm still shaking, and every breath feels like something that requires constant brain power.

"Andy? Are you still here with me?" He asks, lifting my head to look me in the eyes.

"Cam...I'm so tired," I say, struggling to keep my eyes open to meet his.

"No, no, no...you need to stay awake," he says, now rubbing my back and zipping us tighter in the sleeping bag.

"I know – I know. So, talk to me. Make me laugh," I say, struggling to lift my head so I can see the smile that I know is flashing across his face.

Oh no, the dimples...why does he have to have those damn dimples...

"Remember that time you found out that I wasn't actually allergic to mangos?" Cameron asks, giving me his classic, goofy smile that adore.

"Oh, you mean after you *lied* to me for months after you spent half of our first date in the bathroom of that Tapas Bar, throwing up," I respond, poking him in the side with my elbow.

"Look – I was worried I was going to lose my man card that day! There was no way I was going to admit that I was throwing up because I was so nervous about being on a date with the most amazing woman I'd ever seen. The mango allergy was a completely legit cover, and I would've taken that lie with me to the grave had Theo not snitched," he says, a rose color flashing across his brown cheeks.

"Cam..." I say, my voice trailing off.

"Yeah?" He asks.

"I thought it was sweet...and I'm glad Theo told me. I wish...you didn't feel like you had to be all tough guy all the time," I admit, knowing that this might strike a nerve with him given that his father is the source of his "tough guy" persona.

Cameron is silent for a moment and shifts his body as though he's trying to get comfortable. I let the silence linger, wishing I could hear the thoughts swirling around in his head and wondering if he will lower the emotional wall enough to let me see behind it.

Just when I thought he wouldn't, he responds, "I wish that too."

I burrow closer into Cameron's chiseled chest and can hear his heart beating loudly in my ears. The two of us were almost buried alive today and perhaps living through a near death experience with him has me wanting him to better understand the woman I am now. I pause, trying to decide whether I should disclose what's on my mind.

"Did you know the agency encourages female case officers to lead people to think we're prostitutes?" I ask, thankful that we aren't making eye contact now because I'm not sure I could talk about this while looking into his eyes.

"What? What do you mean?" He asks, confused.

"All the guys in station used to joke about how easy it must've been for me because whenever I invited a target out, they'd always say yes because they'd think I was asking them out or they'd have a chance to 'get lucky'," I respond, "they *did* always say yes."

Cameron is quiet for a few moments before responding, "I'm sorry."

"Why are *you* apologizing?" I ask.

"I was mad when I found out that after we'd waited for months for Basir to show up, he'd chosen to come to *you*. This case is the most important one my team has been tasked with handling, but he chose to trust *you* over me and my team," Cameron admits.

"Seriously? After what Basir told us, you still wish he'd come to *you?*" I ask, laughing at the ridiculousness.

"Well actually, yeah. Andy, I feel like a total asshole because now I know you are a target and that's why he came to you. But, I still feel guilty...like there's something I should have known that could have stopped this," he says, placing his lips to my head and pulling me in closer to him.

"You know what was worse for me than the fact that you lied about cheating? I knew it was a lie by the way..." I say, rolling my eyes at him remembering how unbelievable it was at the time.

"Wait, you *knew?*" He asks, seeming to be genuinely surprised at how bad of a liar he was.

"Yes, I knew. But what was worse was how crazy you got over work. You became so singularly focused, and I felt like your entire world revolved around the next career power grab," I admit, closing my eyes and clenching my jaw to try and stop myself from the pain of that time seeping back into this moment like flood gates opening.

"So you didn't think I cheated?" He asks.

"No, I didn't. But it still hurt because I knew the intention behind it was to harm me and that shit was cruel, Cam," I respond, closing my eyes and trying to shake the memory of how much his words hurt back then.

Silence drops between us again before Cameron says, "I didn't realize at the time that I'd gotten so bad. I mean, I wanted this career and I still want it. And I feel like I have to prove myself every damned day, but I never wanted you to feel as though you weren't more important than any of this...I'm sorry."

I let his words hang in the air for a moment, still not sure he knows how to have a career and a family.

"I wish he'd come to you too," I say.

"I know you didn't ask for all this to happen," he replies.

It's quiet again and I can hear him breathing deeply and feel his breath on the side of my face as he holds me close.

"One night, I took one of the men I'd been developing for months out to dinner to celebrate his recent promotion," I say, "I couldn't stand this guy because he oozed lechery, despite how hard I tried to make it clear my intentions were not romantic. I'd constantly tried telling him he reminded me of an older brother – even though he didn't – and that he was such a great friend – even though he wasn't."

Cameron pulls me closer to him and I appreciate feeling anchored in him as I share this.

"While we were out that night, the guy had too much to drink and was going to try and drive home. Instead, I took his keys and offered to drive him home. Once we arrived at his house, he insisted I come up for a cup of coffee. I knew right there it was a bad idea. And my boss's voice rang in my ear, telling me how important it was to keep this guy happy and talking," I say, swallowing to try and clear what felt like a glob of cotton in my throat.

"Oh no...Andy...did he..." Cameron tries to ask before stopping himself, anticipating where the story was about to go.

"As soon as we got into his apartment, he told me he needed to get something for me. Moments after he disappeared into his bedroom, while I was still standing in his doorway, he returned half naked. He charged toward me, throwing me on the couch, and trying to take off my clothes. I broke free, thankfully," my voice trails off before I continue, "but the next day when I returned to station, my arms covered in bruises, I insisted on including the attack in my official report."

"Andy...that's awful. Did Brody give you time off? That's a lot to go through to just come back the next day and be expected to work," Cameron says.

"I wrote the report – detailing everything that happened that night. I even included how his breath smelled, his teeth rotting out of his mouth, as he hovered over me. I remember feeling like I'd throw up," I say, closing my eyes and willing myself to smell what was around me instead of allowing my body to conjure up the memory of that man's breath.

I continue, "Brody edited my report and took the entire assault out of it. He said it made *me* look like I'd done something wrong – like I'd sent the wrong message. And yet, in the next sentence, he told me it was great that this guy assumed I was going to date him because that meant my cover wasn't blown."

Cameron paused before responding, "I'm sorry, Andy. I hate that this happened," pausing again, "and I hate that I wasn't there for you."

"I hate that when things like this happen, we can't even talk about it with anyone outside of the agency. The veil of secrecy protects them against horrors and there isn't even anything we can do about it," I seethe, still angry about how I was treated and worried about what this means for me now.

"We're told it's our duty to stay silent, even if we know something is wrong. Andy, I'm so sorry that happened to you," he says.

Silence takes hold in the air between us again as I sink further into my thoughts. I've spent years trying to put Cameron out of my mind but being in his arms makes me unable to ignore how much I miss him. The sound of our breathing, mixed with owls hooting, insects chirping, tree branches and leaves dancing in the wind – starts to sound like a symphony of nature to my ears. And the exhaustion taking over my body is more painful than the cold.

"Cam, I'm scared. Over the last few years, the overwhelmingly clear message I've received from the agency is that the organization will never choose to protect me. I was able to continue working because I'd convinced myself that I didn't need its protection. But now – I can't do this alone," I say, wiping at a tear that's escaped down my cheek.

"I know we used to talk about why we wanted to serve – for both of us…it was in our DNA through our fathers. But good God Andy, why did you stay? You could've been killed before and almost were this time," he says, now looking into my eyes.

"Remember when I told you that my dad always told me that you can't change anything from the outside? Well, I guess I've just been holding out hope that I can change this place – make it what all Americans deserve in their intelligence organization," I say, worried that it sounds ridiculous after all I've just shared.

"Yeah, I understand…I mean, I'm chasing demons in myself…I just never figured the demons would be on the inside of our agency," he replies, voice somber.

I don't reply, but there's comfort in this shared understanding.

"I'm scared too, Andy," he says, surprising me that he's willing to admit his own fears.

We continue to hold each other for several moments without another word passing between us, still listening to the sounds of each other's hearts beating.

Cameron interrupts the silence, "do you ever wish things were different?"

Yes – that the plane hadn't crashed into the Pentagon – that we'd stayed together – that you'd chosen me…

"What do you mean?" I ask, unwilling to fully expose my heart despite being completely naked in this sleeping bag with him.

The fire is now crackling, joining into the symphony and I'm no longer sure whether this moment is real or if I've started to hallucinate due to hypothermia.

"Andy, I've never stopped loving you," Cameron says, his grip tightening around me.

I love you too – and always will.

I don't respond out loud. *He* is the reason we broke up. Sure, I walked out but I only because of how cruel he'd been when he lied about having sex with that other woman.

"Cameron, you *do* remember what actually happened right?" I ask, shaking my head so if I'm hallucinating this conversation I can come back to reality.

"I was an asshole. And I'm sorry. But Andy, I never cheated on you. I was a punk for lying about it, but I *never cheated*," he insists, now holding my face in his hands and looking at me with those kaleidoscope eyes.

"Cam, I appreciate that you're coming clean, but the real harm was that you chose to tell the lie with the intention of ending us. Why did you do that?" I ask.

"Because I was scared. When my dad died...was murdered...Andy, we never found his body..."

Cameron's voice cracks and he doesn't finish. His body starts to shake, and tears fall from his eyes.

Is this real?

"When he died, I lost myself. I felt like someone had set off a bomb inside my head and I was spiraling to a place that terrified me. I couldn't control my rage and when you got cut on that glass – I freaked out. I started to worry that I would be the reason you'd get hurt and I felt like I needed you to get away from me before that happened," he continues, now audibly crying into my shoulder.

I tighten my grip around him and hold him against me.

"You should've told me the truth Cameron. I knew things were bad after your father was killed and I *wanted* to be your person. You were my person, and I wanted you to let me be yours," I say, closing my eyes and putting my head back on his chest.

It feels like the room is spinning and I know we're still in this sleeping bag and not moving.

"I'm sorry. You *were* my person, but I didn't know how to hold onto you without hurting you. And I wanted you safe, even if it meant I'd lose...my person," he whispers into my ear, while running his hands through the wild curls that he released from the top knot I'd been sporting.

"Cam, what are we doing?" I ask, clenching my jaw to avoid the jarring sound of teeth chattering together.

"I'm here – I'm not going anywhere. I just wanted you to know the truth and I want you to hang on," Cameron says.

Looking up at him, still with that feeling of falling down a dark rabbit hole I'm not sure I'll ever return from, I pull his face closer to mine. He's above me, and his lips are hovering close enough to mine that I can feel his breath. Squeezing my eyes shut, a tear falls down my cheek. He closes the space between us and our lips crash into each other. Both of us shaking and holding on to the other as though clinging to the edge of a cliff, our tongues intertwine with a kiss that leaves me breathless.

"Andy, we can't...you aren't okay right now...and we can't do this right now," Cam protests, pulling back from me and looking into my eyes.

Look, if I die here today...at least I'll die on the heels of what will be an epic orgasm.

"Cam, I appreciate that you're trying to be a gentleman right now, but I am telling you that I want this. I'm okay, alright," I say, pulling his lips back to mine.

But this doesn't change anything...

A part of me knows that I might regret this tomorrow, but right now that small part of me is silenced by the part that just wants to feel good – warm – and wanted.

Cameron moves from my lips to my neck, pouring kisses over my body like he's trying to bring me back to life. When he reaches my collarbone, he traces my skin with his tongue which sends a lightning bolt straight to the folds between my legs that are now dripping wet from his touch. His hands trail over my body, one hand cupping my ass and running the other running along the inside of my leg.

He pauses as he reaches my panties, before looking me in the eyes and asking, "can I feel you?'

I nod affirmatively, because – *hell yes.*

A few moments of silence pass between us, the sounds of our heartbeats intertwine with the rapid pace of our breathing.

"Are you sure you're, okay?" He asks.

"Yes Cam, I'm okay...please just...do it," I respond, shaking with anticipation and need.

He takes a deep breath, and with shaking hands he shoves my panties aside and plunges several fingers inside me. I moan and my hips rock against him, as though they have a mind of their own – begging him for more.

"Mmmm, I love how you feel," he says, the hum of his voice vibrating against the side of my neck and causing my heart rate to increase and a pulsing sensation all over my body.

Oh...this feels so good.

As the speed of his fingers inside me increases, warmth crawls over my body and I let out an uncontrolled moan. He licks one of the fingers on his free hand and starts using it to rub my clit. My hips start moving as though my body has completely separated from my brain – and my body wants all of him. He starts to pull out and I grab his hand.

"No, I want this – I want you...I want you inside me," I say, terrified of the cold that will return if he stops and craving the feel of his dick inside me.

Reaching down to pull his hard dick from his briefs, I match his intensity as I thrust him – begging him not to stop as I pull him closer to me.

"Andy, I don't have anything…I don't have a condom," he says, the rose color returning to his cheeks.

A few weeks after we started dating in college, I went on birth control and haven't ever stopped.

"I still have the IUD. And, I haven't been with anyone since you," I say, biting my lower lip and feeling a surge of embarrassment at the admission of just how painfully celibate I've been.

"I'm clean. I've tested recently and also haven't been with anyone recently. But are you sure you want this? I don't want you to regret this and I…" he says, before I cut him off by putting my lips on his.

"Cam, I want this," I say, holding our faces close together and kissing him on his nose, his cheek, and biting on one of his ear lobes.

As I nibble on his ear, something I know drives him crazy, he lets out a growl before removing the final vestiges of my panties and bra. He continues to play with my clit while he bites and licks at my nipples. Waves of pleasure vibrate through my whole body as I come close to climax.

"Now Cam…now…I need you *now*," I whisper desperately in his ear, an edge to my voice so he knows I'm asking him to knock off the excessive foreplay.

"There she is – that's the Andy I know," he says, playfully.

Cameron moves his entire body on top of mine, bracing himself with one arm so he doesn't crush me with his massive weight, and brushes his cock up against my entrance. Taking a deep breath, I brace myself and shake with anticipation. He hovers before entering me, holding my gaze with his - as though we're downloading pieces of ourselves onto the other. As he enters, I grab onto his shoulders and wince from an initial spark of pain as my body makes room for him.

"Are you alright," he says, pausing to look at my face and check on me.

"It's okay – I'm okay, don't stop. Please…please Cam, don't stop," I beg, panting and pulling him closer.

He slowly pushes deeper into me, and I gasp as my body struggles to adjust to his size.

He stops and searches my face again. Our eyes lock and for a moment and I feel as though I've been thrown in a time machine, looking at the version of Cameron who was my best friend and the love of my life. We're both frozen for a moment, the constant humming of the forest buzzing around us, and I wonder if he can see the same thing I do. He buries himself deeper inside me as he takes my lips in his, our tongues searching and sucking and dancing with each other.

Our bodies move in a furious rhythm as we cling to each other and lose ourselves in a deep pleasure that renders me incapable of speaking or thinking. As the sounds of our unbridled, mind-blowing sex join the symphony of nature around us, Cameron touches the deepest part of me, and I come undone – body shaking and screams escaping from the bottom of my soul.

"Andy, look at me," Cameron says, grabbing my hair and searching my eyes with his as I quake underneath him.

Cameron slams into me one final time before he explodes inside me, his body joining the rhythm of my climax – before both of us collapse in a heap of unimaginable pleasure that for just a moment makes me forget all the pain.

Chapter 13
Hiding

Even while hiding out in this shithole of a shed that Rove tried to pass off as a cabin, I wake up feeling like I've found a piece of myself that's been lost. I must have drifted off to sleep and Andy's naked body is still curled around me.

Andy – oh no, no...no...no...I shouldn't have fallen asleep.

"Andy, Andy...are you awake? Wake up! You need to wake up," I try to scream, though the sound that comes out of my sounds more like a hoarse squeak full of desperation and guilt.

Oh God, what have I done? I should've been responsible. Why didn't I stop this?

I poke at her, desperately trying to remove the large, brown curls that have fallen onto her shoulders and over her face so that I can see her. She's not as cold as she was last night, but she still isn't waking up.

Why isn't she waking up?

Continuing to shake her, panic starts bubbling deep in my chest and it feels like it's threatening to bust out of me in all directions.

"Andy, please...wake up," I beg, terror coursing through my body.

Just as I feel as though she might never return to me, she stirs.

"Mmmm, Cam? What...why...why are you shaking me? Are you trying to kill me?" She asks, clearly unaware of how long it has taken me to wake her.

"Are you okay?" I ask, wiping at my eyes to stop the tears that threaten, and flushing with embarrassment that she's seeing me get teary.

"Cam, yes. I'm okay. Are you alright, what's going on?" She asks, taking my face in her hand and peering back at me with concern in her eyes.

I hate that she's seeing me like this – seeing me panic.

"I'm just...I'm worried. And I...I was worried that I hurt you and just...I feel like I took advantage of you by..." my voice trails off for a moment and I run my hand through my hair.

"Cam, no. Don't do that – I wanted what happened last night to happen. I don't regret what we did, but...you know this doesn't change anything right?" she asks, her body tensing as though she's bracing for my response.

I look at her, still feeling a sense of dread in the pit of my stomach as though I've just fucked up any chance that I have with her long term for one night of pleasure.

Did last night mean to her what it meant to me?

She continues, "Cam, last night was fun...but that's all."

"So, what does last night mean for...us?" I ask, feeling very self conscious about the fact that she is implying that sex was all this was.

Her silence pierces into me like a knife cutting through my skin with tiny little wounds all over my body.

"I...um...I don't know, Cam. It's...we work together...we can't...it..." she's struggling with her words, and I don't want her to feel like she needs to tell me something she doesn't mean to protect my ego.

"Oh, okay yeah. You're right," I say, trying not to reveal my disappointment.

And trying to avoid more of this blatant rejection from her.

"Are you still cold?" I ask, looking away from her so I can collect myself.

Andy lifts her hand to my face, turning me back toward her, before reaching for me and wiping a tear from my cheek.

"I'm okay...*we* are okay, right?" she asks, her hazel blue eyes turning a deep gray as she stares at me.

Andy's eyes always remind me of mood rings, giving away her emotions even when she tries to hide them. And this color is worry - I'm not sure I deserve. I should be the one protecting her right now, yet she's here keeping me grounded after somehow dodging hypothermia in the middle of the forest last night.

"Andy, I love you," I blurt out, immediately regretting it because I know she won't want to return my words of affirmation.

Oh no, the panic is coming back...where is that dog when I need him. I shouldn't have left him with the team...

She's silent again as I sit here in a puddle of regret and worry about being vulnerable with her *again* and continuing to reveal my feelings to her. While she was the one who insisted on having sex, she's clear it was just that – sex. I feel like an idiot because of course she isn't in love with me after all I put her through.

"I'm sorry...I shouldn't have said that," I say, wishing I could take it all back.

"Cam..." her voice trails off, after calling my attention.

I look up, biting my lip, and praying she'll give me even just a morsel of validation.

"I care about you, I just...I can't...we can't..." She says, voice trailing off and pity flashing across her face.

Damn, it's like that?

"Okay, yeah...I mean...of course...this doesn't have to be a big deal," I say, trying to play this cool as I pull her closer.

No, no, no...I fucked this up.

We hold each other for several moments in silence, our past erecting a brick wall between us with each moment that ticks by.

"I'm sorry, Cam but my life is a whole, hot mess right now and adding our mess...it's just too much," she says, placing one of her hands to her forehead and closing her eyes.

Ouch...

"I just want you to know we can be in this together...even if *we* aren't together," I respond, still hurt, and confused by how she's acting after what we shared last night.

"But we *aren't* in this together. You aren't the person who was stabbed with some nuclear serum and is now expected to essentially take down an entire terrorist network...a network that is also after whatever the hell is *inside* me," she says, her voice rising and shaking in anger as her eyes turn grey with rage.

But I wish it had been me...

I stroke her cheek, causing her to shudder in my arms. Even though she seems hell bent on keeping a wall up between us, I'm committed to do whatever it takes to win her back. And whatever is inside her – whatever threat is ahead – I'll walk that path with her.

I just can't lose her...

"Andy, okay...we can just be...friends...or teammates or whatever," I say quickly, just trying to make this moment stop and feeling defeated.

I pull her back into me and we hold each other in silence for what seems like hours while we wait for rescue.

"Cam? Andy? Are you there?" Theo's voice booms from outside the door, followed by loud banging that causes the cabin to shake.

Andy jumps and clings harder to me with her eyes squeezed shut. I hear the familiar whining and scratching at the door that tells me Theo brought Boss along for the rescue.

"It's okay, it's Theo...the team is here," I whisper in her ear, while rubbing her back to calm her down.

"We're in here," I respond, voice raised so they hear me amongst the noises of the forest.

Theo barrels through the door, followed by Boss and several other men I haven't seen before. Boss immediately makes a beeline for us and begins showering us both with dirty, wet Boss kisses.

"Dude, you *know* I hate your dog breath kisses," I say, wiping at my eyes and playfully shoving him off me before patting him on the head.

"That dog can smell you from miles away man. We were headed in the wrong direction, but Boss insisted on changing course when he caught your scent," Theo says, shaking his head with astonishment.

"That's my dude," I say, as Boss rolls over onto his back for a proper belly rub.

Theo and Boss make a hilarious duo. Theo has a distinctive walk, his body always moving as though he shot up a foot during puberty and has never gotten used to his massive size. Given that Theo is an expert sharpshooter, it always surprises me that someone who clearly has control over his limbs still moves like a pubescent teen. Boss, who similarly flops around like a teenage boy when he gets excited, is also fairly exacting with his actions when he's on the hunt. Seeing the two of them walk in immediately puts me at ease in a way I hadn't realized I needed.

"Whoa, uhhhh… ummmm…do ya'll want to get dressed?" Theo asks, awkwardly turning his back to us, and motioning for the men with him to do the same.

Oh right, damn…we're for sure still naked under here.

Andy groans with embarrassment and buries her head into my chest as the reality of the scene hits her, likely at the same time it hits me. I stifle a nervous laugh, knowing that I'm likely to get gut punched by Andy any moment if I can't collect myself.

"Stay turned guys – nothing to see here," clearing my throat and speaking in the deepest and most professional voice I can muster.

As though he's mocking me, Boss sits in front of us and covers one of his eyes with a paw. I raise an eyebrow at him curiously before he saunters over next to Theo and turns around with the rest of the crew. Backs still turned, Theo and the other two men begin setting up a makeshift medical clinic in the corner of the room. I reach for the zipper to release us from the cocoon we've been in overnight. As soon as the air hits us, Andy shivers and burrows further into me.

"Do you think you can stand so I can help you get dressed," I whisper, to avoid the man…and dog… ears that are likely straining to hear some juicy details about our situation.

"Umm, yeah...let me try," she responds, bracing herself on the ground and slowly lifting herself in place.

I hover next to her, ready to catch her if she falls. Once she stands up, I reach over and hand her the clothes I'd taken off her the night before while conspicuously placing my body between hers and the men standing with their backs turned on the other side of the room. She bends over slowly to pull on her panties, breasts reminding me of how they felt against my skin last night. When she raises back up, glancing between my eyes and my obviously swollen dick, I clear my throat and quickly reach for my clothes.

Get a grip man...

Shifting uncomfortably in my boxer briefs and trying to calm this fire before pulling on my pants, I catch a smile forming at the corners of her mouth.

"Y'all love birds decent?" Theo croaks, giggling like a little kid.

"Shut the hell up man," I respond, slapping Theo on the back hard enough to make him stumble forward.

Theo clears his throat, attempting a more serious tone before addressing Andy.

"Before we head out, can I check your vitals?" Theo asks, reaching toward her to encourage her to sit on the stretcher they've brought with them.

I follow Andy with my eyes as she hobbles to the stretcher and collapses on top as though she can barely control her body. She lets out a deep breath and lays back, holding out her arm for him. Theo, a trained medic – because that guy had all sorts of skills up his unassuming sleeves – checks her pulse, blood pressure, temperature, and blood oxygen levels.

"Your temperature is still a bit low, but not at dangerous levels yet. What was happening when Cam called Rove? He made it sound like it was dire," Theo says.

"Last night was bad. After we left the cave, I felt like someone threw me into a tub of ice water that I couldn't get out of," she responds.

"So, it just went away?" Theo asks, skeptically.

Andy's cheeks turn pink as she glances from the sleeping bag to me.

"Well, um...." she starts, hesitating.

"Theo, just get us out of here and stop with the questions," I interrupt, shooting Theo an irritated look.

Theo shakes his head and starts packing away his supplies, giggling under his breath, "haha, sleeping bag sex."

I punch him in the shoulder and walk over to stand beside Andy. The two other guys with them prepare an IV drip to administer fluids into Andy's arm.

"What's that for?" I ask, pointing to the IV bag.

"I said her temperature was still low, just not yet hypothermic. The fluid we are giving her should help keep her stable until we can get back to a hospital and get more information," Theo explains.

"Don't you think that just walking her into a civilian hospital right now is a tad risky given that it looks like our own officers just tried to kill us?" I ask.

"Dude – that's why we aren't going to a civilian hospital," Theo grunts through gritted teeth, growing irritated at me.

I start to pace nervously and Boss's head bobs between me and Andy. I point him toward Andy, and he immediately stands guard next to the stretcher, nudging her hand for pets.

Boss is always here for the love.

Pulling me from my thoughts, Theo grabs me by the shirt and pulls me outside the cabin.

"What the hell is with you man?" Theo asks as he shoves me through the cabin doors and onto the dusty forest ground.

"In the last 24 hours, we've been through some crazy shit. Apparently, that serum the attacker injected into Andy can just spontaneously make her temperature drop, she's wanted by terrorist groups *and* also apparently our own agency...oh and did I forget to mention that we were chased out of the makeshift tunnel before it legit exploded around us?"

I'm speaking so frantically I have to catch my breath, placing my hands on his knees. Theo puts his hand on my shoulder for support.

"We're going to get you both out of here, okay? Trust me to do my job. And hopefully whoever was chasing you all through the tunnel was buried in it," Theo says.

"Alright...I'm sorry man. I just..."

Worry I can't keep her safe...worry she will never forgive me...

"I don't even know who I can trust right now. Obviously I trust you...and Rove, but our own people sold Andy out. This was an inside job," I say, feeling my heart rate pick up as I say it out loud.

"We got this dude. Let's get her out of here and we can regroup back in the city," Theo says, in his best surfer boy voice while kicking up his heels and pretending he's a country line dancer.

I chuckle, appreciating that Theo always knows how to make me laugh by just acting like a fool. After the two of us laugh and I have the chance to breathe in the fresh wilderness air, we go back inside the cabin to gather everyone and head to the rally point.

"Wheels up fellas," Theo says to the two men he's brought with him as they collapse the wheels of the gurney and carry Andy out through the cabin door.

Boss makes a howling sound as though offended that he wasn't specifically included in the rally call and throws dog shade at Theo with his eyes before tossing up his head and trotting out the door.

"Dude, I think Boss might actually be a person trapped in the body of a dog," Theo says, shaking his head and following Boss.

"Guys, I think I can walk," Andy says, grabbing hold of the IV bag lying next to her and trying to get up.

I jog over to her side and gently place my hand on her shoulder, "Andy, I know you'd prefer to walk, but given the fact that you're still having trouble regulating your temperature…I think you should consider letting them carry you."

Andy hesitates like she's about to argue with me and I shoot her a pleading look. She folds her arms across her chest stubbornly as she looks away from me. I love how she's the type of woman who always wants to take charge, but her stubborn nature when it comes to people trying to care for her is going to be a continuous fight as we try and neutralize the looming threat. Boss and I follow Theo through the forest, with the two men hauling Andy between us, as I ponder how on earth we'll get out of this mess. Not even five minutes after Andy insisted on walking herself to the rally point, she passes out motionless on the stretcher under several layers of blankets.

Chapter 14
The Presidential Suite

"Andy"

Waking up without any clue where I am and surrounded by darkness is disconcerting. This bed is not mine and it's too quiet here. No, it's not completely quiet – there are faint voices in the distance – maybe in another room? There's also the unwelcome, yet familiar, beeping of a medical monitor next to the bed.

Where am I?

"Cam...Theo...Is anyone here?"

I hear the faint jingle of Boss's collar and look over at him standing guard at my bedside.

Well, that means Cameron can't be far...

My heart feels like it's racing and going to explode out of my chest. The cold is back, and it feels like my blood is freezing as it cycles through my body.

How the hell am I supposed to help destroy these nuclear sites, averting the next nuclear war, if I can't even regulate my body temperature?

I need to get out of this bed and figure out what's going on. Lifting my body up, and pulling the IV out of my arms, I roll myself off the bed. Boss immediately starts yelping and jumping by the window of the room. I reach for him, trying to calm him when the beeping monitor alarm sounds. It's so loud that it sounds like a siren, causing shooting pain that feels like someone is stabbing me in the head. Falling to the floor, covering my ears with my hands, I curl my body into the fetal position.

"Ahh, turn it off...please turn that off," I scream, begging the sirens to stop and put me out of this misery.

Why isn't anyone coming? Don't they hear that noise?

The alarm is inescapable, and I've never heard something so awful in my entire life. Boss is hovering over me, licking my arms, and nudging me like he's asking me to get off the floor.

Unable to move from the pain emanating from my ears to my head, and throughout my entire body – I helplessly wait and pray someone will stop it. The pain is so intense that I start to dry heave, reminding me that I haven't eaten anything since the bite of that donut Jake handed me days ago. Doors to the room fly open and several nurses rush in, followed by Cameron and several men I don't recognize. Cameron's large arms wrap around me, as he lifts me to him and carries me back to the bed.

"Cam - please tell them to turn it off! It hurts so much…that sound…I can't…" my screams are interrupted by more involuntary dry heaving as I try and catch my breath.

"What sound Andy? What are you talking about?" Cameron asks, looking around the room.

Boss is still barking loudly and is now knocking his entire body into the medical machine that's making the noise.

"Shut it off *please*," I beg, pointing to the loudly beeping monitor next to the bed that seems like it was intended as a torture device.

Even the dog understands! Why don't the rest of them get it?

After releasing me on the bed, Cameron reaches behind the monitor and pulls the plug out of the wall. The torturous sound stops, and I relax back into the bed, placing my hand on my stomach as though doing so will stop the heaving. Now that my insides no longer feel as though they are falling out, and the shooting pain from the noise is gone, I look around the room to analyze my surroundings. This isn't a normal hospital. Several men who filtered into the room behind Rove look like secret service, obvious by the earpieces, the standard black suits, and their expressionless faces.

"Where are we?" I ask Cameron, who's now sitting on the bed beside me.

His eyes dart from me to Rove and I recognize the nervous worry that flashes across his face.

"We brought you to Walter Reed for testing. Don't worry, a very limited number of people know you're here. And this is the Presidential Suite, so nobody is getting in or out of here without going through me, first," Rove responds.

The Presidential Suite? Holy Shit…

"Andy, what did you hear just now? What was that?" Cameron asks, concern still in his eyes.

"You mean that siren of a machine?" I ask, confused by the sea of blank faces peering back at me, "did you all *not* hear that?"

"We heard the beeping of the monitor, but Andy...it wasn't loud enough to sound like a siren," Cameron responds.

Curling a little closer into the bed, growing self-conscious with all the eyes fixed on me – and the reminder that something is clearly wrong with me – I say, "Oh...well, it was...it was different for me I guess."

The nurses swarm around me, and I close my eyes and lean into Cameron.

"Can we talk without all these people in here? I don't want to be...on display like this. Can I just have a moment?" I whisper in his ear.

"Let the nurses take some blood and get you warm, and then I'll get rid of all the people. Rove has information you should hear, but we aren't going to be able to get rid of the medical team until they at least make sure you're stable. Can you give them ten minutes and I'll try my best to clear the room after?" He asks, voice low and eyes pleading.

"You're staying, right?" I ask in a hushed tone.

Cameron shifts uncomfortably, dawning an awkward grin. I realize that I have a fist full of his shirt in my hands and am probably leaning in a little too close given our audience. I clear my throat, letting go of his shirt and folding my arms back across my chest. This is what pet goldfish must feel like, swimming around in a tiny tank while dozens of eyes gaze at them all day long. Nurses continue swarming, taking my temperature, shining lights in my eyes, and drawing more blood.

Will the blood run out at some point?

Do they even care if they drain me dry?

Do I need to worry about where my blood could end up this time?

I close my eyes, trying to imagine being somewhere else – perhaps back in the sleeping bag with Cameron. But when one of the nurses jabs a giant needle in my arm, unable to find my vein, my eyes fly open, and I shriek with pain. Shaking and biting my lip to stop embarrassing sobs from escaping from deep inside, I lean back into Cameron. He's holding me tight and rubbing my back, while whispering in my ear.

"I got you – okay. It's going to be alright," he says.

"Cam, no more blood, okay? I can't take any more of this."

My body is clearly not cooperating, and she continues to fish for a good vein as a portrait of blue and purple bruises begin forming on my arms.

"Stop it. Just...why is this necessary? You're clearly hurting her, and you aren't even getting anything," Cameron says, now standing and placing his body between me and the unsuccessful nurse.

"Sir, the Director instructed us to collect samples. We need to..." the nurse insists before Rove cuts her off abruptly.

Why does the Director want my blood?

What does he know?

"That's enough, we need to discuss some things with Ms. Lynam and samples can wait," Rove says, voice booming.

I breathe an audible sigh of relief. The nurses scurry out of the room, but the Secret Service officers remain posted at the door like statues. Boss stands by the door, watching the nurses leave as though he's ready to pounce if they don't comply, before turning to the Secret Service and growling.

That dog is a real homey.

"You too boys," Cameron says, walking over to the officers and all but shoving them out the door.

Once everyone leaves, except for Rove, Cameron and the dog, Rove pulls two chairs next to the bed. Cameron plops down in one as though his body simply gives out and the chair loudly scrapes across the floor. I flinch at the sound because it's like fingernails scraping across a chalkboard.

And of course, nobody else can hear that like I can.

Rove shoots a look at Cameron, as though the two of them are having a conversation about me with their eyes.

"Okay boys, I'm right here – just say what you're thinking please," I say, growing irritated at this entire scene.

"I told Rove what we learned from Basir. And in the last few hours we've been working to ensure that nobody else inside the agency, outside of our small GS-9 team, knows anything about what he told us," Cameron says.

"What about Brody, Todd, and all those guys who were at the safe house that day of the debrief? Shouldn't we assume all of them know I've been injected?" I ask, knowing there is no way to keep *that* part of the story from the masses.

"Yes, we aren't the only ones with that information, but we think we've neutralized the Brody threat and Todd and Daniel are presumed dead," Rove says, opening a manila file folder that he brought into the room with him.

Cameron takes the file from Rove, and glances at it before adding, "we have the ear of the Director now and that was enough to grind whatever Brody was trying to do to a screeching halt.

"And one of Basil's contacts, a defector now living in Canada, positively identified Body as having credible affiliations with Solaris. We've confirmed that Solaris offered to pay him for the vial," Rove explains.

Did he just say that my boss is a terrorist?

"So what you're saying is that Brody was going to either sell the vial to them...or sell *me* to them," I clarify, swallowing hard and folding my arms across my chest.

Both of them are silent, as though they know confirming the awful truth I just pointed out might make me feel worse.

After a few moments of the two of them looking back and forth between each other and me, Cameron says, "Yes, he was likely also trying to negotiate another type of transfer when he realized a physical vial of the serum was no longer an option."

"How can I go back home if we don't even know who else knows that I've been injected?" I ask, bracing myself for their response.

"There will always be a risk, Andy. We cannot be sure who else knows. All we can do is offer you GS-9 protection while we carry out the operation," Rove responds, the worry lines in his forehead deepening.

"Didn't you say Brody was neutralized? Does that mean yawl killed him?" I ask, my head now feeling like it's going to explode because of all of this.

"Well, he's not dead...but he isn't going to be our problem at the moment," Rove replies cryptically.

"The last person to see Todd and Daniel reported seeing them walk into that tunnel and never come out. That place completely collapsed. Anyone inside would've been crushed like batter in a waffle iron," Rove responds.

"So, what are you suggesting now? I just give the entire contents of my blood supply to the Director like a lab rat?" I ask, looking down at my arms that bear the appearance of someone who's been jumped out of a gang.

"The Director is aware that the agency could have a mole...or errr...several. And I agree," Rove says, "So we've created a small, covert team with the sole purpose of finding these facilities, destroying them completely, eliminating all the vials, and charging those associated with international war crimes. We expect the antidote required to neutralize the serum inside you will be at one of these facilities."

I place my head in my hands and try to focus on breathing.

Am I a prisoner or a co-conspirator?

"So, can I go home? What's *my* role here?" I ask, looking between Rove and Cameron to evaluate their body language as they respond.

Both men are rigidly stiff, making me feel as though my body is part of some sort of a contract. Cameron appears as though he's been told not to speak and the look on Rove's face is a mixture between discomfort and irritation.

"The Director and I don't agree on what should happen next. He thinks we need to send you into one of these places as a double – but Cameron and I think that might be too risky and we aren't sure that's necessary," Rove says.

I don't respond and instead let the silence linger so that he'll share more.

"The Director has agreed to try my plan first – which will require you to publicly resign from the agency. We will give you a full cover within a consultant firm called Hinkley Anderson. Our team, which will include you, will work on obtaining the Intelligence necessary to locate the facilities," he continues.

"Rove – I wasn't born yesterday. I need to understand why you aren't just putting me in a jail and keeping me there until I am no longer radioactive," I say, staring directly into his eyes and challenging him with my glare.

"Well, there's still a lot we don't know about the vial...how it works...or the side effects for you," Rove says, wincing.

"Basir trusted *you* and in addition to being the physical piece of this entire operation... Andy, you got further with him than any of us were able to get. So of course, we need you as a part of the team," Cameron adds.

Rove continues, "I'm sorry about the blood samples, but we're trying to learn as much as we can about how this works and right now you are all we have. I understand that you have no reason to trust any of us here, but I will give you my word that my team is behind you, and nothing is more important here than making sure you remain safe."

I don't believe him.

"Do I have a choice?" I ask.

"Well, of course. But do you want to take your chances continuing with the agency as normal...knowing that is likely not all that safe...and even more unlikely to yield the antidote?" Rove asks.

And who knows how many other moles there are...

I remain silent while the two of them continue speaking. Rove hands me a business card with the inscription "Hinkley Anderson", to which I raise an eyebrow at the ridiculous made-up consulting firm they've chosen as my new cover. I stifle a laugh while looking at the card and the two men look at me with confusion.

"The initials are 'HA'...like it's a joke. Was that intentional?" I ask, still giggling to myself.

Rove ignores my laughter and continues handing me paperwork. Boss has left his post at my door and is now rubbing his body against Cameron's leg for pets.

I know I don't *really* have a choice – well other than just running away completely. But with the way things have been going, I'm not sure how long I can survive this on my own. As I sit in silence, on this hospital bed between two men who are suggesting I join their all-male team – it finally sinks in why Basir came to me. He knew that the stakes would not be this high for anyone else. And that if he wanted to ensure the destruction of this operation – he needed me.

We live in such a sick and twisted, misogynistic world.

Chapter 15
Resignation

"Andy"

"Mommy, It's me, Andy. I'm home," I say, holding the new "Hinkley Anderson" issued cell phone to my ear.

"Oh my Gosh, Andy? Where have you been? Your father and I have been trying to call you for weeks," my mother responds.

"I, uh, got into an accident in Brazil. But don't worry, I'm okay. I'm home now," I say, quickly trying to reassure her without giving her any details that could put us both at risk.

"Oh, thank God, why didn't you call sooner," she asks, clearly not making this lie easy by insisting on details.

"I had to be medevac'd out and they never recovered my old phone from the accident," I lie, thankful the agency trained me to think of lies on the spot when it meant covering up an operation.

"Hmm, okay baby...well, I'm glad you're okay but can we see you? I just want to see you with my own eyes," she says, skeptically.

"Yeah, okay...just maybe give me a bit? A lot is going on and I need to do some work travel that's going to take me out of the country for the next...uh...month or so," I respond.

Mrs. Lynam is no fool. This woman can smell lies and she likely knows something is very off with me. But she also knows what I do for a living and knows when to stop digging for more information. Seeing my parents before I find an antidote to this serum is a bad idea. One ice cold hug from me right now would probably send both into a tailspin of anxiety and in this case – I don't know how I'd explain the state I'm in if they saw me in person.

Would anyone even believe the true story?

"Well promise me you will call us when you can and we can head out to the Eastern Shore and get a big pot of crabs and some hush puppies," she says.

My father is a retired CIA chemist, so this life isn't foreign to them. Having spent most of her married life being worried about my father when he'd travel for work, my mom didn't want me joining the agency. But my dad encouraged me because he said I needed something to pour my passion for justice into and he knew being a cop wasn't something I'd ever have chosen. Though he's never admitted it, I also think that my decision to become a Case Officer made him so proud. Growing up, he told me that he'd always wanted to be a Case Officer but when he started at the agency Black people weren't chosen for that role. I don't have the heart to tell him how jaded I feel about my job and my country right now.

The mere mention of Maryland blue crabs and buttery hush puppies is enough to make my mouth water and my heart ache with homesickness. Growing up by the water in Annapolis, Maryland was like living in a natural playground. In the summer, we could run straight from the house out to the dock in our backyard and fling ourselves into the water as our parents watched from the large, bay windows on the back of our house. Breathing deeply to imagine the spicy smell of seafood seasoning, and the salty spray of the Chesapeake Bay, I close my eyes. In my imagination, I can hear my dad's booming belly laugh, as my brother and I fight for the title of who can uncover the largest chunk of crab meat.

"That sounds amazing Mommy, I can't wait," I say, being honest for the first time on the call and biting my lip to keep from crying.

After saying, "I love you", I hang up the phone and the dread of what I need to do today pours over me like an unwelcome rain shower. Today is resignation day – and I'll need to make this look convincing.

Not to mention act as though I'm not freezing my ass off from the inside out every moment during the day.

After being released from Walter Reed Medical Center, I return to my small condo in the Adams Morgan neighborhood of DC. I didn't sleep well last night, the nightmares of the attack in Brazil still creeping into my subconscious. Cameron wanted to come with me, but I declined. I need time to process all of this, and I haven't been alone in weeks. Curling up in cozy sweats by my gas fireplace, holding a giant cup of steaming coffee, I try to soak every moment of the fleeting warmth.

I don't want to leave the comfort and safety of my place. When I bought this condo years ago, I was so proud. It's a small 550 square feet, one bedroom condo that spans across the floor of a historic DC brownstone. The floors aren't level, and the doors catch when they close because the building is well over 100 years old – but the feeling I get when I walk through these doors cannot be replicated. There's a grand fireplace in the living room, a large plush couch and a giant window that overlooks the busy, main drag in Adams Morgan – perfect for weekend morning people watching. Sometimes I count how many people are conducting "the walk of shame" in the morning, assuming nobody can see them because the street is empty as they quickly slide into their cars still wearing last night's club outfit.

While I wish I could stay inside like this forever, I know today I *need* to publicly resign. Last night, we'd gone over scenario after scenario and the best option requires me to separate from the agency and work with Cameron's team to find the antidote. Surely, even with my resignation, the agency will assign people internally to work on this operation – but I trust Farhad and if he says there are multiple moles, he's probably right. And I'll admit, having the opportunity to go rogue and essentially save the country is a mission I never dreamed I'd be a part of.

Or one that I ever imagined would be this necessary...

I also know that I don't have time for government bureaucracy. If we find out locations, it could take weeks to even get the necessary approvals to travel and destroy. I'm not even sure I have weeks.

So, I get up, dress in an uncomfortable suit and toe jamming heels, and try to cover the bags under my eyes with some makeup.

Who on earth thought naming a foundation color "wheat" was sexy?

After doing my best to avoid looking like an icy, sleep deprived version of myself, I grab my keys off the kitchen counter and head down the stairs to the rental car Rove secured for me to drive. *My* car is still in the embassy parking lot next to the rental that has my blood splattered all over the driver's seat, likely resembling the scene of a shootout. And in the off chance that anyone outside the agency knew about my connection to this nuclear serum, it's probably for the best that I'm not driving my own car anyway. Cam and Rove don't even want me to stay in my own home, but I need to draw the line somewhere. As I drive to work, maybe for the last time, I think of how my relationship with the CIA has changed over the years.

I was 20 years old the first time I stepped foot on the CIA compound in Langley, Virginia. Filled with excitement, pride, and anticipation as I started my internship in the fall of my junior year in college. The buildings were massive, swelling with offices, cubicles, crowded conference rooms, and secrets held through the years. Coming to work each day had me bursting with curiosity and purpose. I was so grateful to be surrounded by an entire cluster of buildings that held the nation's secrets and were relics of patriotism. I was so proud to serve back then.

As time wore on, the place changed.

Or maybe I had – or we'd both changed.

The walls, which held secrets I'd kept and history to protect, were angry. They were cold and off-white, as though they'd been so stubborn that they'd rejected attempts to update the paint. As an intern, I'd excitedly entered conference rooms where the tables glistened from a fresh polish and the chairs looked like they'd been plucked from museums with detailed engravings on the back. Now, after spending time behind the table – never afforded the opportunity to sit at the table with the White men…even when I've written the report – I notice the putrid yellow colored, agency issued furniture. It's as though they'd picked up the couches on the curb, torn off the "free – please take this" sign, and plopped them into the conference rooms.

The last time I sat on one of those horrible, back busting couches, was the day Reef ("No Briefs Reef") sat next to me on one. I'd spent an entire meeting trying to remove his hand from my leg as he tried to cop a feel. Standing during meetings has enabled me to notice the carpets, which offer a strange juxtaposition to the couches. While the couches look like they've survived one too many drunken frat parties, the rugs appear as though they're vigorously cleaned after each meeting – not even a spot of dirt in sight.

I wonder if I imagined the halls bustling with hope and pride when I'd first arrived, because now I can hear these foot strangling heels as they clop loudly across the marble floors. The sound of my body moving through this massive building only reminds me of all the colleagues I've lost. Those stars that I saw when I first arrived, which represent the Agency staff who've perished in service…I walk by them every day now. But what was once artistic – something I couldn't closely identify with – now represents my friend Liz…who's represented there with a single, black star.

Liz slept in the bunk next to me during basic training. I will never forget how sarcastically funny she was and how she was always willing to help others. The week I suffered through weapons training, my hands bleeding from the kick of the gun, she stood next to me in front of the mirror in the bathroom for an hour to help me work on getting the right stance and drawing my weapon quickly.

Have I changed, has it, or have we both?

Walking into my office in the Original Headquarters Building, I don't bother to remove my sunglasses. I have large dark circles under my eyes from stress, crying, and staying up too late worrying. I also haven't been back in this building since the attack in Brazil and am not looking forward to the looks and questions I might receive from anyone who's read any of the reports. I've been told only a few people know what happened, but that never seems to be the case with this place.

"Hey, work wife. Coffee later?" Jake smiles, nudging my shoulder with his elbow as I walk onto the escalator.

I haven't seen Jake since that morning in the trailer at Blue Castle and his sudden appearance next to me startles me. Jake has this tendency to creep up on people and while we were at the farm, I'd routinely tell him to stop being a "creeper", to which he'd laugh maniacally before asking, "what fun would it be if I always announced myself?" He is one of the few people I know who knows what happened in Brazil, but also knows better than to ask me questions before buttering me up with coffee.

"Of course, work husband. I'd love for you to buy me coffee. But it might need to be now because I'm not staying long," I say.

I lift my sunglasses only slightly so that I can make genuine eye contact. Jake pushes up his glasses and giggles.

"Damn woman - you need that coffee more than I thought. Let's go fight that coffee line and you can explain where you're running off to," he says.

I smile awkwardly, without saying a word. It's going to be hard to tell Jake I'm resigning. He's usually someone I can tell anything to, though he's never met any of my non- agency friends, but there's a short list of people on this "need to know" list and Jake isn't on it. The two of us walk through the cafeteria doors and join the queue that's at least 20 people deep.

"I'm going to resign today," I quickly blurt out.

I know that if I wait to address this, I might lose my courage. Jake spins around on his heels to look at me. He'd been gazing up at the menu as though he'd order something new when he hadn't in the years that we'd known each other.

"Wait, what?" He asks, face falling as though I'd just told him his puppy died.

"I came in today for a meeting with the Director and I plan to resign," I say, now looking at the black pumps that are causing my toes to throb.

"Why would you do that? Andy right now is the *worst* time for you to do that," Jake whispers, looking around us to ensure nobody is trying to lurk and catch some Intel.

We are two people away from the front of the coffee line and I remain silent to avoid getting deeper into this conversation while so many people are around.

Flashing a warning look at Jake, gently placing my hand on his shoulder, I whisper, "not here."

Jake nods in understanding before pulling out his wallet to pay for the coffee.

"Get this woman an almond milk latte and I'll take an Americano with extra room for enough milk to make it taste like a shake," he says, flashing a smile full of perfectly straight, white teeth at the barista.

"I knew there was a reason I loved you Jake," I tease, elbowing him in the arm as I grab my coffee.

Though I've been in Brazil for a solid year by this point, as soon as the barista sees us together, she knows what we'll order. It was ready before we arrived at the counter. After Jake pours enough half and half to make me wonder why he didn't just order cream with a drop of coffee, we grab our drinks and walk toward a booth on the far end of the cafeteria. I side eye his coffee, teasing him in the way I usually do.

"Andy, now you *know* this proud southern gentleman likes his beverages sweet – just like I like my women," he defends, giggling before raising his cup to his mouth and exaggerating a pop of his pinkie finger.

"You're a fool, Jake," I joke, laughing at his flamboyance.

The table we choose is in a dark corner next to some of the restaurants that won't open for another few hours. I slide into one of the booth seats and Jake plops down across from me.

"What's going on with you Andy? Are you alright?" Jake asks, his tone turning serious as he puts his hand on top of the hand that isn't holding my coffee.

I jerk my hand away, nervous that he'll feel how cold it is and that will spur more questions. But it's too late because his eyes dart to mine and I can see a mixture of confusion and what looks like pity.

"Why is your hand so cold?" He asks.

"It's nothing. I had to park on the other side of the lot this morning and it was cold," I lie, wracking my brain for a way to shift the conversation from a topic I cannot get into with him.

"Jake, I can't do this anymore. Brazil...what happened there...I just want out and I want to live like a normal person," I say, praying he will just accept this and stop pressing.

"Look, I know you must have your reasons, and I will leave you to those...but promise me...that you will take care of yourself...and be careful," he says.

"You know I will," I say.

"Andy, the Director invited me to the meeting this morning. I think he's transferring your case to me," he says, looking worried.

This is good. I can trust Jake, can't I?

"Oh, okay…I'm glad. I trust that you will do a good job," I respond.

"I don't want to step on your toes, but this is an incredible opportunity for me. I was going to say no, but if you are going to resign…" Jake's voice trails off.

"It's okay Jake – I'm happy for you. Seriously – you deserve this," I say, feeling a bit guilty because I can't tell him our plan.

The Director knows I'm resigning today, but if Jake was filled in on the plan – he'd have known too. So, I pretend with Jake that the Director doesn't know, and I hope the Director is savvy enough to play along.

"Let's celebrate with a coffee toast," I say, hoping to lighten the mood.

Jake smiles widely and taps his coffee cup against mine. Glancing at my watch, with only a few minutes to make it to the seventh floor, I pop up from my seat and straighten the wrinkles out of my suit. Jake walks around to my side of the table and pulls me close to him in a bear hug. I hug him back and instinctively feel several eyes turn in our direction. The CIA is like a little incestuous, small town where too many people have hooked up and everyone's in everyone else's business. Typically, I try to avoid public displays of affection inside these walls, because I don't want to be the topic of someone's lunch table gossip – but I welcome the hug this time.

I'm going to miss Jake.

"We'll see each other soon," I say, not sure I'll ever see him again.

"We better – I'm not ready to sign the work divorce papers and losing you completely is just not an option I'm willing to consider," he responds.

"Okay, no work divorce…just perhaps, a separation," I giggle, wiping a tear from my eye.

I don't want to resign, even though this resignation is a ruse. Nothing about this situation feels safe, but there aren't any good alternatives. And not being able to tell Jake what I'm doing is awful. He's my rock in this place and has been for years. When one of my first agency bosses, who had anger management issues, threw a jug of water at someone for using a verb he didn't like – I ran out of the office and told Jake. When "no briefs Reef" cat-called me in the hallway, in front of a handful of men (all who said nothing), Jake walked straight into his office and shamed him in my honor.

But he can't know this.

"Let's go upstairs together, okay," I say, locking my arm in his.

When we exit the elevator on the seventh floor, there's a pristine red carpet leading to the director's office. That carpet up here is even more pristine than those in the rest of the building, as though workers will be scrubbing the floor after anyone walks on it. Once we arrive at the door to his office, we notify his executive assistant of our arrival and sit on the wooden chairs outside the office.

Clearly, they don't expect anyone to sit on these, my ass hurts already.

"Director Bryant will see you now." The executive assistant motions toward us as she holds the phone to her ear.

I nod toward her before walking into the large boardroom to find the director surrounded by several division chiefs. As I walk to the empty seat at the table, I scan the room, counting the men and searching for other women or brown faces. There are eight White men at the table...nine when Jake sits down. As usual, I'm the only woman *and* the only brown face in the room.

"Thank you, Ms. Lynam, for joining us today. We're thankful you were able to get out of Brazil alive," Director William Bryant nods toward me, completely ignoring Jake.

"Thank you, sir," I say, taking my seat at the table.

"You've been asked to give the counsel a debrief about your meeting with the Assadi family. Please...when you're ready you can go ahead," Director Bryant says.

Taking a deep breath, I begin, "Well...we've relocated the Assadi family and I had the opportunity to debrief them prior to their departure from the Washington metro area."

I know the Assadi's chose to relocate to Los Angeles, California where there's a large community of Iranian expatriates – but none of the people in this room need to know that.

The room is silent, as I stand and walk to the map wall. I scroll through dozens of choices before pulling on the map of Iran.

"To those of you who are wondering whether Mr. Assadi was able to earn his right to resettle in the United States, I want to assure you he did by showing you a visual of what we learned from the debrief."

I keep the details that include the nuclear war materials that are pumping through my veins at the moment out of the briefing, and instead pull a small box of red thumbtacks out of my pocket and place them in over five locations on the map. None of these location are locations at all associated with Solaris, but they are real nuclear facilities and I have to make it look like I am giving them something. Once I finish placing the tacks in their correct locations, I slowly turn toward the rest of the room.

I need to turn around so I can be sure they aren't staring at my ass.

"These thumbtacks represent every single nuclear facility in Iran. My report explains each one in detail, from the exact coordinates to the individuals working inside them."

Speak slow enough so that their mediocre brains can catch up.

"What is your confidence in this report, Ms. Lyman? And did he share anything else?" One, particularly mediocre looking dude asks, wrinkling his nose as though he doesn't think my report is credible.

Andy, you cannot punch someone just because they are dumb.

"Well, sir – I corroborated this information with several other sources and the CIA has confirmed that all sites have been verified and destroyed," I respond, trying to hide the venom threatening to seep into my words.

And you don't need to know about the others outside of Iran...and the rest of the information.

The entire table looks up from their copies of the report as the director stands up to inspect the map. I *always* make sure to cover my bases because I know this question will come and because I'm thorough and good at my job. Several minutes pass as the men look from me to the map and I stand tall and still like a soldier in a platoon lineup.

"Good work, Ms. Lyman. Thank you for your service," Director Bryant says, nodding in my direction and careful not to show emotion on his face.

Director Bryant, and most every other man around the table, looks haggard. Every one of them has dark circles under their eyes and their faces are solemn like this job has sucked their souls right from their bodies.

"Anything else of note to share, Ms. Lynam?" Director Bryant asks, raising his left eyebrow.

"Yes sir, I'd like to give my official notice. I'm resigning from the Central Intelligence Agency – and I'd like for my resignation to be effective immediately, sir," I respond.

A sea of shocked faces stares back at me, and I realize that making this announcement in this meeting is the Director's way to ensure all division chiefs know of my resignation. Which will hopefully also mean the information would trickle down to the moles as well. Silence is permeating through all corners of this room, and I can feel a shiver run down my spine.

Oh no, the cold is back. I've got to get out of here soon.

"Well, I'm disappointed in this news – but I will honor your decision," the director says.

After a few more awkward moments of silence, the director stands followed by everyone else. The crowd of men move toward the door, but the director stops me.

"Ms. Lynam, a word before you go."

A few of the remaining men pause, before the director asks everyone else to clear the room. Once everyone else has left, he motions for me to sit in the seat next to him at the table. Something feels off about the situation and I glance toward the closed door, confused about the change in the director as soon as the door closes.

Am I safe?

"You know…we can and will call you back any time you're needed. And we *will* do that…if necessary," he says, leering at me sternly in a way that makes my skin feel like hundreds of fire ants are swarming my body.

Is this the same man who was just here a few minutes ago?

"Yes, sir," I say, my voice shaking ever so slightly.

Oh God, I have to get out of here…I can't be in here…this can't happen again…

"And I want you to understand that *I'm* in control of this operation," he continues, as his hand moves under the table to grab a hold of my leg.

I flinch at his touch before freezing in place, feeling as though the blood is draining from my face.

Move Andy…don't just sit here…move!

Trauma is a heartless bitch and, in this moment, I'm frozen and cannot get my body to do what my brain wants it to – to kick him in the balls, beat him over the head with the lamp that's sitting next to me, or simply just scream for help. No, instead I'm frozen with fear. My breaths are jagged, and I bite my tongue, desperate to avoid revealing my emotional state. Just as his hand begins to creep up my leg, pushing my panties to the side, the phone in the room rings. As though snapped out of a trance, I shove back in my chair so quickly that it screeches across the floor, causing another explosion of pain in my head from the loud noise.

"Now, now, don't get the wrong idea. I just want to make sure you are alright," he says, trying to defend his creepy actions.

Without a response, I bolt for the door and run down the hallway toward the women's bathroom. Flinging open the door, rushing into one of the stalls, I pull back my hair just in time before vomiting into the toilet. When I come out of the bathroom, the director is standing at the doorway to his office just watching me unflinchingly as I leave. Down on the main floor, my steps echo loudly on the marble floors as I jog through the empty agency halls.

I'm never wearing these heels again.

After pushing my way through the turnstile, I walk over to the memorial wall. Before leaving the building for what might be the last time, I stand in front of the memorial for several moments and gently trace my right hand along the stars.

Tears well up in my eyes as I whisper, "Thank you for your service."

Chapter 16
Girls Night

"Andy"

"**G**irl, we haven't seen you in months and you look paler than a newborn baby's butt – spill the beans and tell us what's going on with you," my friend Loren says, before taking a bite of her giant burger.

After the resignation today, I agreed to go out with my friends Loren and Gina. They've been calling me for weeks, and I told them I lost my phone in an "accident". I've decided to remain consistent with the story I told my parents about a car accident in Brazil. It's a convenient way to explain why I don't look my best and claiming to have amnesia around the details of the accident allows me to avoid additional lies. I hate having to lie to my best friends and in this moment, reeling from what happened with the director and the chaos swirling around in my blood, I'm acutely feeling the sacrifice officers are asked to make by keeping the silence required for this work. I'd rather curl by the fire in my condo, sitting with my thoughts and tears, but instead I'm smiling and laughing about the ridiculous cover story I created to avoid disclosing my work trauma.

"There's nothing more to tell," I lie, taking a sip of my Pinot Noir.

Well, except perhaps that the director of the CIA assaulted me today.

But that isn't a story I want to tell because I want to have fun and I want to forget any of that happened. What else can I do? Go to Human Resources on the director? I'm not exactly able to put more of a target on my back than the serum coursing through my veins already does.

Oh gosh, and what if the Director is now thinking of ways to keep me quiet?

I take a deep breath, and squeeze my eyes shut to erase these thoughts from my head and try to enjoy the moment. We are at a restaurant called Circa on Dupont Circle because it's metro accessible and has fantastic cocktails, including Gina's favorite: Blackberry Margarita. A wine girl for life, I also like Circa because we come here so often that the owner and all the bartenders know us, so I'm able to influence the wine list and ensure a fresh pour.

Loren and Gina are my ride or die friends. We met on the first day of second grade. My parents moved the family from Mount Pleasant, DC to Bethesda, MD a week before the 1991 riots. On my first day at Garden Hills Academy, a small private school, I was nervous being the only new girl in a class of only 22 kids. Loren and Gina quickly pulled me into their small circle of misfits.

Loren is Colombian- American with long, thick curly dark hair and deep brown skin that always seems to glow as impeccably as her bright personality. Her incredibly sweet, and extremely Catholic parents immigrated from Colombia a few years before she was born. They treat me like another daughter, always challenging me to speak Spanish with them and laughing at my horrible pronunciations. I cringe at how much my Portuguese language training has corrupted my Spanish. Mama Cardenas, Loren's boisterous and hilarious mom, is going to have a field day teasing me the next time she sees me.

The only other brown girl in our grade, Loren immediately claimed me as her "sister from another mister". Gina is first generation Greek American, with light brown, straight hair, and dark eyes. Several years of ballet has permanently changed her gait. She walks like a ballerina and complains about how toe shoes ruined her feet whenever someone even thinks about mentioning dance or anything closely related. She's shorter than Loren and me, and small enough that bartenders frequently inspect her driver's license to make sure she's old enough to drink. Both Loren and I joke that Gina is our token, tiny White friend.

"But how *are* you?" Gina asks, sipping her drink.

"I'm doing well," I lie, shifting in my seat.

"Girl, you look like you need to get laid – are you dating anyone?" Loren asks, too casually for this type of question.

"Wow, you just jumpin' right in with the sex questions, huh?" I laugh, rolling my eyes and taking another sip of my wine.

"Told you we want the juice *and* the tea girl," Loren laughs.

Loren's laugh is booming and infectious. She has the entire restaurant smiling and wondering what we're talking about and wishing they were at our table to join in the fun.

Well, I did have sex with Cam...in a sleeping bag in the middle of the forest...

"Do you all remember Cameron?" I ask, shyly and covering my face a little with the wine glass.

Gina's eyes look like they are about to pop out of her head and Loren raises her hand to ask the bartender for a round of Tequila shots.

"You *cannot* mean Cameron...the fuckboi," Loren says.

I bury my head in my hands to hide the pink I can feel creeping up my cheeks.

"Yes, *that* Cameron. And he wasn't a fuckboi – just an asshole," I sigh.

"Andy no, he was such an ass to you before you all broke up. You cannot go back there," Gina yells, banging her fist on the table and making it shake.

"Yeah girl, don't go back. Come with me instead," some guy across the bar yells before laughing and nearly slipping off his stool.

I roll my eyes and turn myself back toward my friends.

"We aren't back together or anything...we just met up," I say.

...and we're working together...and we had sex.

I hate not being able to tell my friends what's really happening in my life. Having to be a different version of myself around them is exhausting, but they can't know the truth. So, I tell them enough and leave out the rest.

"Well, I still don't like him – but I will love you whatever you decide to do. Just make sure you get some of that good lovin'," Loren says, laughing and lightening the mood as she does.

Oh, it was better than just good.

"Look Andy, so many of us have been to CPR class, but nobody has ever been able to resuscitate the dummy," Gina says, forcing a smile to my face at the thought of Cameron as the CPR dummy.

Loren hopped from her bar stool, pretending to dramatically blow on an invisible dummy and then scratch her head as though she expected it to wake up. We all laughed for several minutes, the kind of side-splitting laughter that fills me with a happiness that I haven't realized I've been missing.

"Speaking of dummies though, I think my boss tried to make a move on me today...like right after I resigned," I say, before chugging the last of my wine.

Both of my friends look at me as though a record scratched in the middle of a raging party, leaving the room silent. They just stare at me, their eyes full of concern and tragic empathy.

"What, why are you guys looking at me like I just told you someone died?" I ask, uncomfortable

I don't ever want to feel like a victim and the energy they are giving me makes me wish I could unspeak the admission.

"Andy, you just dropped that in chat like it's no big deal. Are you alright?" Gina asks, placing her hand over mine.

"Yeah, I'm good. I mean…it was crappy as fuck…but I'm alright," I lie, suspecting they know me well enough to know that I likely wouldn't have mentioned something that was no big deal.

"What??! Oh no…girl…I'm sorry. What did you do?" Loren asks, placing her hand on my shoulder in support.

"Nothing, I just ran out," I respond, feeling ashamed that I didn't have a better response.

"Are you going to tell on him?" Gina asks.

"No, he's…um…he has too much power. It won't go anywhere," I respond.

"Before you start thinking that there's something you should have done…or something you could have done to avoid that happening – stop it. There is nothing any of us can do to stop some of these creepy, old men from being shady and lecherous," Loren scowls.

"Thanks," I respond, thankful that she read my mind on that.

I listen as both my friends share stories about uncomfortable situations they've been in at work with men and how many times they've heard women report – only for the report to make things worse for the victim. It's horrible that women have learned to ignore these things for fear of retaliation – but that's the world we live in.

As my friends carry on for several minutes, lightening the mood with discussion of their latest dating escapades or drama from the larger friend group I've missed, I sink deep into my own thoughts. There's more to say about what happened with the chief, but I can't talk to my closest friends about it. I'm ashamed that I froze – worrying that he took that as a sign of consent. It feels awful knowing that instead of being able to kick him in the nuts, I ran to the bathroom and threw up my breakfast. But after the surface level disclosure, I tuck the experience back into my subconscious – messy, disorganized, and alongside the others.

"Ladies, it's been real…but I have to go," I say, sipping the last bit of my wine and waving over the bartender so I can close my tab.

"Noooo, we practically just got here," Gina whines.

"I'm sorry I can't stay longer, but I have to get up early tomorrow and figure out what I'm going to do for the rest of my life," I respond.

Loren reaches over and pulls me into a hug, "I still can't believe you resigned from your cushy State Department job without another job lined up."

Girl, if you only knew.

"I have another job prospect. I told you that I'm probably going to just consult for a while until I figure out what I want to do next," I respond.

"So, you're going to the dark side with the other beltway bandits?" Gina asks, throwing me the shade I expect with a firm name like "Hinkley Anderson".

"We'll do this again soon ladies," I say, putting on my jacket before heading toward the door.

"We better," Loren and Gina both respond in unison.

I hug and kiss both goodbye and blow a kiss to the cute bartender before pushing open the door and stepping into the cold night. When the cold air hits my face, I quickly pull my hoodie over my head and draw in a breath of the frigid outside. It's a Wednesday night, so the streets are dark, and empty compared to a weekend night in Dupont Circle. It's so quiet that the sound of my breathing seems louder than usual. It's risky to walk home alone at night, considering my situation, but getting into a cab seems scarier – so I'll take my chances walking.

Walking on a street I've walked hundreds of times, I should feel safe – but I don't. With every turn, I instinctively glance over my shoulder, taking mental note of everyone. It's disconcerting that I can't walk anywhere without doing surveillance with the expectation that I'm being followed – either by terrorists or perhaps even my own government.

When I turn onto Swann Street, where Gina lives, it's even darker. I didn't notice before how this street is spotty with lighting. As I try nonchalantly glancing over my shoulder, I notice the same man in a ball cap that I saw just as I was leaving Circa.

Shit, surveillance.

Twice...after several turns...

on a non-linear route....

Through an infrequently travelled street.

Picking up my pace substantially and staying close to the shrubbery along the sides of the houses, I try to remain calm. Clutching the pocket of my signature pink peacoat, I fish around for the burner cell phone Cameron gave me and dial the number as instructed.

"Andy?" Cam quickly answers, after just one ring.

"Cam – something's wrong. I think someone's following me," I whisper into the phone, while starting to jog.

Panic rises in my throat, making it hard to swallow.

"Where are you right now?" Cameron asks.

"I'm... turning right...onto 18th street from Swann and...heading north toward Adam's Morgan," I say, struggling to breathe in between words.

My heart feels like it's going to burst out of my chest. I clutch my chest to calm my racing heart. And even though I'm now in a full on run up a hill, my body feels like ice again.

Does the cold get worse with adrenaline?

"Andy, are you still there?" Cameron's voice is loud at my side, which makes me realize that I'd removed the phone from my ear.

"Yes, sorry…I'm running. I don't know where he went. I can't see him anymore," I say, spinning in a circle to verify.

Trying to talk myself off the ledge of this anxiety spiral, I think of all the reasonable explanations for someone following me that don't include a terrorist organization trying to kidnap me from the streets of Dupont Circle. Given that this was DC, perhaps someone is just trying to mug me.

Clearly, I've lost my mind when mugging is the better scenario.

With a mugging, I could throw my purse at the criminal and run to end it. But a terrorist wouldn't be looking for my purse when what's pumping through my veins is far more valuable than a few credit cards and my driver's license.

"Andy, stay on the phone and keep telling me where you are – I'm coming to you," Cam says, with the sounds of screeching tires in the background.

"Okay, I'm running so I'm close I think," I say, now feeling dizzy.

I can see the main drag in sight, so I grab my purse and start fishing out my keys. I run up the stairs to my building, I hold out my keys in a shaking hand.

Something's wrong…the door is ajar.

The temporary relief I felt when I reached my apartment is gone.

I never forget to lock the door.

I pull a container of mace from my purse and slowly push the door open with my foot. Ironically, even with the current threat against my life, I'm not licensed to carry a gun in Washington, DC. I have a handgun in the safe under my bed, but to get there I'll need to walk through the kitchen and the living room. Just as I step over the threshold of the doorway, someone grabs me from behind. Trying to scream, but muffled by a large, noticeably dirty hand covering my mouth – I begin to kick and throw my body around. Every time I try to breathe, I gag at the taste of oil and body funk on the hand.

Of course, this dude didn't think to shower or wash his damn hands or wear gloves before attempting to kill me.

The smelly hand man shoves me further into my condo and the door slams behind us. I struggle to break free, my legs flailing around attempting to latch onto something that could allow me to break free. I scan the room, desperately searching for objects I can use to defend myself.

Can I get to my gun?

As he drags me past an end table near my couch, I manage to grab a spare set of keys. I jab them into his eye, which causes him to grab his face and scream in pain. He releases me enough to break away, and I kick him in the head with the heel of my boot several times before running to grab a larger object.

Just as I reach for a large lamp, he grabs me by the hair and pulls me back toward him. He grabs my neck, and I jab my fingers into his already bloody eye. This time he throws me against the kitchen island. My head slams against the marble counter before I slide to the floor. I grab my head as the pain courses through my body, and I curl up to brace for his next move.

The apartment door flings open and several gunshots ring out, hitting the man square in the chest. Blood pours from his body as he falls on top of me. I shove him off me and crawl behind my couch, taking cover.

Loud footsteps come toward me, and out of the corner of my eye, I see Cameron. I reach out to him, vision blurry and head throbbing in pain. He drops to his knees, grabs hold of me, and places his hand on the back of my head. His eyes widen and the color drains from his face as he looks at his hand, now covered in my blood. Before he can say a word, I lose consciousness, and everything turns black.

Chapter 17
Wardman Operations Center

"Cameron"

There's blood everywhere and Andy isn't responding to my attempts to wake her up. Boss, who entered Andy's condo just a few steps behind me, wastes no time and is searching for the body of the assailant.

"I got you Andy, stay with me, okay? I'm going to call for help," I say, hoping she can hear me.

I reach for my phone to call Rove because calling the police isn't a reasonable option under the current circumstances.

How would I explain the dead man in the corner to the local police?

"Rove, I need backup. Andy's been hit and she's bleeding all over me...and there's a dead guy..." my mind is racing, and I can't seem to get the words out fast enough.

"Wait *what?* Cam, slow down...first, let's figure out what is going on - check for a pulse," Rove says, his voice the reliable calm that always helps me focus.

"Okay, yeah...she has a pulse and she's breathing but she's not awake and not responding to me," I respond, growing more frantic with each passing second.

"Keep your cool Cameron. You're going to get her out of there and we'll take care of the dead guy. Just tell me where you are and I will send a clean-up crew," Rove says in a reassuring tone.

After giving Rove the address, I reach to lift Andy. While in my arms, she begins to stir and opens her eyes.

"Oh, thank God, Andy, can you get up? We have to get out of here," I say, searching her face for a response.

"Ouch," she says, grabbing the back of her head before trying to get up.

Helping her to a sitting position, I put the phone back to my ear, "Rove, she's awake. This dude, whoever he...was...he's enormous and smells rancid. The entire condo smells like a funk bomb went off."

"Search the body and then get out of there," Rove says.

Just as he says this, I glance over at Boss who's managed to pull the dead man's wallet and phone out of his pocket and slide them across the room to me. Boss looks like he's smiling as he trots over to us, pushing his findings closer.

"Good boy Boss. Come on bro, we gotta get out of here," I say, quickly patting boss on the head after he comes over for his expected affirmation.

I quickly pull my shirt up over my nose and give the dead guy a quick once over to make sure Boss got everything – he did. Then I grab the cell phone, remove the SD card, and then smash it before returning it to the man's pocket. I keep the wallet because we need more time to analyze its contents.

"Get Andy out of there, using a back entrance if possible. Leave the guy there, lock up, and put Andy's key in a discreet spot outside the door. We'll send a crew to get rid of the body and work on identifying him here," Rove orders.

"Shouldn't she go to a hospital?" I ask.

"No, she's been made – that would be too dangerous. I worried this might happen when she tried to return home as though things were normal. We'll have a doctor here to look at her when you arrive," Rove responds.

Thankfully I don't have to clean this scene because the rancid smell that's wafting through the condo indicates that the dead man has crapped himself within the five minutes I've been on the phone with Rove.

"Andy, is there a back entrance we can leave from," I ask, searching around her condo.

"Yeah, the fire escape," she responds, trying to sit up before changing her mind and lowering back to the ground, "but I can't...I'm not sure I can..."

"I'll carry you. Don't try to move," I interrupt, recognizing that she's in no state to climb down a fire escape without my help.

I grab a towel from the kitchen counter and instruct Andy to place it at the back of her head to try and stop the bleeding. Then I gently lift her to her feet and place my hands under her knees to pick her up.

"No, no...I can walk...just...give me a min," she says, insisting she not be carried.

Boss brushes up against her and she smiles, "thanks for the extra encouragement, Boss."

He whines impatiently, as though he can read my anxiety levels rising the longer that we wait here. The smelly dude might not be alone, and I don't want to wait around to meet any of his friends.

"Okay, I'm good…just help me up?" She asks, holding out her hand and grabbing onto mine as I lift her to a standing position.

I put the leash back on Boss because homeboy can't always be trusted to stay close during moments of chaos, and we walk toward a window behind the couch that leads to the fire escape. Opening the window, and shoving the screen out of the way quickly, I step through with the dog before helping Andy climb through the opening. The three of us, including the dog, tiptoe down the fire escape. We're all conscious of not drawing attention to ourselves as we creep down the stairs and through the alley toward my car.

A loud explosive noise rings out and we all crumble to the ground, crouching close to the wall.

Gunshots

Our eyes meet for a split second in non-verbal recognition and agreement of our next move.

Run.

Holding onto each other, with Boss following closely behind, we duck down and run through the alley trying to escape the repetitive blasts ringing out in succession around us. Just as we approach the car, I can hear a shot and the intense pain shooting through my arm alerts me that I've been hit. Quickly glancing down, I see blood pouring down my left arm.

Fuck, no time to slow down.

I push Boss into the car as he howls loudly to grab Andy's attention. I swear if that dog could speak, he'd be telling on me right now. As soon as Andy shuts the door on her side, Boss ratchets up his attempts by pulling on the sleeve of her shirt with his teeth.

"Boss, what's wrong?" She asks, trying to remove his mouth from her shirt.

I turn on the car and step on the gas so hard that the tires loudly screech as we make the steep turn onto 18th street. Bullets are still flying toward us, and Boss is losing his mind, howling, and panting. Instinctively, I reach across both Boss and Andy and shove them down to shield them from the spray of bullets. My defensive driving skills are coming in handy as I crash through parked cars to block the path of our assailant. Andy is still crouching down, holding onto Boss who continues to cry because she still hasn't noticed the blood pouring out of my left arm.

"It's okay buddy, we'll be alright," she says, patting Boss on the head.

He's not crying because he's scared of the bullets – Boss is a warrior.

I rest my hand on her back, hoping she stays down even though the gunfire has stopped. Weaving in and out of traffic, driving in the opposite direction on one-way streets, through narrow alleyways, and taking multiple aggressive turns, I desperately try to get us back to our make-shift operations center without carrying surveillance with us.

"I think we're in the clear," I say, taking a deep breath and releasing my grip a bit on the steering wheel.

Andy sits up, and her eyes widen as she realizes that I've been shot.

"Cam, oh my gosh...you're bleeding," she screams, before instructing me to, "pull over, now."

"No, we're almost there, I'm okay," I lie, starting to feel lightheaded.

Boss starts pulling at my shirt, making driving safely nearly impossible. I'm forced to pull over so that I can push his big, furry butt into the backseat. Once I've pulled to the side of the road to get Boss off me, Andy jumps out of the car and runs around to the driver's side.

"Cam, let me look at your arm. We need to take care of it before you bleed out," she says, already pulling my shirt over my head to inspect the wound.

As she moves my arm, I feel pain shoot through my entire body as though the adrenaline of the situation that was numbing me suddenly wears off.

"Oh ouch – FUCK, that hurts," I yelp.

I can hear Boss panting nervously from the backseat where I shoved him. He's hovering to my side, rubbing against my non injured arm as though he's trying to pet me.

Andy quickly snaps into action as though she's been thrust into a warzone. She searches the car, grabbing the shirt she's just removed from me and shoving it into the wound.

"What are you doing?" I ask, looking down as she's quickly removing the belt from my pants.

"I'm sorry, this is going to hurt – but I need to stop the bleeding and it's the only way I can make sure you don't bleed out before we get you to a doctor," she responds.

Making a tourniquet with the belt, she wraps it around my arm and pulls it tight. I bite my lip so hard I can taste blood. I know Andy can't be doing well right now given that she was just bleeding from the head less than thirty minutes ago, so I'm watching her stunned at how quickly she's able to go through these motions as though she's a trained medic.

"Move over," she says, pressing her hand against my side to try and nudge me into the passenger seat.

"I can drive," I protest.

"Fool, I don't care. Stop acting like you don't need me to take care of you. You just saved my life back there. Now let me save yours, okay?" Her electric blue eyes pierce me, like they're looking directly into my soul.

Hesitating for a moment, because I'm stubborn, I sigh before climbing into the passenger seat. I lean my head against the headrest on the seat while instructing Andy to drive to the historic Wardman Hotel. We've taken over an entire floor of the hotel for our ops center and after what just happened at Andy's place, this might be the only place even close to safe for us right now.

"This is where Rove set up the ops center – hiding in plain sight," I explain, forcing a smile through the intense arm pain.

"Okay, that's great and all but we need to get you to the hospital," Andy responds, looking between me and the parking garage as though she isn't sure whether to enter.

"No, no hospital. Rove called in a doctor when he found out you hit your head. They can take care of me here too," I insist.

As Andy drives into the garage, I hand her the access card to open the gate. The sense of relief that even this small layer of security provides is astonishing. I turn on a new burner phone, because I tossed the one I called Rove from last time and dialed the command center to inform them we were headed up. Looking over at Andy, I notice that her eyes are closed.

"Hey, are you okay?" I ask her.

She's silent for a moment before responding, "yeah, I just have a bad headache. But I'll be alright, let's go."

I open the door, glancing back at Boss who needs no invitation before jumping up and following me out.

Andy is at my side, one hand placed gently on my good arm, while Boss is marching on my other side. Our penthouse floor gives us multiple suites totaling near 4,000 sq feet of combined space. Our operations center is large enough to house the core team – which at this point only consists of me, Rove, Theo, Farhad (who's become a recent addition), and now Andy. There are a handful of other GS-19 members nearby and ready to deploy as needed. Rove insists the core team remain small, to reduce the chance of data leaks.

As we come through the elevator doors, entering a corridor with access control, I place my hand on the scanner to let us in. Rove is standing with a doctor at his side ready to take Andy when he spots my arm.

"No, you need to take care of him first," Andy says, holding up her hand to stop the doctor.

"What the hell happened?" Rove asked, looking between us.

"After we left the condo, we got caught in a spray of bullets. I got hit," I admit, shrugging to try and lighten the mood a bit.

Rove directs me to lay on the stretcher they'd brought for Andy while the doctor inspects my arm.

"There's no bullet in there. Looks like you got grazed. I'm going to have to give you some stitches and bandage you up, but you shouldn't need surgery," the doctor says, flatly.

Andy heads to a nearby couch, with Boss following behind, and lays down.

"Hey man, you forget to dodge?" Theo asks, placing his hand on my shoulder and giggling.

"Yeah man, I dodged...well...some of the bullets," I respond, laughing with him at the inside joke that's bounced between us for years.

The two of us have been involved in an unfortunately large number of shootouts and after each, we check on each other by asking if the other dodged effectively.

"Dodge better next time, alright? I'm not ready to lose you, brother," Theo says, only serious for a split second before heading over to wrestle with Boss.

Good, because I'm not planning to go anywhere.

The pain meds effectively kick in, and I hop off the stretcher and walk over to Rove who's standing in the doorway of the communal kitchen that's connected to the living room area where everyone else is sitting. He's staring at the wall behind the dining table where we've hung up a sea of pictures of suspected terrorists with links to the serum and maps with pins indicating location leads.

"Did you already send a team to clear out Andy's condo?" I ask, fishing in my pocket and handing him the SD card and wallet that I grabbed from the perpetrator.

"Yeah, the team got in, cleaned up, and secured the unit about fifteen minutes ago. They didn't find anything else of note, but took prints from the body," Rove responds.

As we chat about the scene, Farhad bursts through the doors of the ops center covered in sweat. He seems like the type of guy who's always wearing clothes that look tailored and as though he's stepped out of a men's fashion magazine, so his disheveled appearance causes all of us to take notice. Even Andy, who's been laying on the couch next to the doctor, sits up to hear what he has to say.

"There's still a mole in your agency," Farhad says, handing a piece of paper to me before he wipes his sweat beaded forehead with the back of his hand.

I'm still skeptical of Farhad's true allegiances, but since I know Rove and Andy both trust him, I tread lightly with my tone, "How do you know this?"

It's against protocol to invite foreign nationals onto the team, even if technically Farhad is a stateless man. I have good reason not to trust him yet.

'What other option do we have now,' Rove said to me when he first proposed adding Farhad to the team.

I'll admit, the guy has the best computer forensic skills I've seen in my entire career, but as a natural skeptic – I'm still not entirely convinced he should be on the team.

"I have...friend...he still works at one of the sites. He won't talk to Americans because he's afraid. But Rove asked me to talk to him...he's here for a conference in DC...he told me that his boss sent someone for Andy after 'the Americans' gave up her location. They know...they all know...about the serum," Farhad responds, still panting and worry on his face that's causing his eyebrows to crease together.

I don't immediately respond, instead looking over at Rove to wait for more information and for him to add his assessment.

"Cam – Farhad is an equal part of this team and while you don't have to like each other – I expect you to treat him with the respect he deserves. This man put himself in a lot of danger for our country and has earned his right to be one of us," Rove says, a stern warning in his tone.

Damn, I guess my tone wasn't as neutral as I thought.

I nod before extending my hand to Farhad as a peace offering.

"This is my country now, and I care what happens to it – and I care about what happens to Andy," Farhad says, reaching out to shake my hand in return.

"I grabbed the SD card from the guy who attacked Andy. Farhad, can you look at it and see who he was? His identity might also corroborate the Intel you received from your friend," I say, recognizing the risk I'm taking by giving this to him while also understanding he's likely the only one of us who will capture all useful data from that card in the shortest amount of time.

"Sure, man. Give me the card – it will take me some time to confirm but I'll go do that now," Farhad responds enthusiastically, causing me to feel a twinge of regret for being so hard on him.

I can see a glint of nerd joy in Farhad's eye as he grabs the SD card and trots toward the room that houses a bank of computers. The doctor, who's been checking Andy out since she stitched up my arm, helps Andy off the couch and into one of the free bedrooms.

After closing the door behind her to leave Andy to rest, she addresses the group, "I'm surprised she was able to drive. She has a concussion and lost a good bit of blood. I ran an IV to keep her hydrated and will stay here to monitor her through the night," the doctor says

"Is she awake?" I ask.

"She's in and out of sleep," the doctor says before adding, "let her sleep tonight – you can see her in the morning."

Well damn, I was just asking – do I look that thirsty to talk to her?

I'm thankful the doctor can stay the night to monitor her, and know I need to give her space. Rove has been watching me with Andy since we walked through the door, and while he hasn't mentioned it again, I know he's quietly keeping tabs on my proximity to Andy. Glancing back at Rove, who's still hovering, I stumble over to one of the couches and try to get comfortable enough to sleep. Boss gives me the side eye as he stands at the door to our room.

"Nope, it's the couch tonight for me. Do you want me to let you into the room?" I ask Boss, laughing as he audibly huffs before walking over and flopping himself at the foot of the couch.

Rove shakes his head before departing to his own room, and I lean over to pet Boss on the head, "Good job today dude, you probably saved my ass...but next time, don't be a snitch."

Boss rolls over, exposing his stomach, clearly expecting more praise for telling on me to Andy. Within seconds of me rubbing him, I can hear the low and steady sound of his dog snores and the humming sound sends me to sleep right behind him.

Chapter 18
Medicine Woman

I wake to another excruciating headache, only intensified with the light shining through a tiny crack in the blinds. I'm in what looks like a swanky hotel room, noting a small coffee maker in the corner, a private bathroom, and that stale hotel room look with neutral colors and standard furniture. The lighting, elegant, classy, and historic, sets it apart from the typical hotel and adds a level of bougie that I respect.

Where the hell am I and how did I get here?

Oh...that's right...The Wardman...

My eyes continue to scan the room and land on Cameron who's peacefully sleeping on a couch next to my bed. Boss, who's snoring on the floor next to him, must be responsible for the noise that woke me up. Cameron's tall, muscular body is splayed out across the small couch, making it look like a small piece of doll furniture that a child has placed a giant stuffed animal on top of.

"Cameron," I call, my voice surprisingly scratchy and hoarse.

At the sound of my voice, his eyes open and he winches and grabs his arm as he sits up.

"Oh no, is your arm alright?" I ask, remembering how both of us must have looked when we arrived last night.

"Yeah, I'm alright...just sore. They didn't need to do surgery, but where they put the stitches still hurts. How are you?" he asks, rubbing his eyes before coming to sit down next to the bed.

"My head hurts, but I'm not shot," I respond, touching his arm.

We both laugh and he shrugs, "I'm just thankful we got out of there alive. That was an ambush. And hey, thank you for taking care of me last night."

I don't respond and instead just nod. Of course, I was going to take care of him.

"Hey, what happened to that dude who was in my condo?" I ask, feeling nauseous by even the memory of his smelly hand on my face.

"Well, smelly dude is as dead as a doornail," he responds, his Louisiana accent peeking through his words.

"What about the guy who shot you? Any word on him? And what the hell happened to the body?" I ask, a little panicked that there could still be a smelly, rotting, dead man on the floor of my condo.

Oh no...my wood floors.

"Smelly guy...Theo and company took care of him. We assume the guy who shot me was connected to "smelly dude". Farhad is analyzing the pocket litter we got on him," Cameron says.

"Oh...okay. Cam, that guy smelled like oil mixed with dirty locker room socks. It was the worst thing I've smelled in...well, ever," I say, shuttering at the memory.

"Yeah, it was bad. I don't know what hole that dude crawled out of, but whatever it was...was a smelly one," he responds, his face twisting before he shakes his head as though he's trying to shake the memory from his brain.

Silence hangs between us and Cameron doesn't have to say another word for me to know this means I've been made – someone snitched, and my location is compromised. The silence between us is palpable as Cameron slips into the bed beside me and wraps his arms around me. I bury my head into his chest and breathe in deeply, hoping that his smell will replace the memories of what happened last night. For a split second I think I should move away because we shouldn't be this close and comfortable, but my body rejects my second guessing and holds him tighter.

"So, have you gotten any Intel about more locations...and finding an antidote?" I ask, breaking the silence and hoping he's learned *something* in the last couple of days.

"Well, Farhad is on the team now," Cameron says, with an obvious non-response to my question.

So...no...they've gotten nowhere without me.

"Oh – well, that's good right? I mean, the part about Farhad joining the team," I say, trying to read into where he's going with this.

"He's identified one of the locations from someone he's still in contact with...and that person told him it was an American who revealed your identity," Cameron responds, a hint of irritation in his voice.

Tears that I'm desperately trying to fight threaten to crawl defiantly down my cheeks. Cameron's eyes shoot to mine, and I know he knows that I'm fighting to stay stoic.

"Why does it sound like you don't think Farhad joining us is a good thing?" I ask, looking away from him to try and collect myself.

"Andy, I want to trust him, but I'll be honest – I can't just easily get over the fact that Basir essentially brought that vial to your doorstep along with the terrorist who lodged it into your leg," he says, with a deep grimace on his face.

"Cam – listen to me closely," I say, touching his face to ensure he's looking at me, "First – Farhad *isn't* his father. Second – he saved our lives by showing us how to get out of that tunnel and if he weren't on our side, he wouldn't have done that."

"I know. I know my anger is misplaced. But Basir should have followed the plan. If he had, you wouldn't be in this situation."

Cameron lets out a frustrated sigh, and turns away from me.

I touch the side of his face and turn his head back toward me before saying, "we will find a way out of this, okay?"

Cameron's large arms wrap around me as he pulls our bodies flush. I take a deep breath, closing my eyes and letting myself pretend we're together in another reality – one where we'd never been apart. A moment later, the moment shatters with a loud knock at the door. I straighten in the bed and push on Cameron's chest, non-verbally asking him to separate. He awkwardly backs away and stumbles a bit on his way back to the couch while Boss moves toward the door tentatively, as though he can't decide whether to be a welcoming party or a club bouncer.

"Come in," I say, before clearing my throat and pushing several curls that had escaped my ponytail back behind my ears.

I should be more worried about the fact that I had blood gushing from my head last night and my blood is radio-active, but I can't have these people thinking Cam and I are together – or my hair looking a whole mess. And while thankful Cameron was there to save me from the intruder and the kitchen counter, I'm still not comfortable letting him back in as though he's suddenly absolved of his past sins.

The doctor enters the room, followed by Rove. She glances toward Cameron, raising her eyebrow and giving him a look of disapproval.

"Couldn't stay away from her, could you?" Rove asks, smirking at Cameron.

Cameron doesn't respond and instead looks sheepishly at the floor, his cheeks flushing. The doctor approaches my bed, checking my vitals. I watch Cameron as he fiddles with his watch nervously.

"Hi Andy, my name is Dr. Rajani Jain. But you can just call me Raj," the doctor smiles, extending her hand to shake mine.

"Hi, it's nice to meet you," I respond, returning the handshake.

Rove announces that Dr. Jain has joined the team as our resident doctor. She's a nuclear radiologist who built her career studying how radioactive materials can cure diseases but was recruited by the agency years prior when it became clear that terrorism had morphed in a way that made the study of radioactive materials and their interaction with the human body critical. She also holds a clearance because she's worked as a doctor on call with both the White House and the Central Intelligence Agency.

That's quite the resume.

"Can I have some coffee," I ask, looking at Cameron.

"Sure, I'll get it," he responds, getting up from the couch.

"Can you get me...something that's *not* from the instant coffee maker I saw in the kitchen?" I ask, hoping he finds me a latte.

"Uh, okay, yeah, Boss could use the walk anyway," he responds, heading out the door with an extremely excited Boss at his heels.

Raj, what Dr. Jain insists that I call her, smiles at me as though she knows exactly why I'd sent Cam for coffee. I turn to Rove, asking him whether the doctor was briefed on the entirety of the situation to which he responds in the affirmative. Then, I ask him to leave as well. While I'm not sure she'll have all the answers, I want to discuss what's happening to me without the men here. My hope was that this will allow me to decide what they need to know and keep the rest to myself.

"How are you feeling?" Raj asks, while shining a light into my eyes as soon as the men all vacate the room.

"My head hurts. It feels like my brain is floating around in my head and banging painfully against my skull every time I move," I respond.

Closing my eyes provides some relief because the light makes it worse.

"I'm not worried about the headache. I know I hit my head last night, so the headache and a concussion make sense," I say.

I'm worried about the serum coursing through my veins.

"Yes, you have a mild concussion, but should be feeling better in about 24-48 hours," she says, examining me with her deep brown eyes.

Raj is a small, middle aged woman of Indian descent with long black hair that she ties back in a ponytail. Though tiny, at only about 5'2", she has a commanding presence that makes me feel as though we're soul sisters. We're the only two women officially a part of this operation and I'm so thankful that her presence means I'm no longer the only one.

"Thank you for being here," I say.

She doesn't immediately respond, but instead flashes a warm smile that reveals two dimples and amazingly white teeth.

"I'm happy to be here. Your reputation precedes you and when Rove asked me to join this team, I didn't hesitate when I learned you were a part of it," she responds, taking my hand and squeezing it firmly before placing it back on the bed and patting my shoulder.

She then pulls up a chair and sits next to the bed, before placing her stethoscope back around her shoulders.

"So, tell me what's really bothering you," she says, as though she can read my mind.

"I assume they've told you what happened to me in the woods – when my body temperature dropped rapidly?" I ask, unsure of where to start.

"Yes, I'm aware of the nuclear agent present in the serum you were injected with, and I understand that one of the side effects you've experienced is impaired thermoregulation," she responds, concern now showing on her face.

"I'm cold all the time, but it gets worse sometimes," I admit.

"Have you noticed anything during the times when it's gotten worse that would indicate a trigger?" She asks.

Feeling embarrassed that I hadn't thought about this prior, I take a moment to think about all the times when it'd been at its worst – with the incident in the woods being at the height of my discomfort.

"Right before it was at its worst, Cameron and I were running for our lives away from Brody's minions who were trying to take me…well, trying to do something with me," I say, never fully knowing what their intentions were for me that day but knowing they weren't good.

"So would it be accurate to say that perhaps…being in a dangerous situation where you're prone to heart rate increase…that could worsen the symptoms?" She asks, now taking notes on her electronic tablet.

"Yes, that could be…" I say, my voice trailing off as I think.

"How did you manage that episode in the woods? I understand you two were there overnight before the team arrived for extraction. Was there something you did that helped?" She asks.

Oh no…this is going to be awkward.

"Umm, well...uh..." I can feel my face getting warm as I think about how to tell this woman that Cameron and I slept naked together and had sex.

"Body heat?" She asks, trying to hide a smile but failing miserably as she looks back down at her tablet.

"Yeah, something like that," I say, stifling an embarrassed giggle while also being thankful that I didn't need to offer additional details.

"Well, that certainly can be a very effective way to increase body temperature," she says, now laughing alongside me.

After we share in the humor of this ridiculous situation, I turn serious and share with her the worries that are keeping me up at night.

"We don't have a lot of credible leads, and I'm worried the only way to find out where all the sites are – and how deep Solaris is within our government – is going to require something extreme," I admit, words flowing from my mouth like a faucet of confessions I can't stop.

"What are you proposing?" She asks, tilting her head to the side and looking into my eyes.

"I'm worried that we won't stop them unless I allow myself to be a double and let them take me," I admit, surprising myself that I've said this out loud.

"That is quite risky and we haven't explored alternatives sufficiently," she replies, pulling a blood pressure cuff from her medical jacket and placing it on my arm.

"This serum scares the hell out of me because I know I'm not alright. The cold is one thing – but noises are...different. It's like certain frequencies send me into a complete spiral and with all this – I'm scared that if I go in there, I won't come out," I admit, words flowing from my mouth like a faucet of confessions I can't stop.

And I know that my ability to go into the Epicenter of the Solaris group is likely my only way out of this...

I bite my lip and try to hold back tears. I don't know what it is about Raj that makes me want to tell her all this but telling her makes me feel lighter – like I'm no longer holding this truth alone.

"Please don't tell the guys – please," I beg, my voice shaking.

"What you tell me is protected under patient confidentiality. They all know this. I'm only able to tell them what you authorize me to say," she responds, in a reassuring tone.

"Okay, thank you. I appreciate that. Do you have any initial thoughts on what might be going on," I ask, hopeful that she can give me some answers that might help give me some hope.

"I have some unconfirmed hypotheses – one, the serum is impacting your nervous system in some way or perhaps its mimicking an endocrine disorder and blocking hormones that help the body regulate temperature – such as your pancreas, thyroid, pituitary gland, and adrenal glands. But the blood work we got from your brief stay at Walter Reed isn't showing an obvious issue with your hormone levels. And finally, if there are parallels between increases in heart rate – there are some meds we can use to try and counteract that" she responds, giving me more detail than I expected.

"So, what do you recommend," I ask, praying she has some options that don't hinge on me waiting for us to find an antidote.

"I have something I'd like to try. I want to prescribe an antiarrhythmic medication for you to use when you feel like your heart rate is increasing and the cold worsens," she responds.

"Okay, I can do that – that sounds promising," I say, hopeful for the first time in weeks.

"But Andy, this doesn't completely remove the urgency of finding that serum. At this point, it's like poking around in a cave – trying to find monsters with a tiny little key chain light – and not being able to fully turn on the lights and see. The pills I'm giving you...I'm hopeful they will help avoid a crisis in the short term, but we're going to need to turn on the lights before the monster eats us," she says, standing from her chair and removing the cuff from my arm.

I appreciate her analogy because I feel like I'm trapped in a dark cave and this description tells me that she might be one of the only people who comes even close to understanding. She pulls a small bottle of circular, white pills out of her bag and hands them to me.

"Don't worry, I'm not leaving. We have a lab inside the operations center where I can continue conducting research. We have some of the vials of blood taken from your last hospital visit. That, plus the Intel you all get from sources who've worked in the labs should give us more answers about what we're dealing with. Try and relax a bit and I'll be back later to check in," she says, rubbing my shoulder before starting toward the door.

Moments after Raj leaves, Cameron comes bounding back through the door. He's out of breath like he's just run up several flights of stairs.

"What happened to you?" I ask.

"I didn't want your coffee to get cold, so I ran back as quickly as I could," he responds.

"Well damn, bonus points for your human Mr. Boss man," I say smiling down at Boss who's panting from the run back to the ops center.

Cameron flashes his classic toothy, wide smile that always makes me melt as he pulls out a cup from behind his back with the label, "Chai Spice Café". Chai Spice is the café across the street from The Wardman and in addition to that cafe being one of my favorite spots in the city for coffee, it also holds special meaning between us. Chai Spice was where he and I had the "define the relationship" talk when we'd officially become a couple.

"Oh, Cam...this is so much better than stale hotel coffee. Thank you," I croon, waving him over to me so that I can hug him and take my coffee.

As he leans over to hand me the coffee, I rub my hand along his head and kiss him on the cheek. Pulling the cup to my nose, inhaling the cinnamon espresso smell of the chai-puccino (a mix between a cappuccino and a chai latte) feels like someone is pouring warmth over me like a silk blanket. My hands shake as I bring the cup to my lips, and I can feel Cameron's eyes on me. He's looking from my face to my hands, and I suddenly feel a wave of self-consciousness.

"I'm fine, please don't treat me like a patient," I snap at him, before immediately regretting how sharp that came out.

"What did the doctor say?" he asks, taking a seat next to me and sipping on his own coffee.

"We need to get to work," I say, intentionally ignoring his question.

"Andy, you can't even hold your coffee without shaking and you got your head smashed hard enough last night that you actually lost time," he says, his face cloaked with worry.

"And...you got *shot*, but yet here you are...still working," I say, pointing out the obvious while gently placing my shoulder on his bandaged arm.

Boss makes a sound that's a mix between a whine and an admonishment before tilting his head to the side and gazing at us.

"See? Even Boss agrees that you're operating on a double standard here," I say, smiling at Boss who's quickly becoming my favorite member of the team.

"That's because he's a traitor," Cam responds quickly, teasing Boss by holding the pup cup full of whipped cream he'd gotten at Chai Spice just out of reach from him.

I carefully put the coffee cup on the table and frown. Silence falls between us as we exchange looks.

"Can you please just let me take care of you? I know you are a badass and I love that about you, but please...just chill this morning and I promise that tonight, after you've had some rest, we'll sit down and get back to business," he says, picking my coffee up off the table and bringing it to my lips.

"You *do* realize you're feeding me coffee while expecting me to rest?" I ask, raising an eyebrow teasingly.

"Andy, since *when* has coffee actually kept you from being able to sleep," he jokes back, poking me in the arm playfully.

He's right – I've always been the type of person who could drink coffee at night and go to sleep five minutes later. And right now, I'm drinking the coffee because it's delicious and warm – and I'm an unapologetic coffee addict and both of us know it.

"Theo got rid of the body and cleaned up your condo, but I think we can all agree that it's too dangerous for you to go back there right now. I had him pack a bag with some clothes for you because I knew you'd want some things. I'm sorry…Theo is…well…Theo…and I can't guarantee there's anything in there that matches but we can order anything you need from here," he says, speaking faster than usual as though I'll be crazy enough to go back to my condo right now after what just happened there.

"I'm sure whatever he brought is fine, please thank him for me," I say, placing my hand on his arm to stop him from continuing with more accommodation options.

Cameron looks like he hasn't slept in days, dark circles under his eyes and his typical clean-shaven look is now stubbly.

"Hey, can you promise me that you'll get some rest too?" I ask him.

"Yes, I will. I'll be in the room next door," he responds, hovering a moment as though he's waiting for me to ask him to stay.

I don't ask him to stay, because we both need to sleep, and I know what will happen if we curl up with each other in this bed.

"Goodnight Cam…and goodnight, Mr. Boss man," I say, glancing at Cam and then the dog before closing my eyes and willing my body to fall back asleep.

Chapter 19
New Plan

I wake up to a giant wet tongue gliding across my face.

"Dude, yuck! Boss, how many times do I have to tell you that I don't want your kisses, man," I yelp, shoving Boss away from my face before tackling him and rubbing his belly.

Shit, what time is it?

I nudge Boss off the bed and the loud clunk of his claws snap me back to the reality that we aren't at home – we're still in this hotel turned ops center, and I have no clue when this mission will end. I promised Andy I'd rest, and I thought I'd just take a mini nap but as soon as my head hit the pillow I passed out. I'll have to thank Doc Raj for those pain meds because I'm sure they helped me get the first solid rest I've had in days.

I stumble out of my room, still a little drowsy like I'm suffering from a sleep hangover.

...Or perhaps the hangover that happens after you've been shot.

In the communal area that connects the rooms, Rove is sitting alone at the table and rummaging through a pile of papers. A quick glance at the clock hanging above the kitchen area tells me that it's ten o'clock at night, meaning I've slept through the entire day.

"Damn man, I'm sorry. I didn't realize I was so tired," I say, walking over to join Rove at the table.

"It's fine, you're going to need the rest for what's coming. Farhad identified the assailant in Andy's condo, but we aren't that much closer to getting the full picture of all the sites and we don't have anyone on the inside of the 'epicenter' of this giant terrorist shit storm," he says, his face flush with anger.

Several of the reports on the terrorist network affiliated with the nuclear serum refer to a location they call "The Epicenter". While we know that getting inside there could be the key to taking this entire organization down, we first must figure out where the hell this place is.

Rove looks like hell. His light brown hair, which is peppered with gray, is a mess. It looks like he's been in a fight with a pack of birds that decided to have a party on his head. He's likely been running his hands through it for hours and greasy spikes of his hair were pointing in all directions. There's a dark shadow under his blood shot, green eyes and I know that somehow, I need to convince this man to take a turn sleeping while I continue the analysis.

"Let me look at this for you Rove. Go to sleep and by the time you're rested, I'll be caught up and we can meet with the entire group," I say, snatching a folder from Rove and patting him on the shoulder to encourage him to leave the table.

"Alright, yeah…I don't think I know what I'm reading at this point. Don't let me sleep late. The TLDR here is that we need someone to debrief some informant who just obtained asylum in Canada. He came from one of the nuclear sites and claims to have Intel on The Epicenter," Rove says, yawning loudly before getting up from the table and heading toward his room.

I watch him leave before looking back at the mound of reports, photos, and maps that are splayed out all over the table. It looks like a hurricane dropped down just over the area and threw papers everywhere. Given that this disaster area is likely to cause Andy unnecessary, additional anxiety, I quickly move my hands across the pile to try and organize the maps and location photos into logical piles.

Before digging into the files, I jog over to the grand, gas-powered fireplace at the corner of the room and turn it on. Boss, who's always trying to find a warm place to sit, trots behind me and practically glues himself to the mat in front of the fireplace.

"Don't get too comfy man, we still have work to do," I say, as though he understands me.

Boss opens one of his eyes and I swear he smirks at me because comfortably settling in like he didn't just get me out of bed to go back to sleep.

Before digging into these files, I head to the mini bar in the kitchen. There are several bottles of Bamma Bourbon from a local distillery in DC that Theo's been raving about. As I pour myself a stiff glass, I laugh remembering the argument that Theo and I had gotten into over a bottle of this stuff years ago. Theo, a DC native, tried to explain to me that "Bamma" refers to a messy person who isn't well dressed, whereas I'll always think of the word as referring to someone from Alabama.

"So, it's Alabama Bourbon?" I'd asked, knowing he would get heated about this.

"No man, it means the bourbon is messy," he responded, pouring another glass, and laughing at the hilarity of pouring a messy Bourbon, "neat".

"You're a clown man, pass me the Alabama "Bamma" Bourbon," I'd said, reaching out for more because it was admittedly dangerously delicious.

Pouring myself a stiff glass, I look forward to the burn as the alcohol makes its way down my throat.

As I walk back to the table to immerse himself in paperwork, Andy's door slowly cracks open, and she emerges from the dark room. She's wearing a baggy sweatsuit and her hair is wet with curls pouring over her shoulders like a golden-brown waterfall. I pause, bourbon in my hand, and take in her appearance. Even recovering from a gunshot wound, I want to drop this drink and run over and devour her.

Good lord, this woman makes me feel like a caveman.

"How are you feeling?" I ask, setting the glass of bourbon on the counter.

"Better, thanks," she responds, eyeing my drink.

I return to the mini bar and get a second glass, pouring some for Andy before raising the glass to her with a questioning tilt to my head. She nods, smiling, and biting her lip before taking the glass from me. She follows me back to the table and sits down next to me and the stacks of papers I've just sorted.

"So, what are we looking at here?" She asks, taking a sip of the bourbon before closing her eyes while she is swallowing, "Damn, this *is* really good,"

"Don't tell Theo that because the man will never shut up about this place. Your praise will just give him more fuel," I laugh, taking a sip of his drink.

"This doesn't taste like a 'Bamma' anything, but I appreciate the good ole' Merlin twang," she says, in her most authentic Maryland accent.

I laugh, remembering how I used to tease her about how she'd fall into her Maryland accent when we'd go to the Eastern Shore to visit her parents. Taking another sip of the bourbon, I look at her and let the silence linger between us for a moment.

"I miss it...all of it. I miss the way the sand felt between my toes while walking the beach at sunrise, the smell of seaweed and crabs, and how you couldn't walk into a restaurant without encountering at least a dash of seafood seasoning," she says, closing her eyes and taking a deep breath as she clutches the glass to her chest.

I don't respond immediately, afraid of saying the wrong thing that will make her feel worse and knowing there is nothing I can say that will take away the worry that she might not ever be able to go home. As if on cue, Boss lifts his tired body from the floor and saunters over to Andy's side to brush himself against her leg. This immediately makes her smile as she pets him with the hand that's not holding the glass.

Way to go my fur dude.

As soon as Boss gets his fill on rubs, or perhaps he realizes he's too tired to continue hanging out with us, he retreats to the floor next to the fireplace and flops to the ground with a loud thud. Andy giggles before shaking her head.

"I think your dog might be a person trapped in the body of a dog," she says.

"Of this...I'm certain," I reply, shooting Boss a glance before turning my attention back to the work in front of us.

Andy reaches over to the pile of maps and begins scanning them while I read through the reports in the folder Rove indicated as urgent.

Damn, she smells good too – like fresh rose petals.

"Looks like Farhad was able to identify the man who attacked you in your condo – his name was Armin Esfahani," I say, turning the pages of the report as my eyes scan the contents before looking across the table at Andy.

At the mention of another Esfahani brother, recognition flashes across Andy's face, causing me to drop the file and focus on her.

"The Esfahani brothers...just like Basir warned of," she says.

"Yeah, Farhad seems certain that Solaris hired them to grab you and they are motivated enough to just keep sending more of them," I say.

"Couldn't he have just come to avenge the brother I killed in Brazil? Him coming here doesn't prove that Solaris knows about me. It just proves that the Esfahani brothers are trying to grab me," she replies.

"Right, we know they are trying to grab you but we already know Solaris was tipped off that you were a host so the most logical conclusion is that they hired the Esfahani brothers," I say.

She takes another long swig of her drink before getting up from the table and walking over to the fireplace. She starts to pace, running one hand through her damp curls while the other holds a nearly empty glass of bourbon.

"Andy, talk to me...what are you thinking?" I ask, now up from the table and standing beside her by the fire.

"Cameron, you know they aren't going to stop coming for me, right?" She says, clutching her hand to her chest and continuing to pace.

Andy reaches a shaking hand inside her pocket and removes a small bottle of pills. She struggles for a few seconds to open it before popping a pill into her mouth and chasing it with the remaining bourbon. I have no idea what these pills are, but pills and bourbon are never a healthy combination. I slowly approach her, wrapping my arms around her and helping her over to the couch by the fire.

"Even though I knew it was unlikely, I kept hoping that my attacker in Brazil was really just there to kill Basir and that I was caught in the crossfire. But the two of them being connected...it just confirms my worst fears," she admits, draining the rest of her drink and placing it on the coffee table next to the couch.

It feels like her body is emitting a frost that even my body heat and the fire cannot calm.

She's quiet for a moment before continuing, "Cam, I don't think we have time to keep hoping that someone will give us the Intel we need to find this place. You just said yourself that they don't want to kill me. We have an obvious way to get them to come to us."

"No Andy. That's a horrible plan," I respond, knowing where she's headed with this.

"If we have moles in the agency, it's no secret this serum is inside me. They will come for me, and when they do, we can be ready. I can lead the team back to the center of this entire operation. We can keep playing whack and mole, trying to destroy the ones we know about, but at some point...we're going to need to go to the source to destroy the entire thing," Andy says, before pulling herself up from the couch and moving closer to the fire.

"Theo and I have the location of some of the sites that Basir handed us during your last debrief. They're not publicly listed as nuclear sites so I think he and I should go case these places before deciding to take extreme measures by sending you in as a double," I say, praying Theo and I can find a solution that proves more reasonable than sending Andy into a terrorist site.

Andy sighs loudly, making her frustration obvious, but she doesn't respond.

"Andy, I can't believe you're suggesting walking into a terrorist cell and offering yourself up to be harvested like a lab rat. We don't even know where this place is so how would we even get you out?" I run my hands through my hair and stand up, shaking my head violently in disagreement.

"Okay, I have some names to go over with Farhad and traces I can run to see if we can find another source. Can your team case some of these sites in the meantime to see if there's anything there?" Andy asks, intensely searching my face with her eyes.

"Alright, that sounds like a better plan. In the morning, we can talk to the team. Theo and I should be able to fly out tomorrow and we can all rally back here, after we've finished collecting the Intel we need, to plan our next move," I respond.

"Cameron, I'll give you this...but I know I don't have a lot of time. I can feel it – my body feels like a giant ticking time bomb. I'm stuck in this hell loop where one moment I feel okay, but I never know how long I'll have before I completely lose control," she exclaims, worry washing over her eyes.

I know this is driving her crazy because she's the type of woman who's always in control. I've always loved her ability to take charge and handle things, even when chaos is swirling around her. It's something that makes her amazing at her job and perhaps another reason Basir came running to her. Andy is one of the best-case officers I've ever seen, but as I've experienced myself - the agency isn't color blind and will likely never see past her color to recognize the truly amazing officer they have in their ranks.

"You're amazing Andy. I hope you know that. I know this must be hard for you and while I have no idea what it feels like to be you right now – I hope you know how much I want you to be alright. I'm on *your* side," I say, moving closer and reaching for her to try and pull her into an embrace.

She holds out her hand to stop me, causing me to retreat immediately.

"I just want to work right now. I'm alright, okay? I feel fine right now so let's get organized before the rest of the team is here so we can hit the ground running tomorrow morning. Where is the pile of maps?" She asks, as though she's immediately shut off the tiny valve of emotion that allowed her to reveal how she was feeling.

I shake my head and walk over to the table, pulling out the pile of maps. Andy grabs her glass of bourbon from the counter, walks over to the table and sits down before grabbing from the top of the pile. We silently pour through several maps, cross referencing them with the notes Andy took from the previous debrief.

"Cam, none of these maps are giving us exact locations. City maps really don't help if we don't know where to look," Andy says, in an exasperated tone.

"We've been to all the known nuclear plants in these places – Peru, Russia, Portugal..." I say, my voice trailing off as I fall into thought.

"Basir said he thinks there was only one site in Iran – located in Taybad and that's the one Solaris destroyed. There's an informant Basir told us about in Canada who we still need to debrief – but first I'd like to review more of these names and get some additional sources. Russia is also not the type of place we want to go poking around without a more precise location," Andy explains.

"Yeah, that makes sense. Russia is not a place I want to spend extra time in and I'm sure Theo feels the same way. Last time I was there, the tires on my rental car were slashed five times in about 24 hours," I complain, shaking my head and cringing because the memory of that trip still disturbs me.

We both fall silent for several more minutes before Andy pulls out one of the maps, stands up, and jogs over to the whiteboard. She uses one of the magnets to hang up the map and then draws a picture of what looks like a church, drawing tunnels underneath.

"What is that?" I ask, moving to stand behind her.

"This...is the Basilica and Convent of San Francisco," she responds while she continues to furiously draw as though from memory, "and these...are the catacombs underneath."

"Why exactly are you drawing them on the whiteboard," I ask, confused, and legitimately impressed that Andy has somehow memorized the tunneled maze of Catacombs in Lima, Peru.

"I studied Latin American history in high school, and I spent a summer digging bones out of some of the walls in these Catacombs as part of an archeological program. There are places under that city that aren't open to the public and several locations that are still being excavated. It's not something I know for sure – but Cam, I think it's worth casing out," she says.

"We don't have any better leads, so I'm up for checking it out. Can you find a detailed map of what is open to the public and then mark some spots that wouldn't be part of a public tour? I'll text Theo and have him help me schedule a flight," I respond, a little worried that we are planning a mission around what seems a bit like a hunch.

"Cam, I can see the skeptical look you're giving me right now and I can't explain this more than just...I feel like there's something there. I looked at the map and it felt like for a moment I was transported back to those tunnels. It's weird...I know it's weird. But trust me...there's something there," she says, a look of conviction and intensity in her eyes.

I'm still not entirely convinced that going to Lima and crawling through the catacombs under the city won't be a wild goose chase, but I'm thankful there's a direction to run in where we might find something useful. Andy's asking me to trust her and since I trust and respect her, Theo and I will be flying to Lima and check it out. And based on the looks Rove's been giving me every time he sees me hovering over Andy, I probably also need to get out of town to clear my head a bit. Even though I want to save Andy, I also know Rove is watching and has already questioned my ability to keep my head in the game.

Chapter 20
Memorial

"Cameron"

It's 2am and I'm pouring through the notes from Andy's last debrief with Basir. Boss whines loudly, brushing his head against my leg before flashing me his classic disgruntled dog side eye.

"I know buddy, I'll be done soon. You do realize that *you* can go to bed without me," I say, patting him on the head and attempting to give him the sternest look I can muster so that he doesn't think his side eye is an effective form of influence.

Boss grunts and collapses the weight of his entire body onto my leg with such melodrama that I think he's possibly missed his calling as a show dog.

Moments later, Rove enters the room. I couldn't sleep earlier but waited for Andy to fall asleep before returning to keep reading. I don't want her to think I'm second guessing the plan we've made, but I just want to be prepared. The sound of papers loudly turning and my pen scratching against the pad holds an urgency, as I desperately work to find connections in the materials that we might've missed. I have a bad feeling about this whole thing and like there's something obvious that will jump off one of these papers and hit me between the eyes.

Andy offering herself as a double is a terrible option, but if I cannot find something better, she is going to insist on doing it anyway.

Without looking up from the documents, I can sense Rove hovering above me. He's silently watching me work for a few moments before joining me at the table. As soon as Rove sits, Boss saunters over to him as though he knows Rove is about to ask me to do what Boss has tried to get me to do for the last couple of hours – go to bed.

"Cam, put down the pen," Rove says, with quiet authority.

I pause, pen still in hand, before looking up at him.

"Are you about to tell me to stop working when we're running out of time and good options?" I ask, annoyance bubbling at the tip of my tongue.

"When's the last time you slept?" Rove asks, raising one of his eyebrows.

Boss whines and dog babbles like a little traitor.

"Shh, Boss...go to bed," I say, shooting him a warning look.

Does the hour I passed out on the chair by the fire count?

"Uh...I've slept," I respond, putting the pen I'd still been holding down on the table.

"Aren't you and Theo flying to Lima tomorrow night?" Rove asks, with one eyebrow raised.

"Yeah, and when we get back, I'm headed to Vancouver with Andy to debrief that defector," I say, looking back down at the papers.

"I have reservations about your ability to accompany her on this debrief," Rove says, a stern look washing over his face.

"Well, she can't go alone," I respond.

"Why can't she? Dr. Raj gave her meds to manage her temperature changes and she's a fully capable officer," he says, challenging me.

I drop my pen and look up at him, folding my arms across my chest. I know he's right – she *is* capable. But that doesn't stop me from wanting to go with her.

"I'm going to send someone with Andy to the debrief in Canada, and whether that's you or not will depend on whether you're willing to adhere to my condition," Rove says.

"And what's the condition," I respond, eager to get this over with so that I can get on with my work.

Boss's ear perks up as though he wants to know as well. I laugh at the fact that the ear Boss always seems to lift, when he wants to be all up in my business, is the one that another dog took a giant bite out of during a fight. Perhaps the chewed-on ear is easier for him to lift since it's only half an ear at this point.

"I set up an appointment for you to see Dr. Kingsley tomorrow morning. Whatever is going on with you as it relates to Andy – or your father – needs to be addressed before you continue with this operation," he says, leaving me feeling as though he's dropped a bomb on me.

What does my dad have to do with this?

"My father?" I ask.

"I know you and Andy have history, and I was willing to overlook that and let it slide initially because you're one of the best guys I have on the team. But if you can't figure out how to operate as a part of the team and stop hovering, you're going to fuck up this entire operation," he responds.

"What does that have to do with my dad?" I ask, purposely avoiding mention of Andy.

"I've long believed that you haven't handled the trauma related to your father's death and I can't tell whether this behavior is because of that – Andy – or both, but I need you to deal with it," he responds, eyebrow furrowing in frustration.

"I've gone to the therapist you told me to see. There's nothing left to do there," I complain, hoping he will drop this.

"Yeah, but didn't Dr. Kingsley tell you the same thing I told you? Have you done it?" Rove asks, knowing that I still haven't gone to my father's memorial bench.

"No, I haven't," I admit, glancing over at Boss who is now covering one of his eyes with his paw as though to indicate that this is like watching a train wreck.

"Okay then, that's my condition – go already," Rove says, clearly not fully understanding the gravity of his request.

Ugh, anything but that...

As though he understands the request, Boss raises an eyebrow and glances at me as though he's about to ask me if *we are* going to comply. I should respond, but I can't seem to find the words as my heart rate increases and my palms start to sweat. On cue, Boss gets up from where he's been sitting and walks over to me. With his human-like eyes, he searches my face and taps my hand with his paw – one of the ways he lets me know I need to rub him.

Way to distract me by centering your need for belly rubs dude...

Several more moments of silence pass between Rove and I before I respond, "fine, I'll go tomorrow. Theo and I fly to Lima tomorrow to check out that possible site. I'll go before we get on the plane, alright?"

Boss sighs, rolls onto his back, and appears to smile as I comply and rub his stomach.

Rove nods, grabs the papers out of my hand, and points to my room before responding, "I trust you won't lie about going, but right now you are going to bed and letting this case rest for the night."

Boss jumps up and starts walking toward my room and I follow, feeling defeated and dreading tomorrow. After what feels like only a few minutes after my head hits the pillow, my eyes jolt open as the sun peeks through the Wardman window shades. It's six o'clock in the morning. Acceptable enough timing to leave without Rove questioning me, while still early enough that I might luck out and get to be alone there.

I jump out of the bed and get dressed to head to the memorial. Boss opens an eye as I walk toward the door, as if pondering whether he wants to insist on accompanying me or whether he'd rather continue sleeping. There are clear reasons this dog washed out of DHS K-9 school. Boss has always loved sleep more than just about anything on this planet.

"Come on man, you sleep too much," I say, nudging him in the side with the tip of my foot.

He opens one of his eyes, clearly not impressed by my attempt to rouse him out of bed. I wait by the door, leash in my hands, and tap my foot impatiently.

"Okay fine...I'd like you to come with me...and I think I might need you there, little dude," I say, sighing with frustration that this dog is making me beg him to get out of bed to come join me.

At my admission of needing him, Boss jumps out of his dog bed in a swift move that makes my head whip around in surprise.

"Boss, you little faker," I laugh, putting him on the leash and walking him out the door.

Driving through the near empty streets of DC into Virginia brings me back to what it felt like the day after my father died when the airport was closed, and people were too afraid to walk the streets. People are probably still sleeping off last night's party-induced hangover, or perhaps leisurely drinking their morning coffee from the window seat of their Washington row homes. All things I'd rather be doing right now than driving across the river to visit my dead father's memorial.

After parking in the empty lot at the Pentagon, I take a timid step out of my car. Boss hops out and I don't bother to leash him since we're the only ones out here.

There's still time to turn around – can I just say I was here?

"What do you think Boss, should we just bounce and go get you a pup cup?" I ask, hoping he will be my co-conspirator at this moment and endorse my plan to just leave.

Boss whines and heads for the sign in front of us.

"Damn, I thought we were friends dude," I say under my breath as I follow Boss and his determined stride.

The air feels harsh this morning and I take a rigid and cautious breath. The fog is so thick around this massive sea of creepy benches. Facing different directions, apparently to depict the direction of each body that was found. This is a crime scene that they're trying to pass off as something peaceful. The fog dances across the concrete benches and I close my eyes and ball up my fists beside me. The viscosity of the air reminds me of the billowing smoke that filled my lungs as I ran through the rubble that day...looking for my dad.

When I open my eyes, feeling Boss nudge my leg, I instinctively look at my hands. I know it's not September 11th and it's been almost a decade since that horrible day, but why am

I looking at my hands and expecting to see them covered in blood like they were that day. Looking out at all the benches, I can still see the bodies and remember how my hands looked after hours of pouring over someone else's loved ones...only to come up empty. I returned to this site every day for the nine and a half weeks it took to clear the rubble, praying I'd find his body so that my mother would have something to bury.

I can still smell that horrible stench that invaded my nostrils, a mix of burning and decaying bodies mixed with fuel. Fighting the urge to vomit whatever is left in my stomach from dinner last night, I raise my head to read the inscription on this sign.

We claim this ground in remembrance of the events of September 11, 2001.

To honor the 184 people whose lives were lost, their families, and all who sacrifice that we may live in freedom.

We will never forget.

I stand in front of that inscription for several minutes, my feet feeling stuck to the ground. This memorial has been finished for almost a year, and I never planned to *actually* come see it. But Rove is right – both he *and* my therapist told me I should come. My mom has also tried to get me to come with her or my brother several times, like this place is some key to the grief process.

I'll never understand why so many think it's alright to tell someone how to grieve. After my dad died, it felt like the world was reeling and there didn't seem to be space or time for my own sadness.

Back then, I heard it all –

Cameron, you should have a good cry. Or...

You should be so proud because your dad died with such honor. Or...

Why are you so angry – you need to get over it, move on, don't blame yourself...

I just wanted what I want now – for people to just let me be and leave me alone to do this my way.

"I think you need to address how this event made you feel, how it's shaped your life choices, and perhaps how it's impacting your relationships," Dr. Kingsley said during our last session.

When we were still together, Andy told me the day my father died I changed. I was angry and distant. There *was* a Cameron before and there's another version of me now. Andy hated that I wouldn't talk about what happened and we fought about it every time she brought it up. I shut her out when I needed her the most.

And I wasn't strong enough to admit that to myself...let alone anyone else.

I paused, letting the realization of how my actions that must have felt to her wash over me. Throwing myself into work was a welcome distraction – it's still a welcome distraction.

But hasn't Andy also thrown herself into the service of her country? She's the one who keeps volunteering to hand herself over to a pack of terrorists...

"This isn't about *Andy*, this is about *you*," Dr. Kingsley *and* Rove keep telling me, as though they've agreed on a party line as part of some therapist-mentor conspiracy plot to keep me in line.

I didn't used to be so cynical.

So here I am – standing in front of this black, stone memorial – trying to will myself to move and find the bench with my father's name engraved into the stone. They found the remains of the hijackers who died that day, but not my dad's...his were never found.

Burned beyond recognition...

I kick the stones on the ground, sending a plume of dust into the air which sends me into a fit of sneezes.

Damn allergies...thanks for those, dad.

Almost as if on cue, Boss also starts sneezing. Perhaps he's trying to make sure I don't forget he's here. I pat his head, silently thanking him for being here with me.

I sigh, closing my eyes briefly to collect myself. I can't walk to my dad's memorial and lose my cool. He'd hate that.

"Don't be a pansy, son. Real men don't cry," he always told me.

When he died, I didn't cry – not once. Looking back on that time, crying probably would've been healthier than what I did.

Like a damn fool...

Searching through a sea of benches, looking for his name, feels so absurd. He was such a large man, in both size and personality. And now, instead of even getting a proper gravestone above his dead body – he gets a bench outside the scene of the crime. I appreciate what they're trying to do here, the small pools of water under the benches providing a soothing soundtrack for mourning. But as I spot my dad's name, the only thing I can hear is the sound of my own heart thudding loudly inside my head.

"What would you say to him if you could talk to him one last time...or if he were here right now?" Dr. Kingsley asked me during our last session a few weeks before I deployed to the sandbox to wait for Basir.

Since he's dead, I have no idea if he can hear me. But since this is the last place that he was whole – perhaps some part of him is still here.

"Dad?" I whisper, self-consciously looking around to make sure nobody can hear me while I talk to my dead father.

"I did what you wanted. I'm serving my country. But I'm doing it in *my* way...not in the military like you wanted. I'm sorry about that," I say, looking at my feet.

"Did you know how much I loved you? Did you know how much I wanted you to just love me back?" I lift my hand to my face, begrudgingly wiping away an errant tear.

I loved my dad so much, but sitting here I realize how incredibly angry I am. I'm angry I couldn't bury him, can't avenge his death, and I'm angry I can't protect the people I love most. My mom still sets a place for my dad at the dinner table, as though she expects him to just walk about through the door after almost a decade. Gabe resents me for signing up to serve immediately – blaming me for saddling him here to take care of our mom alone.

Gabe has moved on with his life, he's married now and I'm an uncle to a two-year-old little boy that I haven't even met yet. I haven't been around because I'm too busy chasing a ghost and chasing just the right amount of power and success to make my dead father proud of me. My chest is heaving, making me feel as though I need to urgently catch my breath. Now, instead of my eyes just tearing, I'm sobbing, and the tears are running indiscriminately and uncontrollably down my face.

No, no...you cannot have an anxiety attack at dad's memorial site...he'd hate that...

I take several deep breaths, trying to remember the exercises Dr. Kingsley taught me to do when I feel anxious. Instinctively, I reach for Boss who immediately moves right up next to me and places his head against my leg in his version of a hug.

It's okay, you can do this.

I collapse onto my knees, burying my head between my legs.

Breathe Cameron...breathe...

What's one thing I can smell – dust.

One thing I can feel – rocks.

One thing I can hear – running water.

Something I can hear – Boss panting and whining in my ear.

My eyes shoot open, and I smile down at Boss, who's clearly doing his best version of a support dog in this moment though also visibly distraught and shifting around helplessly.

Sitting here, having an emotional breakdown, I realize that I cannot fill my father's shadow. Avenging his murder doesn't even seem possible. But this agency – this isn't what I signed up for. It's not the good guy I thought it was...or perhaps it once was. I love my country and while I cannot bring my father back, he'd want me to fight to bring honor back to the country he fought so hard to protect. And I'm going to bring down Solaris to not only save my country but also save the woman I love. And I'll do it as the Cameron I can be proud of – *my* version of a man.

Before getting up from the bench, I place my hand flat against the stone and close my eyes trying to feel him. I never want to come back to this place so as I stand up, I glance back at his bench one last time.

"Bye dad," I whisper to myself, speed walking back to my car with my head focused on the ground to avoid eye contact with the few people who've arrived since I've been here.

Hushed voices dance around us and the constant jingle of Boss's collar forms a beat in my head that carries me back to the car.

As I peel out of the parking lot, I drive toward my brother Gabe's house to meet my nephew.

Chapter 21
The Peruvian Catacombs

"Cameron"

After a nine-hour flight from Reagan National Airport in Washington, DC to Jorge Chavez International Airport in Lima, Peru, Theo, and I are heading to a hotel in the historic district to drop our bags, grab a bite to eat, and regroup. My eyes feel like someone dumped sand in them, which is usual after a red eye because I can't sleep on planes. The Government always insists we fly economy, completely disregarding that my big ass body doesn't fit in plane seats. Theo, on the other hand, can sleep anywhere. He's just as tall as I am, well over six feet, but I've seen the man fall completely asleep while standing up before, so he always bounces off the plane as though we haven't just been packed in like sardines overnight.

Lima is crowded and even though it's a Tuesday, it seems like there's a party in the streets downtown. Between the tourists and the locals darting out in front of traffic, and our driver swerving like a maniac to avoid accidents, my anxiety is through the roof. I'm kicking myself for not trying to push harder to get Boss approved as a support dog so that he could come with us.

He'll make me pay for that when we return.

I've never verbally admitted to him how much I need him, but I think he knows that I didn't just save him – he also saved me. Perhaps he picked me because he wasn't adjusting well to life as a bomb sniffing dog, and I haven't been adjusting well to life since losing my dad. Whatever it was, the fact that my brown knuckles are turning nearly white as I clutch the seat of this taxi is proof that I could really use my DHS reject of a support dog.

"You alright, man?" Theo asks, cracking open the window and glancing toward me.

And apparently Theo also sees right through my attempts to play this cool.

"Yeah, just tired and want to get to the damned hotel," I respond, wiping sweat from my forehead and shifting in my seat.

Hiding the fact that I'm anxious with an air of irritation is a skill I've worked hard to perfect. A few minutes later we roll up to a hotel in central Lima that's just a few blocks away from the Basilica and Convent of San Francisco. The Basilica sits right on top of the catacombs that Theo and I booked an official tour later this afternoon. And in the next few hours, we need to case the outside of the place and plan how we'll inconspicuously leave the official tour to look through the tunnels Andy highlighted on my map.

The two of us hop out of the taxi before Theo turns back to the driver, addressing him with impeccable Spanish that makes me raise an eyebrow. Theo shrugs before flashing a giant smile and throwing his duffle bag over his shoulder. Luckily, we only plan to be here one night so we didn't need to pack much.

"I'm going to go throw the bag in my room, take a quick nap, and then I'll meet you back down at the bar in an hour. We can grab some food before heading across to get a look," I say, securing my backpack on my bag and heading to the front desk to grab my room key.

"Yep, sure thing dude," Theo responds, following close behind to grab his key.

As soon as I enter the tiny hotel room, I drop my bag and fall into the tiny single bed. It's so small that my legs dangle off the end, but I don't care because at least I'm horizontal. After what seems like moments later, my phone starts incessantly ringing.

"What?" I answer, feeling momentarily confused and forgetting where I am.

"Dude, get your ass down here. You've been asleep for two hours and we only have about an hour to eat and plan before catching that tour," Theo's voice booms from the phone.

Fuck – was I really sleeping that long?

I roll off the bed, my body loudly thudding on the creaky wooden floors. After splashing water on my face, I throw my rugged computer into my backpack and head downstairs to meet Theo. Once I arrive at the restaurant bar, I see Theo chatting with the female bartender who has a giant smile on her face. Theo never seems to consider that we aren't supposed to be drawing attention to ourselves on these missions. Sitting on the stool next to him, I nudge him in the shoulder before politely smiling at the bartender and asking her to see a menu.

"Bro, I get that it's hard for you to resist getting into conversation with the ladies, but we don't actually want anyone here to *remember* we were here," I say, as soon as the bartender walks away to grab the menus.

"Well, if you hadn't fallen asleep for two hours, perhaps I wouldn't have had an opportunity to be chatty. It would be even stranger if I sat down here and refused to speak to someone who tried to speak to me," Theo retorts.

"Whatever man, did you eat?" I ask, my stomach reminding me that if I don't feed it this mission will be negatively impacted.

"Nope, I was waiting on you...like a true gentleman," Theo responds, batting his eyes mockingly before laughing.

We take menus from the bartender and both order plates of Pollo a la Brasa. Theo tells me that we also try the Pisco Sour, which the bartender insists is *the* drink to taste before leaving the city. Before our food arrives, we move to a table in the back of the restaurant so that we can review city maps and prepare for the mission. While I was sleeping, Theo acquired some local, city maps of our immediate vicinity that have slight variations from the maps we'd seen prior to travel.

"See this map? It's showing the basilica footprint as larger than what we thought and there's a door on one side that doesn't appear open to the public," he says, pointing to the tourist map.

I look between the two maps, and look up at Theo before saying, "well, hot damned man...looks like a good place to start casing."

Theo grins widely and leans back into his chair, casually waiting on our food and drinks. When our drinks arrive, I must admit that I'm thankful we'd ordered something with alcohol. And when the silky sweet, tart drink slides down my throat, I close my eyes and audibly sigh.

"Damn man, that's good? You sound like you just had an organism," Theo laughs before picking up his own drink and taking a swig.

"Man, shut up! Don't act like you even know what a good one feels like," I tease, punching him in the shoulder before taking another delicious sip.

"Dude, you know I'm a whiskey and beer guy, but this drink might even make me a convert," Theo says, his eyes widening as he inspects the foam on top.

When our food arrives, we both sit in silence and inhale the food like we're two men who haven't eaten for days. Honestly, that's how I feel as I consider that I cannot even remember the last time I ate more than a snack from the ops center stash. Shoving the last bite of this chicken in my mouth, I roll up a few of the maps and stick them in the pocket of my cargo pants. Theo drops enough cash to pay for the meal, leaving a little extra for the waitress he's been flirting with before sending a wink in her direction. Rolling my eyes, I grab him by the shirt and nudge him toward the door.

Theo and I make several laps around the Basilica, trying to act like we were just there on a tour, while scoping all the possible entrances and exits. Our official tour starts in just a few minutes, but the plan is to try and ditch the tour without getting noticed. As we walk past the door Theo spotted on the local map, I approach it as though I don't know it's not a main door and try to open it. Of course, it's locked – but to my surprise the door handle is really hot. Sure, it's hell hot out here, but this doorknob doesn't feel like anything else I've touched today. It's so hot I jerk my hand back from it and shoot Theo a cautious look.

"We gotta get in there, man and see what's making that doorknob so damned hot," I say to Theo under my breath.

Theo nods and scanned the area before pointing toward the small crowd gathering at the entrance of the catacombs for the tour. There's an extremely loud, older couple whom I immediately peg as the Americans and a few others who are looking at the Americans as though they're wondering whether there's another tour they can take.

Perfect – they are just annoying enough to be the distraction we need to duck out.

I smile at the couple, who are now arguing with each other over which one of them said "hola" with a more authentic local accent.

Theo snickers under his breath before fake sneezing and saying, "neither".

Several others standing close by laugh while the American couple looks confused as though they don't realize how loud and obnoxious they've just been. A few awkward moments later, a tiny, dark brown man appears from the entrance way and bounces toward us.

"Hola, my name is Albert, and I am your guide today. Follow me while we go into the grave tunnels," he says, in heavily accented English with a smile so wide that it seems to stretch across his entire face.

We all follow Albert as he continues talking about the history of the building and tells us to watch our heads as we duck down to enter the dark crypt. The moldy, damp smell hits me in the face as I try to navigate my large frame through the small tunnel. Normally, I'd be deeply interested in what Albert is saying as he points to the thousands of human skulls that line the walls of this place, but I'm not here for a history tour. I'm here hoping that within these walls there's a clue that can lead us to an antidote and some answers.

Theo is just in front of me, and I see him trail his hands along parts of the wall as his eyes dart in all directions. We're both trailing behind the larger group, but Albert doesn't seem to notice because the loud American couple continues peppering him with questions. Just as I go to duck through another entrance way, Theo stops dead in his tracks almost causing me to run into him. He swivels around toward me and points to a small portal to the left of the entrance. The two of us pause, watching the rest of the group continue to move ahead.

Instead of continuing to the right, we start left and walk down a noticeably darker corridor. I pull a small flashlight from my pocket and shine it around us as we slowly walk, trying not to make too much noise with our steps. The silence is only cut with the intermittent dripping of water nearby. After what seems like several minutes, the two of us come to a clearing in a dimly lit room full of large steel containers.

"What the hell is this place?" Theo asks, low enough for just me.

"No idea, but it certainly doesn't look like a place of worship," I respond.

"Whatever this place is...or was...it doesn't look functional anymore," Theo says, taking several small vials out of his pocket and collecting samples from the dirt floor and the water streaming down the walls.

I walk up to one of the steel containers and reach to open it. The door swings open and reveals an empty shell. Seconds later, an alarm sounds followed by a plume of thick smoke that billows from all directions.

"Shit, we have to get out of here quickly before whomever is taking care of this place comes back to find us," I hiss while continuing to scan the room.

"Grab everything you can on the way out," Theo replies, stuffing his backpack full of papers from a nearby desk.

I pick up what look like empty syringes from the floor and stuff them in my bag and run toward the door. When I grab the knob, it's as hot as it was on the outside which causes me to grab ahold of the bottom of my shirt to help me get a good grip without burning myself. Footsteps clamber in the distance, but Theo and I escape through the door before anyone sees us. Both of us pull up our hoodies and throw on our sunglasses before heading out. A nearby restroom allows us to change up our clothes enough to avoid immediate identification as we walk back to the hotel.

That two-hour nap in the hotel is likely all for me today because we can't risk staying here the night after setting off that alarm. We both know it's only a matter of time before the local police have this entire area closed off and search for who was responsible for the break-in. Though I guess I should feel panicked, the fact that we found something gives me a sense of relief that maybe we are a step closer to figuring out this nightmare.

In what seems like a blink of my eye, Theo and I are headed to the closest airstrip for extraction. There are no words that can accurately describe the depth of my exhaustion and I can feel my eyelids closing as the cab lurches through the streets of Lima.

"Don't worry bro, you can sleep on the plane," Theo laughs, sure as shit knowing that I don't have his plane sleeping swagger.

To even my own surprise, just moments after the plane leaves the tarmac, I fall asleep.

Chapter 22
Steamy Operations

If food were a love language, it would be mine. As I walk into The Ops center, the smell of vanilla infused Grand Marnier and pastry crust fills my senses, causing me to audibly moan. The smell arrests me in the doorway, as though I've been transported back to another time – a time when Cameron and I were happily together, and him baking for me was foreplay. But things are more complicated now. We aren't college Cam and Andy anymore - when our biggest concerns were which professor we'd have, how we'd done on a test, or how we'd sneak time together in the halls of the CIA headquarters as interns. We aren't together like that anymore and I'm not sure we ever will be.

But sweet baby Jesus – I want whatever he's making.

"When did you get back? Are you baking?" I ask, feeling the full awkwardness of asking such an obvious question.

"We got back a few hours ago," he responds, looking over his shoulder and flashing a toothy smile that makes that one dimple on his cheek pop.

"You slept?" I ask, knowing that Cameron has never been the type of person who sleeps well on a plane.

"Yeah, surprisingly...I did," he replies, looking up only briefly from the art he's making on the counter.

Boss, who looks like he's been sleeping on his dog bed for several hours, opens one eye before promptly rolling onto his back for a stomach rub. I walk over and pet his stomach before following the delicious smell to the kitchen.

I sit across the counter from Cameron on a stool, intent to watch him while he works. His shoulders dance behind a shirt that's grabbing his muscular frame as he vigorously whisks a bowl of eggs.

Cameron grew up shadowing his grandmother, the matriarch of their house, as she worked miracles in their Louisiana kitchen. Despite his father's attempts to convince him that cooking was "a woman's job," Cameron has maintained his love for cooking.

I'm thankful that Cameron's cooking isn't something his father could take. He always told me that being in the kitchen made him feel as though his grandmother was still here. A few times when I snuck into the kitchen while he was cooking, I'd catch him speaking aloud to her as though they were having a riveting conversation.

In addition to making the best seafood gumbo I've had in my life, my friends and I have a running joke that Cameron's tarts are "panty dropping" tarts – as in, so good they make you want to drop your panties for the chef. And tonight, he's making the tarts.

I know that Cameron's just returned from Lima, and while our plan is to reconvene in the morning with the larger group, it's hard not to grill him on what he found. Forgetting this for the night, though, and just hanging out eating tarts sounds like a glorious alternative. Cameron knows that I've just spent the last few days bouncing between research and more debriefs with Basir. I know he wants to know how it went, but I appreciate that he's allowing me to tell him at my own pace.

Bonus points on the strawberry tarts for the amenities to get me talking.

"You're baking amenities? Am I getting debriefed tonight?" I ask, teasingly.

Cameron shrugs, "can't I just want to do something nice for you without needing an ulterior motive?"

I raise an eyebrow and smile before responding, "sure, if that's what this is then I'll accept the tart."

"I have a lot to tell you, and I know you have stuff – but all my stuff can wait until tomorrow. Tonight, let's just hang out and pretend we don't have the threat of a nuclear war hanging over our heads?" He asks, flashing a dimpled smile that makes me melt a little inside.

A few moments of silence pass between us, Cameron chopping strawberries as I inhale the sweet scent. I sit on one of the stools on the counter across from him, leaning my elbows against the marble countertops.

"Dr. Raj asked Basir some follow up questions about the serum, trying to piece together the larger picture on how it works and how to counteract its effect on me. Basir and I reviewed all the names he remembered from his time working in the lab. I got some hits that I'll go over with you in the morning," I explain, still a bit skeptical as to whether he wants to talk business or if this is something else.

"That sounds perfect – now forget about that stuff. We're both here and I have strawberry tarts on the way," he says, with that rogue dimple popping out again.

I nod, thankful for what I hope can feel like a break and praying that my body gives me a reprieve from the chaos for an evening. Preemptively, I reach into my purse and grab the pills Dr. Raj gave me and pop one into my mouth.

"You want to taste the custard?" Cameron asks, knowing there's no way I'd turn him down.

"Umm, of *course*," I respond, leaning forward as he lifts a tiny spoon full of custard to my lips.

My eyes instinctively close as I slowly lick the fluffy, creamy, yellow cream to taste. Just as I open my eyes, Cameron moves around the counter to stand next to me before taking me into his arms. He leans down and runs his tongue over my lips, before pulling me into a deep kiss. He tastes like vanilla bean, and I cannot resist the urge to keep his mouth on mine.

"Do you like it?" he whispers, pulling back to look at me.

"It's delicious," I respond, reaching my hand to the back of his head to pull him back to me.

Reflexively, I start running my hands through his curls – something I always loved doing that I know drives him wild. His body stiffens a little and he moans into my mouth. A clanging noise startles us both – he's dropped the spoon that he was holding onto the floor. I rise on my toes to get closer to him and he cups his hands under my behind, hoisting me onto the smooth countertop. As though I'm part of the dish, he sprinkles kisses all over my neck and shoulders before sucking my earlobe into his mouth.

He takes his arm and moves the custard and the bowl of strawberries to the side before laying me across the countertop.

I'm glad he saved the strawberries...Damn, this feels so good...I hope I don't regret this tomorrow.

Snapping me out of my head, he joins me on the counter, layering his body on top of mine. We both vigorously and desperately remove each other's clothes. Our bodies are like the mouths of a river, one bigger than the other...flowing together but each fighting for dominance.

"Are you alright? Is this, okay?" he asks, pulling away and searching my face.

"Are we really doing this?" I ask, more to myself than to him.

"Oh...oh gosh...do you not want...," his voice trails off.

"Yeah, yes, I'm okay. I want this too. But this doesn't mean…I mean…this is just…" I start to say before he places two fingers on my lips.

I'll be lying to myself if I don't admit that I'm falling for Cameron again, but I'm not ready to admit this out loud and to him. I just need more time and it can't be more than sex right now.

"I know, it's okay," he says, saving me from having to explain that I want sex and don't know if I want anything else from him right now.

"This can just be…whatever…I mean, we can just be two people who want to enjoy each other right?" He asks, that dimple poking out of his cheek seductively again.

Cameron reaches over to the bowl of custard, spreading some across the top of one of my nipples, before pulling it into his mouth. An involuntary yelp of pleasure escapes from me as I dig my fingers into his back. The creamy decadence rolls onto my skin like butter, and he continues to suck, lick, and bite as I soar close to the brink of orgasm. Writhing on the counter beneath him, I can feel the bulge in his boxers expanding and pressing against my thigh.

"I want *this*," I say, using one of my hands to tug at his last layer of clothes before grabbing ahold of him with the other.

He places his forehead against mine, our lips so close that I can feel the steam coming from his mouth and smell the remaining vanilla liquor he used for the custard. Our bodies intertwine and our hearts beat in a rhythmic symphony, alongside the sounds of the kitchen – the knocking of the dishwasher, the humming of the refrigerator, and the fan of the stove. And when Cameron enters me, we drink each other in – like two people who've been without water, desperately trying to take the drink that will allow them to survive.

Chapter 23
Back to Business

"Cameron"

Waking up alone in an empty bed isn't what I expected after the mind-blowing sex Andy and I had on the kitchen counter last night. I know she insisted that she wasn't ready for anything more than sex right now, and I understand why. I'd be lying, though, if I didn't admit to myself that it hurt when she rejected me and went back to her own room.

What's wrong with you man? Shouldn't every dude want sex without strings?

The doors of the ops center open loudly, and I hear several voices filter into the common room. Groaning to myself as I pull my exhausted body out of this bed, I put on a pair of pants and a t-shirt to join the rest of the group. The smell of fresh brewed coffee hits me in the face as I open the door to my room, and I immediately spot Theo at the espresso machine. He's shaking the bag of fancy espresso beans he insisted we buy at some obscure café in Lima before returning.

"That cup better be for me man...for putting up with your coffee bean hunt in Lima when we had business to handle," I say smiling, before placing a coffee mug in front of him.

Theo laughed, "make your own damn coffee dude. I snagged those beans while you got your beauty rest in the hotel."

"Back to business folks, Theo and Cam – what do you have for us," Rove says, flopping down at the table and thumbing through some of the documents we recovered from the basilica.

Theo jogs over to the table and wheels over the rolling whiteboard. He begins to scribble what looks like a poor attempt to draw the basilica for the group.

"Okay, so there we were..." Theo begins, dramatically enough to cause my eyes to roll a little.

Andy laughs, causing some of her coffee to spill out of her lips, which immediately makes me less irritated about Theo's morning shenanigans. Rove looks up from the papers and gives Theo a stern look before prompting him to continue.

"Well, while y'all were getting your sleep on, I was cross referencing some of the information we pulled from the paperwork with the names that Raj and Andy obtained from the debriefs they conducted while we were in Lima," he continues, now jotting down a few names onto the board.

Farhad, who's just spent several moments picking a donut from the box on the counter, joins us at the table with his open laptop. After placing his donut on a napkin next to him, he begins typing a string of code into the command line on his computer.

"I ran a search on the phone numbers you found and tried to see if there were any matches with the names my dad gave us that could lead us to some new leads. There were two hits that I think are interesting here," he says, before taking a bite out of the donut.

Farhad's face twists in a look of disgust before turning to the rest of us and saying, "that is *not* donut. What is that? You said it was donut but that was an assault on my tongue."

Andy laughs, before placing her hand on his shoulder and saying, "oh honey, welcome to America – *that* is an American donut."

Farhad takes a sip of water and shakes his head, as though he is trying to erase the memory of the donut, before continuing, "ick, okay whatever you say. Okay, so...I continue...two hits. One of them, Peruvian scientist Diego Alvarez. His phone popped up here in DC just three days ago and I was able to find him on a list for the Argentinian Diplomatic Reception that is supposed to take place tomorrow."

"Okay, good – we'll get a team to the reception. Andy and Cam?" Rove asks, in a way that doesn't really feel like a question and instead feels more than we're being voluntold.

Andy nods before turning back to Farhad and asks, "okay, what was the other hit?"

Farhad continues, "My father said that Nikolai Popov, a nuclear scientist from Russia, would know where the headquarters is and how to get there. But here's the thing, we know he went to Vancouver, but we don't know his exact location. In the trace I ran, I found several calls between Alvarez and Popov, but I lost the trail on Popov. So, I think, we find Alvarez – we find Popov."

Theo interjects, "and we get a two for one if Alvarez can give us more information on that site we found in Lima."

"And while Andy and Cam are at the party, I'll take the samples you grabbed from that abandoned lab in Lima and run some tests," Raj says, pulling one of the samples from Theo's backpack and holding one of the vials up to the light.

"Cam – Andy, I'm going to mobilize a team to run some counter surveillance for you tomorrow night and we will also be standing by to grab our guy if you are successful in spotting him for us," Theo adds.

"If he thinks he's being cornered, he could spook, so be careful and a light disguise probably wouldn't be a bad idea – especially for you Andy," Rove says, looking over at Andy whose giant mug of coffee is lifted to her face and all we can see is the cascade of brown curls spilling around her face as she finishes the rest of her coffee.

She carefully places the mug on the table, and the entire room watches.

"Stop it guys, I'm not going to break," she snaps at us before shoving her hands into the pockets of her oversized sweatpants.

We all awkwardly look away from her as though on cue, and out of the corner of my eye I see her face drop as she quickly turns away to hide her expression.

"So, when we find this Popov guy, what's the plan Rove? We just casually walk in and ask for a vial of the antidote?" I ask.

"Look, *if* we find Popov *and* he's willing to talk to us *and* he actually knows where this place is, that would be one of the best-case scenarios," Rove responds.

"But you know that I'm the only one here who can get inside that place without breaking in right? And if we go in by force, what happens if a fire fight breaks out and the only chance at getting our hands on an antidote goes up in flames?" Andy asks, folding her arms across her chest and scanning the room.

Her eyes are the deep blue green they get when she's heated about something. I don't want to upset her, for fear that whatever chemical is running through her body will cause another scary medical crisis, I also cannot entertain this idea of her becoming terrorist bait either.

"So…what…you'd just go inside, and we'd never see you again but at least you'd know the information? How would we get the info out? How would we get *you* out?" I ask, questions streaming from my mouth like an involuntary rapid-fire succession.

Fuck – this is a bad idea.

I rub my hand through my hair, which now feels like a messy mop of curls darting out in all directions.

"It wouldn't be *that* hard to make them come to me. We could leak my location inside the CIA to someone we suspect is dirty – honestly, my money is on the director himself. Before I left, he told Jake he would take over my case. So, if I get wrapped up...connected with the CIA...chances are Jake would have the info and I really don't think he'd turn on me," Andy says.

"Jake? No way. The farm washout?" I ask, brows crinkling with anger remembering how it felt to see Andy and Jake interact at the safehouse.

Now I'm pacing and I hate this. I know I look like a jealous teenager and yet cannot seem to stop myself. Boss, who rolls up on the scene with impeccable timing, is now brushing his body against my leg to calm me down. I close my eyes and take a deep breath, allowing him to nudge me over to the couch with his nose.

"Cam, you know it's not like that between us. Jake is like a brother to me," she says, walking over to address me privately.

Didn't look like a brother when his tongue was down your throat in the halls of Langley.

Doors start opening and closing as the rest of the team nervously and awkwardly shimmies out of the room to avoid witnessing what I worry looks like a lover's quarrel. On his way out, Rove gives me a look that I know means a lecture is coming. At this point it must be clear to everyone that something is up between Andy and I, but I'm willing to ask forgiveness from Rove before walking away from Andy again.

"And what happens if Jake doesn't report the information to us? What happens if we can't get you out?" I ask, unable to stop my mind from racing to all the horrible ways this could end.

"You know where I'll be...and if we can't find a way for me to get information out – you give me three days to find as much information as I can...and then you come in after me and we destroy the place," she says, with a calm tone that confuses me given what she's suggesting.

"Andy how the hell do you suppose we find you?" I ask, rubbing my head in frustration.

"Don't tell me you've never placed a chip inside a person before...it's not like that would be worse than the serum coursing through my veins," Andy responds, shrugging.

"Let's table this for now, okay? We can go to this party, find the Alvarez dude and then hopefully Popov and just see how far we can get without considering the possibility of sending you in," I plead, grabbing the hand she placed on my cheek and holding it to my chest.

I pull her close to me and hold onto her as though I've just grabbed ahold of her to stop her from falling off a cliff.

"I don't want to lose you," I admit, "I can't lose you, too."

"Cam, you won't, okay? You won't," she responds, now kneeling in front of me on the couch placing her body between my knees.

We sit there in silence for a few moments, with only distant sounds of our teammates moving through the spaces on the other side of the wall. She pulls me into a hug, still kneeling in front of me, and places her head on my chest.

"I went to see my dad's memorial this week," I say, breaking the silence between us.

She lifts her head to look into my eyes, questioning, "Are you okay?"

"It was the first time I've gone, and I guess...I just didn't know I had so much to say to him," I say, looking away and tightening my jaw.

She looks at me with worry in her eyes but remains silent to let me continue.

"He meant the world to me, Andy. And when those terrorists killed him, it felt like my entire existence and a part of my identity just came crumbling on top of me. And I ran from it – I've been running away from what happened for over a decade and..." my voice trails off because I'm embarrassed to say this out loud.

Andy grabs my right hand in hers and squeezes it tight.

"I'm sorry, Andy. I lost myself that day my dad died," I admit.

Silence fills the space again before I continue, "I searched the rubble for weeks, pouring through bodies and ash and good God the smell...I think I lost myself in that building. And I've been chasing a ghost or perhaps just hoping somehow...I will figure out how to be me again without him here...figuring out how to make him proud...how to make myself proud."

"Cam, you matter - and you lived a life your dad would've been proud of even before you entered service, but honey...you know he would be proud of you no matter what, right?" She asks, bringing her hand back to my face.

I fight the tears threatening to break free from my eyes and let go of her hand to swipe one away before it has the chance to roll down my cheek.

"One of the biggest regrets of my life is that I let that event destroy us. I ruined the best thing I had in my life," I say, looking at the ground.

"I'm still here," she says, crouching down to look into my eyes.

"Will you stay with me, Andy?" I ask, hoping she knows I want her to stay with me forever.

"I'm not going anywhere," she responds.

She slowly raises from her knees, pushes me back into the couch and lays down next to me. We stay like this for hours, holding each other and talking. Tomorrow we will enter another danger zone, but today – and tonight – I want to just hold onto her for as long as I can.

The entire station is quiet now and there's no longer light shining through the windows. Andy's body is curled up next to mine, her legs and arms intertwined with mine as though she's hanging onto me, and I am to her. The crackling of the fire next to us and the soft snoring sounds of Boss, who's body is sprawled out on the floor next to us, cause my eyes to feel heavy. Despite the chaos looming around us, my body relaxes. I don't know how or if we'll succeed in restoring order and integrity in this country, that we're both dedicated our lives to serving – but tonight we have each other. And for tonight, that is enough.

Chapter 24
Something Like a Party

"Andy"

Diplomatic receptions, events cloaked in the appearance of an actual party, are one of the most dreaded parts of my job. Before I became a Case Officer, I loved a good party where my friends would gather to laugh and drink good wine. Only the good stuff though – none of that boxed wine from the convenient store we'd suffered through in college. We're the type of crowd that will unapologetically tell you when that old bottle of wine has turned, but also happily share the good stuff. Together, always over a good bottle of wine, we'd celebrate each other's joys, loves, and jam out to our favorite music (usually hip hop and R&B from the 90s).

In the after, I don't even enjoy parties with friends anymore. I'm always worried about sharing something that might blow my cover and I'll never be comfortable with the lies that I'll tell if someone asks me where I've been or what I do for work.

"Oh...you know...things...nothing sexy," I lie, before diverting the conversation else-where.

Slipping into this curve hugging, red dress feels like I'm putting on a costume. My back is exposed with a fabric that barely covers my behind and the V-neck strategically allows my breasts to peek out and join the hunt. When I go to these parties, I wear too much foundation, lipstick that's too red, eyeliner too dark, and sometimes I even throw in fake eyelashes.

"It's better they think of you as a prostitute than a spy," my bosses always say, smirking in that way that shows they've never had to make that type of sacrifice.

Many of the men I work with float through these receptions, sorting through guests for their next target like used car salesmen ready to sell you something they know you don't want. This has never come naturally to me, so I put on this costume – complete with the foot strangling heels – and brace myself for the discomfort. I walk into this party knowing the targets will come to me – not because they are ready for me to recruit them, but because they hope that I'll end up in their bed. And I feel pressure to smile even when I'm sad, laugh when it's not funny, and flirt with men old enough to be my father. I'm not here to party, but instead, to convince one of these men to do something I'd never be willing to do – betray his country and put himself in mortal danger to do so.

Tonight, I'm going to a reception at the Argentine Ambassador's house with a single purpose in mind – to bump Diego Alvarez and see if he'll agree to talk about the nuclear facility Cameron and Theo found in Lima and tell us where we can find Popov.

"Are you ready?" Cam says, walking up behind me as I put on an earring.

"Yeah, almost...I just have to get my jacket," I respond, turning to face him after grabbing my lipstick off the counter.

"Wow, Andy...you look incredible," he says, running a hand through his wild curls that are glowing as though he's just stepped out of the shower.

"Thanks, you don't look too bad yourself," I respond, smiling and glancing at him before looking away.

He's wearing a navy-blue tuxedo with a crisp, bright red bowtie that makes him look as though he's just stepped out of a men's fashion magazine. The bowtie is probably an attempt to draw attention from his beautiful eyes, but I won't tell him that it isn't working. He smells like a mixture between Louisiana peach soap and the spice of his cologne.

Does he have to smell distractingly good right now?

"Cam, I'm nervous," I admit as soon as we're alone together in the car.

"I understand, I am a little too. But I'll be there too, okay? And if *anything* weird happens or you don't feel right about something, just send an alert. We'll both be connected to the rest of the team in the ops center through the wires we're wearing, and Theo and the rest of the crew are in the mobile unit just outside" he says, trying to reassure me.

I nod, clasping my hands and squeezing to try and calm my nerves. I've done this party scene a million times, but tonight feels different because the stakes are much higher. Typically, I go in and see who's there, get a few numbers, and then bounce after a couple glasses of wine. But tonight, we have one shot at this guy and the wrong move could send him running or ratting us out to the rest of the network.

"Can they hear us yet?" I ask, not sure if we will have to enable the wires or if our mics are already hot.

"Not yet, I'll handle that before we go in," he responds.

The car is silent for a few minutes, neither of us moving to turn on music or trying to engage the other in useless banter. Perhaps he's in his head, thinking about all the ways this could go wrong like I am.

Good God – I hope he can't hear my heart racing right now.

I lean back, place a hand over my chest, and rest my head against the seat while I look out the car window. On our way to the event, deep into the Dupont Circle neighborhood in DC, I focus on all the people in the streets. They're smiling, seemingly carefree, on their way home from the grocery store, on the way to a party, or stumbling out of a bar. Watching them like this reminds me of how caged I feel in this life. With this serum coursing through my veins, and the future of this nation resting on my shoulders, I'm trapped with duty.

"Andy, do you ever feel like the CIA is a giant funnel where all the Black people end up on the bottom?" He asks, jolting me out of my thoughts and causing me to turn in my seat to look at him.

"What do you mean?" I ask, now certain he's been in an anxiety spiral of his own as we've been driving.

"Well, if you walk around the Langley compound...on the upper floors of the buildings where people are Case Officers and GS Officers like you and I...you don't see many of us...maybe just a few here and there. But then when you go to the basement where the support staff work, you see a bunch of Black people. It's as though they put us all into a funnel and most of us fall to the bottom, while the few remaining are hanging on...clawing our way up...trying to stay on the top...and terrified that one day we will fall through," he says, admitting what is possibly the most vulnerable things he's told me in years.

Closing my eyes and taking another deep breath, breathing in peaches and spice, I reach across the middle console of the car and place my hand on his.

"Yeah, I do," I say, letting my words sit between us without needing to elaborate.

I get it Cam – I get it.

There's a silent understanding between us at this moment and for the first time since I returned from Brazil, I don't feel as lonely. Cameron pulls into a crowded, street parking spot a block away from the residence. He turns off the car, but we remain silent next to each other for several minutes in the dark car.

He presses a button on the battery pack attached to his wire, before signaling for me to do the same.

"Okay Theo, we're on the move. Do you have eyes on the front door?" He asks, before stepping out of the car.

And just like that, we're both back in character.

"Roger that – eyes on the front door from across the street. Target arrived ten minutes ago, and he's solo," Theo responds through our earpieces.

Cameron has his arm around me as we approach the door of the Argentine Ambassador's residence. We flash our invitations – which were beautifully forged by one of the guys on Cameron's team – and head inside. As soon as we're inside, we separate from each other to search for Alvarez. I walk toward the giant chocolate fountain first.

Because…it's a chocolate fountain and if I have to be here – I might as well get some chocolate out of it.

Just as I'm about to dip a stick of strawberries into the silky chocolate that's flowing like a river of lava from a volcano, a man approaches me. He's not my target, and I don't want to get trapped into a conversation, so I attempt to ignore him.

"Well, hello there, so happy to have crossed paths with you again…friend," he says, his voice causing me to freeze upon recognition.

I look up from my strawberries slowly, hoping that perhaps he will magically disappear before my eyes meet his.

Ugh, of course – he's still here.

I plaster a fake smile on my face and say, "oh…Omar. Hello, I'm surprised to see you here in DC."

Omar is a Moroccan Diplomat in the Ministry of Foreign Affairs, African Cooperation, and Moroccan Expatriates and one of the slimiest people I've ever had the displeasure to encounter in these circles. He stands just a couple inches taller than me, has olive colored skin, a full mustache and beard, and black hair that has so much grease in it that I always worry a flame will get too close and the entire room will blow up. He quickly moves too close to me – so close that I can smell his breath, which smells like a mix between rotten fish and kitty litter that has not been changed in weeks.

"I've missed you," he whispers in my ear.

Andy, you cannot punch this man in the gut in the middle of this party.

I spot Cameron from the other side of the room and our eyes meet. I shoot him a panicked look and he says, "stage four creeper just rolled in on Andy and I've spotted our target heading to the restroom. Andy, I'm going to come take care of that dude so you can follow our guy. I'll wait in the hall on the other side of the men's room in case you need me."

I nod, mouthing a 'thank you' at him, before turning my head to get eyes on the target. Moments later, as Omar is still whispering creepy things into my ear, Cameron walks past and pretends to lose his grip on his wine glass. His red wine flies out of his hand and heads straight for Omar's white suit, as though it's a wine missile that artfully hits its intended target.

"Oh no, I'm so sorry sir," Cameron says, acting surprised and mortified, as I stifle a laugh and head toward the hallway leading to the restroom.

Cameron grabs a napkin from the table and begins to obnoxiously wipe at the red stain on Omar's suit, causing Omar to be even more distracted as he swats him away.

Just as the target rounds the corner and comes into view, I enter the hallway before he does, lean against the wall, and pretend to be distracted by my phone. As soon as he passes me, I bump into him and then launch myself to the floor, giving the appearance that he's just bumped into me and caused me to fall to the floor.

"Ohh, oh no," I scream, putting on my best damsel in distress act and looking up at Alvarez, praying he will stop and help me up.

"Pardon," Alvarez responds, reaching out a hand to help me up.

"Thanks, I'm so sorry, I can be such a klutz," I say, looking him in the eyes.

As soon as Alvarez meets my eyes, he freezes and quickly drops my hand.

"It's *you*," he whispers.

"I'm sorry, do we know each other?" I ask, confused.

"You need to get out of here," he says, his head whipping back and forth as though he's searching for the nearest exit.

"Why? What are you talking about?" I ask, trying to keep him talking.

"I can't be seen with you – I want nothing to do with any of this. Please, leave me alone," he pleads.

Theo responds in my earpiece, "okay, I'd say his weirdness just now is enough of a confirmation that he's our guy and that he probably has some information we need. Do me a favor and make sure he exits out the back? I'll have the car out there in thirty seconds."

Alvarez starts toward the front door just as Cameron rounds the corner to block his path, then he starts running toward the back door.

"Target headed in your direction, Theo," I say, glancing at my watch to confirm the timing is right.

A moment after Alvarez runs out the back door, Theo's voice crackles through our earpieces again, "we got him. You two can head out."

Cameron puts his hand on the small of back, and I can see Omar glaring at us out of the corner of my eye. He's on the other side of the room, standing too close to another woman who appears as though she's about to vomit – likely from the smell of his breath. We walk toward the front door, smiling and nodding at guests and thanking the Ambassador before rushing out.

As we get into the car, a group of women a few years younger than me, pour out of the row house across the street. Smiles spread across their faces as they walk with their arms linked toward the main strip of Dupont Circle. In the before, I loved a good party.

Chapter 25
"Cover" Me

"Andy"

"**I** think we have this wing of the ops center to ourselves tonight because the team is at one of the safe houses getting Alvarez to talk," Cameron says as we enter through the elevator doors.

Reaching down to remove these wretched shoes, my feet feel like they are covered in blisters from the night.

Why would anyone make a shoe that imprisons a foot like this?!?

Even though my feet feel as though they'll run from me, my eyes can't help but fix on Cameron who's unapologetically taking off his coat, tie, and button-down shirt right in front of me.

"Whoa, cool your fire, man," I say laughing, picking up the red tie and throwing it at his head teasingly.

Cameron jogs over to me and pulls me into a bear hug before exclaiming, "we did it – tonight feels like we might be finally getting somewhere."

"We made a good team, huh," I respond, unable to stop myself from smiling.

Cameron smiles back, the sexy dimple popping out as though on cue, before turning and heading over to the kitchenette.

"Do you want something to drink?" He asks, with his back turned as he begins to boil water for tea.

"Sure, tea actually sounds amazing," I respond, as I walk over toward the fire.

After walking a few steps, I notice that something feels off. I'm dizzy and it feels like my body has suddenly been dipped in an ice bath.

On no...not again.

Trying hard not to draw attention to myself, I search through my purse trying to find my pills.

Shit, they aren't in here.

The room is starting to spin, and I need to find a seat quickly before I go down. I fall on the couch. My body starts to shake, and I don't even think I could get up and walk if I tried.

"Cam, I need…I think I need…I can't catch my breath," I scream.

I think I'm screaming.

Cameron is screaming for help, and now the room is dark. Voices swirl in the air around me and there's loud sounds of doors opening and slamming in rapid succession. A mask is placed over my face and warm air fills my lungs, as blankets are layered on top of me. The tears streaming down my cheeks, that I can't wipe away, feel like they're painting a portrait of pain on my face.

"What's wrong with her? She seemed fine one moment and then the next she wasn't."

Cameron's voice is low, as though he isn't sure if I can hear him – but he's still sitting next to me, and I can hear all of it.

"I think this is the effect of the serum and we just don't know everything yet, but she experienced a rapid drop in body temperature. This can cause hallucinations and seizure-like episodes," a voice that sounds like Dr. Raj responds, calmer than Cameron.

A third voice enters the conversation that sounds like Rove, "we don't have a lot of time. All Intel points to that place called The Epicenter holding the answers, but Alvarez doesn't know where it is – or isn't giving up the information."

"What about the dude up in Canada. Do you think he will know? Did Alvarez at least give up that guy's location?" Cameron asks.

"While Alvarez seems like he's never been a shot caller in this organization, he did tell us about where we can find Popov," Rove responds.

Cameron's voice sounds like it's ringing in my ears now as he says, "Okay, Theo and I will head up there as soon as possible. When can we get a plane?"

"No, Andy has to go," Farhad's voice jumps into the conversation from the other side of the room.

I'm so cold – hang on girl – stay awake.

"What? Do you see her right now?" Cameron asks.

"You both can go, but bro – you know we are one step ahead here. We've already tracked down Popov and he says he will only talk to Andy," Theo chimes in.

"I *told* you. My father already told you that people like this won't talk to you. They will only talk to Andy because they know she wouldn't work against her own self interests. There are too many dirty people inside your government to trust just anyone," Farhad continues, frustration in his voice as he audibly huffs.

So, they'll only talk to me because I have skin in the game...literally?

"Cam, you and Andy will fly out as soon as the doctor can get her stable. If this guy can give us information on how to find this place and how to get in, we might not have to send Andy into the fray," Rove says, the sound papers crumbling in his direction.

"You all know this is crazy talk, right?" Cameron says.

"No...no, I want to go," I say, my voice shaking still as I grab ahold of Cameron who's still sitting beside me as Dr. Raj shoves an IV into a vein in my arm.

"Look, this doesn't make any of us feel warm and fuzzy, but this sounds way better than just waiting for them to come get her," Theo says.

My body is back to feeling like it's my own, but I keep my eyes closed because I want them to keep talking when they don't think I can hear them.

"How can she go to Vancouver in her current situation? And with Solaris actively trying to find her...and the Esfahani brothers on her back...you know there are like several of those motherfuckers, right? *Shit...*" Cameron's voice trails off.

"So, you saw the information Farzad found on the guy who attacked Andy in her condo?" Rove asks.

"Yeah...Andy recognized the name. I didn't know the brother was the guy from Brazil," Cameron responds.

"Why don't you guys take the work talk over to the other side of the room so Andy can rest," Dr. Raj interjects.

No – I want them to stay here.

As Cameron shifts to get up from the couch, I reach out and grab a fist full of his shirt with as much strength as I can muster.

"Andy? Are you alright? Can you hear me?" Cameron asks, now grabbing my hand and covering it with both of his.

"I'm alright. I feel okay now. Dr. Raj – I forgot to take the pills. When I felt cold earlier, I took them and this didn't happen, but this time when the cold started coming – I couldn't find them in time," I say, hoping that my admission will keep everyone from the assumption that I can't hold my own in Vancouver for this debrief.

"How much of our conversation did you hear, Andy?" Rove asks, raising one of his eyebrows.

"All of it," I say, flashing them a sheepish smile.

Dr. Raj is studying my face as she adjusts the IV bag that lays beside my arm.

"Do you need a break from all the work talk?" Raj asks, concern washing over her face as she shoots both Rove and Cameron a stern look.

"No, I'm fine. And we need to have this conversation. I'm going to Canada so we need to do whatever we have to do so that I can go without slipping into another medical crisis," I respond firmly, keeping my voice steady and free of any signs of stress.

Given that the guys migrated to the area where the table sat, I start shifting blankets off me and attempt to stand. Cameron, who's gotten up to get a glass of water from the counter, runs back over to me so fast that he looks as though he's flying across the room toward me, and Rove is close behind. Rove flops into one of the plush chairs next to the couch, and Cameron places his hand on my shoulder with enough pressure to stall my efforts to rise.

"Please stay put, we can come to you," Cameron says, little beads of sweat dotting the edges of his hairline and worry lines spreading across his forehead.

Rove studies the two of us together, raising an eyebrow at Cameron before clearing his throat and speaking, "Hmm, okay. Here's what we know about Nikolai Popov after the debrief with Alvarez. Popov is a nuclear scientist from St. Petersburg, Russia. According to Alvarez, Popov is a gnarly looking dude. When he first walked into a Canadian embassy in Helsinki, they falsely assumed he was homeless and having some sort of psychotic break."

Rove opens a manila folder on his lap and hands us a set of pictures. Between an auburn, bushy, unkept mustache and a long and shaggy beard, it's hard to see much of the man's face. His eyes, the palest blue I've ever seen, peek out from above all that hair and wear an expression that looks like a mixture of fear and menace.

"*This* is Popov?" I ask, hoping I'm wrong because the man staring back at me in this picture is terrifying.

Cameron takes one of the photos from me, silently scanning the image as though he expects information to jump out of the picture at him.

"Rove, I'm a big dude and I think I can take down many dudes twice my size, but this guy looks like he could eat me and Theo for breakfast and then come back for more. Andy can't go in there alone. I mean, I know you can handle yourself Andy...but please don't go alone?" Cameron pleads, rambling nervously.

"Calm down Cam, I won't let him eat you," I respond laughing to myself, "and you can come with me."

"Last I checked, I'm a grown ass woman who doesn't need you to *let* me do anything," I say, shooting Cameron a look out of the corner of my eye as I turn my attention toward Rove.

"Seriously though," Theo says, "this guy looks..."

"Looks shady as fuck?" Dr. Raj interjects, glancing at the picture from over Cameron's shoulder and grimacing at the image.

Rove responds, "yes, that *is* Popov. That was footage taken from the surveillance cameras outside of the Canadian embassy moments before he walked in about a month ago. *This* is how he looked before he smuggled himself out of Russia."

I take the photo from Rove and see a man who looks nothing like the first picture. This version of Popov is clean shaven, showing chiseled features with only slight smile lines on his eyes. He looks serious, but not as terrifying as he did in the first picture. Raj is hovering over my shoulder now, eyes narrowing at the picture in my hands.

"I think I know that guy...I mean, I've met him before," Raj says, placing her hands on her hips and leaning in to get a better look.

"You know him?" Rove asks, raising an eyebrow.

"I met him at a conference years ago. He's a nuclear radiologist who presented at a conference I attended in Stockholm years ago about the use of radiopharmaceuticals to diagnose and treat disease," she says, surprise spreading across her face.

"Well, that's on brand. Before he smuggled himself out of Russia, hiding out in the hull of a commercial fishing boat, he worked at one of a handful of nuclear labs connected to the network we are trying to take down," Rove says, now handing us maps and pictures of the facility where Popov worked before fleeing.

"Didn't the Canadians debrief him? Can't we just get them to ask the questions about the Epicenter?" Cameron asks, looking annoyed.

"They did debrief him, but they didn't get the information we need and when we caught up to him, he agreed to talk to Andy – and *only* Andy. So, we have two choices here...refuse and get nothing or send Andy and find out what this guy knows," Rove responds, matching Cameron's irritation with his own.

As the men argue back and forth, as though I haven't already made up my mind to go talk to Popov, I pore over the rest of the images and maps. Talking to this guy and perhaps getting the information we need to find the antidote seems like a way better idea than just waiting to get wrapped up by the terrorists.

"I'll need a disguise and a robust cover with documents to back it up. And I'll need a way to leave here without anyone seeing me in case we were followed from my condo the other night," I say, interrupting the brewing argument between the two of them.

"Done, I've already worked that out," Rove responds, jumping out of the plush chair he'd been sitting in and moving toward the dining room table in the corner of the room.

Cameron gets up from the couch in a huff and starts pacing back and forth, rubbing his head. Rove grabs two separate folders and practically bounces over to me and Cameron, handing us each a folder.

"You will be husband and wife – Rebecca and Donald Weisman. Start reading because each of you will need to memorize your cover before leaving. In the folders, you will find passports, driver's licenses, and relationship details to make this all believable," Rove says, beaming with what looks like pride.

"You made me a Becky?" I ask, looking up at Rove and twisting my face in confusion.

Rove shrugs, but I catch a small smirk as he glances toward Cameron.

Awesome – my new boss thinks he's a comedian.

"I mean, would you prefer the name Karen?" Theo asks, snorting with laughter.

I roll my eyes, collapsing back on the couch with the folder in hand, and begin memorizing enough information to make this all believable.

Chapter 26
Vancouver

"Cameron"

My face is so itchy with this ridiculous disguise that Rove made me wear. I feel like I'm going to tear off my face at some point during this trip because it feels like there's an angry racoon growing on my face. A "costume crew" showed up early this morning and spent hours meticulously gluing human hair all over my face. They created a mustache and beard with so much coverage that my own mother probably wouldn't even recognize me. The look was topped off with a pair of round glasses that made me look about fifteen years older.

Twisting the gold wedding band on my left ring finger, I glance down at Andy. We're a few hours into the six-hour flight between DC and Vancouver and Andy fell asleep on my arm moments after takeoff. My arm is going numb, but I don't want to move her because she probably needs this rest. Her disguise is also ridiculous, a straight auburn colored wig with tinted glasses and bright red lipstick.

"We have to do whatever possible to draw attention away from your eyes," the costume designer said, pointing out that a Black woman with piercing blue/green eyes is memorable enough to make this process difficult.

The designer is right, her eyes *are* unforgettable. While leaning into me, her hand rests softly on my leg. The large, diamond wedding ring she's wearing as a part of this disguise is gaudy and not at all the type of ring Andy would want in real life. I'd find her a rare stone that the two of us would likely geek out over to represent how unique she is and how special she is to me.

Why am I thinking about this right now?

I can't even get her to agree to acknowledge that we're together publicly, let alone imagine broaching the topic of marriage.

Wait...are we together?

I want us to be together and if she'd let me, I'd propose to her today. But I also know that she isn't ready for all that and now is not the time. We could have had that, I think...had I not ruined things all those years ago. And now, I'm sitting here with this chia pet all over my face having to pretend to be married to the love of my life while also trying to find the pack of terrorists that *might* have a serum that could save her.

The plane lurches violently, jolting me from my thoughts and Andy startles awake. She grabs my arm, clinging tightly as though I can stop us from falling out of the sky. The pilot's voice streams calmly over the loudspeaker, assuring everyone that we're just experiencing turbulence, and everyone should return to their seats. As anxious as I am right now, I know Andy well enough to know that planes scare the hell out of her. Years ago, she told me she'd been in a small plane crash with her father when she was only eight years old.

"The landing gear never came down, and when my dad landed the plane, there were sparks flying as the plane spun around in circles. I thought we'd all be burned alive that night," she'd told me, recounting the traumatic memory moments before we boarded a plane to the Caribbean for spring break.

I know we'll be alright, and *this* plane isn't going to crash, but I don't want Andy to worry. Worrying could cause a rapid heart rate and a rapid heart rate is what Dr. Raj believes is a trigger for the hypothermic episodes Andy's been having.

"Do you have your pills?" I ask, rubbing her back gently as she buries her head into my arm.

"I'm okay...but yeah, I have them," she responds, extending a shaking hand to open the backpack she'd shoved under the seat in front of her.

After taking one of the pills, she grabs my right hand in hers and I can feel the cold emanating from her. I say nothing because I know she will get mad at me for hovering and worrying. She will assume I think she can't handle herself.

"Young lady, are you alright?" An elderly woman next to us asks Andy from across the aisle, looking up from her knitting project.

"Oh, yes...I'm fine. Just a little motion sickness," Andy says, flashing her a friendly, reassuring smile.

She looks pale and like she might vomit, but we're almost on the ground.

"Okay dear...you let me know if you need this bag here for a vomit bag," she replies, tapping the white bag in front of her before returning her attention back to the sweater she's knitting.

"Do you remember when we're supposed to meet this guy?" I ask, my voice low.

"As soon as we leave the airport," Andy says, looking up but still clinging to my hand but no longer shaking.

The plane continues lurching around, making me wonder how I will clean the vomit out of this beard if I start throwing up. Thankfully, the pilot comes back on the loudspeaker to inform us that we should prepare for landing.

"Sorry for the bumpy ending here folks. We should be touching down in Vancouver shortly," the pilot says, in a voice that seems too calm for how much the plane is jolting up and down and side to side.

I lift Andy's chin and look into her eyes before asking, "you good?"

"Yes, I just need to get off this plane," she responds, the color continuing to drain from her face.

As the plane approaches the runway, it continues lurching side to side like a feather blown by a large gust of wind just before slamming violently onto the runway. I brace my body for the impact and Andy whimpers into my shoulder as her entire body stiffens. Pulling her close to me, I begin gathering our things.

"We're okay," I say, trying to convince myself and her to stay calm.

"Thanks...I'm sorry. Gosh, after all these years of flying you'd think I'd have gotten used to some turbulence," she says, color returning to her face as she smiles up at me and awkwardly at the older woman across from us.

I try to wipe the worry from my face, and turn away from her, because I know what's coming next from her.

"Cam, stop. I'm not going to break," she says, placing her hand on my cheek and turning my face back toward her.

"I'm sorry, I know you're tough. But Andy, I hate everything about this," I admit, whispering to avoid anyone around us hearing.

And wish it were me and not you...

Andy doesn't respond because the seat belt alert signals, and she jumps out of her seat. That tiny ping is like the gun in a foot race, turning us both into mission mode. We rapidly collect our belongings, exit the plane, and speed walk through the terminal to the parking garage. I rustle through my pocket, searching for the paper where I'd jotted down the location of the car the lead team left for us in the garage.

"You can stop looking for your notes, Cam. It's on the second floor in spot 162," Andy says, glancing at me with a smirk on her face.

I look at her and shake my head, "of course you just remembered that."

Andy has an incredible memory and she used to tease me for keeping notes to remind myself of things. I can remember useless facts I've read in a history book but forget that I've promised to meet someone for dinner.

As we approach the car, I rush for the driver's seat. She says she's fine, but it wasn't ten minutes ago that she looked like she was going to vomit her breakfast all over the airplane carpet.

"Cam, seriously?" She raises her eyebrows at me, holding her hand out for the keys.

"Nope, no way Andy – just now on that plane…you looked like you were going to pass out or have another seizure. I'm driving," I respond, hopping into the driver's seat, and pulling the door closed behind me.

I smile to myself as she rolls her eyes, walks to the passenger side of the SUV, and flops down next to me before punching me in the shoulder. We sit next to each other in silence for a moment before she turns to me, arms crossed across her chest, and face flushed with irritation.

"Cam, stop…we need to have a conversation before we go anywhere," she says, blocking my hand as I move to turn on the car.

I drop my hand and turn toward her, crossing my arms and leaning back in the seat.

"You want to know what pisses me off about all of you guys?" She asks, piercing me with her eyes that now look green to match the hue of her sweater.

"All *who* guys?" I ask, irritated before she continues about being lumped in with a group of men that I'm sure she is going to berate as being problematic for some reason.

"I've been putting my life on the line, going into places most men at this agency wouldn't even dare…doing it solo…and getting the job done for almost a decade…and yet, ya'll decide to flex in these moments like I can't handle myself behind the wheel of a goddamned SUV to drive to what is likely to be a relatively straight forward debrief?!?"

Her voice is raised, and her eyes look like an angry blue ocean. I don't respond immediately because my anger at the fact that she thinks she's a super woman could cause me to say something that I might later regret.

"I need you to stop – stop hovering and acting like I am always going to break," she says.

"Andy, I *know* you can handle yourself, but I also know that we don't know what the hell is going on with this serum and you need to stop acting like it's not coursing through your veins right now," I reply, dragging my hand through my hair before banging the steering wheel.

"Cam, you're acting like I am about to burst into nuclear flames and it's driving me crazy! It's bad enough that I'm the key to bring down the terrorist cell that's infiltrated our government, but don't you think I also know that I might not even survive this if we can't find the antidote?"

"I'm sorry, Andy. I'm trying not to let this drive me crazy. This entire situation is madness, and I hate that you're even wrapped up in this but why do you insist on this toxic level of independence!"

I'm gripping the steering wheel so tight that I can feel my hands start to sweat and ache.

"But I *am* and if we keep doing this dance where you hover, and I push...it's just not helpful. We need to focus on what we came here for and stop worrying about shit we can't control. Just drive," she says, looking away from me and out the window.

Starting the car, I pull out of the airport garage, and we drive. We sit next to each other in silence for several moments as Andy continues to look out of the windows. My therapist's voice rings in my ear.

Just because you're a man...doesn't mean you aren't allowed to show fear of vulnerability.

I clear my throat before saying, "I..I..um...have been seeing a therapist."

Andy turns her entire body toward me and watches, waiting for me to continue.

"You told me to go when my dad died, and I didn't want to. I didn't think I needed to go. But I did need to go because I was so angry and taking it out on all the wrong people," I admit, my eyes fixed on the road.

"How do you feel now?" She asks, turning back to look at me.

"I'd be lying if I tell you that I'm not angry anymore, but I'm starting to realize that in trying to avenge my father – I've taken on some of the behaviors of his that I'd rejected before he died. There were good reasons for rejecting them...well, you know."

More silence passes between us, with only the sounds of the passing cars ringing in my ears. Making this confession while watching the road, not having to look at Andy as she watched me, feels easier than it would be without the distraction. I can feel her eyes on me though, and I know there's more to say.

"You didn't deserve the way I treated you back then," I admit, keeping my eyes on the road while I clutch the steering wheel so tight that my knuckles are turning white.

She doesn't respond so I continue, "and I know you don't have to trust me, but I wish you'd let me protect you – I wish you'd let me back in."

I hear her take a deep breath and out of the corner of my eye, I can see her turn toward the passenger side window.

"I'm not weak," she says.

"I know you're not weak," I respond quickly.

"Cam, I'm speaking – let me finish please. I've been through *a lot* of shit with the agency, and I don't need you hovering over me and acting like I can't do my damn job."

She's silent for a moment, still looking out the window. I wait quietly to allow her to continue.

Taking a deep breath, she says, "these guys, they never had a problem with me putting my life at risk while they sat back at the office drinking whiskey. But the moment the case got good, and the dangerous part was done – they'd suddenly appear and act like I needed one of them to run the case."

"I know you're good at your job. And it's clear your reputation precedes you given that none of these scientists want to speak to anyone but you," I say, feeling a bit guilty about how jealous I'd been that none of them would speak to me without her.

"Let's make a deal, okay? I know this stuff coursing through my veins is unpredictable, and it's driving me crazy that I feel like I'm in this constant hell loop between being fine and then feeling like I'm gonna die. But when I'm okay, can you just...stop acting like I'm gonna break and let me do my job?" She asks, now placing her hand on my leg.

"Andy, I'm not going to be able to stop worrying, but if you promise to tell me when you aren't okay – I will promise to try and back off and trust that you'll tell me when you need me to help you," I respond, "but can you *also* stop treating me like I'm just another one of these agency dudes?"

Silence drops between us again for a few moments before Andy says, "Okay, I guess...I guess I'm still taking some things out on you and that probably isn't entirely fair of me. I'm sorry."

I don't respond but nod my head, thankful that this argument seems to be coming to an end.

She continues, "and hey, I'm proud of you. I know that stuff about your dad wasn't easy to talk about but thank you for telling me."

Her soft voice pours over me, cooling off my anxiety and making me feel a bit guilty for getting so heated with her. I glance at her out of the corner of my eye, smile, and grab her hand with the free hand that isn't on the steering wheel. Andy squeezes my hand before pulling back and removing a map from her backpack.

"We good?" She asks.

"Yeah wifey, we are good," I respond, before she shoves me in my shoulder.

While typing the location into the car GPS would certainly be easier, we both know better than to do that. We left our cell phones in DC and replaced them with these burner phones, which Theo instructed us to only use in the event of an emergency. While in Canada, we're going off the grid and we need to find Popov via old school mapping navigation.

"Theo said Popov's cabin is an hour and half north of Vancouver, near Whistler ski resort, so let's take the signs that way and that should give me some time to find the exact location on this map," Andy says, comparing the notes she received from Theo with the map.

I smile knowingly, as I've already convinced Rove to let us stay in a ski chalet in Whistler village after the debrief before we head back to DC tomorrow night. And because Theo is my homeboy, he and the chase team made the reservations and I have no doubt that it will be anything less than epic.

"I'm so tired and it doesn't even make sense given how long I slept on the plane," Andy admits, brushing a few strands of hair from the wig behind her ear.

"Our flight back isn't until tomorrow night. So, after this debrief, I've already arranged for a place for us to crash for the night," I say, flashing a smile with this irritating fake beard.

Andy swivels all the way around in her seat to face me, a look of excitement in her eyes that I haven't seen in years.

"Well, Mr. Weisman, did you forget this is a business trip and we have work to do?" Andy teases, poking me in the shoulder.

"If we're gonna be fake married...we should at least get a fake honeymoon," I respond, smirking while rubbing the shoulder she'd just poked.

"Good point, but can you leave the beard on? That way, we can *really* commit, and I get the full, authentic Donald Weisman experience tonight," she says, raising her eyebrows up and down suggestively before erupting into laughter.

"If that's what it takes, I'll take one for the team tonight and deal with an itchy face for a few hours longer. But damn, did they have to make me look like a mountain man," I respond, laughing alongside her.

"Ohh, but the mountain man look is surprisingly sexy," she teases, batting her eyes suggestively.

The drive to Whistler goes by faster than I expected. We spend part of the drive going over our cover story, with hilarious additions – like how Rebecca Weisman ("Rebe" for short since Andy hates the name "Becky") saved Donald ("Donny" for short) from a bear attack during the first few months they dated by whipping out her pepper spray on their hike. We decide Rebe is a planner and Donny is the reckless, and somewhat idiotic, type who tends to do things like follow bears into the woods for a picture. Once we finish coming up with silly cover stories to pass the time, we review our questions for Popov as well as contingency planning should things get dangerous.

"Rove sent a lead team for this right?" Andy asks nervously, as we turn off the highway onto a dirt path through a dense section of the Whistler Interpretive Forest.

I pause before responding, remembering that I promised not to hover or ask if she was alright. Glancing down at her, I see her hands clinging to the seat, knuckles white indicating how hard she's gripping.

"They did Andy – don't worry. They wouldn't lead us into danger. Last time, in the woods, we knew exactly what would happen and we had a plan to escape. We're going to be alright," I say, trying to reassure her while also not revealing my own concern about this entire operation.

She releases her grip on the seat, leans down to grab the backpack she's left at her feet, and takes a deep breath.

"I know and I trust Theo. He told me that he swept this entire area and that we have counter surveillance. I just...Cam, I can't shake this feeling I have...and just...I just can't relax," Andy admits, burying her head in her hands.

"I understand. This is some crazy shit, Andy. And no matter how capable both of us are, this is not a normal situation because the stakes are too high...too personal," I respond, reaching out to grab her hand.

"I just wish this was not...like I was not...in the middle of this, you know?" She says, squeezing my hand.

"I wish that too...like that this was just a mission and that the entire state of the union...and your life wasn't also riding on the information we're able to obtain from this dude," I respond.

There's five minutes before this debrief is set to begin and we were instructed to wait until the exact time before approaching the door. I scan the driveway, only seeing one car which I assume belongs to Popov. I'm not sure how Rove got the Canadians to stand down on this debrief, but I'm thankful he did. We can't even trust our own government not to snatch Andy, given that she's a walking key to nuclear domination. The last thing we need is to also worry about the Canadians and their allegiances.

I turn to Andy, whose face looks like it's draining of color, and place my hand over her heart. I take a deep breath, look into her eyes, and ask her to breathe with me.

Andy closes her eyes, takes a deep breath, and then says, "Okay, I'm ready. Let's go."

Chapter 27
Whistler Debrief

"Andy"

As we walk toward the chalet to meet Popov, my heart feels like it's going to beat out of my chest. I grab hold of Cameron's hand and hold onto him as though he's capable of keeping me grounded in this moment. We need to find out what this guy knows because this might be my last chance.

Keep it together girl.

Cameron lifts his hand to knock on the door, but before his hand connects the door flies open – causing us both to jump back.

"You're here, good. Come in quickly – don't want no one to see you," a man I assume is Popov says, wrapping his hand around my shoulder and nudging me through the door before quickly closing it behind us.

"Hello, it's nice to meet you. Thank you for meeting with us," Cam says, not bothering to tell him our cover names.

Popov knows who I am, given that he asked to speak only with me. Our cover was to safely travel, but I'm growing increasingly concerned over whether we can trust our Canadian counterparts to keep our whereabouts discreet.

Get out of your head.

Popov could be the most intense person I've ever met. He still has a mustache that connects with a long beard and piercing dark blue eyes that look like they've been plucked from the Caribbean Sea. His forehead has a crease in it that gives him a permanent menacing glare and his skin looks leathery as though he spent too long in the sun without sunblock. In contrast to the photos we saw, he looks clean and cared for; however, his appearance is still quite off-putting.

"We don't have time for the 'hello' and 'hi'," Popov says, glaring at Cameron.

I swallow and clear my throat, trying to call upon my most authoritative voice.

"Sir, you called me here for a reason and while I'm motivated to obtain the information, how about we keep this classy and you let us ask our questions and cut the crap," I say, praying my act of bravado will diffuse him without making him angry.

Something that looks halfway between a smirk and a smile washes over Popov's face but disappears almost as immediately as it arrives. He nods and points to a grouping of chairs to the left of the front door. The chalet is scarcely furnished, and I wonder how long he'll stay here before the Canadian government relocates him to a more permanent location. I can't tell whether Popov is angry or if that scowl he's giving us is just his face, but it's going to make this meeting uncomfortable.

Well, I can't fix my face either, bro...so same.

"Your government is infected," Popov says, flopping down on one of the chairs across from where he'd instructed Cameron and I to sit.

Well damn, tell us something we don't know.

Without responding, I shoot Popov a look of confusion to prompt him to share more information.

"Can you please elaborate?" Cameron asks, sitting down next to me on the couch.

Popov glares at him and grunts, seemingly annoyed that he's here.

"Basir is my friend. And he's the only reason I'm even talking to you people. He and I had a plan of how we would rid the world of this vile shit. And your own blood sucking government destroyed the plan," Popov continues, his face contorting and nose flaring as though he's just been accosted by a rotten smell.

"Well, I thought the plan was for Basir to come meet my team in Afghanistan. Given that the terrorists successfully injected Andy, and Basir essentially brought the serum to her – sounds like it was not the best plan," Cameron says, before I kick him in the leg to keep him from pissing this guy off and destroying any chance of us getting the Intel we need.

Popov doesn't respond to Cameron, but instead just turns to him and grunts before turning his attention back to me.

"Okay, well then why are you talking to us?" I ask, not willing to disclose the fact that we aren't exactly acting in any official capacity on behalf of our own government now.

"Basir contacted your government and insisted Americans would help us destroy the remaining labs. But just before he was about to head to Afghanistan his lab was raided," Popov says.

"If his lab was raided, how did he find out about me?" I ask, wondering how I was pulled into all this.

"He got your name because I told him. Before I left Russia, I grabbed whatever I could get my hands on to help give us what we needed to destroy Solaris and the remaining labs," Popov explains, walking over to the counter in his kitchen and grabbing a large stack of papers that he's shoved into a folder that looks too small to hold all of it together.

Popov hands me the papers before saying, "you were named as a target and according to this paperwork, *your* agency sent Solaris your blood from a lab located in your own damned country."

I lean back from Popov as I open the file because he's speaking with so much passion that spit is flying from his mouth. Holding up my hands, to try and ease some of the tension, I respond, "We know that there are problems within our own government and need you to trust us with whatever information you have that you think might help us – help you. Our goal is the same as yours – to take down the network."

"What can you tell us about 'The Epicenter'?" Cameron asks, ignoring the fact that Popov has turned his back to him and is only addressing me.

Popov glares over his shoulder before responding to me, "Nobody can get in or out of that place...well, almost no one. *You* can go there because they know about you and you're...you're the key to continuing their operation."

We're starting to hear his Russian accent popping through the more passionate he gets.

"What do you mean when you say '*they*' know about me," I ask, to clarify what I now suspect he knows.

"How many people have come for you so far?" Popov asks, folding his arms across his chest.

"What do you mean?" I respond, pretty sure I know where he's going but also wanting to hear him explain.

"That night you and the Assadi's were attacked...do you think that man came for Basir? He could care less about Basir, he wanted *you*. But he wasn't the only one and he won't be the last," Popov says, his eyebrows curving with intensity as he stares at me like he is waiting for me to actually respond.

I remain silent and give him a nod to indicate that I understand.

"Basir and I have grabbed everything we could from the labs to try and find the others, but your chances of getting into the Epicenter without being...taken in – impossible," Popov says, shaking his head and throwing up his hands dramatically.

"So you're recommending she just walk out into the street and give herself to a terrorist organization," Cameron says, stepping in front of Popov to grab his attention.

"Well, you can go on a hunt and use the data we got out, but time is a problem for you...well, for *her*," he says, pointing at me with his large, extremely hairy, finger.

"What do you mean time is a problem for me? What else aren't you telling us?" I ask, feeling my pulse start to race.

"When I was working in the lab, I was testing the serum. I never tested on humans, but the serum will make it hard to regulate your temperature and over time that will get impossible," Popov responds, his face dropping and a flash of what looks almost like empathy flash across his face.

"What are you saying?" I ask, as Cameron crosses the room to grab ahold of my shaking hand.

"If you don't find that antidote in the next few months, you might not survive this," Popov says, now looking at both Cameron and I.

Popov's sea blue eyes, now looking like a storm of waves pooling around inside his eyeball, shoot to my shaking hands before looking back up at my face. I quickly shove my hands into my pocket and try to bury the emotions of what he's just said so that I can get through this debrief.

"Andy, you're our last hope. I asked to speak to you because you need to be prepared for what *will* happen," Popov says.

This seems like a suicide mission, but do I have any other choice?

"Andy isn't going anywhere near that place," Cameron blurts out, his eyebrows furrowing to match Popov's expression.

Popov swivels around again, glaring at Cameron before responding, "and who are you?! Some guy who doesn't even know anything about Solaris. You didn't even know your own agency has a cancer."

I can feel my heart rate increase, as the cold returns and starts taking hold of my body. Before continuing this conversation, I excuse myself and ask Popov to point me toward the restroom. Once he does, I jump up from the chair and race to the bathroom, fishing in my pockets for my pills. My body is shaking, and I feel like I'm going through some sort of drug withdrawal. Popping a pill into my mouth and drinking a handful of water from the sink, I swallow before sliding down the bathroom wall. Curling into a ball, hugging my knees to my chest, taking several deep breaths...I wait for my temperature to normalize.

Moments later, my eyes still closed as I focus on slowing my heart rate, I hear a crashing noise in the room next to me. Rushing into the room to see what the commotion is, I see

Cameron and Popov inches from each other's faces – both men with their fists balled as though they're ready to war with each other.

"Stop! Both of you sit down," I yell, pointing at the couch instructing both to sit.

Shooting a look of anger toward Cameron, who reluctantly retreats.

"Look, I wanted out of this mess. Your people found me, and I cannot help it if you don't want to hear the truth," Popov says, backing away from Cameron and shrugging his shoulders.

"Okay, let's all try and calm down. Popov, thank you for telling us all this. What else do you know about the serum and why they came to me," I ask, trying to get this back on track.

"The serum won't work on just anyone. You need the right blood type and there are only a few people on the planet who'd present as a good candidate for...to be host, essentially," Popov explains.

"How do you know someone in our government had anything to do with this?" Cameron asks, leaning forward in his seat.

"Before you deploy overseas, your government makes you do physical, no? Look in that folder and you will see Andy's file from her physical. How would I have that if someone in your government hadn't leaked it?" Popov asks, raising an eyebrow at me.

I slowly open the file, praying that he's gotten this wrong and that my health records aren't going to be inside. As I start reading through the file, my heart sinks.

"Oh God, Cameron..." my voice trails off and I feel as though I am going to vomit.

This file contains my blood tests, details about my body down to the small star tattoo I have on my right wrist and the birth mark on my left thigh. I drop the file, and papers spill out onto the floor. Cameron falls to his knees and gathers the papers before coming next to me and holding me close to him.

"I told Basir to just destroy the vial because it seemed like too much of a risk to bring it anywhere close to you, but he insisted that he needed to turn it over for his freedom," Popov continues.

"If my government knew I was a match and had the serum themselves, why didn't they just inject me sooner," I ask.

"Basir's lab had the newest generation of the serum, the one that everyone believed was viable. In the raid, most of it was destroyed and Basir got out with what might have been the only fully intact vial," Popov responds.

"How does anyone even know this will work if I am the first human host?" I ask, feeling frantic.

"Could anyone have gotten ahold of your blood since you were injected?" Popov asks.

Taking an inventory in my head, I consider when my blood could've been tested. Cameron appears deep in thought as well, before turning to me and confirming, "there were two times they could've gotten their hands on blood – once in the embassy infirmary and then again at the VA hospital. We thought the threat was isolated to Brody and his guys, but if anyone was at the VA hospital that night...they could have gotten it there."

"No way, we were watching you the entire time. Dr. Raj got two vials and we've had them in our custody the entire time," Cameron says.

"But Cameron, were you with me the entire time in the infirmary?" I ask.

Cameron's head drops before he admits, "no, I wasn't. And Basir told my team that you were injected, but when Jake came to debrief you he already knew – which means Brody and his team already knew."

I'm a professional so I know I have to keep my cool during this debrief, but this man just told me that my own damned government stole vials of my blood to confirm that I'm a match for this serum. Even with Rove saying that he neutralized Brody, how do I know this doesn't go deeper than him?

Cameron buries his head in his hands and returns to his thoughts. I turn my attention back to Popov.

"You said they'd be coming for me, what did you mean? Did you tell anyone we were coming here?" I ask, rubbing my head where I can feel worried lines forming.

"Rove and his team coordinated your trip with Canadian Intelligence. These Canadians still think the U.S. is an ally and that means a team could already be waiting for you at the border," Popov says, in a monotone voice as though he's devoid of emotion.

"And what happens if I don't return?" I ask.

"They'll keep looking for you. And you might evade them, but you won't last long without the antidote. And the only place to get it is inside the Epicenter. So, better plan is you go back – you have Rove, and his people place a tracker – and you let them take you there. Then, we can get this done," Popov says, banging his hand on the counter for emphasis.

Popov spends the next hour going through what he knows about the Epicenter, including where they would most likely store an antidote. He explains his belief that our director is compromised, which isn't surprising to me given my memory of his sleazy hand creeping up my leg from under the table. Cameron and Popov never seem to warm to each other, which is also unsurprising. As we leave, I thank Popov for his information, but Cameron simply grunts and nods.

Driving off, I pull out the burner phone Rove gave us before we left and dial his number.

"Rove, I think we've been compromised," I say.

"We know – Farhad picked up on some chatter over the police radio waves a couple hours ago. You and Cam need to stay put until we can plan our next move," Rove responds.

"Roger that, are we safe to head to the spot?" Cameron asks.

"Yes, I'll contact you all in the morning..." the phone went silent for a moment before Rove continued, "and Andy...I'm sorry. But there might not be a way around this that doesn't include sending you. But we won't send you without backup on standby and we will always know where you are."

Silence fills the car as the reality sets in. I don't respond audibly, but instead nod and close my eyes.

Once Cameron hangs up the phone, I utter the thoughts that have haunted me for years, "I've given my life to our country, but I've never truly belonged within it. Cam, I don't even know what it's like to be *wanted* as a part of this country that I keep fighting for...and even if we can save it, I'm not even sure that reality will ever change for me."

Chapter 28
Ski Chalet

The drive between Popov's safehouse and where we're staying for the night seems like hours and neither of us have said a word since I started the car. Andy's words about belonging and country hang in the air between us. I struggle to break the silence, continuing to go back and forth in my head about how to explain how I'm feeling.

Finally, I just say what's on my mind, "I think I've been chasing that feeling...that feeling of being wanted and belonging...and worthy...maybe my entire life. And...I'm not trying to play the oppression Olympics, but I just want you to know that I understand."

Andy asks, "how do we stop this cycle, Cam? Does it ever end?"

"What do you mean?" I ask, not sure if she means our mutually complicated relationship with our country or with each other.

"Just all of it, Cam. I'm exhausted and I just want to feel safe and have peace."

"I still can't believe that our own people turned on us," I say, still stewing over how our own damned agency was involved in this.

I cannot believe I missed this, and that it took me too long to see that our own people were involved *this* deep. We should've kept closer tabs on Andy after knowing that Brody and Todd turned. We should have known something was wrong when Basir missed the initial date and Solaris never should have gotten the chance to get close enough to Andy to inject her. And then we just sat there and let them take her blood and essentially gave them the definitive evidence they needed to confirm that she's a viable host. I rake my hand through my hair and scratch my face, remembering that this horrible beard is still there.

As we round the corner into Whistler Village, heading for a cabin at the base of the mountain, I glance over at Andy who is now fast asleep with her head leaning against the car door. Snow covers the mountain, and I'm thankful the rental car has four-wheel drive as I pull into a driveway that clearly hasn't been plowed since the last snowfall. I contemplate leaving the car running to keep Andy warm while opening the place, but after what we just heard from Popov – even that doesn't feel safe. If someone grabs her now, we wouldn't even have a way to track her.

Yet another thing we need to talk about...

"Andy...wake up...we're here," I say, gently shaking her shoulder.

She jolts awake, quickly lifting her hands over her head to shield herself, before accidentally hitting her head against the car window.

"Andy, it's just me. You're alright, we are just here at the chalet where we're staying. Come inside with me and I'll come back out for our bags once you're settled," I say.

"Cam? Oh gosh...I'm sorry," she responds, rubbing her head in the spot where she hit it.

I get out of the car and come around to her side to open the door for her. Reaching out my hand, I gently pull her to her feet and wrap my arm around her waist.

"Let me help you," I say, knowing she can walk but not wanting her to slip on the ice because she seems only half awake.

The two of us slowly walk across the icy walkway and up a flight of stairs to the front door. As I open the large wooden door to the chalet, it's everything I wanted it to be and more - an expansive 12-foot ceiling, floor to ceiling windows with a view of Whistler Mountain, a giant fireplace in the center of the room, and a large, plush sectional couch overlooking the view. We're both exhausted, but I want tonight to be special. I'm not sure how much longer we can outrun the chaos that's waiting for us back home.

"Wow, this place is incredible. Cam, did you do this?" Andy asks, her face lighting up as she scans the room.

Seeing the light return to her eyes at this moment is amazing and I need to figure out a way to thank Theo when we get home. When I told him I wanted to do something nice for her, I didn't expect him to pull out all the stops like this. Andy's favorite wine, a Pinot Noir from Chateau de la Cree in Burgundy, France, is on a table in the center of the room beside two, long-stemmed glasses. The fire is blazing, reflecting off the large floor to ceiling windows overlooking the snowy Whistler Mountain. Andy shrieks with joy and runs over to the couch like a small child on Christmas morning, grabbing the label to inspect.

"Château de la Crée – Renaissance Gravieras...my favorite. How did you know?" She asks, running her hand across the label.

I can feel my cheeks flush as I reluctantly admit, "Theo is really an observant guy...he outdid himself here."

"Well, this place looks amazing. I love it," she responds, beaming at me from the couch.

I walk over and cover her in one of the throw blankets before heading to unpack the car. By the time I return, Andy has poured us both a glass of wine and is facing the mountain. She's pulled off the auburn wig and is running her fingers through her hair as she takes out the pins that held the wig in place. Her light brown curls now flow wildly over her shoulders and down her back in spirals and the moonlight is shining down on her in a way that makes her look angelic and takes my breath away. I stand in the doorway for a moment, taking in the scene in front of me.

Dear God...she's gorgeous.

Dropping the suitcases by the door, I come sit beside her and intentionally brush the fake beard up against her neck as I kiss her. At the tickle of the ridiculous beard, she erupts into laughter before grabbing my face and pulling it to hers for a slow, deep kiss. We search each other's mouths, licking and sucking with a curiosity as though it's our first kiss and an intensity as though it's our last.

"As much as I love the beard...so much," she says giggling, "I need to shower."

I back away from her, I'm sure my disappointment was evident on my face because I'd be happy just continuing to kiss her here all night.

"Do you want to join me?" She asks, looking over her shoulder as she walks toward the bathroom.

I jump up from the couch and start peeling off my shirt quickly and jogging beside her to take her hand.

"Well, Mrs. Weisman...I think I have a better idea," I say, raising an eyebrow deviously.

"Oh yeah...husband?" She asks eagerly, a coy smile spreading across her face.

Theo told me there was a giant hot tub in this place, and that sounds way better than a shower. I lead her up to the loft where there's a giant hot tub. It's filled and full of rose petals, courtesy of Theo's lead team.

Damn, they are good...

Theo's been teasing me that I will "get lucky" tonight and perhaps he thinks both Andy and I need some luck because he's for sure been a tad over the top here.

Though...I love it too.

"I guess Theo knows something's up between us huh?" She asks, looking between the rose filled tub and me.

I shrug my shoulders and smile, "I'm not sure it's possible for me to hide how I feel about you to most people and Theo is my best friend...so..."

"It's fine...I'm glad the team did this, it's beautiful," she interrupts, placing a hand on my mouth.

She dips a finger into the hot tub before letting out an adorable moan that has my dick raised at attention.

I move to stand behind her and pull her close enough for her to feel my erection on her lower back. She inhales deeply and I help her slowly pull her shirt over her head. Removing her pants, leaving nothing on her body but her underwear and bra, she climbs the steps into the hot tub. Not at all shy, I take off all my clothes, desperate to rid myself of the last remnants of the disguise. I rub off the horrible chia pet on my face and sling it into the trashcan before climbing into the tub behind her.

Before I can make another move, Andy is on top of me, and her hand is stroking my erection. While I'm typically a take charge type of guy, her confidence and willingness to just take what she wants from me is intoxicating.

"Tell me what you want me to do to you," I say, running my tongue along her neck before taking her ear lobe into my mouth and sucking.

She doesn't respond at first, and instead unclasps her bra, causing her breasts to spill out in front of me.

"Oh my gosh, Andy you're so beautiful," I say, admiring how the moonlight continues to shine through the giant chalet windows, making her honey-colored skin glow.

She smiles shyly, never able to take a compliment well. She continues stroking me with her hand while the folds between her legs are now bare and gliding across my leg.

I rub one of her breasts, lifting it to my lips and begin to suck furiously. She moans, throwing back her head with pleasure. While my mouth moves to her other breast, I rub my hands along her back and massage the soapy, floral water all over her body. She pulls my head up and takes my lips in hers before finally speaking.

"I want you to take me back to the couch and I want you to go down on me," she says, looking into my eyes with an intensity that makes his heart skip a beat.

"Are you sure?" I ask, knowing she's never let me go down on her before.

"Yes, I'm sure," she responds, biting her lip, and brushing a few errant curls from her cheek.

Andy wraps her arms around my shoulders as I place my hands under the curves of her behind and lift her out of the tub. Carrying her down the staircase that leads from the loft back to the main room, both of us smelling like rose petals, I'm intensely aware of the way her breasts feel pressed against my chest – and the way the cheeks of her full ass feel in the palms of my hands.

I'm throbbing with need but won't allow myself to be inside her until I can make this experience perfect for her. Anticipation lingers between us and the only sound, outside of our breaths and the beating of our hearts, is the crackling fire. I'm nervous because I want this moment to wash away whatever has made her not want to do this in the past. Laying her on the couch, I hover over her and kiss her gently on the lips. Looking into her eyes one last time, I search for her consent. She nods and her cheeks flush as she closes her eyes and takes a deep breath.

"Relax and let me make you feel good," I whisper in her ear before trailing kisses down her naked body.

When I reach the junction of her thighs, I slowly open her legs while gazing up at her. Pausing for a moment to catch my breath, she opens her eyes.

"Don't stop," she says, unleashing the dominant and animalistic part of me that wants to devour her and make her scream with pleasure.

As I bury myself between her legs, I realize that in her giving this piece of herself to me...I'm also giving a part of myself to her that I hadn't realized was even available for the taking.

I can't lose her – I won't – I need us to be like this...forever.

Chapter 29
Undone

"Andy"

The sensation of Cameron's breath between my legs is almost too much to bear. If someone had told me years ago that it was possible for fear and arousal to collide into an experience so full of pleasure, I'd have told them they were crazy. At this moment, as the love of my life, has his tongue between my legs – I cannot get out of my own head.

Stop it girl, just enjoy this!

Also...did I just call Cameron the love of my life?

My legs start to shake and Cameron strokes them gently and urges me to relax. I want this so bad, but I'm scared. I don't understand why so many people think oral sex is a gateway. To me, there aren't many things that could leave me feeling more vulnerable than being in this position with a man. There's something about this that feels uniquely intense and focused on me in a way that is more intimate than anything we've done together before. And for me, this sensation is colored with dirty feelings of the past – feelings I don't want to feel with him.

I will tell him...but after.

I close my eyes and take a deep breath, urging my body to relax and enjoy this moment with Cameron.

Cam isn't him...this isn't that...this is Cam...

He starts out gently, licking as he massages my legs. Then, he finds my clitoris with his tongue and begins to increase pressure by sucking and pulling as several of his fingers dive into my core. My body lurches up suddenly and uncontrollably as Cameron increases the pressure and makes a humming sound with his lips that causes a tingling sensation to take over my body.

"Oh, oh Cam – I can't...I think...I think I'm going to..."

I'm going to cum.

I try to move him, feeling too exposed and a little embarrassed about coming completely undone by his tongue – and worry I pushed this to happen before I was ready. But also, not wanting him to stop because I want him to change the way I feel – to help me erase the past.

He doesn't move from between my legs and instead increases his pace. I scream out in pleasure as my body twitches under him and I pour out from my core. Collapsing back on the couch, I'm speechless and still shaking from the sensation. A single tear escapes from my eye and Cameron's body stiffens.

"Are you okay?" Cameron asks, cradling my head in his hands and wiping away the tears.

I nod affirmatively, still unable to respond audibly. Reaching for him, I pull him close to me and wrap us both in the blanket before moving my hand to the erection poking me in the side.

"Wait, I just want to look at you for a minute," he says, locking eyes with mine, "we don't have to do anything else."

"I know, but I want to," I respond, shifting my weight so that I can climb on top of him. *Now it's my turn. I want to be in control of this...*

Cameron takes one of my breasts in his mouth and sucks hard, causing even more of a pool between my legs. Slowly guiding myself onto him, descending his shaft, I pause to adjust to his size while maintaining eye contact with him. I control the pace as our bodies collide, which feels like fireworks exploding through every nerve in my body. Flecks of brown dance in his eyes, mesmerizing me as our bodies synchronize in a passionate rhythm of desire.

We lose ourselves in each other in front of an audience of nature, snow falling on the mountains beyond the safety of our chalet. This second orgasm comes as a surprise and my core contracts wildly around Cameron's shaft, causing him to shout with pleasure as he spills out inside me.

Collapsing on top of him, I don't remove myself from him immediately. After several moments of silence pass between us, both clinging to the other as though we're afraid we'll spontaneously combust, Cameron slowly pulls out. With the separation, I start to shake and the cold I've dreaded replaces the warmth of his body. He carefully lifts me from the couch, and my head flops on his shoulder.

"Can we go back to the tub?" I ask, smiling to reassure him and desperate not to ruin the moment.

He quickly carries me back to the tub and turns the hot water to warm the water. Several moments pass, as we soak in the warmth of the tub while in each other's arms.

Damn…this feels so good.

"Cam, there's something I want to tell you," I say, swallowing the knot forming in my throat that's threatening to take my voice.

He's behind me, and attempts to turn me around to face him, but I stop him.

"No, can we just stay like this? I don't think I can tell you if you're looking at me," I admit, already embarrassed about this entire topic.

"What's wrong?" he asks, pulling me closer to him.

"I have to tell you something that I probably should've told you a long time ago," I pause while I work up the courage to continue, "when I first started at the agency…while we were still interns…something happened and…umm, it's why I never felt like I could…have that kind of attention on me."

"What? What happened? Did someone do something to you?" Cameron asks, his body stiffening and his heartbeat increasing as I lay on his chest.

"I can't…I don't want to say more. I just…what happened between us tonight was amazing," I say.

So amazing…

"Andy, I wish you'd told me…I could have been gentler…I could have…" his voice starts sounding panicked.

I swivel around in the tub, placing my legs over his before grabbing his face with my hands and saying, "no, Cam – it was perfect. You have *nothing* to apologize for – nothing."

Cameron takes a deep breath and kisses me on the cheek before wrapping his arms around my shoulders and pulling me into a hug.

"I'm sorry that happened to you and I wish I'd been there to stop it…or could have done something at the time to help you. Thank you for telling me", he says.

"There's more," I say, dreading this next disclosure.

I look down before closing my eyes and covering my face with my hands.

"Cam, the day I resigned…the director…he grabbed me…and it happened almost exactly how the other situation started," I admit.

"What - Director Bryant? Oh gosh, Andy…I'm so sorry," he says, his fists balling at his sides before continuing, "why didn't you tell me?"

And now I'm crying…

"I'm sorry, I don't want you to feel like I'm blaming you. I just…God, I had no idea and while I didn't trust *any* of those fuckers – I didn't know that guy would do something like *this.*"

"I know, it surprised me too. And I didn't say anything because I just wanted to forget it ever happened...but when Popov started talking about the disease inside the agency...Cam – the fish rots from the head," I say, using that famous fish analogy that my dad used when I was a kid.

"Are you going to tell Rove and the rest of the team?" Cameron asks.

"No, you can't...please. I can't...I just...I don't," I start to panic at the idea that the entire team would know about this, "I just...I wanted you to know because as if this crap with the serum weren't bad enough...I'm really worried that Director Bryant is going to worry I'll say something and maybe..."

My voice trails off, as I consider what his next move will be. What I don't say is that I know from personal experience that nothing good comes when you speak up about sexual violence in the workplace – especially when powerful men at the agency are involved.

"That he might try and silence you? Andy...I understand why you'd be worried but what do you think he could do at this point?" Cameron asks, worry in his eyes.

"I don't know. But Cameron, you know what kind of power that man has," I say, trying to catch my breath.

"We don't have to give them any details. But I think we need to make sure Rove knows nobody in that organization can be trusted. Our entire plan hinged on being able to trust the director, and I don't think we can trust even him anymore," he says, raking one of his hands through his now wet curls.

"Okay, but don't we already know that we can't trust any of them?" I ask.

"Andy, how can we send you there? Please don't do this...please help me find another way," Cameron begs, taking a lock of my curls in his hand before rubbing the back of my neck.

I raise a hand to his lips and say, "Can we stop talking about this tonight and just be together? I didn't even want to tell you, but I just wanted you to know what tonight meant to me and that I trust you."

And that I choose you.

I don't speak all the thoughts whirling around in my head, and Cameron certainly doesn't realize that telling him felt more like a confession. We've had an incredible night together that healed a part of me that'd broken years ago when I was barely an adult – and some of it came back up for me during that debrief with Popov. I've obviously suspected the agency wasn't what I signed up for, but the debrief called to the surface my deepest fears. We're alone in this – our tiny little rogue group of CIA misfits...and asylum seekers...we're alone...and I feel a degree of loneliness even amongst my own team because I know whether we succeed in taking back our country rests solely upon my shoulders.

This bliss I feel with Cameron might not last more than this night, but I want to have tonight.

"We'll talk about it in the morning alright, I promise," I add.

Cameron nods, taking my hand, and kisses my palm. He reaches for the glass of wine he brought to the tub and takes a long swig.

***

The next morning, I wake up to the smell of freshly brewed coffee – a luxury unparalleled. I don't remember moving to a bed last night, but I'm curled up in a plush comforter surrounded by giant pillows and there's another giant window in this room that overlooks the mountain. I'm still naked, which means at some point Cameron moved me to this bed without me even noticing.

Where are my clothes? Where is Cameron?

The buttoned-down shirt Cameron wore to the debrief yesterday is lying across a chair in the corner of the room. I grab the shirt, pulling it close to inhale his scent on it, before putting it on to cover myself. My hair is a hot mess, curls springing out in all directions, so I pull it into a top knot before starting down the stairs that lead to the living room and kitchen. Cameron is at the stove making breakfast, dressed only in a pair of black boxer briefs.

Hot damn, he looks so good...

Standing silently at the bottom of the steps, I admire him silently for a few moments. The muscles in his back seem to dance as he moves around the kitchen, humming to himself like he has no idea I'm standing behind him. I tip toe behind him, reaching my arms around his chest to hug him from behind before laying my head on his back.

"Good morning," I say, before he turns around and I stand on my tiptoes to kiss him on the lips.

"Good morning," he responds, wrapping his large arms around me and reaching down to squeeze my ass.

"I smell coffee – can I have some?" I ask, scanning the kitchen for the source of that delicious smell.

"Of course, I made it for you," he smiles, before jogging over to pour me a cup.

"Can I help you make breakfast?" I ask, taking the warm cup from his hands before walking back over to the stove to see what he's cooking.

"Nope, you can go sit under the blankets on the couch and I'll bring the food to you," he says, his smile widening to reveal his dimples.

Good, because I'd probably accidentally burn the toast.

I scurry over to the couch, situating my body as close to the fire as possible, and take a sip of the coffee. As the warm liquid goes down my throat, my body relaxes deeper into the cushions. Last night was amazing, but I'm acutely aware that it's going to make what I need to do today even harder. I don't want to leave Cameron, but I know I'll need to once we return and the clock continues to tick loudly on this operation. There are so many unknowns, but one thing I know for certain is that unless we can identify what Basir and Popov call "the disease" within the CIA – there is no surviving this – not for me or my country. Destroying the facilities won't cure the larger problem of the fractures within our agency.

The loudly vibrating burner phone, which causes the end table to jump, jolts me from my thoughts.

Reality is literally calling.

"Hello," I answer, my voice tentative.

"Andy, it's Rove. We've worked all night to vet Popov's claims, and I think we all should get on a conference call together. Is Cameron with you?" Rove asks.

"Yeah, he's here," I respond, walking to the kitchen to get Cameron's attention.

Placing a gentle hand on his back, I motion for him to join me in the living room. Once both of us are seated at the table with our notes available for review, I tell Rove we're ready to get started.

"Andy, you're the one with most to lose here – I want to know how you're feeling about all this," he says, before falling silent.

"I think the Director is one of the moles," I blurt out, glancing over at Cameron who's looking at me intensely, "that's likely how our location was compromised. Was he aware of our meeting?"

"We've kept our activities close but couldn't meet with Popov without informing our Canadian counterparts. Despite my attempts to keep the meeting from spreading further than Popov's handler, it clearly spread far enough and if the director is compromised...well, we must assume nobody outside of our small team can be trusted," he responds.

"How do we know we can trust everyone on our team?" Cameron asks, skeptically.

"Well Cam – things didn't go sideways until we had to involve the Canadians and their own assets pointed them back to our agency. It wasn't GST," Rove snaps, his voice laced with irritation.

"So, what do you suggest at this point," I ask Rove, not seeing any other way than the one Cameron is against but knowing he will have little choice in the matter if the order comes from his boss.

"Theo is leading a team that's headed to St. Petersburg to see what's left of the lab there and gain additional intel on the network. While it's risky, placing a tracker on you and letting you get wrapped up will serve two things for us – one, the director won't think we are working against him and two, you'll lead us to the location so we can take it down," Rove responds.

"Give me a couple days…I'll go in and try to identify as many people as possible and collect as much as I can remember…and maybe there's someone there who can be turned. But we can't know that from the outside," I say, looking at Cameron and hoping he will get on board.

"Dr. Raj is telling us that without your pills, two days would be pushing it…but Theo is on his way to you all with a tracker that will track your location *and* your temperature. If it gets to the point where Dr. Raj believes it's too dangerous to leave you inside – we go in," he says.

"Okay, good. I'll try and work fast," I respond, laughing a bit to try and lighten the mood.

Cameron is now pacing back and forth in front of the fireplace, "Rove – so what…I'm just supposed to sit back at the ops center and watch Andy via a tracker and just hope they don't kill her in there?"

"They're not going to kill her – they need her," Rove responds, calmly.

"How long before Theo gets here?" I ask, hoping I have time to calm Cameron down.

"He's about an hour out," Rove responds.

"Okay, we'll hang tight until he gets here," I say, hanging up the phone and walking over to place a hand on Cameron's arm.

He moves away from me, which causes my heart to twist painfully in my chest. At the rejection, I slowly walk toward the couch and wrap myself in the cozy throw blanket. Without another word, I watch Cameron and wait for him to engage. My stomach growls, which reminds me that we haven't eaten, and breakfast is likely cold.

"Cam? Are you going to talk to me?" I ask, debating whether to try and touch him again or stay away.

"Andy, you know I don't want you going in there," he responds, looking over at me with stormy eyes.

"I don't want to either, but there's no other way. We don't even know where this place *is*, and we don't know how tied up the agency is in this and who all is involved. We need the proof, and I can't just wait around while we run in circles. Don't you realize...I could also get killed if we do nothing as well?"

A fact I've been trying to ignore despite the hell loop I am in with the serum pumping through my veins.

I'm screaming and so frustrated that I feel tears threatening to break free. I turn my back from him, not wanting him to see me fall apart. Moments later, I feel his hand on the small of my back. I turn, wrap my arms around him, and sob into his shirt. I hate crying, but a part of me feels like these tears needed to come out. Just when I feel like I have no tears left, there's a loud knock on the door. It causes us both to startle and Cameron to grab his gun from the kitchen counter, heading over to look through the peephole.

"It's Theo," he says, setting the gun back on the counter before opening the door.

Well, that was a lot faster than an hour...

"Damn dude, it's colder than a mother fucker out there. You could've moved a little faster than my grandma to open the door, man," Theo says, smacking Cameron in the shoulder before pushing past him into the living room.

"Hey Theo," I say, smiling widely and laughing at his grandma joke.

Cameron rolls his eyes and follows Theo into the living room. Theo sits down on the couch and gets right to business by opening his bag and pulling out a bunch of medical items and some things that look like they've come right from a tattoo parlor.

"Theo, what is this?" I ask, my face twisting with concern over what he's about to do to me.

"I should warn you...this tracking device is experimental and hasn't really been well tested on humans...but Dr. Raj assures me that it will do the job – and that we don't really have any better options," Theo responds, apologetically.

"Okay, so you are about to inject me with something that maybe has only been placed in lab rats. How very apropos of you," I sigh.

Cameron stands in the corner and grunts with irritation, and I glare at him out of the corner of my eye. Transferring his anger to Theo isn't the move, and he needs to knock it off.

"I hate to ask you to do this, but I need to place the tracker in your neck...and this might not feel great," Theo says, wincing at the visual of this that was likely swirling around in his mind.

"Okay, let's do this," I say, moving my hair to the side before holding out my arms for Cameron to come sit with me.

I brace myself for impact, just as I've done so many times before.

Chapter 30
Just Us

My blood is boiling lava hot as I watch Theo pull out a device that looks like a staple gun, telling us that he's about to inject an experimental tracking device in Andy's neck with it. Andy moves her hair to expose her neck and reaches out for me with fear in her eyes. I grab ahold of her, and she clings to me, her body tensing. My eyes widen as Theo places the gun at the base of her skull.

"Holy shit man, do you have to put that thing *there*?" I ask, horrified at how close it is to her skull.

"Look man, if you want to help here you can hold her and keep her comfortable while I do this," he responds, not taking his eyes off Andy.

I can feel Andy's breathing increase and her body shaking under me as she says, "Cam, stop it. Just let him do it so we can get this over with."

Placing a firm hand on her back and grabbing ahold of her hand, the one that isn't clutching the side of the couch, I hold her still and close my eyes.

I can't watch this.

"Okay, take a deep breath and try to relax. I know this really sucks, but you must hold still," Theo warns.

Andy continues to tremble in my arms, taking a deep, labored breath but her entire body remains tense. I try consoling her by rubbing her back but feel helpless because it doesn't seem to provide her any relief from this situation.

"Can you just be quick?" She asks, making her body rigid and as still as possible.

Theo shoots the gun into her neck, and Andy screams before collapsing her entire weight into my lap and shaking uncontrollably.

"What the hell is happening to her, man?" I ask, trying to hold Andy still as her eyes roll back into her head.

"Just hold onto her, Dr. Raj mentioned that the implant could trigger a seizure. Get blankets and let's just keep her warm – her heart rate is likely going crazy and as soon as she's lucid we need her to take the meds," Theo responds, calm enough that I feel like I'm in the twilight zone.

A few moments pass before Andy stops seizing, taking deep breaths and gasping for air.

"I feel like you've just shattered my skull," she says, clutching the side of her neck where Theo inserted the tracker and slowly opening her eyes.

"I'm sorry, it might feel like that for another couple hours while your body adjusts," Theo says.

Andy moans in pain and I grab an ice pack from the medical bag.

"How long before we have to fly home, and what can we expect once we arrive," I ask, punching the ice bag to activate.

"No! No ice, I'm too cold," Andy mumbles, holding up her hand to stop me before closing her eyes again.

"We don't have a lot of time. Yawl need to be at the airport in about three hours. And it's a two and a half hour drive no matter how you dice that apple," Theo warns, handing Andy a pill from the bottle on the table.

"Okay, let's go," Andy says, propping herself up to stand before falling over and clutching the side table.

Both Theo and I rush to her side, putting her arms over our shoulders, and carrying her up to the bedroom. She's still wearing my shirt, which she obviously can't wear to the airport. Once we get her to bed, Theo awkwardly shifts his weight from one leg to the other. I glare at him, causing him to put up his hands in a surrender motion before heading back downstairs to give Andy privacy.

"Andy, I'm going to bring your bag...do you think you can get dressed or do you need my help? We need to leave in the next fifteen minutes to make it to the airport in time for our flight," I say quietly, wondering if delaying the flight would make them all rethink this plan to send Andy into a hornet's nest of terrorism.

"I can do it myself if you get me the bag. I also need my wig from the table, and you need to put the chia pet back on your face," she smiles, reminding me of the fact that I also need to get myself ready.

Since we entered the country in disguise, we need to leave that way unless we want to invite drama from the Canadian authorities as well. And while it's tempting to slow down the inevitable, we can't risk getting stuck in Canada because I'm sure the Canadians will just hand Andy over. If that happens, I don't know how long it will be before I can come for her.

Trying to wipe those thoughts from my head so I can do the job, I run downstairs to bring Andy her suitcase and quickly dress myself. While I'm gluing hair to my face, Theo walks up behind me.

"You alright, man?" Theo asks, putting his hand on my shoulder.

"I'm fine," I respond through gritted teeth.

Not even close to fine...

"Dude, I know you well enough to know you aren't fine. You want to just tell me what you are all sour about?" Theo asks, leaning on the wall next to me.

"I don't want her to go into that place, Theo. I feel like it's happening all over again – but this time, I should be able to stop it," I admit, punching my palm against the sink so hard it stings.

"You know this isn't the same as the situation with your dad, right? We aren't going to let anything bad happen to her. The first sign of trouble and we'll be in there like white on rice," Theo says, placing a hand on my shoulder.

"She's my girl, man. I have to protect her," I mutter, placing both hands on my head in frustration.

Did I just say that out loud?

"Trust us, okay? We'll get her out," Theo assures me, squeezing my shoulder before returning to the living room to collect his supplies.

"And bro, I'm glad yawl found your way back to each other," he says, snickering and patting me on the back.

"Well, we aren't..." my voice trails off before Theo interrupts me.

"Dude, you can try and deny it all you want but you aren't fooling any of us. You two might as well end this charade and just come out with it already."

To my amazement, in less than fifteen minutes, Andy comes down the steps looking like Rebecca Weisman. Despite her ability to pull herself together in record time, I take note of the eerie, glassy eyed look she gives me as she walks to the car with her head down. Andy is tough and I know she'll muscle her way through this, but I'm worried about what this will cost her in the long run.

Once we're in the car, Theo says his goodbyes and wishes us luck. He prepares us by explaining that it's not clear what the next move will be from the terrorist group, but that once we land at Dulles airport anything could happen.

"Let's just try and get you all back to the ops center safely and we can plan our next move," Theo says, before raising his fist and flashing us the goofy smile he makes when he's trying to make people laugh.

Andy and I spend the two-and-a-half-hour car ride to the airport in silence, Andy drifting in and out of sleep while I grip the steering wheel so tight that I worry my hands might break. The flight from Canada back to Virginia's Dulles airport is uneventful, both of us exhausted. We don't speak about it, but I know Andy had to also be anxious about what awaits us now that we've returned home. The anxiety bubbled in the pit of my stomach, but I keep it to myself and just pray for more time to come up with a better plan than sending Andy into more chaos.

I'm deeply in thought when the plane slams down on the runway, popping me out of my thoughts.

"Welcome home," Andy says sarcastically under her breath.

I sigh loudly and run my hand nervously through my hair. Walking through the airport, I transfer my desperately tight grip to Andy's hand not wanting to let go of her.

"Cam, are you trying to break my hand? I just really have to pee, and you can't come with me," she says, squeezing my hand to reassure me.

I hover at the entrance to the women's restroom, eliciting the glares from several older women exiting who likely think I'm a creeper. Typically, when I land back in the US, I feel a sense of peace being home. This time, however, dread fills my body because I'm returning with the realization that things have changed. I still love my country, but we have our work cut out for us. Our team is tiny compared to the mammoth of an organization we're up against. And until Andy gets more information, we don't even know how deep this goes.

"Stay close to me," I say, grabbing Andy's arm when she gets a few paces ahead of me.

"Cameron, stop it. You're making this worse. I'm not gonna get grabbed in the middle of a goddamned airport," she snaps, glaring back at me.

When we get into the car, Andy reaches across the middle console and grabs my hand, preventing me from starting the car.

"Hey, look at me Cam," she says, her eyes piercing with intensity.

"What's up?" I ask, my eyes darting all around us as I worry that we've been followed.

"Can we just sit here for a minute?" She asks, now holding my hand with both of hers.

"Okay, you alright? Do you need something?" I ask.

"Cam, before we go anywhere, I want you to know something," she says, biting her lip while her face starts to flush.

"Should I be worried?" I ask, now looking directly at her.

"I love you, Cam. And I know I haven't given you any confidence that we'll be able to get back to being...us. But I need you to know that I love you and I want that, again," she says, her eyes now glowing a little as they begin to water in the low tight of the parking garage.

I don't immediately respond, as I let the reality of what she's just said sink in.

"Same," I say, before quickly elaborating, "I mean, I love you too. You *are* my past, my present, my future, and my everything."

I don't wait for her to say another word before scooping her into my arms and hugging her tight.

"Cam, you're crushing me," she says, giggling before reaching out to place her hand on my face.

"Oh, sorry," I say, smiling back and wishing that I could slow down time and keep her with me for longer.

"I need you to do something for me," she says, concern now washing over her face.

Without responding audibly, I lean back and tilt my head while waiting for what's coming next.

"Can you trust me? No matter what happens next...can you just trust that I can hold my own? And that no matter what happens I can handle myself?" She asks.

"What do you mean," I respond, not liking what I think she's referring to.

"I'm not trying to say we aren't a team. I know I haven't been the best at letting you help, and the boys club drives me crazy, but I need you to see me as an equal member of this team...and not...just your girlfriend," she says, now holding my face in both her hands and forcing me to look into her eyes, which are now a shade of grey.

Wait...did she just call herself my girlfriend?

"Wait, am I your boyfriend?" I ask, needing to know if we are having the define the relationship talk just before we could be staring down the end of the world.

"Do you want to be?" She asks, raising an eyebrow.

"Yes woman! I have wanted you back from the moment you walked out of my apartment that night we broke up and have been praying you'll let me be yours every day since I saw you again in Brazil," I reply, hoping she isn't playing some kind of joke on me.

"Okay, let's do this then," she says, biting her lip and looking me in the eyes.

I swallow and take a deep breath, before placing my hands on hers. There's never been a question of whether she's capable and she's certainly carrying this team right now, but I know I haven't been the best at giving her the space she needs to lead when she should be the one to lead.

"I trust you Andy and I know you can take care of yourself. But can you promise that on this team – you and I..." I say, gesturing to indicate that it's just us two, "that you'll meet me halfway and let me take care and protect your too?"

"Okay, so we move forward as a team. I have your back and you have mine, alright?" She asks.

"I can do that," I say, kissing her face before putting my lips on hers and pushing my tongue into her mouth.

She moans just loud enough for me to hear, which sends a shiver down my entire body.

We cannot have sex in this car, man...calm your fire.

When my lips are on hers, the world seems to fall away. For moments, while we continue kissing like a couple of teenagers hiding out in a mall parking lot, I forget about the danger looming all around us.

We sit like that in the car, with her in my lap, and hold onto each other as though we're both trying to keep the other from falling off a clip. Some moments later, she climbs off my lap and back into the passenger seat, rubbing at her eyes and resting one hand on my leg. I feel more relaxed than when we got into the car but remain somewhat vigilant about surveillance as we exit the airport garage.

My eyes dart between the road in front of me and the rear mirrors, as I cautiously exit the airport garage and head toward the highway. A few miles from the airport, a feel the hairs on the back of my neck stand at attention and notice Andy glancing in the passenger window.

"Cam, do you see that?" She asks, reaching over to grab my hand.

Just after we exit the toll road, just a few miles from the border between Virginia and Maryland, a police siren sounds behind us. Andy takes a deep breath, squeezes my hand so tight that her knuckles turn white, before turning to me with a resigned level of calm.

"It's go time," she says, with only a slight, almost imperceptible shake to her voice as several police cars surround us.

Within what feels like seconds, Andy's being pulled from the car. I try to exit and chase after her, but several officers block me while holding their weapons at my head. Out of the rear-view mirror, I watch as Andy is thrown to the ground and placed in handcuffs.

"What are you doing? Why are they hurting her? She isn't resisting. Why have we been stopped?" I ask questions in rapid fire, though I know I'm not going to get a response.

Several officers drag Andy's now limp body into the back of a squad car before speeding off. As soon as the car holding Andy is out of sight, the officer who's holding his weapon on my face hits me in the face with the base of his long gun before spitting on me through the car door window.

"Tell your boss...Rover...or whatever the fuck his name is... to stand the fuck down," the officer sneers in a deep southern drawl.

The officer is a plump, pale man whose face is so red that it looks like he's just tried to run a marathon. He's missing a few teeth and I can smell his rancid breath as spittle escapes his mouth with each word he utters. Once the officer lobs his threat, he waddles back to his car and speeds off. I immediately put the car in drive, slam my foot on the petal, and speed to the Wardman Ops center. With the hand I'm not using to drive, I pick up the burner phone and dial station.

"Rove – they took her. Several cops...they grabbed her and threw her...we were on the toll road...and they just grabbed her...and they threatened us...said to stand down, FUCK, FUCK, FUCK," I scream, banging my hand against the steering wheel, and trying to stifle a sob.

"Cam – calm down...I know this is hard, but you need to get back here safely and try to remember as many details as you can," Rove says.

"Okay, I have their names and badge numbers – Officer Sanchez, 1776 – Officer Moore, 1333, Officer Cavender, 1762...Rove something is off...those guys weren't agency...they were like small town cops. She's hurt – they hurt her," I shout, unable to stop from screaming into the phone.

Rove instructs me to end the call and focus on getting back to station safely, reassuring me that we'll get Andy out as soon as we locate the epicenter of the terrorist cell. I still hate this plan and hoped we'd have more time before she was taken.

We should've stayed in Canada.

On the drive from Virginia back into DC, I pass the Pentagon – a stark reminder of how similar this situation feels to when I lost my father. Another person I love is being torn away from me by a pack of terrorists, but this time the terrorists are my own countryman.

But there's still a chance we can save her.

They all said we could track her and that there will be time.

...but what if there isn't?

Something about this entire situation doesn't feel right. I race back to the station, driving over 100 miles per hour, the names and badges of the officers running on loop in my head as though remembering them will get us anywhere. Tears of fear, sadness, and rage stream down my face indiscriminately and I don't even bother to stop them. Barely able to see the road through the blur of my own tears, I try the breathing exercises my therapist taught me.

But they're useless right now...of course.

As soon as I pull up to the Wardman, I don't even bother to pull into the parking garage. Instead, I just abandon my car on Woodley Road, not caring what happens to the car. Racing past security, I flash my identification. Thankfully, I ripped that horrible beard off my face in the car, so I look like himself again – albeit a ragged form with blood shot eyes from crying during the drive.

Before reaching the doorway that leads to the station, I hear several raised voices and the hard knot in the pit of my stomach makes him feel like I'm going to vomit. Crashing through the door with so much force it flings open loudly, the entire room turns to look at me. Dr. Raj, Rove, Theo, and Farhad are all gathered around a large screen in the main room that shows a map with a trail of red blinking dots.

"What is that? Have you found her?" I ask, pointing at the screen.

Dr. Raj immediately looks at the floor, frowning and Theo walks over to me and gestures for me to sit on the couch.

"Well...where is she? Can we go get her?" I ask, my eyes darting between a sea of distraught looks on my teammates faces.

I hope they found the location of the facility and have surveillance on Andy already. From the looks on their faces, though, something is seriously wrong.

"Cam – this monitor shows the movement of the tracker. I'm going to replay this for you so that you can see what we're working with," Rove says, before reaching for a remote and pressing "play".

The map pans out, showing the red dot hovering above Whistler Village where Theo had inserted the device into Andy's neck. Then, it shows a sped-up version where we see the dot tracing where our plane entered the United States, the route we'd taken with their car, and the moment Andy was separated from me. The dot remains active for another hour, tracing her to a building in Manassas, Virginia and then the dot stops blinking.

"Why did it stop? What happened?" I ask, growing more irritated that they aren't just telling me what's happening and instead expecting me to know how to interpret this red dot.

The entire room remains silent, and everyone just looks at me with horror in their eyes.

"Where is she?" I ask, looking directly at Rove who I knew would answer me.

He responds and explains, "we don't know what happened, but about an hour after she was taken – we lost the track."

"What do you mean we lost the track? How? Where? Can we just go to where she was before the track was lost?" My mind is spinning in all directions, trying to hang onto something that will allow me to regain some shred of hope.

"I was afraid this might happen, but hoped it wouldn't," Dr. Raj says, "If they scanned her for tracking devices, and they got any inkling that we'd track her...they'd have checked and removed the device before taking her anywhere of significance. What that officer said to you – telling you to tell Rove to 'stand down'...means that they know enough to know we are on to them...which likely tipped them off to the fact that we wouldn't have left her vulnerable to capture without being able to track her in some way."

I can feel my face heat up and I ball my fists at my side. I want to throw something or punch something, but instead flop onto the couch and bury my head in my hands.

She needs me to think – to be strong.

"We aren't going to just leave her out there. I don't give a flying fuck what that asshole told you – we aren't standing down on jack shit here," Rove says, reaching out and grabbing my shoulder.

"Well, what are we going to do? It's just us and we can't even rely on the agency to help," I say, the reality of how little resources we have without the agency and how screwed we are as a result finally sinking in.

"Cam – in the time since you all left Canada, some very real things have changed for us. The President of the United States just signed an emergency order to re-allocate funds to our group. We're officially operating outside of the CIA and at the strict orders of the president," Rove explains.

"If Congress is aware of us – we're dead in the water...totally screwed. We all know those fuckers can't keep their mouths shut," Theo says, putting his palm to his head in irritation before deeply sighing.

"Nope, this is deep cover – Congress isn't in this one," Rove responds, smirking as though he's gotten away with something.

"How is that possible? Doesn't the President have to ask Congress if he can take a piss?" Theo asks, rolling his eyes.

"Well...the President just took piss on CIA and Congress doesn't know," Farhad says, giggling to himself.

"*My* man, that was funny," Theo says, high-fiving Farhad.

"Not this time man because we're in national emergency territory– and I'm not looking a gift horse in the mouth because we need the cash...and the backing. You got a better plan?" Rove asks, placing his hands on his hips and raising his eyebrow at Theo.

GST-9 is officially rogue – unaffiliated with the CIA and under the radar of Congress.

"Team, we have 72 hours to prove to the President that high-ranking CIA officials are associated with Solaris or the CIA will be informed of our plans and we'll be shut down," Rove warns.

"And we have just about that amount of time to get Andy her pills or she won't come out of here alive," Dr. Raj adds, looking down at a medical file in her hands.

"We need to find Andy, destroy the epicenter, and get the evidence we need to start bringing these moles down," Rove concludes, starting to give instructions to everyone in the room.

Without the tracker, Andy is going to have to find a way to send us a signal. She told me to trust her, but as I stand here and watch the replay of the tracker going dead, I can feel my heart starting to break.

Chapter 31
Captive

"Andy"

Slowly opening my eyes, I'm nauseatingly aware of how cold I am. I'm lying on a cement floor inside a cell. Moving my jaw around and touching my face, I try to see if something's broken. One of the officers, the large one with the *really* red face punched me before I fell to the ground.

Or maybe I was just thrown to the ground?

Pulling myself painfully off the floor, I scurry to a corner of the cell and wrap my arms tightly around my knees to stay as warm as possible in this hellhole. Peering over my knees, my eyes remain fixed on the men in the room. I need to remember as many of these details as possible for the report I'll write when I get back to station. I can't wait to add their pictures to the network visual we're building on the wall.

If...I get back to the ops center.

I don't have my medication, but Dr. Raj told me that the best thing I can do is try to remain calm and keep my heart rate steady. So that's what I'm trying to do – breathe and focus on trying to take in as many details about this place, and the people in it, as I can.

"What do we do with her now?" The officer with the red face and matching red hair says to the other, turning toward me and sneering.

"Hell, if I know. But - she's pretty darn cute. I wonder if your guy would mind if we had some fun first," the other one says.

He leers at me as he licks his discolored, chapped lips. This one is a bit older, with jet black hair styled in a buzz cut, olive color skin, and a beer gut that makes him appear as though he's nine months pregnant. They both seem as dumb as a sack of rocks, so I think it's unlikely they know much about the terrorist plot. It seems like it's mentally taxing for them to even remember their own names on a regular basis.

I close my eyes, and momentarily hold my breath, trying to keep from throwing up all over myself. I doubt they'd give me new clothes and spending the next several days in vomit encased jeans would make this even worse.

"Naw, dude, the guy said we needed to keep her alive. She must be important the way they have us keeping her back here and all," the red face guy says, his mouth hanging open as though he's trying to get additional oxygen to the two brain cells in his head that are trying to connect.

The dark haired one, whose pants are hanging low enough on his hips to reveal a repulsive amount of butt crack, scratches his head as though he's trying to process something.

"Eh, too bad. At least we're getting paid, though," the dark haired one exclaims before pumping his fist in the air enthusiastically.

I let out a deep breath, relief pouring over my body that at least I won't have to fight off these guys in the short term. After a few minutes more of asinine conversation between the two of them, they leave the room without saying a word to me. With my eyes closed, I imagine myself wrapped in Cameron's arms by the fire in Whistler. That memory is my happy place, but sadness creeps in when I think about how much time the two of us wasted.

You can do this...

It's so cold and this cement floor makes it feel like I'm sitting on an ice cube. This place looks like a police station, but there's nobody back here where they're holding me. And oddly, I don't hear the noise I'd expect from an active police station. Other than the two village idiots, I haven't heard anyone else since...

Oh God, Cameron...is he okay?

My heart twists at the thought that they might've done something to him. I reach out to touch my neck, remembering the tracker and thankful we'd placed it before our return. Moments pass with continued silence until the blood curdling sound of a siren alarms. The noise takes my breath away and I cover my ears with my hands, while also trying to curl into a ball. The pain in my head renders me unable to move because it feels like someone is repeatedly bashing my skull against the cement floor with each moment the noise continues.

"Stop! Please stop," I scream, trying desperately but unsuccessfully to escape the noise.

Then, the door to the room outside of this cell opens and the noise stops. Two men enter the room – one is red cheeks, and the other is...

Todd?

Wait, no...

Todd is dead...

The man who looks like Todd walks toward my cell, hands casually in his pocket while his hair tosses about on his shoulders. He's wearing kakis and a polo shirt, as though he's just stepped off the golf course and patent leather shoes that make clicking noises as he walks toward me.

"Well, well...hello again, Andy. You thought you'd escaped huh? You should've known Brody and I wouldn't let you get away *that* easily," Todd says, a smug and cocky smile creeping across his face.

He's alive?!?

"What do you want from me?" I ask, trying to see how much information he'll give me.

Todd begins to cackle, like a trite Disney villain who's about to do something horrible that's sure to give small children nightmares, "you know what we want...so there's no point in us pretending you don't. You're ours now – property of the state...but first...we have some business to take care of."

Business?

Todd turns to the red-faced cop and says, "You can leave now. Here's the money I owe you...now why don't you be a good boy and clear the building for the next hour or so."

Todd hands red face, who's salivating like a vulture that's just caught sight of a fresh piece of bloody meat, a large wad of one-hundred-dollar bills. Red face grabs the cash and scurries out the door with and extra skip in his step, seemingly oblivious to the fact that Todd was just speaking down to him.

Todd reaches into his pocket and pulls out a set of keys. As he begins to open the cell, several other men walk into the room and stand behind him. They pull their weapons on me and instruct me to place my hands behind my head and turn away from them, facing the back of the cell. I slowly lift my hands over my head in compliance. The goal is to gather as much data as I can in the next couple days, so there is no reason to fight...yet.

Once the cell gate opens, several of the armed guards grab me and prod me along while following Todd into an adjacent room. My eyes widen as we enter a room that looks like a mix between a surgery room and a torture chamber.

"What is this place?" I ask, fear starting to feel like it might strangle me to death.

Without a response to my questions, Todd points to the metal table in the middle of the room and says, "Put her there...and make sure she's strapped down tight. She's stronger than she looks."

The men holding me throw me onto the table and begin strapping my arms and legs to the table with thick leather straps. My desire to comply has left the building and I start kicking, punching, and scratching the men furiously. With several men against just me, I'm no match and moments later I'm on my back staring up at a bright light while strapped to this table. Two of the men have scratches all over their face and arms from my fingernails, and one of them has blood gushing from his nose where my elbow connected.

Todd saunters over, looking me in the eyes, only a few inches from my face. I narrow my eyes and spit in his face. With an eerie calm, he picks up a towel from the table beside him and wipes his face. He's always been an asshole, but I notice there's been a change since I last saw him. His eyes look dead and glassy like he's no longer capable of human emotion. Perhaps he never was, but he used to do a better job of hiding it. He walks over to me and places his large, sweaty hand on my face before violently turning my head to the side. This move exposes the bruising at the base of my skull, along with the tiny red area where the tracker was implanted.

Oh no...no...no...they can't...can they?

"Yep, I thought so. Take it out boys," Todd says, glancing at me out of the side of his eye before leaving the room, "Keep her alive...we still need her, but you can make it hurt."

I stare unflinchingly into the light, biting my lip to keep my face from showing the terror bubbling inside. As a large tool that looks like a power drill closes in on my neck, I close my eyes. When it touches my neck, the pain radiates through my body with such a fierce intensity that my eyes fly open, and I hear a loud scream.

Is that me?

I can feel my body shaking with the force of the drill, and then the entire room dissolves into darkness.

I'm eight years old, sitting in the back of my father's black Ford Bronco truck when I hear the police sirens. My mom is in the car behind us, as we caravan home from the marina where our boat is docked. When it's clear the police car is following us, my dad slowly pulls over to the side of the road. We all hope the officer passes us, on pursuit of someone else – but he doesn't.

"Step out of the car boy," the officer says, as my father rolls down his window.

"What seems to be the problem sir," my dad asks, confused because he hadn't been speeding.

"I said get out," the officer yells, pounding on the car door and pulling out his gun.

"Daddy? What's happenin?" I ask, not wanting my dad to get out of the car.

My dad slowly releases the steering wheel, lifting his hands where the officer can see them.

"Okay sir, I'm going to open the door, but first let me reassure my daughter that everything is alright," my dad says, his voice calm and controlled.

I hear my father taking deep breaths and see how hard he's trying to remain calm in this scary situation. The officer rolls his eyes and tells my dad to hurry up and get out.

"Andy, stay in the car baby…your mother is behind us, and she'll come sit with you while I take care of this, alright," my dad says to me, looking at me through the rear-view mirror.

My eyes shoot from my dad's face in the mirror, to the cop, to the gun that's pointing at my father. When my dad exits the car, the officer grabs him by the jacket and throws him to the ground before placing his foot on my dad's back.

"Daddy! Nooo," I scream, pounding on the window of the car.

Moments later, my mother exits her car and starts yelling at the officer. The two of them get into a shouting match, while the officer calls for backup. My dad remains still, cheek pushed against the pavement, and back under the foot of the officer for a long time. Once backup officers arrive, and my mother hands the officer my father's driver's license and insists they run his plates.

Tonight, the police are looking for someone who's stolen a car. The only description they have is that the suspect is a Black man, around six feet tall. They saw my dad driving a new Ford Bronco, and my dad is a Black man. So, they stop us. Tonight, I learn a lesson about survival.

"Baby girl," my dad says, when he gets back in the car, "never show them you're afraid and always keep your cool – hold fast…and you will survive."

When I wake up, I'm surprised to be alive. My body still feels numb, as though it's reached its threshold for pain and simply shut off. I'm still on the metal table, but the room around me is now empty. The light still shines above me, but everything else in the room is blurry. I look down at myself and notice that I'm naked. Turning my head, I notice my clothes in a heap next to me, cut up to shreds.

They didn't find a wire.

Completely exposed, without a chance for rescue without the tracker, a part of my soul shuts down. The door to the room opens, and my body tenses in anticipation of the next atrocity. I turn my head slowly to face my adversary. One of the last people I expect to walk through that door, approaches me.

"Jake? Is that you?" I ask, tears of relief streaming down my face.

Jake walks over, unties me from the bed, and I throw my arms around his neck to embrace him. As soon as I pull him close to me, I realize something is wrong. His body is rigid and he isn't hugging me back. The door flies open again, and Director Bryant enters the room.

"Nice work Jake, I knew I could count on you. Now that we don't have to worry about any unwelcome *visitors,* we can head out," Director Bryant says, lecherously scanning my naked body.

I pull back from Jake and try to cover myself by hugging my knees into my chest. Looking up at Jake, begging him to rescue me with a look of desperation. Just when I'm expecting his humanity to surface, he reaches and grabs a fist full of my hair before dragging me off the table and out of the room. I cry out in agony before a bag is placed over my head. While I'm still being dragged by my hair, the cool air hits my body like a knife cutting through my flesh as we exit the building.

The sound of metal doors opening echo in my ears, and I'm thrown into the back of what I assume is a van. My hands and feet are tied with rope. I start to scream, praying that someone who will help might hear me. A cold, smelly hand reaches under the bag and places duct tape across my mouth. The doors of the van shut loudly, and I start kicking on them as hard as I can until the van lurches to a start and I slam against one of the sides.

I start counting the seconds, minutes, and hours until we reach our destination – keeping track of turns and any noises that might help me figure out where we're going. I need to find a weapon because if I'm going to die here, I'm going to take some of these guys with me and I'm not going down without a fight.

One hour, thirty-nine minutes, and forty-two seconds.

Twelve turns, seven stop lights...

The van doors fly open and there's several hands grabbing different parts of my body as I kick and scratch and desperately try to break free. It's so loud that I cannot make out any single voice. The men are all yelling orders at each other and there's a loud noise that sounds like a generator, consistently humming in the background.

Two minutes, thirty-two seconds...

The bag is removed from my head, and I'm thrown into another cell by two new men who quickly exit the room.

Hold fast Andy.

Outside the cell, I can hear the men planning for what's to come.

"What time will the pilot arrive?" One asks.

"He'll be here in a few minutes. We have to prepare the girl for transport," the other responds.

The Girl?

It feels like hours have passed, or maybe just a few minutes, when a large man dressed in medical scrubs enters the cell. He's followed by several men who wheel in a stretcher. I scurry backward, trying to put as much distance as possible between me and the man charging toward me.

"What's happening? No, stay away from me," I scream, kicking the man as he comes close to me.

The man in the scrubs has wild brown hair that's tasseled about his head, which gives the terrifying allusion that he has snakes coming from his head. He has stubble on his face and menacing green eyes that bore into me as though he's hoping to set me on fire with them. I'm kicking and screaming, but I'm no match for this man who's easily a hundred pounds heavier than me. He grabs me by one of my arms and lifts me to my feet, before pulling a giant needle from behind his back and jabbing it into my neck. I start to see dark spots and the room starts to spin.

I have to keep my eyes open – I have to stay awake.

Despite my attempts at a self-pep talk, I'm no match for whatever this man has injected me with because suddenly, I slump over, and the room goes completely black again.

Chapter 32
The Cave

"Andy"

The first thing I notice when I wake up is the constant buzzing sound of a fly circling around my head. This fly is so loud and urgent, as though it's trying to tell me something and getting annoyed that I can't understand its language.

"Go away," I say aloud, swatting at the fly and then immediately feeling silly that I'm talking to an insect.

Birds are chirping in the distance, and I can see a stream of light shining through the steel door to my new cell.

No, not a cell – this is a cave, posing as a cell.

The walls are made of rocks that look as though they might crumble on top of me at any moment. I reach to grab for my neck, remembering that my last memory was that large man with the snake hair injecting me with that needle.

Is it possible this has all been a nightmare? Perhaps I'm still asleep.

Rubbing frantically at my eyes, I try and wake myself. Water is running through the cave, and there are two levels in this hell. Where there once were stairs to the second level, there's just crumbled rock and the wooden slats above my head have large holes in them. Straining to see the room above me through the holes in the wood, I notice there are windows on the second floor.

Maybe I can climb up there and find my way out of here.

There are two wooden benches in here with me, neither large enough for me to sleep on. Lifting my aching body off the rocky floor, I run my hands across the wall. Some of the rocks crumble as I touch the wall and I gather several in the corner of the room, hoping to use them as weapons when my captures return.

Will they ever come back for me, or have they left me here to die?

Large spider webs line the ceiling and cover the walls. They're so tangled and thick that they look what you'd have a plumber extract from a deeply clogged sink. That fly is still buzzing around my head, and I wonder if the damn thing has been hired to constantly buzz in some sick attempt to make me lose my mind in here.

I'm wearing clothes now, which I'm thankful for. I have no idea how I got dressed, but I'm wearing a pair of green sweatpants and a matching sweatshirt that look like standard military issued clothing. There is a pair of dirt brown combat books sitting by the door. Before I can finish assessing my surroundings, the door creaks open. I scurry to the corner of the room and immediately cover my head with my arms, bracing for another blow.

"Andy, it's me," says a soft, familiar voice.

Jake?

I don't move, because though Jake's voice is soft and he sounds more like *my* Jake, I can't shake the image of him pulling me like a rag doll and playing along with this sick game. I shift my arm to view him from a small slit between my arms. He emerges from the door by himself with a blanket in his arms. I open my mouth to speak but shut it immediately, realizing that I don't know what to say to this man I thought I knew.

This man I thought was my friend...who I'd loved like a brother.

Without saying a word, he slowly lifts the index finger on his right hand to his lips as his eyes dart around the cave. He approaches me with a large blanket and some pillows, cautiously reaching toward me to hand them to me. I'm shaking and I'm not sure if it's fear, the fact that I'm freezing, or perhaps both. I take the blanket and pillows from him and quickly try to move away from him. My back is pressed against the wall and even though I can feel the crumbling, jagged rocks piercing into my skin, I kept attempting to move further away from him. He grabs one of my arms, pulling me close before clasping one of his hands over my mouth to stifle a scream.

"Stop screaming," he whispers into my ear, "please listen carefully. We don't have much time. I need you to act like we don't know each other, and I need you to understand that I'm going to need to do things to make sure I keep their trust. It's how we *both* get out of this alive."

I can feel tears escape from my eyes as I stare directly at him, mere inches from his face.

"And I'm sorry. I'm sorry for what I've done before today, and for what I will need to do. But please Andy, I need you to know that I'm not one of the bad guys here," Jake continues.

Desperate to believe him, I remain quiet and nod my head to indicate that I understand.

"Jake, *where* are we? What is this place?" I ask, keeping my voice barely above a whisper.

"We're in France. I don't know what Intel you were able to gather before you left the agency, but *this* shit is a whole mess. The director is trying to justify keeping you here by telling us you've committed war crimes. What the hell Andy? What kind of mess are you wrapped up in?" Jake asks, a sincere look of concern on his face.

"Jake, you can't possibly believe that I did something to justify this, do you?" I ask, incredulously.

While I wait for him to respond, I search his face and read his body language. I want so badly to trust him, but the world seems to upside down right now.

But what other choice do I have?

"Jake..." I say, raising my hand to his face and gently placing it on his cheek.

There are tears in his eyes, and he quickly looks down at the ground before admitting,

"Andy, the director told me that if I don't cooperate, they'll go after my mom. I can't...I mean...you know she's the only family I have."

"What? He said that?" I ask, my hand dropping to my side as Jake nods affirmatively.

I fall back against the wall, letting out a huge breath of air while I try and think of how to get out of this.

"Jake, you know me, and you know I'd never betray my country. And I'd never ask you to do something that would put your mother in danger, but we must work together. You can't do this on your own," I say.

"Give me time, Andy. I have to figure out a way out of this, but I need time," he responds, nervously rubbing at the stubble that's spotting his cheeks.

"Jake, we don't have time. I won't survive here more than a couple of days without medication – or an antidote," I say, pulling the blanket close and wrapping it around myself.

Jake's eyes dart back and forth from me to the door and he's wringing his hands nervously as sweat beads on his forehead.

"What are they planning to do with me?" I ask, searching his face for answers he's unwilling to say out loud.

"I don't know," he admits, biting his lip, "but usually, they don't disappear people to third countries like this unless there's a reason that they want to avoid drawing the attention of Congress and the President. And Andy, I don't think there's any way the President would have signed off on this stuff."

He didn't.

A loud sound that's like machines turning on reverberates through the room, causing more of the rocks in the wall to rumble out onto the ground next to me. I instinctively grab for Jake, and he pulls me into his chest to shield me from some of the rubble falling from the room above us. Moments later, the shaking stops but we hear voices in the distance.

"I have to go," Jake says, panic entering his eyes as he jumps up.

"Jake, I need you to get a message out for me," I plead, grabbing ahold of his leg before he can leave.

"Andy, I can't promise..." he says, before frantically glancing between me and the door where the voices are coming closer.

"Jake, just please...find Cameron and tell him where I am," I say, now on my knees looking up at him.

"I don't even know where that guy is. I haven't seen or heard from GS-9 in months," he responds, his pale cheeks turning red with panic.

"The Wardman...you need to either go yourself or send someone, but we need to be able to get a message to Cameron," I say, "I need medication and I don't know how long I have in here before whatever is coursing through my veins kills me."

"Okay, I'll try," he responds, tugging his leg free and slipping out of the door.

Moments after the door closes, I hear the crash of what sounds like a heavy lock caging me in. Wrapping myself tighter in the blanket Jake brought me and sitting on the pillow, I lean back against the wall. My mouth is so dry that it feels like I've swallowed a handful of sand and I can't remember the last time I had something to drink.

Was it on the plane? How many days ago was that?

The room eventually returns to the quiet state where I can only hear myself breathe and the buzzing of that damned fly. The light that was shining through the door is now gone and I'm here alone in the darkness.

I'm losing my sense of time...how many days has it been?

I pray that Jake can open communication with the team. That seems like my best chance to salvage this operation, but I know I can't wait here for the men to rescue me. I need a plan to rescue myself. A banging noise rings out in the room, coming from one of the pipes that runs along the floor, and a gush of water is released onto the floor. I scurry over, cupping some of the liquid in my hands and drink.

Chapter 33
Tea Leaves

A giant, smelly, dog tongue sloshes across my face, and I fall onto the floor from a restless sleep on the couch of the ops center.

"Argh, Boss I told you I don't like gross dog kisses man," I say, shoving Boss off me and gathering the giant mound of papers that are now strewn all over the floor around me.

It's been days since Andy was taken and the entire crew has been pouring through reporting, trying to find new sources, and I even have a contact at the National Security Agency (NSA) that's promised to run a script he created through the Intelligence chatter on the dark web for any mention of Andy. Boss is now dancing around, getting his dirty paws all over the maps I was looking at when I fell asleep.

"Dude, take that poor dog out for a walk before he shits on the floor. Ain't nothing you're gonna see on those papers in the next 30 minutes that's gonna make cleaning up dog shit worth it," Theo says, walking in from one of the adjacent rooms and patting Boss on the head before heading to the coffee machine.

He's right, but it doesn't make it easier to walk away from this.

"Thanks man, can you look through these when you're done with your coffee? Farhad sent over a stack of maps and satellite images of places his dad thinks we should investigate."

"Yeah bro, I got it. Just take that dog out and let him walk this time. He's up in here driving us all nuts because homeboy needs a workout," Theo replies reaching for a mug and whatever new bougie coffee bean he's brought in this time.

I don't even have to tell Boss we are walking because as soon as he sees me put on my sneakers, he leaps for the door and practically puts on his own leash. After leaving the Wardman, Boss and I jog across the valet area and head into the neighborhoods nearby. The houses in Woodley Park, DC are mansions and I always wonder how much money people need to be making to afford to live in them. When I was a kid, growing up in rural Louisiana with my dad bouncing in an out from military deployment to deployment, I could never have dreamed of a place like this. Moving to DC as a teenager, after my dad was stationed at the Pentagon, D.C felt like a different planet. Even as an adult, I'm not sure I'll ever walk through a neighborhood like this without being acutely aware that I'm not from here.

"Yeah man, that *is* a big ass house," I say, turning to Boss who's gleefully prancing beside me.

"Woof, arf, ruff," he responds, nodding his head enthusiastically.

I snicker, grateful for him and these moments when he's able to lift my spirits even in a time like this.

"Thanks man, I appreciate you."

I bend down to give Boss a rub on his belly and scan the area around us. Something feels off and the hairs on the back of my neck stand at attention. I've been through enough surveillance training to feel when I'm being watched, and I know it's not my own people.

"Game time, Boss," I whisper to him before handing him a treat.

Boss raises the ear that doesn't have a giant chunk missing and begins to scan the area with me. He puts his nose to the ground and pulls me back toward the main street from the side street we'd been walking on. It's fall in D.C., which means orange, yellow, and brown leaves line the sidewalk and there's no way to walk without announcing yourself. I can't see the person following us, but I know they're nearby because of the distinct sound of crunching leaves nearby.

Starting to walk faster and placing my hand under my sweatshirt to grab ahold of my Glock, I whirl around just in time to come nearly face to face with a man in a black hoodie with black jeans. I draw my gun and Boss starts barking loudly and lunging at the man, bearing his teeth as though he's ready to take a chunk out of the man's leg.

"Don't shoot! It's me, Jake."

He immediately raises his hands and takes down the hoodie so that I can see his face, but I don't lower my weapon. Jake is Andy's friend – not mine and right now I don't trust anyone from the Agency outside of GS-9.

"Look man, I know we didn't get on like old friends last time we saw each other, but you gotta trust me," he says, the words leaking rapidly from his mouth like he's not even in control of them.

"Why do I have to trust you?" I ask, suspicious as hell as to why this dude just popped up in the middle of my walk.

Jake pulls his hoodie back over his head and his eyes dart around us like he's afraid *he's* being followed. I must admit that this dude looks like he's run through a lair of hell since the last time I saw him. His hair looks greasy and is in spikes all over his head, his blue eyes are blood shot, and it looks like he hasn't shaved in a few weeks.

"Not here man, someone could see us here and...look...Andy sent me," he says quickly, his eyes fixed on mine with desperation.

Andy?

At just the mention of her name, I can feel my heart beating faster and sweat beading on my head. I lower my gun but don't move from my protective stance while I reach out to search him for weapons. His hands remain raised, and Boss whines and leans into my leg as though he's telling me to move.

"Come on, follow me," I say, gesturing him to follow me with my head.

There's an audible sigh of relief as Jake lowers his arms, shoves them into the pockets of his jeans, and follows me in silence back to the ops center.

When the elevators open to the ops center, several on the team are crowded around the table in the common area: Rove, Theo, Farhad, and Dr. Raj.

They're all engaged in what sounds like a lively and passionate debate when we walk in, but it comes to an abrupt halt when they spot Jake.

"What is *that* guy doing here?" Theo asks, eyeing the gun on the kitchen counter as though he's not sure whether to make a run for it or offer him coffee.

"He's unarmed – I checked. He said Andy sent him and since right now we don't have any better leads, I say we hear him out," I respond, walking over to the table and moving a chair toward Jake to instruct him to sit.

"You spoke to Andy? Where is she?" Rove asks, glancing at Farhad who's opening his laptop and furiously typing.

"They took her to a remote facility in Western France. They're hiding in plain sight, ironically in a bunch of caves under some sort of monastery," Jake replies, wringing his hands nervously.

"Where, what's the name of the town?" Farhad asks, still hunched over his laptop and undoubtedly scouring satellite footage trying to locate the place where Andy is being held.

"It's called Moirax...it's seriously in the middle of nowhere," Jake replies, clearly under estimating Farhad's abilities to find a needle in a giant pile of hay.

"Who knows you're here?" I ask, raising an eyebrow wondering if he knows even the director has turned.

"Nobody," Jake responds quickly and defensively, "except Andy, of course, because she begged me to come here even though this could absolutely get me killed."

"What happened to my tracker?" Theo asks, a rare flash of anger moving across his face.

"The directer knew about the tracker and when he had her picked up by the police, he and Todd had it removed immediately," Jake responds.

"Wait, Todd? I thought that guy was dead," I say, looking at Rove.

"We did too. I don't know how he would've been able to escape the collapse of that cave. But we can figure out how to handle him later, we need to get to Andy," Rove says, turning back toward Jake.

"Director Bryant didn't notify the White House or Congress because he internally declared Andy a war criminal, which is how he justified her swift removal out of the United States," Jake explains, his pale face flushing as he wipes sweat from his hairline.

After what Andy told me about Bryant, it doesn't surprise me in the least that he would trump up false charges against Andy as a way to make her disappear. I cannot wait to see what claims allowed him to get away with this to this point.

"I don't even know if she's officially in U.S. custody. There isn't any record of what they claim she did or what their plans are at the Agency – I checked," Jake continues, rubbing his hands on his jeans nervously.

"Is she alright? Did you speak to her?" I ask, confused as to how the man who failed out of the Farm got pulled into all this.

Jake doesn't answer my question directly, and his eyes get *really* shifty.

What is homeboy hiding?

"After Andy resigned, the director pulled me into this operation. At first, I thought it was a promotion because it was the first time anyone on the seventh floor even knew my name, but it turned into a nightmare."

Jake tells us that when he caught wind that the director was trying to essentially disappear Andy, he tried to quit and report the situation. According to Jake, his complaints never made it anywhere and when the director found out, that's when the safety of his family was threatened if he refused to cooperate.

"I could be killed, and they could kill my mom if anyone in that circle knew I was here right now, but Andy begged me to get this message here and I honestly didn't know any other way than to just come myself," Jake utters, more to himself than to the rest of us.

"Why are you here then?" I ask through gritted teeth.

Jake starts to stutter; his nerves look to be getting the better of him.

"I um...uh...Andy's my friend," he replies, again not exactly answering my question.

Likely sensing that I'm growing more irritated by the half assed responses Jake is providing to our questions, Rove steps in between us and places a hand on Jake's shoulder before saying, "son, we appreciate that you took this risk, and we need you to take more risks if we're going to get you and your friend out of this."

"Found her," Farhad shouts, jumping out of his seat as though he's just won the lottery and turning his laptop to the rest of us and flashing a giant smile.

We all turn our heads to look at Farhad.

"They took her to Moirax. Not just any monetary, but a Cluniac priory that was founded in the 11ᵗʰ century," Farhad explains, as though we should know what that means.

"A what?" Theo asks, scratching his head and looking confused but ready to nerd out with Farhad.

"A Cluniac priory was a Benedictine monastery or nunnery that belonged to the Cluniac order. And the Cluniac order was founded in 910 and centered around Cluny Abby in France," Farhad replies.

"Yeah, okay. That tracks," Theo says, chuckling to himself.

Given that Theo and I found the remanence of a nuclear facility in the catacombs under an old church in Lima, it seems like this could be a pattern developing.

"Okay, so let's go get her out," I interject, growing tired of the history lessons and wanting a solid plan.

"No, no...you can't just go in there," Jake says, his voice raised and fear returning to his pale blue eyes.

"What do you mean we can't just go in there? You said they have Andy, what's our alternative? Are you suggesting we just leave her there so they can continue to drain her of all her blood like a lab rat?" I'm furious and Jake is someone I'm desperately hoping I don't have to tolerate much longer.

Rove walks over to me, pulls out a chair beside me and sits down facing me.

"We have to move smart here and if we go into that little town guns blazing, we could cause them to move her to a place we don't know about or worse – they could kill her," Rove says, his eyebrows furrowed into a serious glare.

He's right, and I know Andy would tell me to trust her and let her do her job, but I feel like I have to do something, and I can't sign on to just sitting here and waiting for things to get worse.

"I have to go back. They don't even know I'm gone, but if they find out I'm here...well, I don't even want to think about what they'd do. But if they see any of you all anywhere near that place, it's just going to make things worse," Jake says, rubbing his face with an anguished expression.

"Well then, you'll go back, and we'll set up a way to communicate while we formulate a viable plan," Rove replies.

"And please, take this medication to her. She needs them as soon as possible to counteract the cold," Dr. Raj says, handing Jake a pill box and wrapping her hands around his to enclose it in his hands.

After only a few more minutes of conversation, Jake gets up to leave. I hand him a card with the number to the satellite phones and tell him only to call from a number they aren't tracking.

Goddamn, how did we end up in a situation where we have to rely on the dude who didn't pass the tradecraft certification?

Theo and I will set up a command center in the nearby town of Agen, France where we'll be close enough to do some level of casing without drawing too much attention to ourselves. Once we do some initial work and get reliable communication, we'll figure out how we can get her out of there *and* take down this disease that's taken control of the agency.

Chapter 34
Incrimination

"Andy"

*B*uzzzzzzz, hummm, zip, drip...drip...drip.

I'm lying on the uneven dirt floor, curled in the blanket Jake brought me and can feel every rock, bump, crumble, and stick that digs into my back. The ache in my hips is nagging and making me afraid to move, for fear that it will get worse, and I won't be able to run when I need to. I haven't slept but my eyes have been closed because opening would expend more energy than I have right now. Nobody has been here since Jake, which means I haven't had food or water in days.

Does the floor water count?

Every fifteen minutes, during the daylight hours, I hear a church bell that seems like it's ringing overhead. When it chimes, more of the rocks fall around me. It's so cold in here and this blanket feels damp so I'm not even sure it's helping. When I hear footsteps coming toward the cell, I pray that it's Jake coming back with information from the team.

Did he find them? Did he get out of France without the rest of them finding out?

My hopes are dashed when the cell opens and two, large men whom I've never seen before entering the space.

"Stand up," one of them yells in a thick French accent.

Even if I wanted to comply with this request, which I don't, I can't move so I just lay here and brace myself for their next move.

"Get up," the second one, who's enormous and looks like someone who'd be hired as a bouncer to stand in front of a violent nightclub, screams impatiently before kicking me in the ribs.

The blow is so hard that it knocks the wind out of me. Coughing and struggling to catch my breath, while also not wanting to get hit again, I try to pull myself up from the ground. My arms feel like jello and I'm dizzy. If I don't get food, there's no way I can get myself out of here when I can't even stand up. Using the wall, I pull myself to a standing position to comply with their request, but my legs are shaking, and the room feels like it's spinning so wildly that if I had anything in my stomach, I'd probably throw up all over the smaller man's shoes.

"We don't have time for this. The boss is going to get mad if we don't get her on that table in the next five minutes," says the smaller one, who's still at least five or six inches taller than me but not as much of a giant as his friend.

The table?

The giant man, whose handlebar mustache looks like he spends a gross amount of time getting it to curl symmetrically on both ends, violently grabs me by the arms and starts dragging me toward the door. My legs collapse beneath me and the tall and skinny one grabs me by the other arm while the two of them continue to drag me from the cell. Though my body has failed me, I can feel every rock as it scrapes against me, tearing my skin with every step the two of them take. They need to keep me alive, but don't seem to care about the state I'm in as long as my heart keeps beating and the blood keeps pumping.

They continue dragging me along a cold, cement floor, past what looks like wine barrels, until we reach another room. Inside this one, there's a single hospital bed with the rails engaged, sitting next to a metal standing desk on wheels that's covered in medical instruments.

Oh God, what's going to happen in here?

Once we reach the bed, the two men hoist me over the rails with the force, and lack of grace, that would be more appropriate for throwing a sack of potatoes into the back of a truck. Then, they grab my limp wrists and handcuff each of them to the bedrails. Given that I couldn't even walk myself here, I'm not sure where they think I'm going to be able to go. Moments later, a middle-aged white woman who reminds me a bit of a human square, walks into the room. She's dressed in light blue medical scrubs and her face is emotionless. She grabs a forehead thermometer and rolls it across my forehead to take my temperature. An almost imperceptible grimace flashes across her face before she begins barking orders in French at "weird mustache giant guy" who's still standing in the corner of the room.

The giant leaves the room briefly before coming back with a pile of blankets, which he places over me. The blankets are warm, which feels like a slice of heaven in the middle of this shitstorm of hell. I close my eyes and try to imagine being somewhere else, perhaps laying on the beach or back in Cameron's arms. What I would give to go back to that moment with him in the car inside that airport parking garage or in the giant tub at the Whistler Chalet.

The hum of a space heater that's attached to the ceiling jolts me out of my thoughts and the square-shaped nurse grabs my left arm and starts poking the veins on the inside of my elbow.

"Not good. Still too cold," she mumbles under her breath, snapping her fingers at the mustache giant and ordering him to bring her things.

I'm so tired, but I want to stay awake to take mental notes of everything so I can get the information I need to take these people down *and* have a chance of getting out of this alive. It looks like we're still underground, but unlike my cell, this room has basement style windows that are protected with bars.

Would anyone hear my screams?

Still scanning the room for any clues that could help my team, should Jake actually be trustworthy and successful enough to carry my messages, the square nurse comes toward me with a needle.

"What are you doing?" I ask, hearing the panic in my own voice and trying to squirm away from her.

"If you fight, this will be worse," she replies, in a deadpan voice that makes me wonder if she's a complete sociopath.

She wraps a tourniquet around my arm so tight that I lose feeling in my hand, and then jams the needle into my arm. The rest of my body is in enough pain that I barely feel the needle, and I watch as the blood flows from my arm into vial after vial. My heart begins to race and the cold returns.

They'll stop before this kills me, right?

The tall, skinnier guy jogs to the square nurse's side and collects each vial of my blood into a bag. With each collection, his face brightens like she's handing him liquid gold.

"Enough, no more today," the square nurse says after filling three vials.

"No, one more. He's not going to like it if we just bring this," says the weird mustache giant, who joins them from the corner of the room and starts inspecting my arm.

"No water, no more blood," replies the square nurse, as she removes the tourniquet from my arm and replaces the collection vial with an IV needle that's attached to a bag of fluid.

The two men grab ahold of the blood bag, and reluctantly leave the room. While the square nurse cleans her station, I reach out to grab ahold of her shirt. Straining against the cuffs, I can only hold onto a small corner but it's enough to get her attention.

"Help, can you help me?" I ask, hoping to find a shred of humanity inside this woman.

A strange grimace spans across her face and she replies, "I don't respect or help women who betray their own country."

"What? What are you talking about?" I ask, defensively.

My country betrayed ME.

"Oh, you don't know what they have on you, do you? There's video of what you did. You want me to think you're one of the good gals, but you are nothing more than a lying, cheating little bitch," she exclaims, spittle flying out of her mouth at a force and distance that causes me to turn my head to shield myself from getting her spit in my face.

"I have no idea what you're talking about," I reply, hoping that I keep her talking and she'll reveal what on earth she's talking about.

"Sure, you don't," she says, with sarcasm laced thick in her voice, before plunging her square face so close to mine that I can smell her fishy breath, "you're never going home. You belong to us now – we paid for you so shut your mouth and you might stay alive long enough to be worth the investment."

She stares at me, still inches from my face and breathing heavily, for several silent moments before shoving her large body away from the bed and storming out of the room. The church bells chime again for one last time before darkness pours in through the tiny windows. I'm alone, I don't know if Jake is ever coming back for me.

Chapter 35
Agen

"Cameron"

"We have to get into France without coming across the radar of the local authorities," I say to Rove and Theo, while the three of us crowd around the kitchen island making travel plans over a bottle of whiskey.

Boss leans heavily against my leg and looks up at me with his large puppy eyes.

He can sense when I'm getting ready to leave for a trip and he doesn't want to be left behind this time.

"Don't worry homey, I'm taking you with us," I say to Boss, patting him on the head for reassurance.

"Dude, you speak to that dog like he's a human," Theo says, shaking his head and smirking at Boss.

Boss lifts his paw and swats at Theo, as if he understands what's been said and is offended. I ignore Theo's jab because I don't have the energy to argue with him about why I am not leaving Boss behind when we don't know how long we'll need to be gone.

And we could use his unique skills – like super smell.

"I contacted one of my former platoon mates who works in aviation. He transports planes back and forth between the United States and Toulouse, France regularly. He's offered to let the two of you hitch a ride with him early tomorrow morning at 02:00," Rove says, without looking up from the paperwork in front of him.

"What about customs? Don't those planes get inspected when they come into the country?" I ask, skeptical about this plan and wondering why we can't just get the White House to arrange something given the urgency of this mission.

"If there's anyone who can get you both in and out of that place undetected, it's my guy Phillipe," Rove replies.

I don't know this guy Philippe, but if Rove trusts him, I'm cool with it. My main goal right now is to get to Andy as soon as possible. And as soon as I get to France, I plan to figure out how to see her. For now, I need my team to believe I'm willing to go along with whatever plan they have. If Rove knew that I don't plan to wait while Jake tries to save her, he'd probably never let me go to France. So instead of protesting the plan to simply case without entering, I publicly agree to go along.

As soon as Rove is done delivering instructions to Theo and I, I head to my room and start packing. Boss is running circles around the room, nudging his leash over towards my bag and giving me his best tongue out dog smile. As a sign of good faith, I make a point to grab his travel dog bowl, hold it up for him to see, and throw it in my bag. At the clear sign that I would bring him with me, Boss takes a seat at the foot of my bed and relaxes while he watches me finish packing.

"Let's go boys, Philippe is waiting for you on the tarmac at Andrews Air Force Base," Rove yells from the kitchen area.

Rove's ability to get this flight together on such short notice is amazing and a testament to that man's global connectedness. Within 15 minutes of the plan, Theo and I - and boss, of course - are headed out the door on the way to the air strip. It's just past 1:00 AM in the morning and I'm so amped up on the hope that I could see Andy again, maybe even within the next 24 hours, that I'm not even nervous about the danger and magnitude of the operations we're about to undertake.

Theo and I raced through the streets of DC so that we can get there before the 2:00 AM takeoff. This guy Philippe is on a schedule that has nothing to do with us, and if we mess up that schedule, we risk his exposure and ours. As we pull up to the tarmac, I immediately see Roves guy Philippe because he's the only guy standing in the area next to a giant, empty commercial airplane. Philippe is easily 6 foot 3, has a mess of wavy red hair, and a long red beard.

"Howdy, you must be Rove's guys – Theo and Cameron. I'm Phillipe, it's nice to meet you," Phillipe says, extending his pale, freckled, heavily tattooed arm and revealing a jolly, toothy smile.

"Hey man," Theo said, fist bumping him instead of shaking his hand.

I snicker under my breath, because I know Theo has always been weird about germs and is the type to explain why handshakes are gross. Sensing Phillipe's confusion at the awkward switch up to a fist bump from Theo, I extend my hand to give him a firm handshake.

"Don't mind Theo, he's always been a little extra about germs," I say, glancing down at an excited Boss who'd have extended his hand too had he been at the appropriate height.

"Rove warned me about the dog. If he's not going to piss in the cabin, he can come," Phillipe says, raising an eyebrow at Boss before laughing and giving him a pat on his belly.

Boss audibly huffs likes he's offended at the assumption that he'd make a mess.

Before takeoff, Philippe sets us up in the cabin of the plane. He explains that upon arrival we need to be as quiet as possible. While he's never been checked on previous trips, any noise from us could lead the locals to be suspicious and decide to inspect. The flight itself is uneventful. Both Theo and I are stretched out in first class and boss has taken over a large portion of the aisle floor. Sleeping on planes has never been my superpower, but for once I find myself closing my eyes and then what seems like moments later, we're landing in Toulouse, France.

As we prepare for landing, Theo hands me a stack of maps with annotations and circles all over them.

"What is this man?" I ask, rubbing my eyes and running my hand through my now crazy looking curls.

Boss pops up from his sleeping position, as though he plans to read the maps with me.

"I took a cat nap on the plane, but then got started planning the best possible locations to set up an ops center here," Theo says, pointing to the map he's placed on the top of the stack.

The city of Agen, France is about halfway between Bordeaux and Toulouse. The city center lies on the east bank of the river Garonne, and the canal of Garonne flows through it. Our challenge is that we need to be close enough that we can pick up chatter from the bugs we hope Jake is willing to place for us, but far enough to go undetected by Solaris loyalists that could be roaming this tiny city.

"Bro, this city is the size of my big toe," Theo says, laughing and shaking his head.

"Dude, you have a big ass toe, but I get your point," I say, throwing one of the airplane pillows at his head.

Thankfully, because Theo is always prepared, as soon as he found a suitable spot during his plane research, he sent a message to Rove. Now, all we need to do is grab the vehicle Philippe is letting us borrow and head to the apartment to drop our bags.

We pull up to a three-story, several hundred-year-old building. It has a wooden barn like door and a quaint looking balcony that overlooks the canal. The first two floors of the building are empty, and we've rented the top floor which has an amazing view of the city and the countryside beyond the city limits. On the other side of this canal, about a fifteen-minute drive from here, is Moirax – where they're holding Andy. Under different circumstances, this place looks like the perfect romantic getaway, but I want to get Andy and get out of here as soon as we can. From the moment I arrived in this place, I've felt a nagging sense of unease that I can't shake.

Once Boss and I are alone in the room I'm claiming as ours, I turn to him and say, "Okay little dude, let's go get our girl."

Chapter 36
Bloodline

"Andy"

Darkness peaks through the tiny, barred window in the torture room where I'm still laying. Big Bertha, my nickname for the mean nurse, has left the room so I'm here alone. My mouth is no longer dry, which I guess I have the IV drip to thank, but my stomach growls loudly reminding me how hungry I am. My eyes dart around the room, searching for a way out of this mess. With the tracker in my neck gone, Jake getting word to the team on my location would be a damned miracle at this point, but I need to find the info we need and a way to get myself out of here.

Big Bertha isn't as bright as she thinks she is because the metal table full of torture devices, scalpels and scissors, is just sitting here close enough to this table that I might be able to reach it. My wrists are still tied to the bed, but if I strain or try and move the bed I might be able to get myself close enough to grab something. I need to find a way to get there without falling over because I don't want these fools knowing I've gotten a weapon. Thankful for a bit of strength back, because I'm no longer as dehydrated, I knock my body against the left side of the bed.

Shit, that wasn't enough force.

Taking a deep breath, closing my eyes, and saying a silent prayer, I shove all of my weight into the side of the bed with as much force as I can.

It moved, oh my gosh...it MOVED!

The table is now mere inches from my hand. I strain to reach it, the cuffs creating red indents in my wrist and causing it to bleed. I grab ahold of a pair of sharp scissors with my finger tips and gently pull them off the table and back to my bed. I shimmy myself in the bed to get the scissors into my pocket so that whomever comes in to take me back to the cave won't see that I'm armed. The scissors won't get these cuffs off my hand but they haven't cuffed me inside the cave so there's a chance I can attack the guards the next time they come for me. I have to move the bed back to where it was, though, so nobody suspects what I've done.

Oof, if only my entire body didn't feel like it's just been drained of all its blood.

I fling my body weight to the other side multiple times and the bed moved back into place. When I hear a key in the door, my entire body tenses.

Oh no, someone heard me.

No, no more blood...

I squeeze my eyes shut, bracing for more pain until I hear Jake's soft voice.

"Andy, it's me. It's okay," he says, gently touching my arm.

I slowly open my eyes and reach for him with one of my hands, but am stopped by the cuffs that still chain me to the bed.

"Jake?" I ask, voice scratchy and barely sounding like myself.

My eyes start to water and I look away from him, unable to wipe the tears from my eyes and embarrassed that he's seeing me in this state. Jake touches my cheek to gently turn my face back toward him and wipes the tear from my eye.

"Hang tight, I'm going to take you out of here," he leans over and whispers in my ear.

I nod and he pulls a small key out of his pocket, gently removing the cuffs from my hands. My arms fall to my sides, a clear indication that I couldn't have escaped this place even if they hadn't cuffed me to the bed. It took all the strength I had to grab the scissors. Jake lifts one of my arms and instructs me to place it on his shoulders while he lifts me out of the bed.

"Do you think you can walk?" He asks, cautiously and still whispering.

"I don't know," I admit, briefly closing my eyes to try to stop the room from spinning.

"Okay, let's get you out of the bed and if you aren't stable I'll will carry you," he says, lifting me out of the bed.

When my legs hit the ground, they buckle underneath me. Jake catches me in his arms and pulls me back to standing.

"I guess we have our answer," I say weakly, laughing to myself as I close my eyes.

"Okay, I'm going to lift you and carry you out."

Jake lifts me into his arms with a strength I had no idea he had. Despite the strength, though, he looks like he's about to pee himself with worry. His pale face is flushed and turning an unnatural red and his eyes are darting around the room like he's afraid of who might burst through the doors. I won't tell him about the scissors because I don't know if I can trust him not to take them from me to protect himself.

I still haven't forgotten how just a few days ago he dragged me by my hair.

"I need to get you back to the cell. I barely made it back in time for my shift and if I don't follow the order quickly, Bryant won't trust me and we need him to trust me," Jake says, words racing from his mouth as though he's talking to himself more than he's talking to me.

"Barely made it back in time? Does that mean you found Cameron?" I ask, desperate for good news.

"Shh, we can't talk about any of that here," he whispers into my ear, his heartbeat thumping against the side of my head as he pulls me into him.

When we were at the Farm together, one of the reasons Jake washed out was because he doesn't operate well under stress. Jake is brilliant, but he isn't the one you want in your corner in the field – his skills are best utilized at headquarters behind a computer with a cup of that horribly over-creamed coffee he likes. But his nerves are likely what made him a target for this operation. Bryant wants someone who is a bad liar and will show their nerves.

I might have to teach this man how to lie before he gets us both killed.

"Okay, I understand. Do what you gotta do," I say, raising my hand slightly and prompting him to move.

Jake carries me back to the cave cell and as soon as he places me on the dirty, rock filled floor, he reaches into his bag and pulls out a pill box.

"Take one of these now and put a few of them in your pocket. When you hear someone coming, take another one," he instructs, before pulling a bottle of water from his pocket and prompting me to drink.

I quickly shove a pill in my mouth and guzzle the water, afraid it will be too long before I have a chance to get more. Then, he pulls another bag out of his backpack and hands me a turkey and cheese sandwich on a croissant. My eyes widen and my mouth starts to water, as I grab it and inhale the first meal I've had in what feels like a week.

"Did you talk to Cameron? Does he know where I am?" I ask, tears running down my face as I remember our last moments together.

"Yes, I met up with Cameron and the rest of your team. The doctor with them gave me the pills and told me that you needed to take them as soon as possible," he says, his eyes watering too.

"What else did they say? Are they coming?" I ask, desperate for answers.

If I have backup, it will make breaking free much easier than I expected. I'm not sure Cameron would trust Jake to reveal any plans the team has for extraction, but maybe Jake can figure out a way to bring Cameron to me.

"We have to be really careful, Andy. They know where you are, but I told them they can't just come rushing this place or they could get us all killed," he warns, rubbing his arm across his forehead to wipe the sweat dripping down his face.

"Whatever happens, you need these people to trust you because the moment they stop trusting you, we're all hosed," I say, lifting a hand to Jake's cheek.

"Theo and Cameron are coming and once they're close they'll contact," Jake says, packing up the backpack he brought with him.

"Thank you, Jake. I know you're risking a lot for me and I..." my voice trails off.

Jake interrupts, "Andy, you know I love you and would do anything for you. Of course I want to help. I just want to make sure we don't all die in the process."

"I know. Thank you for the pills. I'll be alright, just go find Cameron."

"I will. We're all thankful we got you the pills, now try to rest so you're strong enough to run if we find a way out," he says, packing up his bag.

"Jake, where are they keeping my blood? And where would they keep information about other sites?"

"I don't know. We're under the church and there are some closets that I have the keys to. I can't be caught snooping where I don't belong, but I'll do my best to unlock them whenever I walk past one," Jake responds, flashing that sweet southern gentleman smile that I love so much.

"Thanks, Jake. You know you're my favorite work husband, right?"

"Girl, I better be your *only* work husband now – don't go workplace cheating on me," he giggles, his face flushing pink again.

Jake pulls a warm, dry blanket from his bag and wraps it around my shoulders. He pulls me to into an embrace and we hold onto each other for several moments until both of us hear foot steps in the distance. I jump at the sound of others, worried they'll come to try and get more blood.

"They won't be back for at least another day or two. Before I came to get you, I overheard a few of the lab attendants talking about how they'd need to wait several days before attempting to draw more blood," Jake whispers, rubbing my back.

"Good, that gives us some time. But Jake – I need to try and get out here before they get more. I'm not sure I could survive another session like that, and the last thing we need is more vials of my radioactive blood floating around," I shutter, trying to avoid imagining this terrorist group creating a weapon with my blood.

Both of us are silent, and I hold my breath, as the sound of footsteps pass right in front of the cave.

"I think we're in the clear," Jake says, his voice still low as he presses his lips close enough for me to feel his breath.

"When you're walking around out there, I also need you to locate where they're keeping the control rods so we can shut down the nuclear reactor," I say, as Jake pulls away from me.

"Andy, I didn't study this stuff at all. I'm the guy who specializes in normal diplomatic relations with Latin, Central America and Africa. I stayed away from nuclear proliferation for a reason – it scares the hell out of me and I'm not a science guy," Jake mutters, nervously pacing the Cave.

"I'll help you, it's okay. Every nuclear facility has control rods because that's the mechanism that allows the operators to adjust reactor power and just down the reactor in an emergency. Once you find them, get that information to my team – they will know what to do to make sure that we can destroy this place without blowing a hole in the entire city," I say, forcing a smile in an attempt to calm Jake down.

"Okay, I'll take a look around on my watch shift later. And I'll be back as soon as I can without drawing too much attention," he says, walking toward the door and glancing at me one last time before he leaves the cave.

The loud clank of the grate and the distinctive thwacking sound it makes when he locks it behind him remind me that I'm still a prisoner. While I have more hope than I did a few hours ago, I'm still acutely aware that in order to survive this I'm going to need to make some big moves.

Chapter 37
Moirax

"Cameron"

The irony that a sadistic terrorist organization, planning to harvest human blood in hopes of world domination, has chosen an 11th century Cluniac priory as their headquarters isn't lost on me. Theo is busy setting up long range listening devices, but Boss and I are headed to Moirax to case the city. Because I know that I can't just walk into this place looking like myself, I've made sure to cover my face with a fake beard and wear sunglasses and a cap. For an additional layer, I attach a velcro ankle wait on one of my legs to change up my walking gait. I look in the mirror and smile at the unfamiliar face smiling back at me.

This should do it.

In addition to housing a pack of terrorists, Moirax is also an off the beaten path tourist destination with 11th century architecture, a grand church, and even a Michelin rated restaurant. I still think their church trend is a bit odd. Perhaps Solaris thinks that nobody will suspect evil lurking and commingling on such sacred grounds, but I think history has proven that even the most pious aren't immune to evil.

"Lets go Boss, I can't promise I'll find you a pup cup in this town, but if you can pick up Andy's scent – I'll order you a steak tonight," I say, patting Boss on the head and grabbing his leash from the top of the dresser by the door.

Boss practically dances to the door, sitting in front of me and raising a paw.

"Ah, so you're gonna be cocky now, huh? You think you can find her without having ever stepped foot in this city?" I ask him, knowing he won't actually respond to me with words.

He tilts his head, before sticking out his tongue at me and running in a circle as though to say, "you know it, now let's get this party started."

I attach the leash onto his collar and head for the door. There's been a near constant ache in my heart since Andy was taken; however, since we've arrived in Agen it feels like my entire body can sense that she's close. I know it's insane to get my hopes up that I'll see her today, because surely these fools are smart enough to keep her in a place that a tourist couldn't just stumble into. But if anyone can pick up her scent, it will be Boss.

So there's *a chance...*

Theo and I rented a car when we arrived, if this tiny little box can be considered an actual car. As soon as I open the door, Boss jumps into the passenger seat and I fold my body into the tiny driver's seat. I'm so large behind the wheel that I feel like I'm driving a clown car, but Theo insisted we go with something small so that we didn't draw any unnecessary attention to ourselves.

"What's the most common car you have here," he'd said, flashing a wide tooth smile to the rental car agent.

And she'd pointed to this little thing, gushing about the incredible gas mileage and giggling to herself. No doubt she and her coworkers laughed at the two of us as we tried to navigate our large frames into the car and somehow find space for the bags we'd brought with us. I just hope this little clown car can make it up these hills to Moirax and that by the time we return Theo has been able to pick up some audio on these assholes.

Boss and I bump our way up the hills for the fifteen minutes it takes to get there and my heart feels like it's in my stomach the entire time. I have no real plan, and frankly should have stayed to help Theo, but I can't stay away when I know she's somewhere in there. Jake warned us not to come without a plan, but he made the mistake of telling me the main facility is under the church in the middle of the town. So when we get to the tourist parking area next to the church, I peel myself it of this car and taking quick strides to the path leading to the entrance of the church. Boss bobs along beside me, glancing up toward me as though he's waiting for permission to work.

"I don't think I can bring you inside the church, man," I say, leaning down next to Boss' ear to whisper quietly.

Spotting a black metal fence on the outside of the church, I tie Boss' leash and pat him on the head before assuring him I'd be back for him after taking a quick look inside. Boss lets out a disgruntled growl before flopping on the dusty ground with a thud that sends a billow of brown dirt billowing around him. The town has an eery quiet that feels like something out of a horror film. Besides the hum of the birds and and the occasional stray cat roaming around, it looks like Boss and I are alone. The large, faded green doors of the church are open so I walk inside.

As I walk down the pillar lined hall leading to a grand organ, my head swivels around looking at the faces carved into the wooden pews that line the walls. There's a single lit candle on the alter and an empty chair next to it. While it doesn't look like anyone's been here, someone must have lit that candle. I take a seat on one of the pews toward the front of the church and pull out the rosary I'd brought for a prop. If I just stand here obviously casing there's more of a chance someone will suspect that I'm here for something other than praying. Before returning to Boss, I look around to count the doorways or cracks that could indicate a trap door.

Since there's nobody in here, I stand up to get Boss. We might only have a few minutes in this church alone so I need his radar nose. As soon as I open the door, Boss stands at attention.

"Come on man, I need you to find us a way under this place," I whisper, causing his damaged ear to pop up to listen.

As soon as we cross the threshold inside, Boss' nose drops to the floor and he pulls me to the corners near the wooden pews with the eyes. He walks just past pews and looks toward a door in the back of the church before circling back on the pews.

"What is it Boss? There's no door here," I say, running my hand along the pew to look for a possible hinge in case it's like one of those secret doors.

Running my hand through my hair, now damp with sweat, I wait to see where Boss will go with this lead. Instead of moving on, Boss looks up at me and whines. I start pulling on the pews, but they won't budge. A few moments pass before Boss huffs loudly and throws his body against one of the pews, which causes the entire thing to creak and a small crack is exposed.

"Damn dude, how the hell…" I look at him amazed that he didn't even need two minutes to find this strange opening.

Before we enter, I look around the church to make sure we're still alone. Pulling the pews open large enough to get both of us inside before closing the gap behind us, I pull out my phone and send a text to Theo.

"Hey, I need backup, I think we found a way in – Boss and I are going under the church," I write, quickly seeing bubbles while Theo writes his response.

"Fuck man, I told your ass not to leave without me," he replies.

"And yet, I know you knew I would anyway," I type back.

"Dude, I just picked up audio from the bug Jake planted for us. They're going to move her in a few hours and once they do, who knows how long it will take us to find out where," Theo responds.

Shit, already?

"Roger, find the control rods and I'll find Andy," I type.

Boss' nose is already to the floor as we slowly walk down a dirt path that looks like it's going to cave in on us at any moment. There's a low hum of machinery in the distance and I can hear water running through some pipes above our heads. My heartbeat is loud in my ears and Boss starts tugging harder on the leash, leading us to a darker corner for the hall. He stands at attention right in front of a steel door that has bars at eye level. Peering through the bars, I see a small body curled into the corner of the room and my breath is suspended for a moment as I recognize the light brown curls that cascade down her bare shoulders like a waterfall.

"Andy," I whisper, terrified that someone will find us before I can figure out how to get her out of here.

She doesn't move and I lift my arms to the bars and shake them hard enough to make noise. At the sound of the rattling grate and the stones that fall from the ceiling around her, she startles and crawls further the back of the cave like she's bracing for impact.

"Andy, it's me – Cam," I whisper, pressing my face to the grates and trying to be loud enough for only her to hear me.

She slowly lifts her head, brushing the hair out of her eyes before returning her arms defensively across her chest.

"Cam? How...no...you can't be here. They can't see you here," she says, her voice shaking and hoarse.

"It's okay, Boss and I are alone," I reply, trying to reach for her through the grates.

She braces her arms at her sides and struggles to a standing position before grabbing ahold of the wall beside her to hold herself up. My heart twists watching her struggle without being able to go to her. Limping over to me, her face comes into the light enough for me to see the dark circles under her eyes and the bluish tint to her skin.

"Your pills...did Jake get them to you?" I ask, grabbing ahold of her ice cold hands between the grates.

"Yes, I took one. I'm alright, but you need to leave – NOW," she says, fear gripping her features.

"Andy no, we're not leaving you in here," I respond, moving my hands from hers to hold her face and checking for injuries I can't see.

She stands on her toes to come closer to me and puts her hands on mine before kissing me. For a moment, it feels like the rest of the world falls away as we hold onto each other. But almost as soon as her soft lips touch mine, she's pulling away.

"You have to go, they can't see you here and we don't have enough information yet," she says.

"Andy, they're going to move you in just a couple of hours. We don't have time to search this place with a fine tooth comb because once they move you, we might not find you again," I reply, keeping eye contact with her.

"Go find Jake, I told him to look for the control rods so we can shut this place down. You know we can't leave without doing that," she says, now shoving me away from the grates.

I know she's right, but my feet feel like they're welded to the floor. I grab ahold of her arm as she pulls away, trying to hold onto her for just one more moment.

"Theo's on his way to give us backup," I whisper through the grate.

"They aren't going to take me anywhere. I have a plan. I grabbed a weapon and I'll be ready when they come for me," she says, squeezing my hand before pushing me away again.

The sound of footsteps come crashing down the hall and Andy retreats to the back of her cell.

"Cam go, there's a closet at the end of the hall. Hide in there and grab whatever you can from inside. I'll come find you," she insists, pointing in the direction she wants me to run.

Her body falls back on the floor and her eyes plead with me to run. Boss whines at my side and nudges me to move, snapping me into action. The two of us run down the dark hallway, searching for the closet Andy mentioned. I don't know how close the people are or whether they're in the hallway with us or in the church above, but I know we need to get out of dodge. When we make it to a door, just as we round a corner, I grab for the handle and pray it's a closet and not a room full of people.

After we throw ourselves into the room, I quickly close the door behind us. Boss, crouches down and puts his nose to the floor and I reach for the flashlight on the Swiss Army knife in my pocket. I can feel walls close, and it's pitch black in here until I shine the flashlight.

"Holy shit, Boss...what is all this?" I whisper out loud, only to hear a low toned woof of acknowledgement.

The walls of this closet are lined with vials, several dark red and labeled with Andy's name. I grab a few vials and put them into my bag along with several other vials of a clear liquid. There's two laptops in here, and I grab both of them along with several external hard drives that are just laying on the floor in here. I can't fit all the vials of blood in my bag, so I reach to start destroying the rest. Before we leave here, we can't leave any of her blood behind that could be used to create whatever weapon they're trying to create here. Now in addition to footsteps, we hear voices. Both Boss and I freeze, listening and waiting for the sounds to pass so that we can get out of here and look for Theo.

In the distance, I hear Andy's cell open and moments later I hear screams and what sounds like fighting.

"We have to help her," I say, turning to Boss before taking off his leash.

This dog is a weapon and our best change is to have both of us fighting unrestrained. I take a deep breath before bursting through the door, just in time to see Andy running toward me with blood all over her tank top and more blood that's stained the legs of her pants.

Chapter 38
Solaris Rising

"Andy"

The two French wardens have come to fetch me again, but this time I'm ready for them. Now that I know Cameron isn't far, I just need to wait until I'm beyond the confines of this cell to strike. The pill I took earlier, along with the croissant Jake gave me, make me feel strong enough to fight; however, I need the guards to believe I can't walk so they won't think to bind my arms. I slump against the wall and wrap my arms around myself, waiting for the to grab me.

"Get up," one of them says, before kicking me in the side with his heavy boot.

He's kicked the wind out of me and I just roll over, trying to catch by breath. The one with that hideous handlebar mustache folds his arms and sighs impatiently, as the skinny one walks closer to inspect me.

"I can't get up," I lie, trying to sound as helpless as I can.

"Just get her up, we don't have time for this," mustache guy says, rolling his eyes and grabbing one of my arms before gesturing for the other to help him.

As they lift me off the floor, I make a point to appear as dead weight while evaluating where I'll strike. My legs drag along the floor as they pull me through the door. As soon as we're safely in the hallway, I start screaming and pretending to be in distress. The two morons drop my arm to look at me, which is just long enough for me to to reach into my pocket and pull out the scissors I grabbed from that hospital room. I launch myself at mustache guy, grabbing ahold of his ridiculous facial hair before stabbing him right between the eyes with the scissors. He screams while lunging for me, but before he can reach me he falls to the ground seizing and blood is pouring from his head.

The skinnier guy with the heavy boots just stands there in shock, giving me enough time to grab him from behind and slash the carotid artery in his neck. When he drops, I reach down and grab the gun from the holster on his waist and run toward the closet I told

Cameron to hide in. As soon as I round the corner, I run straight into Cameron. He grabs me around the waist and I fall into his arms.

"Andy, are you hurt?" He asks, staring at my blood soaked clothes with wide eyes as Boss stands ready to attack anyone else who rounds that corner.

"No, it's not my blood. I killed two of their guys," I say, trying to catch my breath while I wipe blood from my hands on my sweatpants.

"I just grabbed a bunch of stuff from that closet – good call, by the way. But, I have no idea whether Theo or Jake have found the rods," Cameron says, taking one of my hands and lacing our fingers together as he looks for an exit.

Cameron's phone vibrates in his pocket, and he grabs it with his free hand and answers, "Speak of the devil dude, where the hell are you?"

While still on the phone with Theo, Cameron starts pulling me further into the tunnel. He quickly puts in an ear piece and plays the phone back in his pocket, replacing it with his flashlight.

"Theo says there's a room down here where he thinks we'll find what we need to shut down the reactor," he says, trailing his flashlight up and down to locate whatever Theo is telling him in his ear.

"We don't have long before the people those guys were taking me to find out something is wrong and come looking for us," I say, wracking my brain to think of anything I've seen in the past few days that can help us.

"Theo and Jake have been working together to place bugs all over this crypt and the emergency shut down for the reactor is close to where they were keeping you," he says, his eyes still focused along the walls.

I keep one hand on the gun at my side, and the other still holding his hand as we continue walking along the dark halls. It's gross down here and a part of me is thankful I can't see the rodents that I know must be running around at our feet. Once we get to the control room, if Solaris isn't aware of the threat they will be when we initiate the emergency shut down. A few moments later, Cameron stops walking and shines the flashlight on a spot on the wall that looks like a giant frame without a picture.

"Do you hear that?" He whispers, pointing toward the wall.

There it is – the faint hum and bubbling sound of a nuclear reactor. I nod and Boss drops his nose to the floor, scratching with his paws around the frame for an opening. I gently press the wall and to my surprise it just opens, revealing a giant room full of nuclear reactors.

No lock?

Just when it seems like it's too easy, a loud alarm sounds and flashing red lights blink furiously above our heads. I immediately cover my ears because the sound makes me feel as though my brain is about to split into a million pieces. Cameron pulls me into him and heads straight for the control panel.

"Theo, we found it – but we set off some kind of alarm when we opened the door. How do we initiate shutdown so we can get out of here before we have company?" Cameron asks, inspecting a giant panel with dozens of unmarked buttons and levers.

The alarm is still sounding, making standing upright nearly impossible, but I push through the pain with my weapon pointed on the entrance. Cameron runs to the corner of the panel, and pulls a large red lever. Almost instantaneously the alarms warn of shutdown. The control rods deploy from their suspended positions above the reactors, making a loud clang as they drop into the cores. Steam hisses and I start to hear what I assume is other members of Solaris, running down the hall toward the sound.

"We have to go," I scream, looking for a way to exit that isn't going to run us smack into the people who're coming for us.

We both know there's no time to find an exit so moments before the door bursts open, the two of us look at each other and dive behind one of the reactors.

"She has to be in here somewhere. Nobody leaves until we find her."

When I realize the familiar ring of the voice barking the orders, my heart feels like it's going to stop and by breath catches in my throat.

Jake?

I look at Cameron as my eyes widen in recognition. Boss silently bears his teeth in Jake's direction. Confusion clouds my mind as I try and figure out why Jake has led them right to us, after presumably helping us shut down the reactor.

"They won't shoot me. Get out of here and bring Theo for backup," I whisper in his ear, before squeezing his hand and coming out from behind the reactor.

I haven't dropped my weapon, but I raise my hands above my head, which causes the two men at Jake's side to run for me. Before I can reach for my gun, gunshots fire from different directions and both men drop with kill shots to their heads. Jake has killed one of them and seconds later Cameron emerges from the shadows as though he and Jake planned the ambush all along.

"Well played man," Cameron says, fist bumping Jake whose smile is so wide it looks like it might break his face.

As soon as the shock of the moment wears off, and the alarm is disabled, I run for Jake and wrap him in a big hug. I can feel his tears on my shoulder and now both of us are crying. As we hug, and Jake jokes about how I'm getting someone else's blood all over him, Theo runs into the room.

"Oh snap, I guess ya'll already handled business in here," he says, holstering his gun and petting Boss who runs up to him and demands pets for a job well done.

Jake pulls away from my hug, but his smile has faded. Theo and Cameron are also now looking somber and I feel like I'm the only one in the room unaware of what they all seem to be thinking.

"We have an extraction plan for the three of us and Boss," Theo says, glancing awkwardly at Jake.

"What do you mean? Jake just saved our asses. We need to take him with us," I reply, grabbing Jake's arm and pulling him toward me.

The four of us stand there, soaking wet because the sprinklers have turned on in reaction to the hot steam coming from the reactors.

"Andy, I can't come with you all because if I do, you lose your asset," Jake says, looking at the ground to avoid eye contact.

Oh no, he's right. He's our asset now.

Despite the fact that I know he's right, and that we need him, I still can't fathom the thought of losing him to these monsters.

"They trust me, and when you all leave here – and you very much should – they'll keep hunting you if we can't bring them down," Jake insists, his deep blue eyes searching mine.

"But we just destroyed their headquarters, shutting down any chance for them to pick up activity here," I say, hoping that this was enough for us all to get back to some level of normalcy.

Theo steps out of the shadows of one of the reactors he'd been standing by as he collected a sample and interjects, "we won the battle today, but this war is far from over Andy."

"So how are you going to explain what happened in here?" I ask Jake, folding my arms and looking around at the smoking reactors and the two dead bodies lying at our feet.

"You're going to shoot me, and make it look convincing without killing me so that I can walk out of here like I didn't just help you escape," Jake replies, nodding to the gun at my side.

Without responding, I look at him like he's just lost his mind. But everyone is just looking like they're accepting this crazy plan.

"You've got to be kidding me. Can't we just punch you or something?" I ask, rubbing my temple to ease the throbbing headache that started when the alarm sounded.

"The other two men who walked in here got shot, so the cleanest way to handle this is to make it look like you all escaped in a gun fight," Jake replies, sweat dripping down his head and face turning an even darker pink than usual.

The four of us take the next few minutes to discuss the insane plan of where to shoot Jake to cause the least damage and make it most realistic. While Cameron offers to shoot him, I refuse because knowing their history – there's too high of a chance he'd get some level of satisfaction out of it. As the three guys argue, while Boss looks annoyed enough to grab a gun himself and handle business, I quickly pull out my gun and point it toward Jake.

"Jake, I'm really sorry," I say, before shooting him in the arm.

He yelps in pain, but I've intentionally grazed his arm instead of shooting him in a way that would require them to remove a bullet. For additional credibility Theo punches him in the cheek to make it look as though there as also a struggle.

"Get out of here. Take the south exit that will bring you to the backside of the village, and I'll wait five minutes and run in the opposite direction," Jake instructs, handing me a map of the walkways and pointing to the direction he wants us to run.

I grab the map from Jake before reaching in for a final hug and whispering in his ear, "take care of yourself, man. I'm not ready to be a work widow."

Jake squeezes me close to him with the arm that isn't bleeding before replying, "don't worry, I have no intensions of going anywhere before we take these assholes down. Now go before our entire plan falls apart."

Cameron, Theo, and I run for the exit with Boss bobbing along side and enter the dark hallway. Cameron pulls out his flashlight and I hold the map to help us find the tunnel exit that Jake mentioned. Once we find the exit, Cameron shoves open the heavy steel door and the sun hits me in the face as I squint to adjust to a level of sunlight I haven't seen in at least a week.

"Check it out, that's our escape vehicle," Theo says, grinning as he points to an open bed truck filled with fruit and vegetables.

"Did you hijack a fruit truck from the market?" I ask, raising an eyebrow at Theo and promising myself to follow up later for the full story.

"I have connections everywhere," Theo replies, grinning and showing all his pearly white teeth as he flexes one of his muscles and giggles to himself.

To my astonishment, he moves a few boxes of fruit to the side, revealing two hidden seats and gesturing for Cameron and I to hop in while Boss joins Theo in the front seat of the vehicle.

"Well, you didn't think we'd be able to roll out of here with you in plain site did you?" Theo asks, slapping a reluctant Cameron on the shoulder before helping me into the hidden seat.

Cameron hops up beside me and Theo moves the fruit boxes back in place to hide us from onlookers. Amongst the fruit, bobbing along on these jumpsuits, I reach for Cameron and he pulls me into him.

"Did you find anything we can use to get more information?" I ask, anxious for more details.

"Yeah, that closet where you sent me to hide was a gold mine. I picked up hard drives and some vials that Dr. Raj can test for an antidote," he says, pulling me closer to him as though he's afraid I'll disappear.

"We did it," I say, tears of relief rolling down my face.

"*You* did it, Andy. I was so afraid of letting you go and in the end you freed yourself and we got out of there with more Intel than we'd have ever found on our own," Cameron responds, pulling back from me long enough for me to see his golden brown eyes sparkle with the small stream of light shining through the fruit boxes.

I reach up to run my hand through his wild curls before pulling him into a kiss that makes my body relax for the first time in weeks.

For the first time in my entire agency career, I feel like a part of a team. And though we've yet to win the war, being in Cameron's arms makes me feel like I'm home.